The Diocese of the Britains in the year in which
Fl. Lupicinus and Fl. Iovinus were consuls

Britanniæ

M O'Sullivan

The Starbank Press 2011

Published in 2011 by The Starbank Press

The right of M O'Sullivan
to be identified as the author of this work
has been asserted in accordance with Section 77 of
the Copyright, Designs and Patents Act 1988

A CIP record for this book
is available from the British Library

ISBN 978-0-9569812-0-2

*The Starbank Press is an imprint of Resource Synergies Ltd,
58 Greenway Lane, Bath, Somerset BA2 4LL*

CHAPTER 1

'"For it is impossible to disbelieve the children of gods, even if their statements have neither likelihood nor corroboration, and when they claim to speak of family matters we must follow custom and believe them"'

Flavia tilted her head absently, and pulled a comb through her hair. She peered through its pale hazy curtain at the words she had written last year. Then she compared them for yet another time with their original. Her attention was still failing. It was an enigmatic sentence, anyway, she thought with a moment's rebellion. Did it have a simple meaning? Was it some subtle parable, about all the thousands of angels and invisible powers that might link God to mankind? Or was it just a rather mannered little joke, about how implausible it was that the gods might get up to the naughty deeds described in the myths? She sighed: she was evidently a flawed messenger of Plato's thoughts, and disloyal to philosophy. She abandoned her desk and turned left out of the door.

Her garden was hidden from the house by a tall box hedge, and from the home park and the paddocks beyond it by a belt of evergreens and beeches. Its secret peace began to soothe her. Oaks were just showing the tender leaf of the new spring. Cropped grass was studded with clean white saxifrage. Daffodils clumped under the trees, ungainly and cheerful, a yellow promise of summer sun. Through the lawns a stream rippled. Suddenly an image from childhood came momentarily to her mind: herself playing hide and seek with her brother Titus among the firs and hollies. The problems of the translator turning Greek into Latin began to fall into perspective, and she began to disengage, opening her senses to the chaffinches chirping in the trees, and a thrush hopping clownish on the lawn.

Behind, the gate creaked, and Atra came up busily with a writing-tablet: "It's just arrived, Lady Flavia." Flavia looked at it, incurious: an ordinary letter, two wafers of wood four inches square, routinely bound with string and sealed with wax at the knot – a smudged military seal. On the front was a thin spidery hand: *deliver at Cormerick, by Durobrivæ*, to the Most Perfect Lady Flavia Vindex, from the Most Perfect Junius Alfenus.* She took it, broke the seal, opened the two leaves, and deciphered the cramped writing:

To the Most Perfect Lady Flavia Vindex, from the Most Perfect Junius Alfenus, Tribune of the Petriana Horse at Uxellodunum on the Wall, greetings.

It grieves me much to have to communicate to you this third day before the nones of March that your brother Titus left this post eleven days before the kalends of September to travel among the northern Picts on official business. No news has been received of him since, and he has not returned. It is my opinion that he must be regarded as lost on active service. He has left some personal effects which will be sent on to you at Cormerick by the waggon-post. Please accept my sincere condolences.

Farewell.

Flavia read the letter with increasing difficulty, realising that it contained a message, but that she did not understand what it was. She went through it three times before she put it aside, slowly, careful of the motions of reading but not of what she read. Then she raised vacant eyes. She had feared this, she thought to herself, all those months ago, when Titus had been here at the villa, proud of his new appointment, telling her the gossip, being evasive about his relationship with that girl in London.

Her mind seemed to leap, skittering through things that

---

* *The site of Durobrivæ is now that of Water Newton, a village outside Peterborough. A sketch map is provided as the frontispiece, and a note on names and a list of those used is at the end of this book.*

would have to be attended to, shying away from something heavy. She ought to write to Constantinople to their mother and their aunt...but, then again, no, perhaps it was not so urgent, perhaps this Alfenus would have done that; the army was often organised about such things. Then again, she ought to find some way of tracking the London girl down, of getting the news to her: what was her name? Antonia? how could she trace someone with as common a name as that? Another thing: she ought to get the body sent back for burial in the plot on the farm...but no, of course not, that was foolish, he was lost, there wasn't a body, there was nothing to do there. Where was the courier who had brought the letter – would he have more news? No, she realised, he was probably already gone, and the chances were small that he even came from Uxellodunum: he would surely know nothing more.

The thoughts raced into oblivion until, still half-aware of the cold saxifrage, the weed rank in the noisy stream, the misshapen daffodils besetting the solitary trees, she stared vacant at the hedge that towered between grey sky and manicured grass. So much for her childhood games among the fir and holly. Chaffinch-twitters ghosted from the trees; a ponderous thrush patrolled the lawn. Flavia felt alone in the garden.

"What's the matter, Lady Flavia?" came a voice, uncertainly, rather shrilly. "Was there bad news in that letter?" She looked down, and Atra was still standing there, a brown duster clutched under her arm, her small aged face wrinkled up deeply with concern.

Frustration gathered in Flavia: she needed to be quite on her own, to hug this pain to herself and smother it in secret, and here was Atra, faithful and uncomprehending as she had been all Flavia's life, still wanting attention, still wanting a response. And how, she thought, was she going to tell Atra that her 'little man', whom like Flavia she had nursed from babyhood, who had grown up over long years and gone away to London and then the army – how was she to tell her that he was dead? She did not want this responsibility; she did not need it; she had enough to deal with for herself. She frowned as she struggled to control her anger: she well knew that Atra acted only from love and loyalty, and did not deserve her hostility and rejection, but she still could not bring herself to look at her as she said, "Very bad, Atra. I'm afraid Titus is dead," and then dredged up in herself the resource to add something, to invent some consolation. "He fell bravely, fighting the barbarians. This letter is from his commanding officer, who was there at the time. He says he was killed cleanly with a spear-thrust, and did not suffer at all. He says his death was noble, like those of the great soldiers of old."

But unlike Flavia, Atra had paid no attention when Florian told his children the ancient story of Scaevola, who had withered his arm in the flame to impress the Etruscan king with the quality of Roman courage. Atra had never cared about the great soldiers of old. The aged slave seemed not to hear Flavia's words. Her eyes enlarged, her mouth fell open and gulps of shrieking came out of it as she buried her face in her duster, turned round, and trotted toward the kitchens as fast as she could. Flavia looked after her, her feelings wrung further by Atra's distress, recognising with despair that she could do nothing to help.

The rest of the day, Flavia found, had a sense of emptiness that reminded her of the time when her father had died: she hoped, with foreboding, that she would not feel as hollow as she had then. At first, at a loss what else to do, she returned to her books. But, sitting at her writing-table, she kept looking around at the pale yellow plaster of the walls, the honeycomb of little compartments holding scrolls, the shelf of bound volumes below them. The room insistently reminded her of Titus' last visit, the autumn before last.

She remembered her own eagerness at her work when he had arrived: until then, the Dialogue had been occupied for page after page in picturesque but unimportant stories to establish the mood, and now, with the opening of Timæus' speech, Plato was at last introducing fundamental thoughts and moving forward to expound them in action: the main argument was now beginning, and it was exhilarating to have reached it. Paradoxically, it had been at this point that she had felt most unsure of herself. She had been, she recalled, worried by a sense that the word "judgement" was not quite right, and this had broadened into a familiar despair at translating into Latin a Greek which was so unsophisticated and lacking in technical terms, yet seemed to use its very ambivalences to achieve a wonderful clarity. She might have done well enough in the introductory passages, but now that the great theme-words were beginning to appear, words which would ring down the Dialogue punning on each other and knitting the whole together, it had seemed impossible to find adequate equivalents. It was at that moment, when she had been staring at the corner of this bookcase, lost in the problem, that Titus had burst in, full of energy even after his long ride, and grabbed her enthusiastically around the middle before she had had a chance to get up.

She got up now, and stared unseeing at the fresh green on the birch trees across the flower garden. Word of the calamity seemed to be spreading through the house, provoking a new outburst of weeping somewhere as each of the maidservants heard the news. He had been in a curious mood that week, she thought; he had even, as so seldom, spoken briefly of their ill-fated journey to discover Rome together, seven or eight years before. She bent, rummaging in an oak chest, and opened the abraded string round the leaves of the letter he had written from London just before that last visit.

To my dear sister Flavia from her brother Titus in Augusta, greetings.

The new emperor Valentinian's arrived in Gaul at last; he set up his court in Paris in July or August. There's a bad atmosphere here. He has had to send an army against barbarians from across the Rhine, and there's been a revolt in Asia – a relation of Julian's called Procopius – a minor-sounding problem, but one never knows. There's also news of a flood in Alexandria, and an earthquake in Greece, so it's as if there's ill-luck everywhere. But the main thing here is that so many of the officials were appointed under Constantius or Julian, and everyone is afraid for his position. Marcian, the governor of Maxima Caesariensis, put on a lavish wild-beast show for the festival of Vulcan, with African lions which must have cost a fortune; they say he hopes that, if he's seen as popular, Valentinian won't replace him.

Look: Dagwald, the tribune in command of the arcani, asked me to dinner last week. He told me that it's more serious than we've thought among the barbarians: things may go wrong this time. He's been talking to someone in Second Germany about sending people across the frontier into Saxony. Three of his people left for Ireland last month, as well, and that's very unusual. Now they're drafting in new men to go north, too, as political agents among the tribes beyond the Wall. He's asked me to join the arcani and go there as one of them, with the rank of a military tribune of the third class.

Please think again about getting a dog about the place. I know you hate them so, but I worry about you in that house full of women. I shall try to come up towards the end of the month, before the harvest festival as usual, to get some time away before the winter.

> *Look after yourself, little sister. Farewell.*

Flavia remembered him filling in the details of the new post when he had come to stay. His shining eyes had seemed to hint at derring-do and valiant exploits: bold strikes saving grateful border villagers, barbarian princes kidnapped and led in triumph, or the Emperor looking paternally down as he awarded him the insignia of a Count for services which could never be divulged... It was no wonder that such service seemed more attractive than the staidness of a financial administrator. But she was sure that his principal reason for the change was one he had made less of. Titus had been no fool: she knew that he had been well thought of in the Bureau of the Sacred Largesses. His decision to move to the army would have been a considered one, and with both a financial and a military office behind him he would surely have been well-placed for a successful public career.

She closed the leaves of the letter, and tied them thoughtfully. Another letter had arrived, after his visit, but before he had gone north. She dug that out of the chest as well.

To my dear sister Flavia from her brother Titus, greetings.

When I returned from my visit to you I reported to the arcani as arranged, and I was assigned to Senopian's command, which is the unit supporting the Vicar and Count of the Britains, here in Augusta. I have just got back from a month's training near Verulamium, which was very vigorous. I don't think I've ever been so fit, even when I was going to the gymnasium every day.

They say there is unusual restlessness among the barbarians, and also worries about the arcani on the Wall themselves – that's a unit attached to the Duke of the Britains at Carlisle, under Serquina. In a week or two I am to go north on secondment to his unit, and may have to travel north of the Wall. I may not be able to write again for some while; do not worry if you do not hear from me, or if rumours get about – you should be safe enough at Cormerick. But be careful what you say of me; this may be a difficult time.

Look after yourself, little sister. Farewell.

What was all that about? It was so brief. He had never been expressive in his letters. Or had he not been allowed to say much, and should she try to read more into it than it said? Yet the letter was surely indiscreet to imply that this unit on the Wall was untrustworthy; it wouldn't make sense to be so open about that and yet hide some concealed message. Indeed, it was so indiscreet that, if seen by the wrong people, it could itself, she supposed, account for an attack on Titus, not by the barbarians but by this Serquina. As far as she could recall, the seal on the letter had been quite intact when she had received it. She thought back: as a child he had tended to wear his heart on his sleeve – she had always felt older than him rather than younger – but after he had joined the Sacred Largesses he had seemed to grow more politic, and he had certainly been reluctant to be drawn when he had spoken to her about joining the *arcani.* Had he after all been too innocent for this post?

Then again, the end of it was rather elliptical. 'Do not worry if you do not hear from me, or if rumours get about – you should be safe enough at Cormerick' – that looked like reassurance for her about her own safety in the event of military trouble, such as a worse version of the three or four small Saxon raids on the east coast last summer. But it was ambivalent. Was it meant to imply that the rumours might be ones not of barbarian attack but of his own movements?

Flavia sat back on her couch, the phrases of the letters beating at her. She was the wrong person for this task. Remote in the country, lost in her farm and in her books, what could she hope to know about current politics? Maybe the remarks about Serquina were *meant* to be intercepted... But if he was on some kind of secret mission – who knew? – reports of his death might be misleading. It was not like her to give herself unnecessary hope, she thought, but the letters made no clear sense. And the notification of his death had come from the military establishment on the Wall, the very quarter about which his earlier letter had expressed doubt – though even that was uncertain, she thought, and might refer simply to the *arcani* themselves, who were maybe different from regular army units like the Petriana Horse. There was no certainty in it anywhere. But she could not, even simply on an intellectual plane, entirely convince herself that her brother was really dead.

Part of the problem with the letters was that he'd been away in London too long, and she didn't know any more how good a liar her brother was. As a child he had been very bad at it, and deep within herself she approved of this. In her moral code, lying was wrong in principle. Moreover, doing it convincingly was difficult if you were not used to it, yet if practised it had a heady allure, so that in a moment you were so deep in equivocation that you couldn't tell truth from lies. And lying didn't only lead to muddle, she thought. You could do it for bravado: Cæcina Priscus (his memory would not, it seemed, fade with time) had told her that when younger he had often lied as a dare to himself, to see if he would be detected, and had only stopped when he had found that, despite his ingenuous appearance, others were beginning to mistrust him.

She noticed that she was distracting herself from thoughts of Titus, and was sure it could be for no good reason. He was her brother, and he was dead: it was her simple duty to grieve, as nature and the heavens demanded, and if she avoided it this was surely a moral failure, and showed her as a bad woman. Yet she was used to deeper inquiry through her sporadic attempts to examine her behaviour each day in the Stoic way (what bad habit had she cured, what fault resisted, in what way was she better?); and thus she started to wonder whether somewhere in herself she might feel that, if he was dead, it was his own fault, and that it was characteristic of him to have been careless, and whether she was ashamed of this feeling of blame for someone who in death deserved nothing but family piety. And immediately she caught herself shying away again, returning to the letters, and to the question of honesty and lies that they raised, and asking herself if there was self-deception in them, and comparing Plato's arguments in the *Gorgias*, where he clearly had nothing but contempt for the unscrupulous politician Callicles who was so ready to manipulate his own sense of the truth. She turned to her mirror, and spent some time staring at the pale skin, the clear cheekbones, the grey eyes flecked with green. What would Epictetus say? That a fair face oft hides an undisciplined heart, one corrupted by the passions?

She went to bed early, exhausted by her thoughts and emotions, and irritated with herself. Today, if ever, she realised, had been a day to subject her passions to her reason, as a philosopher should, but she felt she had failed miserably. She settled on her bed, oppressed by huge, vague fears, and eventually grew drowsy.

Suddenly Flavia's eyes were wide open in fright, staring at the reddish decoration on the plaster wall of her own bedroom; there was a light of dawn, and the muffled noise of Atra raking out last night's fire in the kitchen. All in the house was in order, she realised, and her heartbeat slowed. But her dream nagged at her with its incongruity. She realised that she really had, once, been told a story like that dream. Yet the man she had spoken to had been not Titus but Cæcina Priscus, the sea not the Channel but the Tyrrhenian. Suddenly the loss of Titus came back to her, spinning her awake like a blow and recalling immediately her efforts to interpret the letters last night; but the realism of the images and the emotions of the dream still lingered with her confusingly, and she was also vexed at the continued presence of Priscus in her life, as if she had been cursed to be haunted by a savage ghost.

She threw back the bedclothes, dragged on some leggings and a shift, and forced herself out into the chill morning. She went straight to the stables and gave her stallion Xerxes a mouthful of lucerne with a bit of green vetch while she settled a pad saddle on his back; then she put a loose snaffle to him and jumped up astride, urging him out up the hillside as the dawn augmented.

For some time her mind was full of its struggle with the old, sluggish horse, and her senses were engaged with his rank smell, with the passing woods and paddocks, and with the vigour of her own activity in the evanescent dew. But after a while, almost against her will, she was drawn back again to her circumstances, and to her dream.

Dreams were sent by the gods, she said to herself. Most people believed that; even the Christians believed it, after their atheistic fashion. Homer and Virgil, in their famous image of the dreams coming from the horn and from the ivory gates of Sleep, had made a clear division between the true ones and the false. But really it was not as straightforward as that. Her dream was clearly false, for the place and characters were wrong, but even false dreams were not all awry; and did it carry some message? Might it mean, for example, that Titus was not dead at all, but gravely ill and would recover? Or was that too easy? Was it not so personal? Was it meant to warn that the Christians are powerful and to be conceded to, or for that matter that the Christians are powerful and to be fought? Or simply that life is fragile? She wondered what Artemidorus said about dreams like that: she must look it up when she got back.

Cæcina Priscus himself had claimed to be a "semi-Christian", though how he managed that she could not understand, when Christians seemed so uncompromising about their ideas. All his male relations had seemed to be priests of the gods, anyway, and he certainly hadn't been baptised, though admittedly they said that Christians often postponed baptism to get a better chance in the after-life. From nowhere a looming memory of the villa at Præneste flashed up, and she shrank away from it, attending to her path. She had left the stud-farm long since, and was now reaching the end of the raised sandy heath country, where the hazel and box gave way to bramble, dogwood and alder buckthorn.

Along the ridge marched a line of flourishing pines, planted generations ago to break the cold east winds. She reined Xerxes in, and looked out across the flatlands. The early mist had quite gone. From here the dilapidated canal was hidden by the hill, but she could see the curve of the river Farcet, lined with alder and with hawthorn just first breaking into flower, while beyond it was a patchwork of little plots. Those marsh-pastures stretched for miles, the sedge grazings studded with little flocks of sheep or goats kept together by half-naked children and their dogs. Interspersed were clumps of willow and of berry and currant bushes left to grow for firewood and fruit, and laboriously-drained fields where the parents were already up, hoeing weeds from the young bere shoots. Here and there were family huts built of wood and reed, a few of them the big old-fashioned roundhouses not much seen so far south; each had its midden, and most a pig rooting in the yard. Beyond, the fens became gradually wetter and less cultivable, sometimes losing themselves in extensive pools studded with reed-beds and alder carrs, until, remote on the horizon, a line of tall sand dunes suggested the sea beyond.

Suddenly her eye was caught by a movement in a bush close by. She turned. "*You!*" she shouted in British at the hawthorn. "*Come here!*"

A dingy cloak disengaged itself from the hedge. "Most Perfect Lady..." it began hesitantly in Latin, then paused. Clouds in the east were still streaked with red.

"Who are you?" asked Flavia, riding right up to him. His clothes looked old and torn, though all she could see were a drab cloak, a battered tall hat, its brim misshapen from much rain, and unusual Gallic-style bands round his leggings. She could not see his face from her horse, but she was pretty sure that he was not from the estate.

"Good morning, Most Perfect Lady," he repeated, "and a very fine morning it is for the time of year. I suppose you would be the Lady Flavia, daughter of the Lord Florian Vindex?"

"I might be," she replied, drawing her hood over her hair to make her appearance more formal and respectable, and surreptitiously loosening her illegal dagger in case of trouble. "But it would be more courteous for the stranger and the gentleman to introduce himself first."

The other bowed in an Italianate way, a gesture polished and curiously at odds with his appearance, and looked up at her, evidently undaunted by the bulk of her horse, and showing a sharp nose set in a freckled face fringed with red hair. "My name is Theodorus, Lady," he said, "and I have business with your brother, the Most Perfect Titus."

She looked at him doubtfully. What was he doing hiding on the heath like this? "Then present yourself at the lodge in the ordinary way, sir," she replied.

"I should not want to put your brother to the inconvenience of entertainment at short notice," he replied, as if it was not perfectly common for people to make unannounced calls during the morning. "Perhaps you would convey him a message. Tell him that Theodorus has arrived and will be resident at the Lucky Fisherman in Durobrivæ for two days."

This was a very strange character, and Flavia was disinclined to reveal the news of Titus' loss. "The Most Perfect Titus Vindex is away from home at present," she conceded slowly.

The other turned away for a moment, staring out over marshes swept by the spring breeze, then back. "I have a letter for him that is most urgent, most urgent. I can leave it in your hands, Lady, if you will. Please to inform him that the dark servant has been given the key; he will understand this. I must make a condition, for which I apologise, and which is imposed by officials of greater dignity than myself whom I cannot name; but I would ask you to swear to transmit the letter only to him."

Flavia pondered and agreed, swearing the oath by Jupiter and Mercury. Then the other reached into his knapsack and fumbled for a bone scroll-cylinder with indecipherable but official-looking seals on the frayed wooden caps. "May the gods protect you," he said, swinging the bag back over his shoulder and setting off at once on foot towards the river. Flavia sat on her horse, holding the cylinder as his form diminished in the distance. An air warmed by the sun touched her leg; she smelled a hint of sap from a pine tree. She turned and rode home.

Handing Xerxes to Argulus, she ran in through the main door, straight past the funeral masks of her forebears and the little shrine, then across the peristyle courtyard to her study. She studied the box briefly. It bore a label in Greek: *Deliver to the Most Perfect Titus Vindex at Augusta*. She broke the seals. To her annoyance her hand trembled as she prised the cover open and extracted a small sheet of papyrus. She unrolled it. More Greek letters stood out dark against the page, the continuous script written rapidly and fluently in a thick, expensive ink. But they were nonsense: six lines of unintelligible jumble.

Tears welled into Flavia's eyes, whether of grief or anger she was not sure, but she mastered herself and ordered breakfast, and went through to get properly washed and dressed. What were the words this Theodorus had used? she asked herself as she sat in front of her mirror brushing her hair. "The dark servant has been given the key"? Some kind of cypher, presumably. But what? And what was the "dark servant"? It might itself be a code: perhaps a veiled reference to some pre-arranged syntax of meaning which she would never be likely to guess. Or it could be a real servant; a man on the farm, perhaps, whom this Theodorus had already spoken to, either as a confederate or simply in a way which would not arouse his suspicions. This would be one of the days, she thought, when her bailiff Sallienus would call at the villa before lunch to discuss the management of the stud-farm. He would be someone she could talk some of this through with, at least, though she did not like the idea of breaking the oath she had had to swear.

❊ ❊ ❊

Atra called her to breakfast, but she could manage no more than a little stewed fruit. After a while fretting uselessly, she reminded herself of Seneca's '*There is no virtue without work*': a repetitive task might help with uneasiness. She went into the sewing-room. But her mind was too disturbed, and she squatted down to study the papyrus. She had never seen such a thing before, but she had read of cyphers often enough, in Herodotus and Plutarch and Cæsar. Maybe some kind of letter-substitution was used – that had been done in the past. She knew no better way to tackle it than to try various specific substitutions and see if they worked, though she could see that this could take a very long time. Perhaps some letters were more common than others in Greek – σ was surely more frequent than most – and that would be a way of approaching the problem.

Even on this task her concentration flagged, distracted by speculation about whether she knew something important she had not realised. Theodorus and his masters, who might have access to all kinds of knowledge, had clearly expected Titus to be here at the farm. She could see that hope based on this was irrational, but she could not dismiss it. In fact, as the morning went on, that hope seemed to grow in plausibility and importance, and the looming pain of loss which was Titus' death appeared to recede. Yet surely the commander on the Wall himself could scarcely be mistaken? She tried to compose her mind into grief, but it felt empty and agitated. More and more she felt that she could only still it by action, and the action that offered seemed increasingly to be to go and make inquiries where Titus had last been seen.

That place, however, she was aware, was a very long way off. She had only once before made a long journey, the trip with Titus to Trier and Rome, as much as nine or ten years ago; and she had never been north of York at all. First she might enquire after this Theodorus in the town, perhaps; he might not have got far. And before all else she should see if he had been seen about the estate, and whether there was any trace of a 'dark servant' with the 'key' to the Greek letter.

She called Banta, and sent her to fetch all the indoor servants from their tasks. They lined up in the entrance hall, in sight of the household gods and the family memorials. As Flavia went in and stood facing them, they fell silent. She looked at them for a moment, care in her brow and an affectionate smile on her face: tiny, wizened Atra, whom she had known all her life; tall, placid Banta, unaccustomedly grave just now; moon-faced Curatia, half-child, who had come in from the stud-farm only last year, now bewildered by the solemn changes from routine; Prudentia, containing some sense of mischief or amusement. Was any of these a plausible 'dark servant'? Prudentia's unruly hair was dark, but she was scatty. Atra was dark-skinned, but surely now too old and forgetful to be a reliable messenger, even unwittingly.

Flavia invoked the gods and turned to her slaves. "I think you all know the tragic news of the Lord Titus," she began. "I have decided to travel north to pay my respects where he was lost. This will mean being away for some months – possibly until the autumn. I shall be discussing the practical arrangements with Sallienus this afternoon." She paused and looked at them carefully: Prudentia was interested, but she was not sure that Atra had taken her words in. "When I was out riding this morning I met a stranger, a man with a lot of red hair, a big hat and bands round his leggings. Has any of you seen or heard of someone like that recently?" But none of them had anything to say, and she had to send them about their business.

As she awaited Sallienus' arrival, she became eaten up with impatience: he was the linch-pin of the estate, and she was uncertain of his reaction to her plans. She made herself sit in her study unoccupied till he appeared. Then there he was, massive and imperturbable as ever, his bristling red moustaches radiating competence, kissing her hand, and saying as usual, "Sallienus greets the Most Perfect Lady Flavia Vindex. Long life and good health to the Most Perfect Lady!" He settled himself in a chair, which gave a creak. She forced a conventional smile, and he stared at her under his bushy brows. "Lady Flavia," he went on, "Atra tells me that you received an official letter from Carlisle yesterday. I understand that the news was bad?"

"The news was very bad, Sallienus," she answered, and taking the leaves from her desk passed them to him.

He read them, and raised his gaze, his white-flecked red eyebrows narrowed in pain and the creases beside his eyes more pronounced. "My Lady Flavia, the news could not be worse. May the gods and the spirit of your noble father comfort you in your loss. You will permit me?" He took her hand between his heavy paws: the gentle pressure and sense of strength that they conveyed was comforting, but the reminder that she must rely on her bailiff for comfort reawakened pain, and she got up, disengaging, pacing up and down.

"What is this place Uxellodunum, Sallienus?" she asked. "Are you saying it's in Carlisle?"

"It's a fort on the Wall, just north of the city," he answered simply.

"Sallienus," she said. "I know that the commander there is most unlikely to be wrong, and that surely everything possible will have been done for Titus. But I have now had other news, and I must know more. I plan to look in Durobrivæ for the messenger who brought this second message, and, if I don't find him, to go to Uxellodunum myself. It will be difficult for me, a woman, to travel alone. I have no-one else: will you come with me?"

The bailiff pondered this, and looked at her

sorrowfully. "Lady Flavia, please consider. You have just lost your brother. Your father is dead; your mother's in Constantinople, at the other end of the world. You're naturally upset, but you have no family to console or advise you, and you must not act hastily. You know my view, that you direct the management of Cormerick as well as any man. But all the same you are a woman, and you can't expect to be in full command of yourself at such a time. I do not believe you should now rush into something which in a week or two, far from home and help, you might come to regret."

This was not the support she was looking for. She drew herself up slightly, and felt strength enter her. "I have thought this over, Sallienus. I am no girl. I am a woman of mature years, and of full status to act on my own account. It is my misfortune to be without family, and on account of that I should have thought I could have expected more support from my friends, not less." She should not rub his face in his debts to her; that would be too much.

He looked uncomfortable. "Lady Flavia, I am sorry to have said that. Perhaps it went too far. But I would also ask you," he paused for a moment, awkwardly, "I would ask you not to demand this of me. I know this province, I know London, or Augusta as they call it. But I am not widely travelled. I have a wife and family here on the estate, and I have duties to them. I ought not to put myself at risk in the frontier regions. Moreover, I have no-one I can easily hand my tasks on to. Next month the procurator comes to discuss the purchase of the new year's military horse-drafts: who but I can negotiate a price, and a bribe to support it?"

This was true, and a problem she had overlooked. Anyway, she realised, if the bailiff felt he should stay with his family, it would be unfair to press him, and he would probably do little good if he came. She would indeed have to go without him. She sighed. "Yes, Sallienus. You are right, I suppose. But I shall go myself, all the same. Pray to the gods for me: I'll need their protection. Now, is there a man or boy you can send with me? I can't travel quite alone, and none of the house-servants will do. It doesn't need to be someone who can be ready at once: I can't set out for a couple of days, because tomorrow night's the Beltane festival, and Tuesday is the annual feast of the Good Goddess, when I need to be at Aculeius' villa as usual."

Sallienus' worried face, which had relaxed somewhat, tautened a little again. "No, the house-servants wouldn't do at all, though obviously you should take a maid: how about Prudentia?"

At this suggestion Flavia realised that she did *not* want to take a maid, telling herself that it was not good to be dependent, that a philosopher is above such things, that while travelling she had a chance to avoid the expectations of service even if she could not do that at home without offence or scandal. But a maid was not the main point, and Sallienus was already going on.

"Let me think," he said, doing it out loud as he often did. "There are one or two slaves, but that wouldn't do. Ideally you want a freeborn citizen to handle difficult tradesmen and officials, but I can't think of any suitable. What about the freedman Philip, who was manumitted a while back now? His wife is pregnant, but only recently: the child isn't due until the autumn, by when you ought to be back, the gods willing. He's been very capable and reliable, and though he has no education he's quick-witted and can stand up for himself."

He peered at her anxiously. "You do remember Philip, don't you? Your noble father bought him in Trier, in the year of the fourth consulship of Constantius, I think. He's been in charge of training in the northern paddocks for four years, but now it's time to bring Calenus on, I think; he could fill the place for a while. It's a difficult time to take over, mind you, right in the middle of foaling. And there are so many other problems at the moment, too. I suspect mould in some of the feed in Tertius' Barn. And Soranus xii, for example, that promising half-Thracian stallion from last year, is getting very difficult, and needs to be put to the mill for a bit to settle his mind; Calenus would be good for that, rather than being called off to Philip's work. But perhaps it can't be helped.

"You need to take someone else as well, though. And the second man *could* be a slave. Tell you what: that Irish fellow of Aculeius', Rúari – if you should have to go north, I believe he's been up there, and he's a good man all round; maybe we could arrange for you to rent him." He frowned slightly as a new thought came. "I suppose it's possible he might try and make a break for home: he's got a wife and three children on Aculeius' estate, so he probably wouldn't, but we should need to agree to compensate Aculeius if so. One of the ordinary usufruct contracts would do. And if any of the arrangements for the servants doesn't work you could sort it out at York – I dare say that if you were going north you'd be stopping there with your cousins."

"Excellent," said Flavia. "Yes, I do remember Philip: he *is* a good man. But I shan't take Prudentia: I can't be taking a huge entourage so far, and we live in Britain, not in luxurious Campania." As she heard herself she felt uncomfortable. For a moment she suspected that, when she rejected a maid, her motives were somewhere or other not quite as she admitted either to him or to herself, and that a maid would add to the burden of expectation on her, and prevent her enjoying some of the freedom of travel, a freedom from the constraints of household concerns that women did not always get, and that she had had once before, on her journey to Rome with Titus.

Sallienus sighed, and shot her a sharp look. "Now, practical matters, Lady Flavia. You say you may be only going to Durobrivæ, but on the other hand you may be away some time? It'd be best to be sure of that before we settle matters with Aculeius, and then we'll send Rúari and Prudentia on if they're needed. Go into town with Philip, and stop at Marcius' works: he knows we're about to place a good order for tack with him, and will be specially keen to help; you can leave your stuff there while you make enquiries, and send a message back for Rúari from there too, if need be. We can find travelling gear for both Philip and Rúari on the farm."

"Thank you, Sallienus," replied Flavia. "I also need money. I want gold and silver from the strong-boxes on the stud farm: say 60 *solidi* and 200 *siliquæ*, if that won't give you difficulties. And we should get more to hand in case there is need for a ransom for Titus, for example. I'd like you to call in debts of around 300 *solidi* and hold them ready in coin."

"I will do that, Lady Flavia. The larger amount will take a while to find, though: I couldn't get a sum like that together before August at the earliest, I think."

"That will be well enough," said Flavia. "I'll leave Banta in charge of the household here while I'm away, and tell her to pass visitors or messages on to you. Make a list, will you, of things we should talk through – anything coming up on the stud-farm over the next few months – and bring it in tomorrow morning?"

"I will, Lady Flavia. And of course I'll look in whenever I'm up at the home farm, just to check that everything's all right."

"We'll speak again about this tomorrow, then." Flavia still felt a residual annoyance at the suggestion that she might be acting impetuously because she was a woman, and did not now wish to confide about this Theodorus whom she had met this morning. But she should at least ask. "And talking about visitors, Sallienus, have you heard of any strangers in the neighbourhood over the last couple of days?"

"Nobody unusual, Lady Flavia, apart from Cautilla and her daughters from Durovigutum, staying with Aculeius for the Good Goddess festival."

That was strange, she thought: they would joke that a shrew could not move in the area without Sallienus hearing of it; but even Homer nods, of course. They moved on to discuss the arrangements for the Beltane festival the next night. After Sallienus had gone, Flavia hunted in a chest in her study until she tracked down an unhelpfully vague map of the Britains – there was a better one somewhere, she was sure – and a rather more detailed written itinerary listing the places on the main roads, annotated with distances and observations.

❋ ❋ ❋

The night celebration was to be in one of the paddocks, about half a mile away from the house, where a tall lone ash tree marked a place hallowed since time out of mind. The next day a rota of slaves, of free farm-hands and of tenant farmers was plodding there all day from the wood stores, heaping up two great bonfires downwind of the tree; the weather was overcast, but it did not look like rain. Flavia made time to pen, and send to Durobrivæ, orders for tradesmen to run up various travelling requisites, including a leather cloak and a new pair of boots, but then found herself spending the whole morning giving instructions to her own household and answering queries sent from Sallienus and from the home farm: a batch of cider found sour, two Christians from the stud-farm refusing to do their share towards the festival, a message from the officiating druid saying that he was delayed. Her life was always busy with the household and the farms, she thought in the midst of the medley, never allowing her enough time for herself; but this was the worst time of year, this time when the festivals ran together. At last she escaped to her study and gratefully to her books.

Flavia was lost in another age and another country, a Thebes where Antigone was courting death by piously insisting on her brother's burial, when Atra knocked at the door. "Mistress, it's getting late. Do you want anything before we put out the fires?" She roused herself, and replaced the scroll of Sophocles in its pigeon-hole. Already dusk was falling. She went out onto the veranda and along to the downstairs dressing-room near the vestibule, where Atra came in with a bowl, washed her face, hands and feet, and then helped her to put on a thick dress and a heavy cloak against the chill.

They went out, Flavia snuffing the last candle as they left the front hall, and walked across the fields together. Sallienus stood by the ash tree with the bard, quietly chatting. People gradually arrived; they spoke of the last year's harvest, and the highest points of the winter flood. Some youths larked by the hedge, their voices occasionally lofting across the gathering. Then a light carriage approached with the druid from Duroliponte. Now everyone was crowded round: the women from the house were there and the people from the home farm and the stud farm – even the two Christians, who in the end had baulked at staying on their own in the cold darkened buildings, among the night-noises which might be ghosts or worse. Men, women and children, there were over a hundred and fifty people, with only a few tenant families still coming in.

The druid took off his fustian cloak, revealing the white ceremonial robe. He called to his assistant, who brought a decorated cap and placed it on his head, and as he did so a great cheer went up from the company. Flavia was reminded vividly of the Beltane two years ago, when Titus had been there – so active, even down to taking part himself in the fire-leaping at dawn. His absence was an ache, and though her eyes were dry, she could not pay proper attention to the ceremonies. The torches were extinguished, down to the last, and then all was black, save for daubs of moonlight leaking through ragged clouds. Half-silvered by it, the druid invoked the gods, and then started a fire with a bow, spindle and birch bark. As the tinder flamed, a gasp of excitement went through the crowd. He lit a torch from the tinder and crossed to ignite first the northern and then the southern bonfires; their blazes leapt, and men all over the gathering went forward to light torches. The druid took a bronze crown from his assistant, and placed it on Flavia's head. Then he took a drinking-horn, filled it from a large earthenware bowl, and put it into her hands. As Titus had done the year before last, she cast a hornful of mead first into one fire and next into the other, where the roaring flames ate them up. Then the druid filled the horn again and passed it back to her; she offered a prayer, drank a mouthful, and passed it to Sallienus, then to Luonercus who ran the home farm, and finally to the druid and the bard. Then he filled five horns with the mead and passed them round the other heads of household.

Meanwhile the stable-lads had fetched over the seven first-born foals of the year – some only six weeks old, and all alarmed by the flames – and were holding them still, out of the firelight, cozening them with soft clucking words, just a murmur behind the bonfire-crackling. The druid strode to the centre of the circle and raised his arms, chanting a loud prayer, then brought his staff firmly to the ground. At this sign the lads started off, running between the two fires, hustling the startled foals with them. They ran on to take the animals home from their ordeal, and the voice of the bard rose up as cups of cider and barley-cakes were distributed, singing an ancient tale of the gods. Flavia's public role in the ceremonies was now over, and she listened with half an ear, still conscious of Titus' absence, but remembering at the right time to invoke Epona privately and pray for the mares to be fertile this year. She kept an eye open for the mysterious Theodorus, and asked after him occasionally as well, but learned nothing until much later, when she was about to leave and found herself standing for a moment near Junilla, a woman of about her own age and one of the granddaughters of Tranquilia Severa, the neighbour who would host the festival of the Good Goddess the next day.

"You look worried, Flavia," said Junilla. "This is the night of Spring, a night to be happy!"

"I've had bad news of Titus," said Flavia, and then before the other could enquire added directly, "Have you seen or heard of a stranger about, a man with a shock of red hair, a large hat and banded leggings?"

Junilla's face was only vaguely distinguishable in the firelight, but seemed to change. "That sounds familiar," she said, and paused a moment. "Paulina mentioned something about someone like that," she added. "I think she said she saw him near your stables."

Flavia's heart leapt. "At the stud farm?"

"No, your own stables, at the house. I can't remember what else she said. You won't catch her here now: I saw her going home a while back. You know she's just got engaged to be married? It's a busy time for her. But she'll be at the festival tomorrow."

Flavia's first instinct, to make her way at once to Paulina's house and find out what she had to tell, was obviously unrealistic: it was too far, too late, too dark. She made her farewells and set off home.

❋ ❋ ❋

She slept uneasily and late, and awoke tired, blinking at the sunshine that streamed through the clear glass windows. She reached out for the water that Atra must have brought when she had drawn the curtains back, thoughtfully leaving Flavia to sleep. This was the first day of May, the day sacred to the Good Goddess. The ceremony would begin in the early afternoon, about the seventh hour from dawn, at the villa on the imperial land where Aculeius was bailiff. By the time it began, all the men of the estate would be gone to neighbours to continue the Beltane revelries, but Aculeius' wife Tranquilia Severa would remain, along with the women of her household, and of course they would be joined by guests from all around. Flavia's own women-servants would be there too, and she should send them over early, in the mid-morning, to help prepare for the ceremony. She struggled up and gave them instructions, then dressed normally but with sturdy boots, and set aside to take with her later a white lambswool dress and good jewellery, putting them in a knapsack with a neat pair of shoes.

Going downstairs, she went to the stable, and made much of old Xerxes, giving him bits of beet to nibble. There was no sign of Argulus, who, despite the lavish amounts of cider she had seen him putting away the night before, must have taken Ario out for exercise. She looked around: the stables were where Junilla had said that Theodorus had been seen. To the left was the ladder going up to the hay-loft where Argulus slept. Beyond it, hanging from hooks on the wall, were a collection of girths and breast- and haunch-straps. On the opposite wall hung two four-horned military saddles. "The dark servant has been given the key": might there be some written message after all? Flavia examined all the leatherwork. It did not seem to carry any intentional marks other than its ordinary tooled decoration, nor had either of the saddles been unstitched so that anything could be slipped into the wooden frame. There was a shelf with a blanket on, and Flavia opened this out carefully and found it unmarked. Might Theodorus have gone up into the hay-loft? She sighed, and went back into the house, pondering frustratedly over the letter with the aid of a wax tablet until long after the last of the serving-maids had left. But before too long she had to set off: the walk would take an hour or more, and she felt it showed respect to the goddess to go on foot rather than ride.

The day was perfect: warm and sunny, with a few tufts of cloud, and the limitless bowl of the sky stretching from one edge of the flat horizon to the other. The early part of the journey was on well-beaten tracks through her own paddocks and fields, but later the way led through tenanted smallholdings where the paths were poorly kept. Here the streams were more errant, and the woodland patches thicker, with carpets of bluebells and scatterings of white anemones and delicate woodruff. She often had to push her way carefully through furze. After a while she was sweating heavily, and wished she had given her bag to the slaves to take. Occasionally she waved and called out in British to greet a man who had already done with Beltane and returned to his crops.

She visited the Aculeii often enough. But going this way, walking rather than riding, it made her think of past feast days, both at this festival of the Good Goddess and at the other in December, when the journey back was always long and dark, and rather fearful. She remembered the time when three women from Athens had been visiting, and had explained that the Good Goddess was known in their city as the Women's Goddess; Flavia had liked that.

As she neared the house of the Aculeii she saw someone approaching along another path: it was Paulina, the girl who was supposed to have seen Theodorus. "Congratulations on your engagement!" offered Flavia, though privately she did not think much of the Italian style of early marriage: in her view eighteen was quite early enough for bearing children, as the writer Rufus of Ephesus had recommended; and Paulina was still only thirteen, even though quite tall for her age.

"Thank you, Most Perfect Flavia!" said Paulina, kissing her on the cheek, a bit too casually and clumsily. Her recent efforts to treat Flavia as an equal aroused both amusement and compassion. Flavia was readier than some of their friends to say that a girl of age to marry could not be treated like a child, but Paulina's attempts to take advantage of this were sometimes painfully transparent. "News travels fast round here," Paulina continued. "But, you know, Flavia, though my Marcus Troianus may be rich, he lives a long way away, in London. And he's quite old: he must be at least thirty! I don't think he's a good match. And the idea is that we should marry as soon as I'm fourteen: it's only in a few months. I've a good mind to run away."

Flavia was unsympathetic to this childish mood, and wasn't sure there was a good response. Besides, she badly wanted to change the subject to what intruders Paulina might have seen over the last few days. But it would be impolitic to lose her temper, and she said simply "Oh yes, and where to?"

Paulina was impervious to the coolness of the response, and basked in a self-admiring smile. "Maybe one of the Saxon pirates who were prowling around last year will come back," she mused coquettishly. "Perhaps he'll be so smitten by my beauty that he'll take me off to be one of those fierce barbarian women they talk of. Or perhaps the new Governor will be impressed by my piety and recommend me to the Emperor as a Vestal in Rome."

What that girl needs is a hard slap, thought Flavia, recalling a Rome very different from Paulina's fantasies, its oppressive atmosphere reeking of precedence and of the carefully-negotiated expectations of the great families. She needed to lead this conversation, she told herself. "Paulinilla," she began, "Junilla tells me you saw a stranger at our house recently. Can you tell me anything about it?"

Flavia watched closely as Paulina decided whether to allow the discussion to be diverted from the more pressing issue of her own future, and with relief heard her say, "Was this the man with red hair and a big, battered hat, a bit like the apprentice bard there was at the summer festival last year?"

"That's right."

Paulina was obviously capable of becoming interested in this as well. "I saw someone like that the day before yesterday," she said. "I was up very early and over your way, and I saw someone in your stables. Your own stables at the house, not the stud farm."

"What was he doing?"

"He was coming out of the second box along, as you look over from the path. I think it's the young black gelding which you often ride, but I've seen Titus on him too when he's been at home. You gave him a foreign name."

"Ario? Ariobarzanes?" Ario was black, thought Flavia: might not he be the "dark servant"?

"Yes, I think so. What's it about? You make it sound mysterious. What is this man – a thief, or a buyer? He had a nice smile."

But, opportunely, they were just coming in sight of the villa of the Aculeii, and a servant came out to take their bags – a woman, since on account of the ceremony the steward Pappitedo had withdrawn.

"Welcome, ladies," she said. "The Lady Tranquilia Severa has asked me to take you directly to the pool, unless there is anything you need from the house." They went past a number of carriages and tethered horses and donkeys, then through, well beyond the house, to where a small river, lined with trees, gathered itself in a pool. Already nearly thirty women from all parts of the neighbourhood were sitting or lying on the grass in the warm spring sunshine, and they were not the only ones still arriving. Two, young girls, were already in the river, and gradually more slipped in.

Then Tranquilia Severa herself appeared, a tall, ample woman of about fifty, seemingly unaffected by the previous night's celebrations. She unbound her long red hair, stepped out of her clothes with great dignity, and entered the water, swimming a little and greeting her guests with easy banter. Then she called her maid to wash her body, and approached a small turf altar under an alder tree beside the pool. She called for silence, and in the middle of the stream extended her arms. "Corinus, lord of the river, and Fimmilena, guardian of this pool, we praise you for your glory and for the pleasure you give to us. Purify us today, so that we may praise the Good Goddess with true hearts and with unpolluted bodies." She left the pool, and her servant patted her dry and robed her in a long white dress and a close-knit yellow woollen shawl, then put a yellow girdle round her waist. The others dressed or tidied their clothes, and followed her in silent procession up to the villa.

She led them to one side of the house to a small thatched building of heavily-weathered flat bricks, and they gathered round its closed yellow door on an area of rough grass. Severa laid a posy of flowers on each side of the door, then turned and gestured, and two women struck up a melody on flutes. They played for a while, and then six girls near Paulina's age began to dance in the open space before the door, sedately, with complex movements. Four women to one side began to sing an ancient song:

> "August and triumphant goddess,
> Good Goddess,
> We praise you who have helped us;
> Powerful goddess, protector of women,
> Good Goddess,
> Come, show yourself in our worship.
> Mighty goddess, worker of wonders,
> Good Goddess,
> You will live in the lives of women for ever."

They repeated the hymn three times, each time at a higher pitch, and then a woman approached the door and gently opened it, revealing an image of the goddess with rich brown hair, dressed in a red and yellow robe. The music ceased, but the dance continued. The four singers called in sequence, each chanting on a single tone:

> "Good Goddess, you watch over the young girl
> as she grows strong and learns her skills."
> *"Garmangabis, you give a woman courage in her work*
> *and comfort her in childbirth."*
> "Good Goddess, you heal the sick and comfort
> them in their pain."
> *"Garmangabis, you are with your supplicants in their*
> *dying hour."*

The dancers stopped, and three little girls came forward with gifts for the goddess: small white fine spelt loaves, a bowl of honey, and a pitcher of beer flavoured with caraway. Tranquilia Severa took these and laid them before the image, and then stood upright and prayed:

"Mistress, Good Goddess, Garmangabis, wonderful goddess, protector of the household, keeper of the family, renowned through all the world: accept these gifts from your servants. Give us peace in our households; give us a prosperous summer and an abundant harvest. Give us contentment on your holy day."

She walked all round the little temple, in silence save for the birdsong, and then clapped her hands boldly three times. A toddler, startled, began to cry, but the noise was drowned: the flautists struck up again, the dancers resumed with a more vigorous set of steps, and the singers began a different hymn. Meanwhile four servants had been bringing in bread, butter, honey and beer, and putting them on trestle tables to one side. Some worshippers started to move towards it and help themselves to food and drink, while others began to join in the dancing.

Flavia found herself standing near Paulina and also Junilla.

"You look worried, Flavia," said Junilla. "This is a day to be happy!"

"I always feel that we oughtn't really to use beer as the offering," admitted Flavia, a bit apologetically, fearing she was laying herself open to being made fun of, and not quite yet seeing how. "In Italy everyone accepts that wine isn't suitable in her worship."

"Flavia's just trying to show off that she's been to Italy and we haven't," said Junilla to Paulina, laughing, while Flavia made embarrassed gestures, reddening slightly. "She suggested this a couple of years ago when we were talking through arrangements for the December festival. Apparently it's quite true that wine is banned in the worship in Rome. But the women there use wine all the same: they just call it 'milk' during the ceremony, and expect the Goddess not to notice!" All three giggled at this evidence of Italian greed and expediency, and Junilla directed a meaningful but good-natured glance at Flavia as she continued. "The priestesses have decided beer is perfectly appropriate. They say that the Goddess' traditional offerings are milk and honey, and beer's also a kind of natural fruit of the field. No, you're quite right to make the point, Flavia: you're our conscience, aren't you, our Vestal Virgin, keeping the ritual pure and making sure it's acceptable to the Goddess. But you might accept a priestly ruling now and then..."

After the formal prayers and ceremonies everyone fell on the food and drink, talking enthusiastically, but Flavia stayed as short a time as she decently could, and made off briskly back to Cormerick, trying to keep Junilla's ambiguous sobriquet of Vestal Virgin out of her mind. She went straight to the stables. They were as deserted as before, and she started to examine Ario's loose-box in minute detail. Suddenly there was a creak at the door, and she turned. Argulus came in, a small ageless man with short straight fair hair, and strabismus in his brown eyes. "*'Afternoon, ma'am,*" he said in British, setting a couple of saddle-cloths briskly down on the shelf by the blanket, and was turning to go. Flavia stopped him, and asked about Theodorus.

"*Ar, happen, I sees 'im, morning of the day before yestern. I'm back from a ride on Brightear; he's blowing a bit, and I'm worried about his wind. He asks me which of the horses is Ario: says he'd heard you might be racing him tomorrow. I hears later you'd been asking after him. Hope I shouldn't have said something earlier.*"

"*Did you notice anything strange about the place after he'd been?*" responded Flavia.

"*Don't think I did. I checks fairly thorough, because I has to leave him alone in here for a few minutes while I'm settling Brightear, and I ain't seen him before, for all he holds hisself out as bein' known to ye. But all the stuff's still here, just as before.*"

"*Nothing at all?*"

Argulus stared downward, thinking. "*I did, Ma'am. I can't see it'd be connected,*" he hesitated, "*but I notices afterward that there's a bit of a mark on Ario's foot. Kind of thing he wouldn't do in the normal course, like. And it's true that I didn't notice it before the gen'leman come.*" He glanced at her, and she looked back encouragingly. "*I'll show you now.*" He went to the horse and picked up the rear left hoof, beckoning her over. There were three lines on the bed of the hoof, not deep enough to do the horse any harm, but looking too regular to be accidental.

"*The gods guard you, Argulus. I think you've found it.*" Ideas leaped in Flavia's mind: was this a "three" or a "six"?

"The dark servant has been given the key": might it mean that the code in the mysterious message was a Cæsarian letter-substitution, with each letter standing for one a number of places away in the alphabet, either earlier or later? *"You'll have five siliquæ for this work,"* she added, and ran indoors.

The first essays were fruitless, but it did not take long to reach an intelligible result:

To the Most Perfect Titus Vindex, from the Most Renowned Orestes, at Constantinople, the seventh day before the ides of February, in the consulships of Fl. Lupicinus and Fl. Iovinus, the tenth year of the indiction, greetings. I rejoice to hear of your health and safety among the barbarians. Tell the primicerius of the schola arcanorum at Carlisle that he may mention the name of the Illustrious Phronimius. Do not disclose your presence thereafter. Farewell.

Greek was hardly a complex code, but Flavia's triumph turned to dismay as she stared at the message. This meant nothing to her, save that important people seemed to be involved: "Most Renowned" meant a senator, while "Illustrious" was a title reserved to Consuls and to palatine Ministers in the Emperor's Consistory. This did not obviously take her much further than the mere existence of the letter. But, again, perhaps it did a little... There was that sentence "Do not disclose your presence": could that imply that Titus had planned to go into hiding, so that he might be falsely thought to have died? Moreover, this Orestes had obviously thought, on the seventh day before the ides of February, that Titus was alive and north of the Wall, and would be in London by now. That was about five and a half months after Titus had left Uxellodunum, she calculated. Did it imply that the Uxellodunum commander's assumption of his death could be wrong? Their mother's infrequent letters from Constantinople took five or six months to come; but the letter she was now holding in her hand had taken only, what, about eleven weeks to get to her. She could not see her way through this confusion. But it seemed at least to heighten the chance that Titus was still alive.

Even if there was such a chance, though, it was a finite one, and she surely ought to write to their mother Helpidia with the grim official news, whether or not anyone else might. She sighed, picked a blank tablet from a pile, and drew pen and inkwell toward her. She had never been to Constantinople herself, but from reports by others, and comparing her own visit to Rome, she had a clear vision of it – just as luxurious and extravagant as Rome, but softer, less marked by reality, and without Rome's problems: no low-lying areas flooded by the Tiber, no intractable enmities among ancient aristocrats; instead, flocks of Christian clerics condemning each other's small differences in doctrine, a new meaningless politics unrelated to the world – or else inviting themselves to old ladies' parties and charming them and angling for gifts, just like the legacy-hunters of Italy, but with the grand pretence that it was all for the poor, never for themselves. The place must surely be heaven for her mother, with all her petty snobbery and incessant demands for attention. Flavia struggled against her own instinct for distraction, and contrived a kind if conventional note, then put it in the tray where in due course Prudentia would find it and see that it reached the posting-house with an appropriate fee.

The thought of legacy-hunters was worrying at her somehow, and she suddenly with a shudder saw why. Any position in the *arcani* was obviously a politically sensitive, vulnerable one, and the mysterious message she had just deciphered suggested that Titus' situation was even more delicate than she had given it credit for. He could, she realised, be involved in some grand conspiracy, say to unseat the Emperor or one of the palatine officials. Even if he hadn't, there might be those who would claim that he had, in order to bid for his patrimony as a reward. And, legally, little of her father's property was hers: only the small farms in Lusitania and Second Germany which had been set aside as her dowry. All the rest, Cormerick itself, the land near Winchester, the house in London, the house and shop in York – it all belonged to Titus. If he was dead and there was any question of political manœuvring, then it could all be vulnerable to bounty-hunters with a good *entrée* to the Court. She had lived all her life at Cormerick. The place was bound up with her soul, and she had found the idea of losing it literally unthinkable. Yet it was not unthinkable, she now realised, nor impossible: if she were not so naïve, lost in her books and her farm, she would have seen this at once. It could be all stripped away from her in a moment, if an accusation could be made, and made to stick – together with all that she had built up since she had begun running the estate, and all her people there. If she was to know the chance of this, and the best way of standing against it, it was all the more important to find out exactly what had happened to Titus.

She called Atra and the other indoor-servants together again. Together they all went to a corner of the living-room, to their own little shrine to the Good Goddess. Atra bent with some difficulty to remove Flavia's shoes, and washed her face, hands and feet.

Flavia faced the Goddess' image at the head of the group of women. She raised her arms away from her body. "Good Goddess," she said clearly, "Goddess of sound counsel, hear our prayer. You know the tribulations of women, and you help them in their hour of need." She signed to Atra, who replaced her shoes for her.

"Mistress of land and sea, in a few days I set out on a journey. Favour my road and keep my steps safe, and grant, if it is pleasing to the gods, that I achieve my goal."

She turned to face the others, looking over their heads, her mind focusing on the Goddess. "Guardian-goddess, powerful over anxieties, watch over this household in my absence. Preserve it from all dangers, and give its members peace of mind." She turned back to the image, and let her arms fall to her sides.

Atra led the others away quietly, but Flavia stayed at the shrine for a while, lost in thought. She could, she knew, be leaving Cormerick for the last time, and she realised that she was in almost everything behaving entirely routinely: she told herself that this was so as not to alarm her servants, but she knew that it was also to quiet her own fears of being away from home. She went to her study, and looked out a dozen waxed tablets for making notes. There on one low shelf stood two small bound volumes of Plato's *Timæus*, one the Greek original, and one a recent copy of her own translation so far. She wrapped both in soft leather, and then in a cover and a separate bag of fine-woven oiled silk, and placed them at the bottom of one of the packs she would take with her.

Before retiring she went out, crossed the garden, and made her way to the family tombs, pausing at her father's grave for perhaps half an hour. The sight of it recalled to her the day of his burial, when she and Titus, after everyone had gone, had made their way down to the river Farcet to give his best dagger to Proserpine, the dagger he had always taken when travelling. Perhaps his *genius* still waited here. "Guardian spirit of my father," she prayed to it, "watch over me on the long journey which I start on tomorrow. Grant that my actions do justice to the confidence he always showed in me. Ask of the great Gods that they keep my steps safe; that they keep me, a woman travelling alone, from the hands of evil men; that they grant my heart's desire and restore my brother to me." She stood immobile, staring into the dark bushes behind the grave, a hovering sense of numinousness reaching toward her heart, and felt a single tear travel slowly down her right cheek and neck, and lose itself in her stole.

❈ ❈ ❈

She pulled the trap to a stop in the yard of the leather-works, put her weight on the worn blue dashboard, and jumped out herself before Marcius could hand her down. As her skirt settled about her, he took the reins from her left hand and gave them to a servant passing back from the cutting shop, while her freedman Philip followed to check that everything was done properly. The buildings, mostly wooden and two stories high, huddled about them in a reek of hides curing, and of smoke from the tanning. "Welcome, Most Perfect Flavia Vindex!" said Marcius, wiping his fingers on the leather apron drawn tightly as usual over his broad belly, and kissing her hand. "Will you be in town all day? We usually see you come to market in a rather more utilitarian vehicle. This elegant little trap of yours is lasting well."

"Thank you, Honourable Marcius; I hope you won't mind my leaving it in your yard again." she replied. He spread his hands in magnanimous reply. "Oh, that's kind; thank you. Yes, I shall be here all day. I may even stay overnight: it depends how the day goes." She looked about at his works, which seemed busier than ever. "It must be a couple of months since I was last in town. What is the news?"

"On the council we have problems again, Lady Flavia." He turned away for a moment: "Nonico, a cup of wine for the Most Perfect Lady; she's come a long way! Now where was I? Yes, the most venerable Emperor has decreed that municipal lands must be transferred again to the Privy Domain, and without the income from them I don't know how we are going to maintain the walls, or even the streets and sewers and water supply. We are making a case to the Governor that the law should be taken to apply only to property bequeathed since lands were returned to the cities by the Emperor Julian, but I'm not hopeful: the Privy Domain has its own special privileges at law. The temple lands are being treated the same, and the priests are distraught too: without money, how can there be sacrifices, and food and drink for the worshippers? I know that our own Corielsolilian canton is a small one, but even so our responsibilities go far outside the city itself: there are the temples at Collyweston and Brigstock to be thought of as well, for example. And all this on top of the ordinary task of the tax-raising! Your brother is very fortunate that his Imperial office exempts him from service as a councillor."

"I'm very sorry to hear it, Marcius," said Flavia, realising that this was a complex grievance whose history she was only vaguely familiar with, and that now was not the best time to be brought up to date. "I wish you the best with the lawsuit, in any event."

"Is there any news of the Most Perfect Titus? We have not seen him now for well over a year, I think."

"No firm news recently. You knew he had been posted north? But I've heard of someone called Theodorus who may be staying in town and have news of him; I was hoping to find him while I was here. Have you heard of him? I'm told he might be about thirty, with red hair and a courteous manner and Gallic bands on his leggings. He may well be staying at the Lucky Fisherman."

Marcius laughed. "You're very precise: there's some story there, I'm sure. Yes: I've passed a man like that in the street a couple of times over the last few days; he was at the baths on Tuesday, I'll be bound. I'll make enquiries, if you like."

"Would you, for me, Marcius? That would be kind. I must go and make my duty calls."

For, she thought glumly, as accompanied by Philip she passed a pile of raw, stinking, salted hides, and set off from Marcius' works towards the main street, it would not do to be seen in town and not to pay her respects to the *curator*, the Emperor's representative in the city-canton, and also to at least one of the two duumvirs who were the council leaders; she could probably leave the rest without giving offence. These were people who could certainly have helped her find this Theodorus, if she asked: none better. But she felt that would be foolish, given Titus' status and Theodorus' secrecy: better to rely on Marcius, whose discretion she trusted. In the meantime the courtesy calls would have to be endured.

She emerged from the works onto the paved main street of Durobrivæ, and the reek of the tannery began to diminish. To the left was the city's south gate, to the right the way to a central cross-roads, lined with public buildings and shops. She turned right and browsed along, stopping to chat with a few shopkeepers, pausing to buy a pound of dried apricots, a small pot of frankincense and a dozen small leather purses for tips, and giving the shopping to Philip to carry. Near the central cross-roads she arrived at the house of Felix, the *curator*, and the doorkeeper recognised her and called for an usher.

She was shown through a passage lined with busts of Felix's ancestors and three bronze tablets recording votes of thanks by the city council, and into the business-chamber. It was a medium-sized room painted in brown-red and yellow ochre with *trompe-l'œuil* panelling, and one wall had a number of small bronze plaques recording formal patronage relationships between Felix and various trade or other associations in the city-canton. Attended by a secretary and a clerk, the *curator* was volubly upbraiding a work-gang leader for the poor quality of a recent sewer clearance. Felix was a short, fat man of about fifty or so, clean-shaven and wearing a rather worn green tunic, informal but girded with the elaborate bronze-ornamented military *cingulum* belt that marked official rank. Something in his voice suddenly gave Flavia a feeling that a bribe was not far off, but on seeing her he abruptly broke off his discussion, telling the other man to wait, and turned to her, smiling.

"Most Perfect Lady Flavia Vindex, I am delighted to see you," he said, kissing her hand. "How kind of you to call! It is all too long since we saw you last in the city! You spend too long in your country retreat, and deprive us of your delightful company."

"You are very kind, Most Perfect Lord Felix," she replied. "On my estate I miss the life of the city, and especially the society of yourself, the Lady Chrysippe and your daughters. It is always a pleasure to see you again."

He offered her Gallic wine spiced with cloves and cinnamon, and asked how long she was staying in town. She replied that she expected to be leaving the same day, although she might stay just overnight. She asked about the city's affairs, and he lamented the heavy financial charges on the council, and that despite their undoubted generosity it was difficult at present to see how they were going to fund certain problems of the water supply in whose details a lady could have no interest. She sipped politely at a little of the wine, which was watered correctly to morning strength, exchanged a few more words, and took her leave, as Felix resumed his admonishment of the contractor.

They passed down the street, and came to the house of Blescius, the leader of the council. She explained to Philip, whose ideas of the world outside the estate seemed a little erratic, that Blescius was one of the wealthier of the many owners of pottery works in the district and that, while his kilns were outside the walls on the Lincoln road, he himself was usually to be found at his home in the city. The brick house they stopped at was two floors high, with an additional wooden storey added, perhaps for servants' dormitories. She spoke to a doorman, and they were admitted and led through the house to a reception room.

Blescius' room was decorated mainly in blue, with a tapestry hanging showing a hunting scene. Flavia and Philip were shown in to find Blescius and his wife gossiping with another earthenware manufacturer and a carpenter whose business was nearby. They were drinking mead spiced with nutmeg, and as he greeted her Blescius gestured for some to be poured for his latest guests.

"I tell you, back in the autumn," continued the other manufacturer, "Mainacrius brought down fourteen geese in one afternoon with those Scythian arrows. It was like magic."

"Perhaps it was," said the carpenter, dryly. "His young lady at Newbridge is said to be a dab hand with the spells."

"Now that's not what I meant! I have it on good authority that the only enchantment she can cast is that of her own natural allurements – which they say are not inconsiderable. I say that as a disinterested party, you understand. Your pardon, of course, Lady Flavia, and yours of course, my good lady."

Blescius' wife let a curious glaze pass over her cheerful expression for a moment, and continued to knit.

"You should know, Honourable Abascatus," continued the carpenter, "I'm not one to be offended by references to Mainacrius' vices. Though he'd better watch out if word is getting about. You can still be indicted for adultery."

"Anyone except yourself, perhaps, Lady Flavia," said Abascatus with the ever-so-slightly-nervous laugh she was used to, then realised that he had expressed himself badly, and blushed.

"What's the news on the council at present?" she asked to cover the gaffe, and in his determination to override it he gave a relentlessly detailed description of the legal moves being taken to evade the confiscation of city lands.

"Why, that estate where the Nene runs over the city-canton boundary, which was left to us by the deified Emperor Severus," concluded Blescius, "that must be at least 800 *iugera*; and in itself it would bring in 200 *solidi*. You know how quick they make the councillors pay for public works themselves if the city doesn't have the funds.

Even our own Felix did that last year, you remember, Abascatus, when he fingered Viridianus for the temporary tribunal and the reception at the Governor's visit?"

"Yes," replied the other. "Your family is very fortunate, Lady Flavia, to have got exemption from the city council."

"Yes, you are," interposed Blescius, evidently reluctant to lose control of the conversation. "Do you know that though it's, what, two years now since the Emperor decreed that the land-tax should be collected by Imperial officials rather than us poor councillors, none of the governors in Britain have done anything about it?"

"Though that may not be so much of a problem," said Abascatus smiling. "We may be expected to make up any shortfall in the tax, but if any taxpayer...offers to pay us more than is due, then in those cases we do stand to benefit a little."

"I suppose we must be lucky in our family to have exemption," Flavia said, hoping to nip in the bud a topic she preferred not to explore, "though I dare say poor Titus has his own problems. I must take my leave now, if I may: I have much to do today."

But her round was not yet ended, and she drove herself on to call on the *exactor* who saw that the taxation-assessments were made and complied with. She introduced him to Philip so that the latter would know him if sent into town on some future date, and spent time making conversation until well into the afternoon.

She felt she had had a long day when she got back to the leather-works and was approached by Marcius. "Well, I've tracked down your Theodorus," he said. "He left on Thursday, headed for Lincoln. To judge by your bags, you're on your way elsewhere yourself: perhaps you'll be going that way and meet him." He was looking at her shrewdly. "Will you join us for dinner? We have some pike caught fresh this morning, I'm told."

Flavia was happy to accept. She was brought some elderflower water, which she drank thirstily, murmuring endearments to the household's pet, one of the few dogs that she had as a friend; then she and Philip joined Marcius and his wife Ateanctos, his children and his two assistants in the dining-room. The invitation became extended to an overnight stay, and Flavia was able for a while to relax. Eventually the slaves cleared the dessert tables away, and Marcius got up to decant another little jug of wine and dilute it to a proper strength. Ateanctos seemed to think they had spent too much time talking of the city's affairs, and asked after Flavia's estate.

"I don't think I've been into town since November, and we seem to have had a very busy winter. We lost nearly a dozen head of stock over the cold spell, mostly weakly foals with chills, though there were two animals running out on to ice in the spring and going into the water, a brood mare and a yearling."

"There's been a lot of that this year. There's been more illness among people, too. Manillius says it's a malevolent conjunction of the stars. He says that an important man like Lycontius never dies in office by chance."

"Lycontius, the Vicar of the Britains?"

"Yes, didn't you hear? It was, what, the Ides of March, the same day as Julius Cæsar. He had arranged for renovation work in the reception suite at the Vicar's Palace. There was a hurry because he had called all the provincial governors in the Diocese of the Britains to a meeting in Augusta at the beginning of April. You know they're still building a new city wall along the Thames waterside? Apparently it was just reaching the palace, and he was out on the terrace seeing how it was going to affect the view when he tripped on some decorating gear and fell from the balcony. He was badly injured, and only lived about two weeks."

"What happened to the decorators?"

"I don't know. Did you hear, Marcius?" asked Ateanctos.

"He ordered them to be thrown to the beasts in the arena." said Marcius. "But then he found there wasn't going to be a beast show at the Games for a few weeks, so he changed his mind, and had them thrown from a tower on the city walls, then picked up and burned alive."

And Lycontius had been a Christian, Flavia reflected: so much for all their talk about brotherly love. What cruel punishments there were. Sometimes she forgot that, spending so much of her time reading things written under the Republic or the early Emperors, when evil things had indeed happened, but surely fewer. She recalled her father telling her of the severed head of the usurper Magnentius fifteen years ago, being carried round the western provinces on a pole. Though hadn't that happened to Otho too, centuries back, in the Year of the Four Emperors after Nero's death? "Has he been replaced?"

"Not yet," said Marcius. "Unlike our other master, Nepotianus at Lincoln. His replacement, Sanctus, passed through town two weeks ago on his way to take up office."

"I'm going on to Lincoln. Did you hear anything about him?"

Marcius glanced at her. "Not much. He had a small escort: his wife is joining him later, I think, and his children are probably grown up now. He's obviously a stickler for protocol, though. I wouldn't forget the courtesy call."

CHAPTER 2

Flavia slept uneasily, and knowing she slept she saw Socrates, Timæus, Critias and Hermocrates grouped round. Socrates – ugly like a boxer, bearded and in a tattered, stained himation – said: '"And we spoke about women too: we said that they were to be brought up and educated in the same way as the men, and share the same occupations both in war and in the rest of their lives."' She turned to him with tears in her eyes and tried to say that he must speak to the Emperor at once, but no words would come, and he did not seem to notice her. Then she saw that behind him was the Parthenon; the doors to the temple were open, and showed the great statue of Athena with her spear, ægis and helmet. On the goddess's face a smile began to form, proud, weary, bitter, and contemptuous.

The old road through Stamford and Grantham would be hilly, and Flavia and Philip took the newer, which was easier for the trap. They got to know each other a little better as they travelled. Philip had been freed five years ago, a delayed manumission from her father's will. He was in his late forties, spare and anxious, with thinning hair, delighted at his wife's pregnancy and obviously yearning that the baby would survive and be a boy, though he claimed that he did not mind being away from her, and that in fact the journey would distract him from the risks of the confinement. Despite what Sallienus had said about his lack of schooling, he had on the farm been taught to speak good Latin, and to read and write. He was also naturally considerate, Flavia found, though ponderous in his manner; she suspected a long-held ambition to become a senior household servant, so that he was trying to mould his behaviour to an often-imagined and regularly-rehearsed part.

They took two days getting to Sleaford, where the iron tyre on one of the wheels broke. The next day they spent at a workshop, while wood-pigeons croo-crooed in the forest behind. The tyre was now mended, and they were watching the smith and his mate filling a circular trench with hazel-bundles, preparing to fire the metal before shrinking it to the wheel. A horse arrived. They looked round, and found that Rúari had caught them up: a tall, classic Irishman in his late twenties with red hair, a heavy brogue, milky skin, and freckles already accelerating with the spring sunshine. With much digression and reported speech, he explained that Prudentia had taken ill at the last minute and had been pronounced unable to come; triumphantly, without any of the masculine hesitation which might have impeded Philip in such a gesture, he handed over a huge bag of sewing and darning equipment which he said Prudentia had been told to bring. Flavia was relieved for her own complex reasons, and not dissatisfied to be spared the burden of watching over a sheltered slave-girl on the road, but looked askance at the pile of needlework materials, concluding that she could safely dump them soon without causing offence.

A further day saw them approaching Lincoln. As they made their way down a long slope past a thin string of farmers with donkeys, they had a spectacular prospect for a mile to the north. Before forming a broad estuary, two rivers, Witham from the south and Till from the west, joined in a great pool nearly half a mile across and crowded with shipping, and the city walls towered on the steep hill above, looking all the higher against the fenland plains to the west and east. They made their way past great roadside cemeteries, full of decaying tombs of the Ninth Spanish Legion, and then across a bridge, admiring the water-mills to the left beyond the harbour, three or four more than a few years back when Flavia had last been there. The road wound its way uphill round the city to the east gate, not far from where an aqueduct brought water from the distant chalk downs.

Flavia had hoped to stay with family friends in the older northerly part of the town, and sent Philip to enquire. He came back to report that they had gone on pilgrimage to the shrine of Jupiter at Lydney, and that there was only a caretaker in the house. She knew nobody else well enough to visit, so they lodged at an inn. While they unpacked their gear she learned that the new governor was away, having gone to the port of Skegness to meet an old friend arriving from Gaul by sea. She made enquiries after Theodorus, and was told that he had been with the governor's party: the best thing, no doubt, would be to wait.

But she felt that she had not done enough to further her search for Titus, and she was frustrated being idle. So the next day she went to the temple of Mars in the north of the city, a god appropriate to her brother's military status, and had the priest sacrifice a sheep for the success of her search for Titus. A small boy started to play the double-pipe, and she composed herself as the priest began the ritual. He washed his hands, invoked the god three times and sprinkled flour and salt on her chosen sheep's head. Next he cut off a few hairs, signed for his assistant to bring the axe down on its neck, and then himself sent the bronze dagger straight to its heart. She had not commissioned her own blood sacrifice for over three years, and it gave her a feeling of effectiveness, of completion: she saw animals die every now and then on the farm, but as her sheep moved its last on the broad low altar she felt somehow that a vigour had passed into her petition that might move even Mars – a god to whom she had never felt close or sympathetic.

Deftly the priest eviscerated the offering, set the intestines and some slices of fat to burn for the god, and put the remaining pieces to roast. As usual the smell drew a number of votaries who might be suffering less from spiritual hunger than from a more commonplace appetite. With the good weather, the worshippers' table was set outdoors; she invited a few of the more presentable bystanders to join herself and the priest, and the acolyte brought out bread and wine. She nibbled some of the meat for the sake of the ritual, but was not hungry. She looked around, and saw a dark man of about thirty with his eyes on her, standing at a distance on the edge of the temple precinct; she found that she did not resent his gaze but returned it, though shortly he drew his cloak around himself and made off. After the sacrificial meal was over she stayed chatting to the priest, a retired junior army officer, and she learned to her dismay that he thought that Theodorus had been in town a week earlier, and had pressed straight on northwards towards Isurium.

Once back at the inn, she decided that there was no point in gambling on the priest being right and her earlier informant being wrong: she should wait for the governor to get back. It would not do to make calls on the municipal dignitaries before visiting him, so she commandeered a sitting-room for reading while Philip and Rúari explored the city and its environs, but she told them to come and see her when they returned, wanting to make sure they were getting on together: it would make her life difficult if they should fall out. A while after the bugles had blown for the dusk closing of the gates, the two knocked at her door. She was sitting in front of a brightly-burning hazelwood fire in a small room panelled in oak on the first floor, and called them in, gesturing them to a couch.

"*How are you finding Lincoln?*" she asked in British, not having yet really tried Rúari's Latin.

They looked at each other, and Philip replied. "*Of course it's a lot larger than Durobrivæ, madam,*" he said, "*but it seems a pleasant enough place.*"

"*Are you occupying your time?*"

"*Certainly, madam. We have already been fortunate with one or two prudent investments at the racecourse. Rúari here proves to be a fine judge of talent, do you not, Rúari?*"

"*Do you now?*" she said, smiling.

"*I do what I can, your honour*," said Rúari somewhat complacently, "*And it helps that in the Kingdom of Ulster where I come from there are the finest horses in the world, descended, as we say, from the mares of Queen Medb. You have to have known a good horse to recognise one, and Kingcup in the race this very afternoon was a horse to be proud of, though these sorry Lincoln people didn't seem to see it. I've seldom seen a brighter eye or a clearer line in the flanks, not even in the great races of my boyhood, and not even among your honour's own herds.*"

But as the door closed behind them she heard their voices through the wood. "*Ha, ha!*" came Rúari's. "*I see you did not admit that you were too timid to put on the accumulator!*"

"*That was prudence, and not timidity, boy – a virtue that you can scarcely lay claim to, I think.*" The injured dignity of Philip's fading response caused her some concern, but it was not long before events put it out of her mind.

On the Sunday there was much commotion at a timber church in the southern suburb where the large Christian community gathered to worship. The uninitiated among them, and those penalised by their priests for breaking the Christian code of conduct, were not allowed inside, but crowded round the door in the light rain. These wrongdoers were dressed in rough clothes and had rubbed ashes into their hair, and some of the uninitiated wore clothes much too good for the weather: loafers hung about, partly for the fun of watching both groups get wet, and partly in hope of handouts from the almoners. Flavia and her party, cloaked in stout hooded *birri*, went to the ramparts, where there was a good view. Suddenly the idlers started into movement and were running round the walls. Themselves they followed above, and saw a party approaching along the easterly road: half a dozen cavalry troopers, then three carriages, seven or eight horsemen, a number of gentlemen or their servants, and another six or seven soldiers. Clearly the governor had returned. Philip took round a note paying Flavia's respects, and received an invitation for her to a reception after dinner that evening. But further enquiries showed no news of Theodorus.

Flavia bathed and dressed carefully for the event: she did not move much in high society, and though she supposed it was true that one should pay respect only to those whose virtue earned it, the fact was that it would be important to make a good impression. She knew nothing of the governor beyond what Marcius had told her, but he would probably be in office for at least a year, and there might well be instances where his judicial power could help or harm her. Moreover, there would be many other influential people at the reception, and, if she met the right ones, that could be useful too. Above all, Theodorus might be present; but even if he were not, there might be others who knew him or who if approached correctly could report his plans.

Binding her breasts in a linen band, she could have done with help; the chambermaid was busy, and Flavia for a moment rather wished that Prudentia had come after all. She put on a good blue-green woollen dalmatic dress with lines of a deeper green towards the hems; her hair, already dressed carefully at the baths, she shrouded in a grey-blue chiffon *maforte* with a gold-embroidered border; she added a polished copper neck-torc, which emphasised the base of her throat, and matching ear-rings. When the time came she made her way with Philip to the governor's palace, and he announced her to the soldiers on the door. One of them shouted within, and a house-slave appeared to escort her through the peristyle to the reception room.

She looked around the room. It was painted in a red and black colour-scheme, with delicate *trompe-l'œuil* effects of panelling and pillars. There was an elaborate coffered ceiling, and a huge mosaic on the heated floor depicting a luscious scene, probably the Judgement of Paris, with little faces towards the corners which might be meant as satyrs or genii. On one wall there was a large hanging of embroidered wool, showing a view of heroes hunting in chalk hills. The governor was seated in comfort behind a draped table on a daïs, probably his tribunal on judicial days, and deep in conversation with a small group of men whom he seemed to know well: he looked to be in his late sixties, bald, brown, still seemingly wiry, maybe a

Spaniard or an Italian. She approached and greeted him formally. He looked up giving an off-hand gesture, but as his eyes met hers they quickened with unexpected interest, and he turned to his nomenclator to get her name.

There were about forty guests there, at least thirty of them men. She could not see anyone she recognised...oh yes, there was the Deputy Head of Secretariat of the Diocese of the Britains, visiting from London...and a former colleague of Titus', an accountant in the diocesan division of the Office of the Sacred Largesses. There was an Imperial Messenger she had met somewhere, but whose name she couldn't remember, and a woman she'd spoken to briefly at the baths on Friday, the wife of the deputy commander of the cavalry unit in the city. She spotted the dark-haired man she had seen the other day at the temple; she craned her neck to try to make out his rank badges, but failed.

She caught fragments of conversation: expectations for the harvest, the winds which had brought the governor's guest to Skegness rather than straight in to Lincoln, the virtues of a horse. Then someone standing next to her cleared his throat. He looked to be in his late forties – rather fat, of medium height, and dressed in dark green velvet. He inclined his head, doubling his chin. "The Most Perfect Julius Limisius Noricus, Most Perfect Lady. I am honoured to make your acquaintance."

She gave a similar bow. "The Most Perfect Flavia Vindex. I think I detect from your intonation that you are not from the Britains. Have you travelled far to be with us?"

"Only from Gaul, Most Perfect Lady. You divine my provincial accent, for they say that in the Britains is spoken the most perfect Latin outside Rome." He inclined his head again briefly, as if acknowledging the compliment on her behalf.

"Would you be a companion of our new governor?"

"I fear not, Lady. I have no official or semi-official position. I am a simple private person."

"Then you've come a long way on private business. I hope you've been successful in whatever it is."

"We shall see. These are difficult times, and like I

think a number of others I have decided that there would be advantages to acquiring land in the Britains; we were all most impressed a few years ago when the Emperor Julian was able so promptly to summon up grain from the Britains for the armies on the Rhine. And land is, how shall I put it, less vulnerable to disorder here than in the Gauls. I am fortunate in that my wife has inherited interesting salt-mines near to the town of Middlewich. We propose to buy in that area. Perhaps you know it?"

Flavia was about to apologise for her ignorance of the west of the province when he interrupted gently: "Ah, look." He indicated something behind her, and at that moment a gong boomed. She turned. She was conscious fleetingly of the governor's gaze. A butler was clearing his throat importantly.

"Honoured Gentlemen and Ladies!" he cried. "Your host the Most Perfect Flavius Sanctus, governor of the province of Flavia Cæsariensis, has an entertainment for you! His own brother-in-law, the Most Renowned Decimius Magnus Ausonius, tutor to the most noble Flavius Gratian the son and heir of the immortal Emperor Our Lord Flavius Valentinian Augustus, having just arrived from Gaul, will now give a recitation of his own verses."

A portly man, his thinning hair dyed, unexpectedly sloppily, to disguise its greying, stepped forward holding a sheaf of papyrus. "Most Renowned and Most Perfect Gentlemen and Ladies," he said (though Flavia had seen no senators of Most Renowned rank, and quite a few of the guests seemed to be merely Honourable), "I shall, with your indulgence, read a selection of poems on which I am still working. You will, I know, have the generosity to recognise that they are still unpolished. One of the collections I am putting together is a series of tributes to my most excellent former colleagues among the teachers at the University of Bordeaux, and the first poem I am going to read to you is drawn from that little garden of verses." He shuffled through the papyri rather nervously.

Flavia's heart sank. She had read some of Ausonius' poems in Trier, and they were widely praised, but not by her. Some of them were quite nicely turned, but the man had been a teacher at Bordeaux for thirty years, and let it show: he was usually pedantic, contrived, and ponderous, lacked a sense of humour or even wit, and had disastrous forays into lubricity (though with luck that was High Table stuff, and they would be spared it in mixed company). She studied the simper on his face and decided that it had appeared when he was introduced: perhaps he wasn't entitled to the rank of Most Renowned himself, but was now so important that he couldn't be held to account if he let others use it of him. How had this man become the tutor of the Emperor's son? Probably simply through connections well cultivated. She told herself, as often before, that she should make more effort at her correspondence: you never knew when you might need the right contact.

His voice had become surprisingly orotund, though rather plummy.

> "*Leontius the Grammarian, nicknamed 'Naughty'*:
> "If you respect the jovial and content,
> And keep the festal days with merriment,
> Recall the name Leontius each year
>   With heavy tear.
> "Although they call'd him 'Naughty' all his days,
> A name unworthy of his blameless ways,
> He ne'er complained and never took offence:
>   It pleased his friends.
> "An arts degree of such a class he won
> Sufficient for his post as Lecturer 1.
> Among grammarians he would seem a mellow
>   And worthy fellow.
> "As students we were never far apart,
> My inoffensive friend! And yet my heart,
> Leontius, grows to you never colder,
>   Though you were older.
> "This is a pleasure sad, not to forget
> You, but with weeping words to spell regret:
> It is a task both thankless and perverse,
>   Owed by my verse."

There was a round of applause led by the governor, Sanctus. Flavia looked around carefully, trying to work out whether people who weren't clapping very hard were bored by poems or thought this one as bad as she did. One or two of her acquaintances seemed to be leaving already.

"The next is a dedicatory poem, which I think should be fairly self-explanatory." Ausonius cleared his throat.

"'*A pretty new book, now who's to receive it*?'
Long ago said a poet of Verona – believe it . . .'"

Her attention was distracted by the first line. It was a quotation from Catullus, a great poet in the ancient days before the emperors, and a memory invaded her mind, a recollection of another time she had heard a man quoting Catullus, years ago, in Rome.

It had been in the majestic palace of the Petronii on the Cælian Hill, where a great ball had been in progress. She remembered that she had been delighted with her white dress, woven of a mixture of fine linen and silk that clung to the body, and subtly decorated with white damask; proud too of the silver snake-band defining her high breasts, running close above and below, and with a sardonyx set where it crossed itself between them.

Out in the gardens the three of them had found a kiosk, but Titus had gone off with a band of youths, and she had been sitting alone with Cæcina Priscus, having eaten and drunk lightly but well; she had been offered a glass of vermouth flavoured with Pontic wormwood and cassia, something she had never tasted before. Priscus had been wearing a toga, a fogeyish affectation of his, and its quantity of cloth had flowed over him generously as he walked, hiding the clear lines of his muscles beneath the floating oscillation of the drapery. He had looked at her with his quickening clear brown eyes, and quoted a poem of Catullus, saying, "Some people give it a title: *Accountancy for life and love*:

"'Let's live, my Lesbia, and let's make love,
And write off the murmurings of sad old men.
The sun and stars set, yet they return again.
For us, once our brief light is spent,
The darkness, and the silence, are for ever.
So pay me...a thousand kisses...then a hundred...
Then a thousand more...then another hundred...
Then yet another thousand...and then a hundred.
Then when we have had many thousands of kisses,

We shall jumble the records,
So that no-one can ever calculate the number,
And so no envious curse have means to hurt us.'"

He had paused, waiting, and she had found herself moving closer to those magical eyes. Her mouth had met his, and he had felt both safe and exciting at the same time. Her sense already aroused by the unfamiliar smells of Rome, she had been overwhelmed by his sweet breath, and the interesting fresh scent of his sweat. Recollections began to come tumbling to her of that meeting and of how it had developed, but now she was becoming aware again of the room she was actually in, and of the continuing reading; and she was unsure how long her attention had lapsed.

She was beginning to realise that there seemed to be a lot of eyes on her, and a rather strange atmosphere. Ausonius was clearing his throat again.

"I think you'll follow the conceits of the next little poem best if you remember that the Greek letters referred to are in capitals," he said. "It's entitled *To Eunus, a Schoolmaster with Delicate Tastes*." He gave a sort of giggle, which Flavia didn't like, and she suddenly realised that she was the only woman left in the room. The men's expressions varied: some were watching her with interest, as if expecting something; others seemed embarrassed or withdrawn.

Ausonius went on, tittering at the pauses:

"Syrian Eunus, you're a gastronome of groins,
And under Phyllis' teaching you're a Master now of Loins!
You see a woman's bush, with four corners, and you know
That drawn in they'll, triangular, the letter *Delta* show."

Every eye was on her, and she felt a surge of anger, and a bright flush burning in her cheeks. Anxious not to lose face, she set off straight for the exit, briskly but at a measured pace. Ausonius continued, affecting to ignore her.

> "The female valley set about with clefts upon each
> side
> *Upsilon's* shape you'd swear it is, when cunt is
> open wide.
> Now when he goes to lick at it, his tongue a *Lambda*
> finds,
> And he detects within, set in a *Phi*-shape, certain
> signs .."

Suddenly on the daïs the governor rose to his feet.
"One moment, please," he said, in a voice which, though
not loud, carried perfectly and stilled every sound in the
room. Thank the gods, thought Flavia, breaking her stride,
he's going to stop this.

"One moment, friend Ausonius," he repeated, though
the rhetor had stopped reading already. "Lady, come here,
please." Yes, he meant her, she realised. Yet more self-
conscious, hardly aware of choosing what to do, Flavia
paused and went over to the tribunal.

Again there was a curious light in his eye. "Madam,
what do you mean by seeking to depart the room without
properly taking your leave of your superior in rank?" She
could not find an answer. It was not a question that had an
answer. Her eyes beseeched his cold face for help. She
suddenly recognised the look in his eye for what it was:
lubricity. His voice became quieter, and more frightening.
"Madam, what is this insolence whereby you stare me in
the face? I am the Most Serene Emperor's representative in
this province. Cast your eyes down humbly in my
presence." She lowered her gaze to the floor. "Madam,
what is your rank?"

She heard her voice come out of her of its own accord.
"Most Perfect, Most Perfect Lord Governor. It is Most
Perfect, as was the rank of my father."

"Your father?" The voice was growing oily and
luxuriant. "Am I to infer that you have no husband to
regulate your doings? Madam, I have doubts of what you
say. Is there any man here who can vouch for the rank of
this lady?" She could not see the room from where she now
stood, but, thinking frantically back to the last few
moments, even though this was her own province she could
not remember any of her acquaintances still being there. A

numbness had invaded the whole of her lower body. Now she could think of nothing but fear.

A deep hush, electric with attention. He cleared his throat, at leisure. "Madam, you are aware that it is a serious crime to assert a rank to which one is not entitled. I believe that your case merits further investigation. Today is Sunday, and under a constitution of the Emperor Constantine judicial proceedings do not take place. I shall judge your case tomorrow. In the meantime you will be detained in this palace. *Biarchus*, take her away! Let the woman be brought before Our tribunal in the morning." She could hardly breathe, forcing the air in, in little shallow pantings. A soldier left the doorway and gripped her by the arm. She drew her shawl round her and allowed herself to be led out of the room.

They passed through the door. She moved mechanically. She was aware of something: the rough skin and hard pressure of the soldier's thumb; he was in his thirties, with thinnish fair hair, and dandruff on the shoulders of his uniform. "Don't know what I'm to do with you," he said in a German accent. He led her back into the peristyle and paused, then called towards the gate: "Rautio! I've been sent on special duty. Alert another man for the audience-chamber, will you?" He started off round a decrepit statue of the Emperor Diocletian towards the north-west corner of the courtyard, where a lamp showed an entrance. Some way along a poorly-lit passageway he suddenly said, "In here, Lady," and she went through a door. Taking a spill to a lamp in the corridor, he lit a candle fixed to the wall, and in the yellow flickering light she saw that the room was small and quite plain, with a little window to the courtyard and three stools. "Sit down, then," he said. She stood staring at a stool, where he had pointed.

He went back through the doorway propping his spear against it, turned, and bent to pick up a heavy wooden staple which would bolt her in, but as he straightened there appeared at the door the dark man whom Flavia had noticed at the temple and then today at the reception. He nodded pleasantly at the soldier, and moved his cloak apart to show the emblem of a Count on his tunic. "Tricky one you've got there, *biarchus*," he said in a deep, friendly, man-to-man kind of voice. "Never know quite whose protection they're under, these class women."

The soldier's gaze became more alert, and he put his head outside the door for a second to check whether there was anyone else out there, then lowered the beam to the floor again. "Oh, yes," he said sardonically. "And what's it to you, mate? Emperor's mistress, is she?"

"Not quite, soldier. And are you sure you want to know? Let's just say," a purse appeared, chinking slightly, "that someone might be prepared to think that a fee of four whole gold *solidi* would be a fair one, if you were to find that the prisoner wasn't in this room after all when you got back to fetch her in two hours' time."

The soldier paused, his eyes on the bag. His hand drifted, as if for reassurance, towards his spear. "A man could get into a lot of trouble for something like that, especially if the Governor had his eye on a lady. One might think that ten *solidi* wouldn't be enough."

"A man doesn't get into trouble only by getting across his present master. But it may be that six *solidi* wouldn't be too much."

The soldier considered. "Six *solidi*, but one hour rather than two," he demanded.

"Very well," said the stranger and reached into a pocket, drew out two *solidi* and added them to the purse, then handed it to the soldier, who looked in and counted the contents carefully. All three of them left the room.

"We'll need a proper veil," said the stranger.

"Haven't got anything like that," said the soldier. "Nobody's told the gate guards. Nothing official, anyway." He set off down the corridor, his shoulders slumped. Flavia took her cue from her rescuer, and they crossed the peristyle quietly. She raised her *maforte* to try and conceal her face, and they walked together past bored, gossiping doorkeepers out of the palace. Philip joined them in the street, having evidently been waiting outside. Then all three went up to the main crossroads and round a corner out of sight.

Her protector turned; he seemed for a moment to look like Apollo, and she told herself not to be foolish. He gave her a formal nod. "My name is Arctus."

It was a curious name, the Greek word for a bear, Latinised. It didn't reveal any family links; it wasn't very promising. "The Most Perfect Lady Flavia Vindex," she replied automatically, a little puzzled, trying to put into her voice the warmth she felt, looking in vain for words that would convey something more than formality. "Thank you so much. I don't know what I can do or say..."

"I think we both need to get out of the city. Indeed, it would be wise to get out of the province. One hour isn't long, even if the man keeps to the bargain: we must move fast."

"But your rank, Most Renowned Sir: would that not protect you?"

"Only Most Perfect, not Most Renowned. But in any event we are in Sanctus' own province. Here he's likely to act first and listen to recriminations afterwards, if there is anyone to bring them: we should do better debating the question in Doncaster, which is probably the nearest place outside his jurisdiction. Do you have transport?"

"Yes, and two servants."

"We had better leave at once. I have things to collect from the posting-station. Let's go now to your carriage."

A damp mist was coming in from the fens as they walked quickly through the streets to the inn, in silence, Flavia not yet ready to digest her experiences, and simply watching and listening for pursuit. Philip had run ahead, and he and Rúari were already loading the trap when she and Arctus arrived, and she went in and settled her bill, while he paid two inn servants to assist with the loading and then joined in the work himself. The four of them climbed up. "I hope wheeled traffic at night is legal here within the walls," said Arctus, taking the reins. "If not, we shall have trouble at the gate."

"I can't remember any restriction last time I was here," said Flavia, realising that she was making conversation as one might at a party. "Should it not be?"

"There must be towns in Britain which imitate Rome on that; there certainly are in Gaul. We ought to have a few minutes yet unless we're very unlucky: I don't think they'd move against me, given my own rank, without Sanctus' personal authority. And his reception may be over by now: he could be anywhere at this time of night, even though I suppose his whereabouts will certainly be well known." And a minute later: "Ah, here's the gate. One moment." They were at the east gate, with two great fifteen-foot arches, and ghostly birchwood scaffolding reaching up to where the towers were being extended. Arctus slipped down and disappeared into the further guard-house, where the window showed a dim light. There was noise of a barking authoritative voice and a surly unco-operative one; a faint chink of coins. Then two figures emerged, and one reluctantly opened the gate while Arctus re-mounted the trap and started through.

Outside the road turned right and – so slowly, Flavia thought – wound half-way round the walls. She waited for shouts or a noise behind, but nothing came. Then they stopped again. "Here we are at the posting-house. Just a minute or two. If anyone comes after you, take off by yourself for Doncaster." He jumped down and disappeared round the corner, maybe to the back door. Minutes passed: long, long minutes. Who was this man Arctus, she wondered; would they be caught? What would happen if they were? Sanctus couldn't have people of their class tortured, not for something run-of-the-mill. But what about the way he had been looking at her? And what about the slaves? She looked about, not caring to pursue this train of thought. The mist swirled and visibility worsened. A muffled roar of cheery laughter came from somewhere indoors, already deadening with the fog by the time it reached her. Nobody was on the road. Suddenly the gate to the coach-houses was opened and a strange man led out two horses, one of which, even in the gloom, she could see was a notably fine mare; another man closed the gate again and ran up to her. "Right, we're all set," murmured a newly familiar voice. "Call out something in Greek, not too loud, if you spot trouble – you can manage a bit of Greek, can you?"

She reassured him on this, and he and his companion began to ride through the suburbs of Lincoln and then away northwards, the trap following sedately. It was about twenty miles to the province-boundary, but, as Arctus said to her on the way, going just beyond it would do no good, for if Sanctus were offended he would have no trouble sending soldiers into Second Britain in pursuit of them: they must get all the way to Doncaster before stopping. He seemed to be following their progress carefully on a map or an itinerary, as far as he could make it out in the broad moonlight, and after a place he said was Riseholme they came to a junction, meeting a gentler way for heavier traffic, and turned off the faster main road.

After midnight they arrived at the river Trent, its waves glittering black and silver into the distance like a sea: two arches of the long bridge here had been carried away by flooding and were under repair, and they took over an hour to rouse the ferrymen and persuade them to haul a great raft across, then (even more difficult) to get the men awake at the posting-station on the other side, and induce them to part with new horses for the carriage; but at last a mixture of money and threats sufficed. As they began to get up speed again they heard in the distance shouts on the east bank of the river – a sign at last, perhaps, of pursuit.

She slept fitfully for a while, propping her head on a spare cloak folded over the wooden seat back, her dreams haunted not just by Titus and by Priscus, but by vague runnings-away in which time and again she was caught and nearly caught. For a moment they were changing horses again at some little settlement, and then it was dawn and they were coming into a sleepy town, a mass of brick and indistinguishably red sandstone, huddled against the walls of its fort. Somewhere the voice of a cockerel made its claim against the slumbering world as they knocked at the doors of the posting-house, a large one that served official visitors to the garrison regiment. A slave who was already making up the fires answered, and went off in search of the housekeeper: they got three rooms without difficulty. In one of them they settled their luggage with Philip, Rúari, and Arctus' manservant Erdigorra. In the other two they each threw themselves on a bed and slept.

Flavia woke from another troubled sleep, registering the braying of a donkey somewhere outside. She dozed, avoiding thought. Then there was a buffeting at her door. "*Lady!*" came a woman's voice. "*It's midday! The baths close to women at the ninth hour, if you want them!*" It was a good idea, she realised, and thanked her invisible adviser. She put on her shift and cloak, shoved a change of clothes into a bag, put nine or ten silver *siliquæ* and a big handful of copper *nummi* into a purse, turned right out of the entrance and made her way up towards the fort.

She had glimpsed its mass in the twilight, but saw it now properly for the first time. The walls, based on three massive courses of ashlar sandstone, rose forty feet to battlements in small well-mortared red bricks. Sixty-foot round towers stood at each corner and on either side of the gates in each wall, and two catapults were mounted on each tower. Above three of the visible towers flew square banners. One she recognised as the ensign of the Count and Vicar of the Britains, who must be the high commander of the garrison; the others she supposed were the colours of the regiment itself, and some other flag.

The baths were just under the walls, blazoned with a plaque explaining at some length the pious concern for the people of Doncaster which had led some wealthy veteran to build them. At the door an aged slave demanded a siliqua for admission. "What are you talking about, you silly man?" cried a voice from behind Flavia, who turned to see a large busy matron with two young girls and a little boy in tow, already dropping a pile of copper coins into the attendant's hand. "Just because this lady's a stranger is no reason to try to steal from her! One of these days you'll try that on the wife of a new commandant, and then you'll be in trouble." She turned to Flavia. "The price is twenty *nummi*, dear, and expensive at that; it'd be half as much in York, of course, but I suppose in a small place we have to be lucky to have a bath-house at all. Come on dear, that's right," she hustled Flavia in as she put the money into the slave's palm.

In the changing room, the little boy became over-interested in women's anatomy, and his mother became preoccupied with her brood. Flavia took her clothes off and gave them to a washerwoman who promised with excessive conviction to have them back washed and dried in half an hour, then let down her hair and gave her bag to an attendant. She went straight through to the hot room and lay down on a towel. She didn't want to worry about Titus or whether she was being followed, and set herself to remember poetry, choosing a cheerful passage from the end of the *Odyssey*:

> This pass'd on earth, while in the realms above
> Minerva thus to cloud-compelling Jove:
> "May I presume to search thy secret soul?
> O Power Supreme, O Ruler of the Whole!
> Say, hast thou doom'd to this divided state,
> Or peaceful amity, or stern debate?
> Declare thy purpose, for thy will is fate."
> "Is not thy thought my own?" the God replies
> Who rolls the thunder o'er the vaulted skies,
> "Hath not long since thy knowing soul decreed
> The chief's return should make the guilty bleed?
> 'Tis done, and at thy will the Fates succeed.
> Yet hear the issue: since Ulysses' hand
> Hath slain the suitors, Heav'n shall bless the land.
> Each future day increase of wealth shall bring,
> And o'er the past Oblivion stretch her wing.
> Long shall Ulysses in his empire rest,
> His people blessing, by his people bless'd.
> Let all be peace." He said, and gave the nod
> That binds the Fates, the sanction of the God . . .

She grew drowsy, then awoke as two heavy old ladies in shifts came in, speaking at each other loudly in British. They had been to an army festival, commemorating the dedication of the temple of Invincible Mars in the Circus Flaminius at Rome. One was talking noisily and greedily about the quality of the sacrificial meat this year compared with last, and complaining that it had been unfairly distributed, while the other seemed more interested in her own sciatica. Whether they were listening to each other at all seemed doubtful.

Flavia liked these little military baths, though: they didn't have great marble halls or a host of variously-heated rooms, but neither did they bother to lower the temperature during the women's times, and besides they were relaxed about letting civilians in, and it was easier to talk to strangers if you wanted. She got up, went through and let

herself into the cold plunge pool, first hissing through
clenched teeth and then letting out a small shriek as she
submerged. She swam up and down rapidly a few times,
then climbed out smiling at someone waiting to get in,
dried herself and took her towel to the warm room. A
woman approached her selling green glass phials of
perfume, swearing implausibly that they were Cosmian.
Flavia, recalling Seneca's advice, "*The best scent for the
person is no scent at all*," firmly refused them, but
consented to hire a pumice stone; she scraped at stray hairs
on her legs, and rested for a while until she was quite sure
she was dry.

Who was this Arctus, she wondered, and what was this
all about? She was sure he was the same as the man who
had been watching her at the temple of Mars Rigonometos.
Why should he, or anyone, take the huge risk of suborning
a soldier in the governor's palace to set her free? And what
was she to do now? Cormerick was in Sanctus' province:
perhaps that made the decision for her – she couldn't go
home now, and might as well go on. She tried to imagine
the map, to think of routes. Would Theodorus have come
this way?

Once out of the baths, she went to leave her bag at the
posting-station. It was the ninth hour after dawn. A flash
came from the gate of the fort as she passed, and looking
up she saw a bugler chatting to a sentry, his eye on a
sundial, preparing to blow the change of watch. It was his
instrument that had caught her eye: bronze and about four
foot long, with a narrow straight shaft and a wide bell at
the end. She had not seen one since Gaul, though the
watches had been called at Lincoln, and she realised now
that there had been bugle calls regularly ever since their
arrival at the fort. She was coming into the realm of the
army, and this was not like the civilian world: time was
closely defined.

The paths to the east were full of workmen going to and
from shifts at the potteries. She walked westward up the
Don to its junction with another river, and back: hawthorn
was all along the banks, and was coming, busy and white,
into full flower; behind it ordered fields stretched, worked
by men hoeing out weeds and throwing creepers into

water-barrels to rot, while small naked boys, brown from the sun, ran about chasing away the wheatears and starlings.

Back in the posting-house she kept to her room, spoke to Philip and Rúari, went through her belongings to check if things had gone astray, pondered. About the eleventh hour, as the gradual dusk began to gather, Arctus knocked and asked if she would join him for a meal. She tidied herself and went through to his room, finding him mixing wine and water in a large bronze bowl chased in tin with figures of deer. The room was simple, with a small brazier in a corner giving some welcome warmth. She saw him now more clearly than in the night: a tallish, tanned, slim man in his early thirties, clean-shaven, with curly dark-brown hair and perhaps a slightly crooked mouth. He looked up, and she saw in his brown eyes a keen, perhaps sexual, warmth of interest, and also a kindness that bid to seduce her at once, but seemed too soft to match last night's events. She smiled.

"I still haven't thanked you properly," she said, "though I'm not sure what to say. It's not a situation one gets practice with, not if one has any sense."

"I think I surprised myself by rising to the occasion like that. I'm still wondering whether I did the right thing."

"I should be in a very nasty situation if you hadn't. But I suppose it could seem different from your point of view."

He raised one eyebrow. "Well, we'll see about that. You could say I had my own motives. The immediate question is, what next?"

She had been thinking this over all afternoon, and was clear at least that she did not want to travel alone right now. Her tongue searched a corner of her mouth for a moment. "Well, I'll be straightforward," she ventured. "Will you come with me as far as Isurium?"

He grinned. "Certainly. Is that really as far as you would like me to come? Or would it be more prudent for me first to ask where you're going?"

She laughed, embarrassed, not sure how to take this; what was it about? "What did you tell them here about us? You're not going to get into trouble?"

"I've made some inquiries today. The local commander's not under Sanctus' thumb. He's well aware that he's in Second Britain and his supplies come from York, not Lincoln; and Sanctus and his colleague in York have some sort of history which means there's little love lost between them." His grin continued and he raised an eyebrow. "But perhaps you mean the Emperor Constantine's law about abducting young girls: don't worry, the penalty of having molten lead poured down your throat is only for complicit nurses – Counts don't count."

She inclined her chin and widened her eye disapprovingly.

"I'm sorry," he added somewhat insincerely, then abandoned the irony. "No, I told them here only that we are cousins and that you're travelling under my protection." He paused a moment. "And now, my freed Andromeda, perhaps you would tell me who you are and where we are going?"

She accepted a cup of wine and peered into it as if it might offer advice. She was in a difficult situation, she thought, and needed help; she already owed this man much and had no reason not to trust him. "Hard to know where to start. My name's Flavia Vindex, as I said. I live on the family estate near Durobrivæ: a place called Cormerick. We raise horses." She put her hand to the back of her head to check her hair. "My father's dead and my mother's in Constantinople. I have one brother, Titus, and I'm travelling north to find him." That would do for now. She took a sip: the wine was white, light and good, much better than the common run in a posting-house: either from Verulamium or from Germany, she guessed.

Arctus looked at her: a slight frown, piecing information together. "So you live in Sanctus' province, is that right? May I ask, then, how he didn't know you?"

"He didn't know me because he's only been here a week or two. Did you not know? I don't know where he comes from, but he's not British."

"No, no, he's from the Seven Provinces, from near Narbonne. But that in itself isn't so surprising; after all, no-one is governor in their home province. And why did no-one speak up for you?"

Was he being too curious? "I think they were all strangers; it was probably just bad luck. That awful poet Ausonius was from Gaul, and someone else I met was from Gaul too, just visiting to buy land. There were one or two people I knew earlier on in the evening, but they left without me noticing."

"I see. Well, despite what I said about the local commander, we should still move on briskly. As I say, I judge that Sanctus won't pursue you, but one can't tell for sure. And one can never know quite what debts people have to call in. Does he know your name?"

"He's bound to. There are any number of people in Lincoln who know me." Another thought. "Anyway, Philip announced me when we arrived; the nomenclator will remember."

"And do you mind going northwards?"

"No." How much should she say? "I was following someone, and I think he went north anyway."

"What do you mean?"

He was certainly asking too much now: she needed to parry this. "He had a message for my brother, and set off before I could ask more about it." A knock came at the door, and a waiter came in with a tray of food, muttering that they were short-staffed and he would not stay to serve it.

"Have some of this," said Arctus, investigating. "They've done us well: there's oysters and a pork dish and something with beans in, and some stewed prunes." He put out a plate for her and helped himself, fetching a basket of bread across. "Who was this messenger?"

No, that was too much. "It's your turn now, I think. You don't sound British. What were you doing in Lincoln, and why did you help me?"

Arctus paused, a sauce-soaked piece of bread already half-way to his mouth, looked up, tightening his brows and smiling at the same time. "Why did I help you?" He sighed. "I suppose there are two answers to that. One is that, though Sanctus doesn't know me, I have a personal score to settle with him. And I think I am fairly safe in doing it. Even if he should find out who I am, since, as you say, I'm not British: I live at Bordeaux, in Second Aquitaine, in the Seven Provinces."

"What?" she interrupted, puzzled and a little anxious. "Ausonius' Bordeaux? Are you a friend of his?"

Arctus chuckled sourly. "On the contrary," he said. "But I don't spend much time in the town. I live on our property outside the city."

"Don't you have an official life? How come you're a Count?"

He stared into the cup of wine. "Let's just say that someone did me a favour."

She looked at him. It hadn't taken him long to reach the limits of confidence, either: a cautious pair. "A significant favour." She pondered. "What's your family?"

She stared, curious to see how he would answer. But he was turning a ring around on his finger, and did not reply. They sat for a while in a silence which grew rapidly uncomfortable. She did not like his not answering that question: he had something to hide. But it would be something private, she realised, for if it had concerned her he could have lied easily enough: in choosing silence instead he was paying her the compliment of truth. His gaze was inward, and she felt embarrassed at her own ingrate sensitivity to questions. "What about the other reason?"

He swam into awareness. "Other reason?"

"...why you helped me," she supplied.

He gave a laugh, recalling himself. "Oh, yes." He looked at her, the mischievous light reappearing. "The other reason, if I'm to be honest, is that since I saw you at that temple of Mars I was looking for an opportunity to get to know you better. When you were arrested I acted on impulse."

She narrowed her brows and grimaced at him, a what-a-fool look. Could he really have acted on impulse like that? But perhaps she was too suspicious: people do do such things. Her initial resentfulness at his presuming that he could join her lessened, as did her suspicion of his reticence about his family; she became more aware that she owed him a real debt, and that somewhere she had a basically good feeling about him and wanted to feel able to trust him. Yet could she depend on that intuition? And what about her own feeling of being flattered by his interest in her? She also wondered if his reserve was shyness or gaucherie, or policy. It seemed to be up to her to take things forward. She reached for a fresh piece of bread, and took a spoonful of stew, redolent of meat and raisins and rosemary. "Tell me about Ausonius," she said. "You must have seen quite a lot of him."

"Not a lot," he answered. "I wasn't educated in Bordeaux: I went to Vienne, where the teachers are much better, and then to Beirut to the law school."

She smiled. "The law school! Is that why you remember imperial constitutions so well?"

"Probably."

"So what are you doing in the Britains?"

"Well, I have an aunt, my mother's sister, in York. She's been ill, and I came over to visit her. I was on my way home when I stumbled upon you and Sanctus." Then his eyes worried and his mouth smiled. "I shall have to find another route now..."

There was another pause. She rinsed her fingers and took a sip of wine, thinking. "Arctus," she said, "could Sanctus take action against my estate, to revenge my escape from Lincoln?"

A look of involvement, intelligence. "I doubt that he would. You are of Most Perfect rank, aren't you? I think it would be one thing to arrest you under a plausible plea of confusion, quite another to interfere with your property on deliberate reflection and after taking advice from locals who knew you." Arctus considered. "Who stands to inherit from you?"

She thought. "My mother, I suppose. She's of the *gens Valeria*, a daughter of the ex-consul Lucius Valerius Proculus."

He widened his eyes. "Ai-ai! Well, I wouldn't worry: I'd think that, once Sanctus learns that, there'll be no trouble," he said. There was another short pause. Then, tentatively, "But your brother is in some difficulty, by the sound of it..."

She now felt more ready to confide. "Yes, that's the reason for my journey. Let's see; where to begin?" She put a spoonful of beans onto her plate and pushed some onto a bit of flat bread with her fingers. "Give me some more wine, will you?"

She held out her pewter goblet. "Titus used to have an appointment in the Sacred Largesses, but about eighteen months ago he got a commission in the army and went north to the frontier. I heard that he had gone missing on patrol, and then a man who called himself Theodorus arrived to call on Titus at our farm; he seemed to expect him to be back. He gave me a message and left. I opened it, but it was rather curious, so I decided that I would try and find out what had happened to my brother."

He looked at her, perhaps wondering how blunt to be. "I don't quite see why you think that this letter casts doubt on the report of your brother being missing."

"I can't altogether explain that, it's partly a sort of hunch. But the letter was strange. It mentioned very important people, as if it came from them. And it came from Constantinople, but took far less time than normal to get here. And it was addressed to him at Augusta, when he ought to have been on the Wall, as if the person who sent it knew better. And it was sent quite a long time after he went missing, as if they might know that he wasn't really. And it implied that he..." she hesitated a moment, and then decided she could not reasonably stop, or perhaps should not, "...that he was...more politically involved than I had realised, to a point where maybe a feigned disappearance by him might be convenient to a number of people, himself and others."

"Where was your brother last seen? On the Wall?"

"North of the Wall, I think. The letter I had was from the commander at Uxellodunum. That's where I'm headed, if I don't run into this Theodorus first."

He looked at her in a speculative way. "Would you show me the letter that this Theodorus brought? Do you have it here?" She remembered her oaths before Theodorus, and smiled a little cynically to herself: it always made her feel uncomfortable to go against her promises, even though this was evidently a situation for the spirit of an oath rather than its letter. She got out both messages, that from the Uxellodunum commander, and that for Titus from the East, and Arctus examined them. He pressed his lips together at one point, and she wondered if he was remembering his slightly patronising question at Lincoln, whether she could speak any Greek. "Well, as you say, the Constantinople letter is certainly mysterious. And even the other raises one or two questions, perhaps. Would I be right in guessing that your brother wasn't part of the Uxellodunum cohort?"

She thought again for a moment, looking at the glowing charcoal in the brazier. "Yes, you would," she conceded. "He had joined an unusual regiment based here in the Britains called the *arcani*. Have you heard of them?"

"Perhaps. Tell me about them."

"I don't know a great deal. They've been about for a long time. I think they were formed when the Saxon Shore forts were set up – what would that be? a hundred years ago? – but I've never heard of anything quite like them elsewhere. They're an intelligence unit."

"Are they based on the Wall?"

"The main headquarters is in London – that is, Augusta – but there are other bases elsewhere, including one on the Wall."

"What do they do?"

"I think they're supposed to support the military commands. Those are quite complex here in Britain. The Duke of the Britains has the Wall forts and those behind, the Count of the Saxon Shore has the south and east coasts of the Britains as well as the north coast of Gaul, and the Count of the Britains combines the titles of Vicar and Count, running the civil administration as well, and has a small field army in the cities, like Counts elsewhere. This unit here will belong to the Vicar and Count, I imagine from the flag, though there isn't a Vicar and Count at present, since Lycontius died in an accident a month or two back."

"So is there a separate head of the *arcani* in each place?"

"I think there is, yes, with the rank of *primicerius*."

"So Titus was subject to an officer on the Wall?"

"No, I think he was reporting directly to the command at Augusta: Dagwald I think is the name of the tribune in overall charge, and Senopian the *primicerius*, both in Augusta. Titus seemed to think it was normal for him to report to Augusta when he was on the frontier, but I've been worried that there could be other things going on. I mean, why should they not want him to report to the Wall people? It might be some complicated allocation of responsibilities between the commanders, but it seems to me more likely that they just don't trust each other. And look at this letter from Constantinople: don't tell me that doesn't suggest some kind of conspiracy."

Arctus examined the letter again. "It says that the *primicerius* of the *schola arcanorum* at Carlisle may 'mention the name of the Illustrious Phronimius'. Yes, it does sound like intrigue. It sounds like a reassurance that this Phronimius supports the *primicerius* and whatever faction he is involved with. Now Phronimius, I think, is the name of the current Prefect of the City of Constantinople – the eastern Emperor's immediate representative in the city, just like the Prefect of the City of Rome in the West. I'd doubt there are any others of that name who would be of Illustrious rank. But I'm sure he was appointed by the usurper Procopius, not by the emperor Valens. I haven't heard what's happened to him since."

"Since what?"

"Have you not heard about Procopius?" She shook her head. "Nasty story. He was a relation of Julian's, and set up as Emperor in competition with Valentinian and Valens – the gods know why, because they had clear army support; one story I heard was that he was manipulated by a Christian faction which was afraid of persecution by Valens and preferred a pagan emperor. Anyway, Valens confronted him in Phrygia, and suborned his troops. Procopius escaped to the forests but was betrayed. Valens had him torn apart: two pine trees pinned down and then suddenly released, so you had an elegant, middle-aged, rather academic aristocrat suddenly spattered all over the forest. Valens had Florentius, his Master of Soldiers, and a tribune executed too, even though they were the ones who betrayed Procopius and brought him in. I think the chances must be that the Illustrious Phronimius isn't a very good person to have connections with."

Flavia could not put this together. "What does that mean for Titus?"

"Hard to say, I think, until we know a little more about all this. Your brother may not have been involved in anything, and even if he had been we can't tell what sort of thing it was." He sighed. "The letter's quite old now. Even if it's genuine, it may reflect people cultivating Procopius against Valentinian and Valens, or Valens against Valentinian, or even both Valentinian and Valens against some local interest here (though that last is a bit unlikely, I suppose; it would scarcely grip them in Constantinople, where the letter came from). And anyway the letter may not be genuine: it could be an attempt to entrap Titus, or Theodorus, or this *primicerius* in Carlisle, or again I suppose Phronimius himself. Do you know anything else about the *arcani*? Do you know who their tribune is himself accountable to? The letter talks of the *arcani* as a *schola*, and the ordinary *scholæ* report direct to the Master of Offices, not up the ordinary military line – though I suppose they are at least part of the Emperor's palatine Court, and that does give them special status. Do you know anyone we could approach for news or information?"

"The only people I've heard of who would know anything relevant would be Dagwald or Senopian, the tribune and *primicerius* in Augusta, but I don't know them personally, and I daresay they wouldn't be likely to take us into their confidence. And we can't easily get to Augusta now, anyway, not with Sanctus' province in the way. I think the thing to do is to press on to the Wall. If we can track down Theodorus, well and good. If not, then the commander of the unit at Uxellodunum must know at least something."

"Yes, that sounds as good a plan as any," said Arctus. He paused, and looked at Flavia carefully. "But I would add a word of warning. I really don't think you should entertain hopes of finding your brother alive."

Flavia felt he was getting to take too much for granted

again. She shook her head as if dislodging a fly and felt her hair slip a little. "I'll be the judge of that, Arctus." She reached for the prunes and put a few in an earthenware bowl. "Mm, these are good. They've got honey and cinnamon in. Is that cream in that little jug?"

But he was not to be deflected, and went on looking at her seriously. "Flavia, I will come all the way north with you, if you wish."

She looked at him levelly, and inclined her head. "If you don't have to return to Gaul, I should be very pleased if you would."

"I'll make one condition: you need a new vehicle. If we end up going north of the Wall, there will be no posting-houses and few inns, I expect. Your trap is attractive and fast, but you will need a bigger, enclosed van that we can all camp in easily. It will help to put Sanctus off the scent too, if he is still after us. I suggest we see to that in Isurium; if we go off the road north into York it will only delay us." He caught her eye and grinned as if he found the formality of this exchange humorous; she felt herself suddenly respond, her solemn features softening into a smile.

CHAPTER 3

Dawn was still glimmering in the east, but despite the earliness of the hour the place was abuzz with activity, with one team of slaves riddling and setting the fires, another getting food out of the pantries for breakfast. A clerk sat in a corner adding up residents' accounts, from time to time barking to a runner to go to check on items; the delicious smell of baking bread drifted from the kitchens. A major-domo with a bushy moustache like Sallienus' sat at a small table finishing an omelette, his sharp and competent eye taking in all at once, an occasional word issuing in good time to correct some potential error. Flavia looked on. *'"The Goddess founded this whole order and system when she framed your society. For she chose the place in which you were born with an eye to its temperate climate, which would produce people of high intelligence,"'* she quoted to herself with a grin, ironically applying the utterance to the posting-house, and maybe the whole of Britain.

She went out of the door into the yard, her mind moving on from Timæus' ancient Athens to what she had seen in Rome on her travels. It was still chilly. There the others were, harnessing the trap and loading it up with their bundles; across the way some slaves were mucking out the stables. "It's the Ides of May," she said to Arctus. "Do you know what happens today in Rome? The Vestal Virgins will be casting straw puppets into the Tiber in an ancient ceremony, and nobody knows any more what it means."

"You don't say," he replied. "I expect the Christians

won't be leaving them to get on with it in peace and quiet."

"Are you a Christian, Arctus?"

"No, certainly not." He turned to face her, evidently deciding what more to say. "I think too many of them are hypocrites. They preach such high moral standards, but they don't keep to them themselves. And too many people have just become Christian because the Emperors are, and because they think it's the way to get on. And some of the things they do are just wrong, I think, like encouraging mothers to leave their families and live what they call "Christian lives" as celibates, or attacking people viciously for their beliefs, or just giving a lot of new anxieties about sin and death to poor people who already have real worries enough. But we must get away if we're to make progress." He turned back to the loading.

Flavia was disturbed by the anger in his tone, and wondered what caused it. Well, she told herself, she *liked* the Vestal Virgins pushing the dolls into the Tiber – it came from time beyond counting, it was a small part of Rome's ancient contract with the gods that made sure that everything was all right. It was just *because* it had no overt meaning that it became meaningful, like everything that scored the immemorial traces of tradition. That was why she had mentioned it, to reaffirm its value, but, if Arctus did not agree and was more interested in some private vendetta against the Christians, she did not have to pursue the matter with him. She went over to his horse and petted her, admiring her lines. She was a bay with hard black hooves, about fifteen hands tall, broad-chested and small-bellied, and with classic Libyan sloping shoulders, which Flavia always thought more graceful than the more conventional upright shape that only looked right on the parade-ground. Flavia ran her fingers though the thick silky mane, and blew familiarly in her nostrils.

The day was fine, with frequent woolly clouds that stopped the heat from being troublesome. The road was bordered with box and thorn bushes, and they made good progress through a countryside full of growing wheat and barley, interspersed with vegetable plots and patches of woodland, and with rough pasture cropped by cows, and by sheep accompanied by shaky-footed lambs. Men laboured in the fields, weeding out crowsfoot flowers and piling them up like golden coin in a treasury. As they passed villages or isolated farms they saw people busy peeling and plaiting osiers, or carrying new-made cheese to store, or out in the yards clearing manure, or hunting for eggs mislaid by errant ducks.

From time to time they met a waggon or a lone rider, and once an enclosed carriage attended by closed-faced apparitors, presumably some great man or his wife on the move. Four times they were overtaken by horsemen pressing on to the next posting-station. Once they passed a long mule-train laden with pig-iron, the animals wayward and fractious, the drivers clumsy and aggressive.

In the evening they reached Pontefract, and again they got three rooms at the posting-station. The settlement was straggly and dirty, huddled under the remains of a fort abandoned many years ago, and the posting-house itself seemed little better, as if it too had never recovered from the departure of the garrison and its regular supplies of pay. Two ill-disciplined dogs came to clamour at them as they arrived, and Flavia shrank back, to Arctus' evident surprise, until they were led away. There was a scuttling of mice or rats in the corners of the common-room, and the bread was gritty.

After their meal Arctus voiced concern about dampness in the stable floor and disappeared for a while. Re-emerging, he suggested a walk up the river, and Flavia was glad to stretch her legs. The two of them wandered first past an orchard of apple and plum-trees white with blossom, and then through an open woodland of oak and ash. "You mentioned Rome this morning as though you'd been there," said Arctus. "Maybe I was a little sharp. These mountains ahead, the Pennines, are they anything like the Apennines? I wonder if the names are related."

Flavia looked up through the tree-branches at the moors, small green woods patched into large spaces of heathland where sheep and goats were attended by tiny, agile lambs and kids, and considered. He was wrong about the derivations, she was sure – many hill-names used the British word for head, *pen*; but the other question was more interesting. "I was only in Italy for six months," she said, carefully. "It wasn't yet summer by the time I left. But it's much more green here. And there are more trees: much of the forest that there used to be in the Apennines must have gone for firewood or houses or ships. And they're different trees and bushes there, ilex and olive and laurel. But you'd know that, wouldn't you? You have similar countryside in the Seven Provinces, surely. You said you'd studied in Beirut, anyway: didn't you get to travel through Italy?"

"No. There were family reasons why it wasn't a good idea. I went to Tarragona and then by ship via Carthage."

They rambled on along a well-defined track, coming out of the wood into pastureland. "The mountains behind Beirut, though," said Arctus, "are amazing. They're quite as high as the Pyrenees or the Alps, and they have snow on them even in the summer: there was no problem in Beirut about getting chilled drinks. Are there snows here in the summer?"

"You make Phœnicia sound very beautiful. No, I don't think there are any mountains in the Britains which have snow in the summer. We used to have a sort of tutor, Titus and me, who said that there were such places in Caledonia. But he was very unreliable."

They began to approach a lamb which, startled, ran suddenly off to its mother. "An unreliable tutor?" said Arctus with a sly smile. "You give the impression of being very well-educated."

"How would I know he was unreliable unless I *was* well-educated? No, I had a good tutor too, earlier on, a proper one. Alexander, he was called."

"Was he a Greek?"

"In a way. He'd been a slave among the Goths. But he had been a Greek earlier, or rather he'd been captured with his parents in an attack on Panticapæum in the Crimea. He was grown up when he was enslaved, and had been to university in Constantinople."

"Tell me more about him."

Flavia frowned as she remembered Alexander, a gaunt figure with a dragging left foot. "He was a sad man," she said. "One habit he never lost: you would be talking about something, and his attention would fail for a moment, and he would sigh, and sometimes he would mutter "*Woe, woe, wretchedest of mortals!*", like someone out of an Æschylus tragedy. I think he could never understand how he could be sold by the barbarians to Roman slave traders and not regain his freedom."

"Life can be very cruel."

"Yes; I used to feel so sorry for him. But my father always treated him like a philosopher, and nowadays I think that his life may have been no worse as a slave than it would have been as a free man: his own father was a doctor but a drunkard, I think, and had never acquired any property. And Alexander was never happier than when reading the ancient authors and discussing them."

"Who did he have to discuss them with?"

"Oh, my father, when he was about, or Titus or me. And he used to go into Durobrivæ once a week and give classes for the municipality. My father let him keep the fees for his own."

"What happened to him?"

"He got his freedom in my father's will, when I was fifteen. He stayed with us for a couple of years, but when we came back from our journey to Rome he had gone. My mother said he had gone home to Panticapæum, and we never heard from him again."

They turned and started back towards Pontefract. The dusk was thick now, and Arctus walked closer to the path so as not to miss his footing by the river, so that he blundered into Flavia occasionally and she caught a faint odour from him. In the darkness she was becoming more aware of where he was. A squirrel scurried to their right in a rufous streak. "Arctus is an unusual name," said Flavia idly.

"It's because it's the Greek word for a bear," he replied.

"Yes," she said. "And are you a bear?" she added, seized by a moment's mischief. "Perhaps you're grumpy enough!" She darted at him, flashing her hands apart in his face like a child at a scaring game. Taken unawares, he started to his left, then realised he was on the point of falling into the stream, and tried to recover himself by throwing his weight to his right and grabbing at her. She reacted indecisively, and they toppled over, she clinging to his clothes to try and climb away from the fall, he trying to sway back the other way again. They fell to the ground heavily and lay winded for a moment, both laughing. Flavia had surprised herself, but found she liked the feel and the scent of Arctus' firm body. She snuggled her head recklessly into his armpit, shutting her eyelids in the spurious hope that this would make the action demure. "Mm, it certainly smells like a bear here," she murmured through his heavy woollen cloak. "Is it dangerous?"

She felt one of his arms enclosing her, and his body raise itself a little as he drew his head back to look at her. "It could be," he said, in a voice thickened with tenderness or desire. She opened her eyes. In the dark his face was indistinct. She pulled him down by the collar of his cloak and kissed him slowly, enlivening a feeling of hollowness in her chest.

Gradually he returned the kiss. She wanted to respond, but instead decided that she ought to take command of herself. Gently she took his head and pushed it away. "Later, perhaps," she murmured, her voice smiling, "it's too cold and damp." He chuckled an acknowledgement that might hint at disappointment; they helped each other to their feet, brushed down their cloaks and started again down the path, hand in hand. She was startled by her own feelings and reactions, and wondered what to do when they got back. At home she wouldn't dare run such a risk of public shame, but here she was anonymous. Besides, she thought, after Lincoln and their long flight, she felt she was exposed in a dangerous world outside her sanctuary, and had a real need for rest and comfort.

The household had already gone to bed when they returned. A tired old woman let them in, asked if they wanted anything, gave each a candle reeking of tallow, and made off towards outbuildings where perhaps she slept. They sat in the common room for a few minutes together watching the embers glow erratically in the draught, and a newly-hatched chick peeping out of a hole in a stocking where someone had put it for warmth, making it roll around the hearth like a snake. Flavia let Arctus lead her into his room.

They put down their candlesticks and sat on the bed. He was still holding her hand, and he sheltered it firmly in both of his: it felt protective, reassuring. He kissed her fingers slowly, then moved his head close and put his cheek to hers. She could feel comfort, delight, something somewhere holding back. She nuzzled at him in return, at first experimentally, then with growing release and enthusiasm. He put his arm around her and squeezed her gently, then somehow teased the pin from her brooch so that her cloak fell to the floor. Now she could feel his fingers on her breast through thin linen, her nipples erect. He slipped his tongue into her mouth: it was sudden, and vivid. She pulled herself away, smiled at him and kissed him lightly on the lips. "I must go to my room for a moment," she said. "Wait: I'll be back in a minute."

She caught up a candle and slipped through the corridor into her room, hunted in her bags: a little pouch, unused for years, with a badge of womanhood revealed to her long ago now by her cousin Proculina: a glass phial of opoponax distillate and a handful of raw wool. She soaked the wool in the liquid and, lying on the bed, pushed it up inside her, adjusting till it was right. Now she felt at the surface of her mind responsible, pressured, focused on her task, and was trying to hold onto the feelings of tenderness and excitement underneath, not to let them go. She got up, pulled her tunic down and darted back into his room. He was sitting on the bed still, waiting patiently, his elbows on his knees and his chin in his hands, and he looked up and lightened as she came in.

"Was I long?" she asked.

"An age," he smiled, standing and reaching out for her. He pulled her to him, hugging her, kissing her deeply, stroking her hair with one hand and pulling her in to him with the other, then moved the lower hand to hug her tight again and stroke the edge of her breast through the fabric. They stayed like that for a moment; then he leaned back and raised his wrists, and gently undid the other brooch-fastenings at her shoulders, while she regarded him seriously. Her tunic fell to the floor and his smile showed his wonder as he saw her naked in the candlelight.

She returned his gaze levelly, enjoying his admiration,

seized him round the neck and kissed him, then swayed back on her heels and pushed him, unresisting, onto the bed, falling on top of him in her turn. Something still lurked somewhere in her mind, but she ignored it as she was grasped with arms and legs, turned onto her back; his hands ran up and down her flanks, his mouth was on her breast; she tugged playfully at his hair with one hand and ran the other underneath his tunic up his thighs and haunches to the muscles in his lower back. She was her mouth, her skin, a hungriness below her heart. He knelt up for a moment and threw off his tunic; then he was everywhere, moving so fast, his touch grasping her, stroking her, deliberately, accidentally... Suddenly he was still, expectant, looking deep into her eyes. "Flavia..." he said. Outside the window a dog barked twice, then again three times. Arctus rocked his hips, edging a fraction up the bed.

Abruptly, from nowhere, a red panic overwhelmed her, irresistible, drowning everything. Desperately she pulled herself back up the bed as if her life depended on it, ten inches, twenty, her knees striking heedlessly against Arctus... She was propped up on her elbows, breathing hard, then sitting up, her legs still apart, her head moving sharply from side to side for a moment. Then she focused on Arctus, sprung back on his feet on the floor, baffled, hurt, angry. She saw him look into her eyes, and recognise the fear; his face changed, she saw the beginnings of pity fighting to emerge. She felt a rush of warmth, of tenderness, of guilt; she leapt to the edge of the bed and threw her arms round his waist, burying her face in his side, bursting into tears though she didn't know if they were for her or for him or for both of them. "Oh, Arctus, I'm so sorry, so sorry. I just don't know what happened. Something happened to me suddenly, I just don't know..." Arctus sat down and put his arm around her, and they sat like that for a time silently.

The next day Flavia woke miserable. Guilt and bewilderment at her behaviour nagged her relentlessly. She had a fear, surely irrational, that Arctus would leave and make straight off home to Gaul; and finding herself covered with painful bedbug bites added humiliatingly to her misery. But when Arctus greeted her, though his manner was rather cold, he showed no sign of a change of plan, and they returned to the road. As they came towards Tadcaster they found themselves part of a growing procession of women carrying jars of milk home on their heads from the plots where their cows were grazed. They lodged at the posting-station, and passed a quiet evening finding common cause in lamenting the poor stable practice, where, for example, the first bridle that came to hand was being used for each post-horse, regardless of what sort of a mouth it had.

The next morning they left early. The hawthorn-hedges were already in full flower along the way. About the third hour from dawn they began to pass through a different kind of country, with huge fields of wheat and much less tree-cover, reminding her of great estates she had seen in Italy and southern Gaul. After five or six miles this gave way to parkland with artfully planted oak or elm trees, full-grown and well-shaped, patched with woodlands giving out the echo of a cuckoo or the laugh of a woodpecker; once, a pheasant clattered out of one of these woods and startled the horses. But after half an hour of this the arable fields returned.

On the Thursday, in brilliant spring sunshine, they arrived at Isurium, the capital of the Brigantian canton. Red sandstone walls rose tall in the plain of the Ouse, and towers of contrasting grey gritstone rose taller. Suddenly a distant trumpet call sounded, and after a moment a gigantic spear embedded itself in the ground a hundred yards to their right. They hastened on anxiously, and were soon met by slaves of soldiers of the Sixth Legion, who explained that catapult training was in progress, and that Flavia's party should use all caution and not leave the road suddenly. As they approached they saw the catapult crews on the ramparts, as well as other legionaries training with crossbows against straw targets, dressed in sleeveless mail coats and pillbox fur hats, and sweating as they wound the bows taut.

They made their way towards the gates. Flavia had not been in mountains for many years, and still expected her own country when she looked around, the huge open skies of the fens. On Monday, in Doncaster, she had been aware of the Pennines to the west; but now she saw the shadow of moors drawing in from the north-east as well, and thick woodland coming not far from the road to the left. She felt the hills as an oppression, and was glad that they were making this journey in the growing light and warmth of spring, and not in autumn.

Then she spotted a field-mouse nibbling at the side of the road. It reminded her of their verminous lodgings the night before, and hence of the scene in last night's bedroom, and this revived her feeling of self-reproach. It nagged at her insistently, and would not let her go. Philip had not been this far north before, and caught her eye. "I'm told that Isurium is the capital of the Brigantes, my Lady. But while it's a decent town it's not a large one, even if the Brigantes may make up the largest canton in the Britains."

"We're only ten miles from York, Philip, which is the second city of the island. I daresay that has something to do with it." As soon as she spoke the curt words Flavia suspected they would wound the freedman's fragile pride, and she heard in her mind the reproach in Horace: '*Words that have once been uttered have already flown past recalling*'. Philip coloured slightly, and did not reopen the conversation, leaving her leisure to reflect that she had been letting loose on the servant the anger she felt against herself.

Meanwhile they arrived in the forum, right in the middle of the town, and hot from the journey asked after the baths. But there was only one public baths, attached to the post-house south of the west gate: the furnace was being repaired, and the whole place was in confusion. They made for an inn and rested, and then Flavia and Arctus went out in search of a waggon. They went round two carpenters who were said to make vehicles, and found nothing suitable, but were impressed by the city: though small, it seemed busy and well-off. In the late afternoon they tracked down a farmer who had the kind of thing they were looking for, though Flavia had to steel herself to go on into the farmyard with its noisy dogs. They looked at the waggon closely, finding it would need some repairs and re-equipping before they could set out, so they had it taken round to one of the carpenters and did a deal with him involving the sale of the trap.

The carpenter, perhaps sensing their impatience, had under-estimated the time the work would take, and towards the end of the next day Flavia realised with frustration that it would take another day and perhaps more, so that, if she had known, she could have gone down to York to visit her cousin Ïullinus and his family. She relieved herself by spending the evening writing him a letter, giving all the news she felt prudent. The following morning, her conscience once pricked, she found herself writing also to her mother and to Antonia, Titus' friend in London – the second letter very short, since the address instructions she could give were vague, and it might well not be delivered – while Arctus took Erdigorra hunting in the nearby woods.

When she had finished, she went out of her room to look for one of the servants to arrange the sending of the letters, but they had both gone out. Flavia told herself that it was a small place and they could not have gone far, and went into the streets to look. But nobody seemed to have seen them, and she wandered exploring the streets until after perhaps half an hour she stopped at a small bar for a cup of cider. It was a clean place, and two other women were there, much younger then Flavia. She sat lost in vacant thoughts for a while, and suddenly her attention was caught. "It was a few weeks back," the barmaid was saying. "The stranger he went off with had red hair and freckles like a Caledonian, but Gallic bands round his leggings, don't you remember?" Red hair and Gallic-style leggings? Surely Theodorus. Flavia listened carefully.

One of the other girls laughed, with a hard edge. "Well, I'm not surprised Eumolpus wanted to get out of town," she said. "Not a lucky place for him. After all, it were only at Saturnalia, weren't it, that he fell off the edge of the tall fountain and broke his leg. And then Babudius and Rufus picked him up and took him to the military doctor and got him patched, and then fetched him away afterwards in a barrow."

"That's right," said the other, softer-spoken but suddenly enlivened. "And then Eumolpus is so grateful he says as they're passing the bar on the way home, 'It's sad to pass a bar like this, boys. Here, that doctor hasn't had all my money off me. Take this *siliqua* and buy yourselves a drink.' And they leaves him in his barrow and goes into the bar, and they comes out at last the worse for wear and picks him up and tips him straight into the gutter and he breaks his other leg!" They chuckled together, but rapidly drank up and left.

Flavia asked the barmaid about Theodorus, speaking in British in the hope that it would have been her childhood language and encourage confidence. "*Yes, I'd say it was him from your description,*" she replied. "*Had a Greek name too: I'm sure it was Theodorus, now you mention it. But it would've been a good two weeks ago now.*"

This was not disconcerting; Flavia had now accepted that he must be far ahead of them. "*But where was he going?*"

"*He was on his way north: Coria-way, I have an idea he said, rather than Carlisle. I might be wrong there, though.*"

Flavia asked where he had been staying, and whether she remembered anything else, but drew a blank; she pressed on to put her inquiry at the posting-station and the inns, but did no better.

It was at the inn nearest to the east-gate that she finally ran into Rúari, supporting a somnolent Philip out of the door. "*Rúari! What in the name of Ceres is going on here?.*"

Rúari beamed. "*It is Philip that it is, Madam, and he has been imbibering a little keenly.*"

Philip, hearing his name, looked up with a solemn, worried expression, which contracted further as he recognised Flavia. "*Madam,*" he began, and paused, standing up and swaying a little. "*I am ve'y so''y to be nuizance. Quite unpardonavle to... so late – early in the day. Quite...*" he looked about vaguely, "*quite....*" He lost his thought and paused until another hit him. "*Game of dice, you know. Rúari quite exceptionarry favoured by Goddess Fortune. Quite ex... excettional. Blessed by the Goddess.*" He put his arm back on Rúari's shoulder.

"*Have you been gambling with forfeits, Rúari?*" asked Flavia sternly.

"*It is not so, I would not say that exactly, Madam,*" said

Rúari. "*But it is true that we have been playing dice, and I have been fortunate. Do you know the expression 'the luck of the Irish', Madam?*"

"*I do not and I have no wish to,*" said Flavia shortly. "*You had better see him back to the inn carefully and put him to bed. And when you've finished I have a task that should keep you busy for the rest of the afternoon.*" She would have to keep an eye on Philip, she thought: he seemed accident-prone.

The following day they set off north, the waggon a good deal less elegant and fast than the trap and offering worse views out, though much more comfortable and practical for a long journey – especially in the rain, though during the first day the weather continued fine, with only a few showers in the night. For several miles out of Isurium they accompanied a band of farmers pushing hand-carts, diminishing as they fell aside to begin the day's hoeing or cabbage-planting. Now for the first time they were beyond the ambit of York, and in territory which Flavia did not know at all, though the landscape was not yet very different, as they passed through meadows of mowing-grass white with waving umbels: men were ditching at the sides to secure the irrigation, their presence keeping titlarks and rails at a distance.

They stopped for the Sunday night on the road, drawing the van off the paved way in case messengers should pass urgently in the dark, and manœuvring it carefully as it lurched over the shallow gutter. They gave the horses a drink from a nearby stream. Arctus took off Hipponoë the high-horned saddle and riding-harness, together with the bright red plume on her head, then offered her a lick of salt, groomed her down with a dandy-brush and then a body-brush, wiped down her face and neck, and then took a curry-comb to her pale mane and tail and to the generous feathers round her feet, while Rúari looked to his own mount and the waggon-horses. Then they let the animals drink their fill and set them loose to graze by the roadside; Hipponoë was a little restive at first, but then quietened down. Meanwhile Rúari drew water, and Philip gathered wood nearby and lit a fire; both of them prepared food while Erdigorra rigged a curtain in the back of the vehicle to give some privacy to Flavia, and set stools for them to sit on.

Rúari served his masters and withdrew to a respectful distance along with the others. Flavia murmured to Arctus, "I think we should eat with them while we're travelling, don't you?", then seeing surprise in his eyes, added, "In the waggon it's cramped and it isn't possible to be distant all the time, and it would be a waste of time and effort to have them eat later just for that." Don't let him reply, she hoped to herself, by saying 'What does a waste of effort by slaves or freedmen matter? That's what they're for,' and she searched her memory rapidly for authorities: there was Epictetus' suggestion that one should share food with one's slaves, and wasn't there something in Seneca? The truth was, she thought, that seeing slaves as so wholly inferior, as no more than a man's property, was an old way of thinking now, when all over the world they worshipped in the same Christian churches as free citizens did. Perhaps it was only in the Britains, where there were fewer Christians, that it was such an issue, though even after her trip in the Gauls and Italy she didn't really know much about how things were done elsewhere.

But Arctus just nodded and called over to the servants, "Bring your food over here now and join us. We shan't stand on ceremony on the road." All of them sat together and ate a stew of broad beans with bacon, enlivened by fish-paste and rosemary, along with bread bought that morning in Isurium. "This is good!" said Arctus, "Who's responsible?"

Philip confessed that the food was largely Rúari's doing, and there followed a discussion of cooking, comparing the plain British with the florid Roman style which used fish-pickle as well as asafœtida and other exotic herbs and spices. Flavia noticed that Rúari was unusually quiet, given the fact that it was his cooking which was being praised – even more so than could be accounted for by the natural reticence of a slave before his masters. Arctus seemed to notice it too, for he made efforts to draw Rúari out, but without success. Then, concealed by the dusk, Rúari said something to Philip in British which the others could not make out, and Flavia suspected the problem could be that Rúari's Latin was not very good.

"Ah," she said, letting out a satisfied sigh, "whatever anyone says, I think that was a meal to match the wedding feast of Matholucos and Branvina, of which it was said '*they caroused and made merry in peace and amity*'."

Rúari at once reacted. "*That is an unlucky thing for the Lady Flavia to say. For after that wedding Branvina's brother Evnissienos took revenge on Matholucos by attacking his horses, cutting off 'their lips at the teeth, and their ears at their heads, and their tails close to the body, and where he could seize the eyelids he cut them off to the bone'.*"

Flavia took a pinch of salt and threw it over her left shoulder. "Let it not be an omen!" she said.

But Arctus had picked up the point. "*And since our meal had British qualities too one can say that it mixed up the virtues of British cooking and Roman cooking,*" he said, in a Gallic accent that seemed a little outlandish, but not too much so, and Flavia did not pick him up for saying 'mixed up' rather than 'combined'. The conversation continued for a while, largely in British, and they went to sleep early.

The following morning, the Monday, they had water and raisins and set off promptly. After a long day's travelling, much of it through forest, they arrived in the late afternoon at a large town called Catterick, passing on the outskirts a cluster of market gardens where women were still weeding despite the hour, and then a row of blacksmiths' and wheelwrights' shops. The place sprawled, its houses and flats dominated irregularly by huge stone storehouses and warehouses which made plain it was a supply depot for the Wall garrison. Most of the people, or at least the many in uniform, looked well-dressed and well-fed.

The next two days they stopped at smaller towns, clustered round forts; the countryside here was more broken, and away from the settlements fields were few by comparison with woodland and rough grazing. Arctus started to put to good use his enthusiasm for shooting and trapping, and would disappear for half an hour at a time, returning with a finch or a hare. Flavia accompanied him on one of these forays, and was surprised by his practised ability for silent movement in the woods. She had been puzzled by Erdigorra, whom Arctus treated as a menial servant but who was evidently free, not a slave, and who seemed cultivated and intelligent beyond his station; on the way back from their little expedition she mentioned this. Arctus was not forthcoming: "He comes from Cantabria," he said, "and the agreement is that he will serve me for three years until he's eighteen: the time is up next March. It's an old family arrangement."

The next evening, to their surprise, they fell in with a party from the exotic Tigris Boatmen's Regiment marching back to their base. Many of these claimed to be descended from Mesopotamians settled there three generations ago, and they seemed a curious mixture. All spoke fluent British and swore by British gods, but nearly half of them were swarthy, with jet-black hair and able to put on a lingo which they swore was Assyrian; all boasted of their ancestral skill at handling boats in all weathers, whether on the Tyne River or on the German Ocean. As they marched they sang songs with outlandish oriental quarter-tones and melismata. They reminded Flavia, interestingly but rather frustratingly, of things she could not remember very clearly, such as the rituals of Isis, or oriental dance-performances in the theatres of southern Gaul and Italy; Arctus remarked that the atmosphere they created made him quite nostalgic for his time in Syria.

About noon of the next day the party reached a junction, and the soldiers turned off along the road to South Shields. Flavia's group pressed on to a small grey settlement distinguished only by two aqueducts leading to its fort and by the garrison, the *Numerus Longovicariorum*, a unit formed only the previous year, they learned, by local recruitment after the barbarian attacks. As they came into the village they saw the roadside cemetery full of flowers, and Flavia realised with a start that it was the Rose Festival. She recalled with guilt that she had forgotten to leave any instructions at Cormerick about this day and how her father's grave was to be honoured in her absence – she, who had always been so scrupulous about duties to the family! She muttered her regrets to her father's shade; and the grief she had felt at his death – feelings of loneliness and abandonment and frustration and anger, lurking behind a determination not to reveal any of it – seemed for a moment to be renewed, until she was distracted by their arrival.

The officers who filled up the posting-station for a drink or two of an evening made clear their pride in their new unit, a replacement for odd detachments which had previously garrisoned the fort, and they boasted they were eager for action which would prove their mettle. They complained about the accommodation they had inherited, and claimed that their regiment had a character quite different from that of the troops which Flavia and Arctus had seen earlier in the day. It might have no ancient traditions or hoary battle-honours, they said, yet all its troops were present, and still being drilled: none were on detachment in aid of the civil power, or on leave, or sick, or present only in name so that the commanding officer could pocket their pay and allowances.

They mentioned high proportions of other units which suffered these fates, and Flavia, digesting this information, started to think it was perhaps not so surprising how few soldiers she had seen since leaving Isurium, for all that they were approaching the frontier; and began to wonder exactly how many troops there really were defending the Britains from the barbarians. Before going to her room to sleep she asked after a shrine to Proserpine, and finding there was none went outdoors for a moment and peered down into the dark of a deep well at the back of the building. "I have always been scrupulous in my observance," she prayed to the goddess. "Grant, if you will, that Sallienus will see to the rites for my father and have them done correctly this year." She dropped a *nummus* into the well, and returned to the lamplit posting-house.

The next day, a Friday, they reached a town preoccupied with the festival of Fortuna, its lodgings full of country people and grudging to strangers. Now they were coming into the border zone, where the Emperor spent huge sums in maintaining his armies. Business was brisk for tradesmen, who could often pick and choose their customers, and it was late before they found beds. At last, on the Saturday, they arrived in Coria, the only really substantial town by the eastern part of the Wall.

Evening was falling after a long day as the little party, with all five sitting in the waggon and the two riding horses following, went down a slope to a stone bridge. As they crossed, they heard the racing of the River Tyne, and were aware of ghostly linen flapping on washing lines stretched over the meadows to one side. At this hour there were few people on the streets. Only about forty yards past the gates of the town was a group of large buildings on the right: the posting-house. They pulled into its yard, and Philip went to look out the duty clerk, while Rúari and Erdigorra saw to the four horses, and Flavia and Arctus, with help from the posting-house servants, set to unpacking. The manager made difficulties and needed a bribe, but eventually, as the night came down, they were all installed in the building: Flavia and Arctus in rooms on the stone-built ground floor, and the others in a barrack-room in the timber upper storey.

Flavia went into her room from the central corridor and straight to the window at the other end, finding that it opened on a verandah overlooking a fountain with a splendid statuette above it, an amphitheatre scene of a lion crouching powerfully over a man – such pieces were common in cemeteries, and she wondered if it had been looted from a tomb. She stared out at it for a while, then got out her copy of the *Timæus* and soon lost herself in the text.

After some time, however, she became aware of a muttering below. She looked down, and saw Rúari and a boy of about twelve with their heads together in earnest conversation. There was a chink of coins; then they rapidly disappeared, and Philip entered the courtyard, still in his travelling clothes, deep in talk with a woman: she looked to be in her early thirties, perhaps, with very elaborate hair (surely not all her own) and a green silken gown; Flavia thought she was made up with white lead and rouge. Suddenly the boy burst into the courtyard, threw his arms around Philip, and reaching up kissed him on the mouth.

Philip expostulated loudly, but when he turned back to the lady she had gone. The boy ran off giggling.

Some minutes later there was a knock at the door, and Philip came in. "Lady Flavia," he said in a voice with a rough edge. She turned. "I have news. I've met someone who knows Theodorus."

"Excellent, Philip. Will they come in?"

Philip looked inscrutable for a moment. "They're not here: they were just passing through. I urged them to stop, but they wouldn't."

Flavia looked at him. "Who were they?"

"They were a very," he coughed, "*flamboyant* Syrian lady and her slaves. She claimed to have an appointment with the commander of the fort at Banna, and on that account was unwilling to delay."

"But by the itinerary it must be..." Flavia paused to work it out, "twenty-five miles from here to Banna! She surely can't be leaving for there at this hour?"

"No, Madam, I don't think she was. I understand that the officer from Banna has been here today at a meeting with the local commander. I gather that she was on her way to the baths, outside the town to the west, and plans to stay with him at the residence here tonight."

Flavia raised her eyebrows. "It sounds as if she will not be easy to meet."

"Perhaps not, Madam. But she did tell me that she met Theodorus here in Coria about a month ago. He was pressing westward in great haste. She said that he spoke of visiting Carlisle, and also of going north out of the Province a little further west of here."

"Philip, that's important news. Well done! But she seems to have told you a good deal."

"I had the impression that she was dissatisfied with him in some way, Madam."

"Did you find out anything else?"

"Yes, indeed, Madam. She may have seen the Lord Titus, about a year or more ago. I described him to her in detail, and she said she recalled seeing him at Carlisle."

That evening Flavia sat in Arctus' room, debating whether they should try and speak to Philip's Syrian lady or press straight on westward. Eventually they shelved the question and bent over a game of "soldiers" they had found downstairs, played with twelve stones on a board twelve squares by twelve. The game had subtlety, and they became engrossed. Eventually Arctus won both the first and the second games. Flavia sat back on her couch, laughing, speaking unthinkingly in childhood British. *"Enough! You've had far too much practice for me!"*

"I have not!" protested Arctus. *"I haven't played in years!"*

"A likely story! But tell me, you speak British, though not quite like a native. Do you speak the same language in Gaul? I've been there, but I don't remember ever speaking any other language than Latin."

"There's much less Gallic used there than British is here, especially in the south: a few of the farm labourers use it, but nobody in the towns. I live in the country, so I have to use it occasionally, though all the house-slaves speak Latin, of course. But yes, I think the languages are quite similar. I've tried to adapt myself to the British way of speech since being here; it's good to hear that I've had some success, especially from so discerning a critic." He smiled back at her, making gentle fun of her precision, and she realised that she was pleased to be friends again after their misencounter at Pontefract. It was true that since then they had slept either in their own bedrooms at posting-houses, or in the van in the company of the servants, but Arctus had made no physical approach to her at all; he must be either put off or waiting for a signal from her, but she had felt confused and inhibited, and found she was very content to leave the matter.

The following morning they left Coria, having to make their way all along one of the main streets, past men and women already sauntering up and down shops and stalls that were selling scent, shoes, rissoles, metalwork, medicines, and a hundred other things; Philip had difficulty manœuvring the waggon through, and added his own warning cries to the medley of calls from the traders. Smells of fried garlic, stale urine, spilt vinegar hung for a moment in the air, then were swept away by a keen cold waft from the hills. Children darted between the shops and stalls making deliveries or carrying change, and groups of women or soldiers knotted unpredictably, absorbed in gossip. On the way out the travellers passed the baths favoured by the Syrian courtesan – sited outside the walls years ago, someone had mentioned, by a prudent commander with experience of fires.

To begin with, the military road ran westward up the river for a couple of miles, beset by thickets of gorse. Flavia saw no other travellers, but suddenly an eerie braying rose up, first on one side and then another, then seemingly all around, as though an army of ghosts was upon them. Suddenly it dawned on her that the noise was the bugle call for the changing of the watch, and must come from army camps just out of sight. Shortly the road bent to the right and climbed a rise. They came to the top and saw the Wall, running along the hill-tops to the north, its nearest point almost two miles from where they were.

It was several times the height of a man, and painted a startling white: it ran irresistibly, a vivid and impermeable barrier, following the contours of the land from east to west, and running out of sight in a course that went, they knew, from sea to sea. Every now and then there was a small fort housing a guard detachment, with gates for passage, and occasionally a stone watchtower with a timber walkway about twenty feet up; Rúari, who had known it many years ago, told them that these defences were known as 'milecastles' and 'turrets' respectively, and that in ancient days there had, it seemed, been many more of them in a regular series. The north side of the Wall and the tops of the milecastles were crowned with battlements.

Feeling closely watched, they went on, following their path on Arctus' written itinerary. The road took them to within a mile of a large fort called Cilurnum, and then ran on in full sight of the Wall: from here they could clearly see gaps in the surface plaster and missing stones which showed how little effort went into its repair. They passed another large fort on the Wall itself called Brocolitia, and then yet another, Vercovicium, perched on an impressive crag. As dusk threatened, they arrived at the town of Vindolanda, set south of the Wall on the main road. The next morning it was a short journey, in brilliant weather, to Magnis.

As they approached that fort, a curlew uttered its

plaintive *courwee, courwee*. Their road ran through grassy mounds, the remains of some ancient field-fortification exercise, then down across a stream and up the side of a hill, the Wall at its summit about half a mile to their right, and the towers of Magnis directly ahead. Soon in front of the fort they could see roofs and a haze of smoke, and found that the ridge had hidden a substantial village at the foot of the south wall, sprawling westward away from their approach.

At the end of the graveyard, the start of the township, a man sat on the ground; he wore a scruffy military belt and a scrap of blanket and had lost both legs, one above and one below the knee. He held out his hand, keening words that constant use had distorted out of recognition, but his meaning was evident; Arctus unbuttoned a pouch and tossed him a *nummus*. Behind and opposite the beggar there were houses of turf and of wattle-and-mud, but stone buildings soon began to appear among them, some of them quite handsome and of two storeys, with tile or slate rather than thatched roofs. Idling boys of eight or ten, wearing only tattered dun-coloured kilts, saw the travellers and ran up, demanding to show them to a bar, an inn, or a brothel, their enthusiasm attracting a couple of stray mongrels.

The road was busy, like that in Coria, though not to the same degree. They had to push through people buying at shops and stalls, and Rúari was sent forward to clear a way for the horses. There was a clamour of street-cries and beggar-musicians, and urban smells began to invade the waggon: grilling sausages, meat or spices from a passing stall, peat-smoke from the doorway of a tumbledown house with no chimney. Soon it was clear that the village was larger than it had seemed and that there were two other streets, one on each side of the main road, with trading spilling down some of the paved cross-streets as well. Then they came to a point where another broad paved way joined their own, a road striking off up the south branch of the Tyne towards lead mines at Epiacum. Now a right turn took them to the south gates of the fort, seemingly the gates used by all traffic.

Arctus put a hand on Erdigorra's wrist, and he stopped the vehicle. Flavia and Arctus climbed down and went on foot to enter, while the others stayed to mind the waggon and horses and to bargain for food. The regiment stationed there was the Second Cohort of Dalmatians, its name proudly inscribed on the standard which faced them as they walked up between the lines of buildings to the headquarters complex. Arctus went straight through into the mess, but a soldier stopped Flavia from going further, and she was left waiting in a hallway. Time went by, and she was alone, save for the occasional glint of sun on metal equipment, or the noise as a squad was marched past. Somewhere in the background there began a whistling and a rubbing sound, as if someone had started a cleaning task. She noticed that along one wall was set a number of bronze plaques, and she started reading them.

The tablets set out the rules of the Magnis Iobacchi, a sodality formed by the devotees of Bacchus in the area. They had a president, a chief bacchus, and a patron; there was an admission fee, with a discount for relatives; there was a fixed contribution to the wine at each monthly meeting and at festivals; there were fines for singing, shouting and clapping at meetings; wardens were appointed by lot, with the power to eject a member from the room; anyone who insulted a fellow-member was judged at a special meeting of the whole society. During meetings, the priest would offer a libation for the return of Bacchus and preach a sermon, and other interventions were only allowed by his leave. When a member died, the society would provide in his honour a wreath not exceeding 204 nummi in cost, and a jar of wine to be shared only by those who attended the burial.

She pondered the lives of the members of the fraternity. It seemed a lot more procedural than her own experience of religion, but she had never belonged to such a formally-defined group: anyone could turn up for the worship of the Good Goddess that she attended at home. But perhaps it was different in towns, where there were more people about; she couldn't really make comparisons, because when she had been in cities, even in Trier and Rome where she had spent some time, she had been travelling and busy and a stranger, and disinclined on the whole to seek out any worship other than the grand public ceremonies which offered spectacle as well as food and fellowship and a link with the gods. There again, she thought, perhaps there was more to it than that. Was there something specially masculine about all these rules? Or was it just to do with the army, that people who spent their lives in a world of rules and order would bring this into the way they dealt with the sacred as well? Though the Christians seemed to have a lot of strict rules as well, and very many of them were women, and very few in the army... But suddenly Arctus broke into her reverie and shepherded her out of the camp.

They walked down the southward road a little to get space to talk, cursing at some urchins to shoo them away. "I got to speak to the camp superintendent rather than any of the regimental officers," said Arctus. "Unfortunate, because he's the one who handles pay and supplies, and I suspect he jumped to the conclusion that I was an auditor: he seemed to be on his guard at once, and sizing me up to see how much money I would want. And there may be no shortage of things for an auditor to concern himself with: I'd guess there are about a third of the number of troops that there ought to be, and I daresay he pockets the others' ration-allowances, along with pay and donatives. I have a feeling many of the Wall garrisons may be like that. It's no wonder everyone looked so sleek in the supply-base at Catterick; there must be excellent opportunities to fiddle the books there."

"Did he have any news of Theodorus?"

"He said he'd been here, but was a bit evasive about where he'd gone. When I pressed him he said he thought he'd turned northward here across the Wall – I gather there's another fort called Banna, just a couple of miles away, and then you go north for ten miles or so beyond the Wall to a place called Cocidius' Temple, on a road which goes on as a track into the country of a barbarian tribe called the Attacotti. But then he said he wasn't sure, and that Theodorus might just have gone on west to Carlisle. That may have been second thoughts, to lead us off the scent. But you never know."

"What do you think?"

"Now we're here, I think we might perhaps best go to

Cocidius' Temple and see if they have any news there. Apparently there's a fortlet, and an outpost is still kept, though the garrison proper was withdrawn during troubles some years back. This fort here and Banna take turns to supply the outpost detachment, and it's this unit's turn at present. The soldiers have been there for over a month, so there's a good chance that if Theodorus went that way he may have been seen."

They were already half a mile from the fort, and turned back. Arctus sighed. "I feel bad about Erdigorra," he confided suddenly. "By the agreement I have with his family I should be teaching him the skills of a gentleman, but I've done little while I've been with you, apart from the occasional hunting expedition, and he's pretty good at that anyway." They returned to the posting-station, which was small and managed by a kindly couple, who when Flavia complained of a sore throat looked out the best of remedies, supper of a dormouse preserved in honey. Muffled up, she went out alone for a walk later on, and on the edge of the town someone demanded a *siliqua* for her to go further; she complied and found a beaten field with three ropes strung between tall poles, where girls in nothing but leather briefs were giving a virtuoso acrobatic performance, watched by an enthusiastic and noisy crowd; a pimp was moving through the throng, taking bids for the gymnasts to provide other services later on. Some of the looks that men gave her were becoming leers; Flavia drew her scarf over her head and set out back to the posting-station.

From far off they saw a sentry standing under a square blue flag on the top of a corner-tower, moving as he caught sight of them. They crossed a ford across a shallow but turbulent river; then, leaving the waggon with Rúari, they climbed a short steep path to the camp, which huddled behind extensive walls following the five sides of the six-acre plateau. The gate towers had been demolished. Stones from the walls had been pilfered for sheepfolds, and the patrol was camped within the fort on ground where wooden barracks had once stood. Another sentry challenged them as they came up to what had once been the gateway. Here they were high in the hills. The view to the west gloried on for miles, but to the north-east mountains rose still higher. The outpost's name, the Temple of Cocidius, came from a timber building heavy with moss, hidden under three hoary yew trees in the remnants of the huge old fort, and adjoined by a small house where, they said, an aged druid lived, solitary, morose and silent.

Lucius Palatinus, the commanding centurion, made the travellers welcome without ceremony, and he and his three decurions were clearly pleased to have fresh gossip. There were twenty-seven in his detachment, though he complained that there should have been thirty-eight. Three of them were from Dalmatia, originally drawn by old regimental ties and a curiosity for change; but most were not. Seventeen were sons of former members of the cohort, five had been conscripted elsewhere in Second Britain, and two recruited in Noricum on the Upper Danube and immediately transferred to the Wall by some military whim – though these last seemed to be making the best of their abrupt separation from the borders of Italy, and were clearly deferred to here, if not in the whole cohort, as arbiters of style, fashion and general good taste. A slight special sense of excitement and professionalism in the camp was perhaps down to being in the open and in a place where barbarians bore arms, though Arctus suggested quietly to Flavia that, since he had spotted a couple of girls lurking around the tents, some of the liveliness might have more to do with the soldiers having left their wives and children twenty miles away in Magnis.

These troops had relieved another detachment five weeks earlier, but knew perfectly well everything that had happened anywhere in the neighbourhood for some long time, including that Theodorus had for certain not passed that way from Magnis but gone due west, headed for Carlisle. But to Flavia's excitement they also knew of Titus himself, and said that he had appeared at Magnis maybe a year ago and set off north to Traprain Law, the chief place of the Votadins near the Firth of Forth.

Moreover, they said, he had been seen in the area much more recently – they thought in October. He had not been to the Wall, nor yet to the Temple of Cocidius: he seemed to have come down from the north travelling alone, and then, having bought food from local shepherds, doubled back as if he had had news. A soldier, one Gervidianus, had actually met him at that time while on patrol, and told them that he had said he was headed westward far beyond the end of the Wall into the country of the Novantans.

It was the end of May, and dusk came late this far north. The soldiers turned in while it was still broad day, and Flavia stood for a time staring northward into the barbarian lands. They seemed to be strange places of perpetual light, and she wondered if Titus was really still there, and if he was dead what had happened to him: whether his spirit wandered these green moors with their sheep and trees, or had gone to some happier or sadder place. At least if you were a Christian, perhaps, you could take comfort in such thoughts. A soldier on sentry-go came up, and Flavia asked him how he liked the spot.

"This place seems eerie at this time of the year," he said. "I come from Dalmatia myself, from the coast near the great Palace of the Emperor Diocletian, and I've never got used to the summer and winter here. Winter's worst, dark all the time, like death; and you know what they say about Britain: winter for nine months and bad weather for three." He laughed a little, and it broke into a cough, as if to bear out the remark. "But in truth summer's strange up here as well: it sometimes feels sort of light-headed and magical. And this is a sacred spot anyway: it makes sense that there's a temple. They say Cocidius was a powerful god once, worshipped all over the north-west. Perhaps he still is. There's certainly other temples round about. I make an offering each time I come – most of us do."

Flavia was slightly taken aback by this, not by the piety itself, which was common enough in the army, but because she had always found soldiers much more down-to-earth. "We have to decide which way to go from here," said she, making conversation to assess the man better. "Perhaps it would be a good place to ask the gods for help."

"I remember my uncle telling me of his consulting the

oracle of Trophonius at Lebadeia in Greece," said the soldier. "There was a shrine of the Good Daimon and Good Fortune, he said, and he stayed for several nights. Every day he had to avoid hot baths and sacrifice a ram, and the diviners examined the entrails to see if the favourable night had arrived. Then he was washed and anointed with holy oil by two young boys, and the priests took him to drink of two springs called Memory and Forgetfulness. After that he looked at a secret image, prayed, dressed in a linen tunic with ribbons, and put on a pair of special boots. Then he was taken to the oracle's entrance, a deep hole in the ground, and had to climb down a rickety ladder into the dark, holding honey cakes. Underground he was taught about the future. He said that it's not always in the same way: 'one person sees and another hears', he said, but he wouldn't explain what he meant. He came back feet first through the same narrow hole (I suppose he must have had some help with that) and was revived by the priests, who put him on a stool called the Chair of Memory and made him repeat everything he had seen and heard."

The soldier stopped speaking but did not move, regarding the horizon as if something of interest were to happen. A falling star? More likely some reply from Flavia. She felt that his story seemed to shunt aside as trivial her own half-formed ideas about tossing a coin so that the gods could decide the way to go next. She kept her silence, but after a few moments the Dalmatian simply moved on.

She went aside to the wooden temple. The building was dark and forbidding. A large insect scurried against a light patch of moss. She directed her thoughts towards the god. "Lord Cocidius," she muttered. "My companion Arctus and I are strangers to you and to your worship. But we are in the country where you are guardian, and now we may be setting out into it further, on our own. We need your protection, Lord, and if we remain safe and come to Carlisle I shall make an offering of a lamb in your temple. Hear me, Lord Cocidius!"

She fell silent. Above, dark clouds sped ruggedly across a luminescence in the misty sky; below, the cold wind of the moors sang in her chilled ears. She looked up questingly. Soon, she knew, the moon would rise, and somewhere on the western horizon, beneath the belly of the Lion, was Jupiter in its dance through the zodiac. But none of this could be seen. She was turning away, when the oak door of the temple creaked, and the ancient druid priest came out, a faint flickering candle shielded by a fold of his robe. As he passed her he croaked, as though not to her: *"The blessings of the Lord Cocidius be upon you, my child."* He shuffled towards his cottage, and hauled the door shut. Flavia made for her tent. After she closed the flap behind her there came from somewhere the rasping bark and wing-clap of a long-eared owl.

CHAPTER 4

'"If he's away," said Socrates, "It's for you and the others to play his part as well as your own."' That was almost the beginning of the dialogue, remembered Flavia all of a sudden, and as its potential reference to Titus dawned on her she was dismayed, and allowed herself superstitiously to reach for and touch the ring of her father's which lay on a cord over her breast. She was dressing the next morning, in a mildewed tent reserved, she suspected, for unimportant visitors like women.

That day Flavia and Arctus spoke to the soldier Gervidianus at length. They ended convinced of his story, and resolved to leave the trail of Theodorus and strike out directly after Titus. There were no roads where they were going, and they would have to leave the waggon behind. They discussed the situation frankly with the servants, and decided that they themselves would go on into the land of the Novantans alone, while Philip, Rúari and Erdigorra should take the waggon west to meet their return at Carlisle. They went through their belongings and left the richer and more luxurious clothes with the Carlisle party. Arctus seemed confident of hunting some of their food on the way, which reduced the load to take.

Flavia had been studying the local women, especially those from north of the Wall, and the next morning she spent some time braiding her hair into plaits like theirs.

From outside, voices at drill drifted in, Palatinus bellowing "Are you ready for war?" and the soldiers shouting back "Ready! Ready! Ready!". She put her delicate ear-rings away in a pouch, and replaced them with plain silver studs to keep the piercings open. She put on a tightly-woven woollen jacket and a loose skirt that stopped well above the ankles, and listened to the rain on the tent. She had forgotten the heavy downpours of the west, and got out the long leather cloak she had had made in Durobrivæ: it was mannish clothing, but she would have no other shelter on the march.

Their route lay westward down the stream next to the fort and across a tributary, then north-west across two ranges of hills and an interposed river. Arctus' horse, Hipponoë, could not carry them both, and they had to walk and use her as a pack-animal, which the mare resented and made some trouble over. Flavia herself, though, was not unhappy with the irregular progress they made on the first day: she had never done such long and sustained walking, and she needed to conceal not just the blisters that quickly appeared on her feet but a developing feeling of overall malaise, especially in the evening. The initial absence of roads also stopped them from making a rapid pace, though they found that with effective enquiry of the few people they did meet they were able to find paths that did not seem greatly inferior to pavement.

With all this, they made a late start and a slow journey before halting for the first night by another river flowing south-westward. They had not brought a tent, being wary of its encumbrance and weight, but when Flavia declared she could go no further, and they saw the forested mountains before them on the other side, they decided to stop for the night, though the area seemed deserted. Arctus relieved the mare of their bags, putting them under a spreading oak tree, and rubbed her down. Flavia felt deathly tired. She forced herself to find pans and draw some water from the river, and then to gather some sticks together for a fire outside the tree's canopy, but it took her a good while, and by the time she had got so far Arctus had settled the horse and taken over the main burden of work, using a fire-bow to light a flame and boiling eggs, which they ate with bread from that morning and with ham and butter. After their meal they lay down in blankets on either side of the fire.

"Will you be cold?" asked Arctus.

"I don't think so," said Flavia, conscious that this was her first night alone with him, and wondering if the question was intended to carry any special meaning. Beforehand, when they had been discussing the division of their party, she had wondered whether he might make a forcible advance on her once they were alone, and rejected the possibility. But now, of course, they really were alone, and she was disconcerted to find that despite his gentle and considerate behaviour, and the friendship she herself had developed towards him, she all of a sudden felt faint traces of an unforeseen panic bubbling within her. She was furious with herself for this irrational reaction. She fought it down, and kept her voice level, deepening her breathing. "How far do you think we might have to go, at most?"

"It might be six or seven days, I suppose, if we had to go far west," said Arctus easily, routinely. "But a lot would depend on what kind of progress we made. We'd have to do a lot better than today." Flavia felt her anxiety ebb. "But it will be natural to improve our speed, the more we and Hipponoë get used to this way of travelling. Anyway, we may later be able to use some of the roads laid by the army further west in the old wars. Though we can't rely on that, I suspect." Already fatigue was overbearing her, and she did not have the energy to reply.

The next morning she woke refreshed despite, or because of, the dampening dew. A blackbird sang cheerfully in a nearby oak-tree, and the fresh green hills looked inviting rather than threatening. Arctus' bed-bundle was there, but he was not. She stretched, feeling a callus on her left foot and a tenderness in her calf muscles, but ready to meet the day. She splashed her face with water, and through a hazel-bush saw Arctus approaching: "Hallo! I limed some branches last night in case it would take a songbird or two for breakfast, but I've been to look, and no luck." They drank some water and munched some raisins, packed up and set off.

Stiffness in her joints wore off rapidly. After several

hours they found themselves making their way round the garrisoned fort of Blatobulgium, and picked up a paved road running westward – the main road north from the Wall, they worked out, built perhaps by Agricola's army centuries before. Grass grew between its stones, showing the scarcity of traffic, and this reminded Flavia of some of the local by-roads near Cormerick. Once on the metalled way they immediately noticed the difference in their pace, and were sorry when it turned northward outside the village of Dumfries, and they had to travel on west without it.

There they came across someone else who remembered Titus, an old lady, the priestess of a little round wooden temple. She clucked disapprovingly until Arctus gave her a snipe he had shot the day before, and then grudgingly said she would offer it to the god, and squirrelled it away in a moment. She admitted that she had seen Titus some time back, and that he had been heading for a place called the White House a week's journey further, a place where a Christian priest had settled, a full day's travel short of the princely palace at Rerigan on the far coast; she gave directions, laughing dismissively when they mentioned the road they had seen marked on maps. They set off westward on a track across the mountains.

In the late afternoon Flavia began to weary again, and was increasingly glad of the pauses Arctus made from time to time to stalk a bird or a hare. At last she prevailed upon him to stop and ask shelter at a farm. The people were grudging, but let them shelter in a barn and sold them cow's milk and porridge. Again she slept heavily.

The next day was mostly along forest tracks, with anxious discussions where the way forked, and they saw scarcely a soul. But the weather held good, and they bivouacked again in a sheltered glade. That evening Flavia, though tired, felt stronger, and they stayed awake for some time after supper chatting of the difference between these forests and others they had known, and journeys they had done in the past; from walking, they strayed on to Arctus' enthusiasm for sailing, and the time he had spent on ships in the Cantabrian Sea – a stormy place, he said, where you needed to judge the wind and the tides well. She realised that she was warming towards him, but also found herself using irony to hold him away, as if she did not want to get too close; she sensed on his part both interest in her and a respect for the distance she set. She wondered if it would last.

The following day, after a long day's hike, they reached a settlement called Goatend on a river they called the Fleet, not far from an ancient Roman fort, its walls covered in moss and with gaps where it had been raided for stones. The people gave them lentil soup with stale barley-and-acorn farls, and showed them a corner of one of the smaller roundhouses, where they rolled themselves in their cloaks next to each other. Flavia saw that they were expected to be husband and wife and felt invaded by the thought; she would have liked to sleep head to foot, so as to keep her distance from him more decidedly, but feared what the other people might think.

She woke early, and crawling to the doorway saw the first streaks of dawn. A man encumbered with a wooden slave-collar was already up, reviving the cooking-fire; they gave him a *siliqua* for their lodging and set off south-westward away from the river into a birch forest. After half a mile or so the path turned north-west into a tumbled landscape, and they found themselves marching across high moorland where long-billed curlews cried, and then down the other side to the west towards the huge mud-flats of a great river-estuary. At mid-morning, already tired, they arrived at the seashore alongside a stream, where yet another little river ran in from the north-east, and found a clump of roundhouses which they had seen from miles away up in the hills.

Their approach must have been watched, but no-one troubled them, and they went up to ask the way of a woman grinding barley in a hand-quern outside a little turf hut, built on a bank lined with two rows of limpet-shells for decoration. Three little children ran off shyly into the house as they came forward, but the woman was courteous. She said there was no fording the river nearer than Minigaff, ten miles away to the north, but offered that her cousin would take them over the Cree by boat, now the tide was in, for one *siliqua*; for two he would take them three miles down the bay to set them ashore to the south of the river Bladnoch, which ran in from the west and would otherwise also give them trouble.

The cousin was a small, dark, taciturn man of around fifty, who, once their bargain was struck, seemed to take forever in getting his coracle out and ready. But about midday they were set down on the southern bank of the Bladnoch. They took a brackish drink of water from the river and munched a farl before marching inland, where they found a clear enough track going south. The way led up into low hills, with straggly woods of pine, oak and rowan. After a couple of hours they found themselves down on the coast again, in a sheltered bay where fishermen's families lived, with a spectacular view for miles back along the undulating coast to the east; here again they asked directions. They set out south-westwards back into the hills and walked for an hour or so before wading a stream, then, making their way around the eastern end of a hill, they saw behind, up another stream, a little group of buildings: one of these was long and squared, rather than round.

This house was about fifty feet long and twelve feet wide, and built heavily to give protection from the elements. The walls were of dry stone, about three feet thick and roughly whitewashed, and as they came up to it they could make out through the chinks an infill of earth and peat. The thatch on the roofs was of barley straw and rushes, held down against wind by long ropes of braided heather anchored with stones. A couple of dark pigs rooted about one end. They looked in at the open door. A hearth in the middle of the clay floor gave warmth, the smoke ventilating poorly through the thatch. The light from the peat fire was supplemented from the door, and by a few small square openings in the eaves. In the gloom an elderly man was patiently plucking a grouse, and watching them.

"*Good day, Sir,*" said Flavia. "*My name is Flavia Vindex, and I have travelled here from the Roman Province in search of my brother Titus. Do you have news of him?*"

The old man was motionless apart from the jerking of his right hand as it tugged feathers out of the bird, and Flavia feared that he had not heard. Then he spoke in a dry, breathless voice. "*You are welcome to the White House, you and your husband. You must await the return of Stephanus. But in the meantime I shall show you the place.*" He put the bird down on the ground, wiping his hands, and advanced towards them. As he came into the light they saw that he looked at least seventy years old, clothed in a threadbare, faded blue woollen smock. He pushed past them, muttering to himself, made his way with long practice round a flaughter spade propped against the wall, and led them behind the house and about a furlong to the south west.

Then with an icy shock Flavia realised she was looking at a small, smooth, upright stone. Her eyes filled with tears as she made out the words carved roughly on it in Latin:

A DEDICATION TO THE GODS BELOW. TITUS VINDEX, MOST PERFECT GENTLEMAN, WHO LIVED FOR THIRTY-ONE YEARS, ACCOUNTANT OF THE SACRED LARGESSES, TRIBUNE OF THE FIFTH PARTHIAN LEGION

She heard the old man speak again. "*The blessed Stephanus said that we should add the first words out of respect for the dead, though he was not a Christian, and that in any case it was true that he would be with the demons.*" The meaning of his unfamiliar Christian jargon sank in; she felt a prickling of anger at the man's tactlessness and stupidity before the finality of the stone overwhelmed her. Fighting to retain her composure as she did so, she gradually, unthinkingly, fumbled the braids in her hair apart in the sign of mourning, and then bowed her head, shrouding it with the strands, burying it in her fingers, tears welling in her eyes. All these miles, all these days of travelling – in more hope and fear than she had admitted to herself, she now realised; all were ended in dust. And she, who should have been there at Cormerick to see to the horse-drafts, there for her father's grave at the Festival of Roses, there for little Vellibia's wedding and the birth of Turianilla's child, she who ought yet to be there for Lughnasa which was not far off – here she was gadding about on a futile errand far away. "I would like to rest now," she heard her voice say;

and then there were murmurs between Arctus and the old man, and someone led her to a dark hut and a heather bed.

Flavia scribbled an emendation on her tablet and turned the page of the book on her knee, and then realised that behind it someone was approaching the roundhouse. The rain was heavy: the emerald countryside was almost invisible.

"Stephanus is ready to see you now, if that is your will."

"He has returned already?" she said.

"Last night, late, after the household was to bed."

She put away her books, pulled on her boots, grabbed her cloak, and went out into the rain, breaking into a run to shorten her exposure. In a few minutes she was at the White House. She pulled her hood down and went through to the book-room, where a man was seated at the open window, staring at the downpour. She sat on a stool, not disturbing him. He did not look round. There was a pause. Then the door opened again, and Arctus came in. He looked at her cautiously, and she waved him to another stool.

At last Stephanus turned. He seemed in his fifties, rather older than she had somehow expected, with long grizzled beard and hair. He was wearing simple undyed woollen clothes, a hooded tunic and a cloak, along with worn military boots. He appraised her, giving her somehow the feel of someone who was genuinely wise and perceptive, and she submitted to his scrutiny without offence. At last he spoke: *"Your brother was here for nearly three months, Lady Flavia, before he went beyond the grave."*

She felt a coldness at her heart again at the words. *"How long ago did he die?"* she asked.

"This year, the tenth day before the kalends of March," he said. *"I remember it well. It was a cold day, unusually cold, and flakes of snow were in the air. Your brother was weak and feverish, but very lucid. It was that day that he asked me to see that his headstone bore the usual inscription. He seemed to know that his life was running out."*

"*Tell me more.*"

"*Well, it was a long time since he had told us of you, and written his letter to you. Even at that stage he was too feeble to write himself, though he tried most pitiably, and I acted as his clerk,*"

"*What letter?*"

"*The letter he wrote to you shortly after the Ides of October.*"

"*But I've had no letter.*"

Stephanus looked at her, perhaps understanding something. "*I am sorry. He feared as much, though I entrusted it to one who seemed worthy of the confidence.*" He turned and opened a chest. "*I have a later one. I think that you should read it now.*"

He brought out a bulky packet of thin wooden writing tablets and handed it to her. She took it calmly and untied the simple bow. She opened the leaves, and saw unfamiliar writing in an open, clear hand.

To my dear sister Flavia from her brother Titus, greetings.

I remember all those months ago, in the orchard at Cormerick, when I told you of Dagwald's offer to me of a commission in the arcani. You looked doubtful and worried, though you didn't say very much, and I realise now that you were right. I believe I am going to die here among the Novantans, and that I am the victim of cynical and wicked men. I am sorry now not to have written to you earlier, even though for the sake of confidentiality my commander advised me not to. I did write some weeks back, but I fear that that letter may not reach you, and will say again here some of the things in it.

I arrived in Carlisle in late winter. You may think it can get very cold in Cormerick in winter, but it is much worse on the Wall. Even by Saturnalia it is snowing, and when I arrived the drifts were thick, and vehicles could not move, only pack-animals. My orders were to put myself under the command of Serquina, but to observe him and to report back to Augusta.

All the primicerii of the arcani are appointed from far away, just like provincial governors. Serquina is from Galatia in Asia Minor, where there are some who still speak a kind of Celtic language, and he has acquired a native's command of British, along with contacts all over the world. He gets as a matter of course all the official information about what goes on north of the Wall, apart from the military reports from the army garrisons at Cramond, Castra Exploratorum and so on, but he has arrangements for getting copies of those as well. He has agents among all the Attacottian and Pictish tribes, even far off in Orkney, Shetland and the Hebrides, and among many of the Irish tribes as well. His headquarters are in Carlisle, but the Duke of the Britains' main offices are in the fort at Uxellodunum, a mile north of the city, so Serquina is the most influential official actually based in Carlisle, and also has a lot of pull with the military supply officers there. In short he is very powerful in the Wall zone.

I think now that he must have realised at once what I was doing here. As part of learning the job, I was sent on a tour of the western forts down to Ravenglass, and till then I heard nothing untoward. But when I was back in Carlisle I got talking to a young man in a bar, full of excitement and enthusiasm, who let slip that there was a barbarian attack being planned, involving not only the Picts and Attacotti from north of the Wall but also the Irish. It seemed that steps were not being taken to head it off. I reported this back to Augusta. Then I was sent to carry a despatch to the political agent at the chief place of the Votadins, one of the Attacottian tribes, at Traprain Law. I tried to keep my eyes open on my way north, and heard at Traprain Law that Serquina is not only not taking action against the conspiracy, but is actually encouraging it.

It seems he is in league with one Valentinus Faber, a senator once important in Pannonia, who was exiled to Britain for political crimes. Flavius Lupicinus, when a commander in Britain seven or eight years ago, fell in with this Faber, and now that Lupicinus is Master of Soldiers of the eastern Emperor Valens, and Consul for the current year, they have conspired. Faber is to stir up trouble in Britain, which will occupy the western Emperor Valentinian; Lupicinus will march against the West on behalf of Valens, and because of the British invasions expects to catch Valentinian unawares and defeat him;

meanwhile Faber is to take command of the British armies and defeat the barbarians here. Once Valens has both parts of the Empire he will, in thanks for Faber's part in this, recognise him as co-Emperor for the whole of the Prefecture of the Gauls, from the Britains to Mauretania. Then Faber, of course, will reward his own followers generously.

I was very afraid of going back to Carlisle, knowing this, and not being sure that news of my knowing it wouldn't get back to Serquina. But it was clearly my duty that the news should get to Dagwald in Augusta. I composed a report and slipped out of Traprain Law a day's journey to the fort at Cramond, our furthest outpost; I insisted on seeing the commander, revealed that I was one of the arcani, and put my report into his hands for transmission, if possible by sea rather than land. I stayed at Traprain Law as long as I dared, trying to find out more, then set off back. I had been very much in two minds whether to return, however, and I planned to stop off at a tribal village of the Novantans, where I had been given an introduction, and which is an area less used by people going between the Wall and the Picts. But first I made for the Wall to see if I could get news.

Near Cocidius' Temple I unexpectedly ran into a fellow-officer of the arcani called Venocarus. He had with him the eldest son of the High King of the Northern Picts. This young man, named Tiotagus, had been smuggled by the conspirators out of Trier, where he was being held hostage under the usual pretext of education. Venocarus belongs to the Saxon Shore division of the arcani and is uncomfortable in the North; he was happy to give up his charge for me to escort home.

But when I got to speak to Tiotagus alone, he proved to be something of a scholar – indeed, I think you might get on – who had been tricked into accompanying Venocarus, and who in fact was not at all keen to go back to his family and their barbarian ways. I did not find it hard to persuade him to return to Gaul. But I could not let him travel openly. The conspirators are clearly active all over the Britains and in the Gauls as well. Any civil or military official could be one of them, and he would be in too much danger of being recaptured. I could not see how to do it. Then I realised that time was not that important, and that so long as he did not get home his father would still feel just as constrained as if he was still in official hands in Trier. I have made a friend of a boatman who lives on the River Tweed, and often goes out into the German Ocean, a man called Cipius. I promised him twenty solidi, half then and half later, to take Tiotagus to you at Cormerick, and told Tiotagus that he could expect me there later to see that he gets back to Gaul.

Heading westward, however, I soon found myself being hunted by someone. I was attacked at night, and was wounded in the leg, though I escaped. Following my plan I went westward, and eventually came across Stephanus. He took me in and sheltered me, and tried all the healing he could, but the leg would not get better, and has now become infected; I do not think I have many days left. If I could get to a military surgeon they could take off the leg, but there is no prospect of that now, and nobody here can do it.

I am so sorry, little sister, for the way this has gone, and especially for involving you: you will have to sort out the Tiotagus business as best you can, and if you read this letter and not the other you will already be at the White House, far from Cormerick and not in the best place for the problem, perhaps. I am sorry that I did not take your advice, even unspoken, and that we shall not meet again this side of the Styx. Pray for me to the gods. Tell our mother, and Atra, that I died bravely, doing my best in the service of the Emperor and Rome. Give generously to Stephanus here (he protests as I ask him to write these words, and I have to insist), who for all that he is an atheist Christian is a good man. Marry, and do not let our father's legitimate line die out.

I have some debts to pay in Augusta. Antonia should have a memento of me, perhaps the gold penannular brooch with the rubies. Also, there is a slave of mine called Melania, about 25 and pretty with dark hair, whom you will remember my mentioning – I bought her when I went to Augusta. I have leased her to a friend of Antonia's called Julia, and she has had a daughter by me. You

should make sure she's well and reclaim her and the child
for the estate. Be kind to her, as I know you will.

 Gaul may not be safe either if there is civil war: I think
you should go to the farm in Spain. I still doubt that
trouble would get to Cormerick, but I now think you can't
be sure. Warn Sallienus and tell him to make what
preparations he can. You must get out of Britain as soon as
possible.

Farewell, my sister.

 The last words were in his own hand. Flavia watched
herself, remote and astonished, as her eyes filled with
tears. She saw Arctus put his hand on her arm and squeeze
it gently, but she could not seem to feel his grasp. She
looked up at Stephanus, who regarded her sadly. "Did he
suffer much?"

 "He was in pain when he arrived. I have some
knowledge of healing, and I was able by the help of God to
relieve some of his suffering with medicines. He was
courageous, and was not distressed by the pain. I am sorry
that I could not prevent his death. He was a very
honourable man."

 Memories paraded past her unseeing eyes as they filled
again: conflicts in childhood when she had been unfair to
him or manipulated their father to his disadvantage,
playing in the garden at home together, his manhood
ceremony at the age of fourteen...

 "*Speak, child,*" said a voice, and it was Stephanus. "*I
would not intrude, but it's not good to keep thoughts to yourself
at such a time. If you wish I will leave you alone with your
friend.*"

 "No," she said, blinking back her tears, "*No, I should
like you to stay, if you would.*" Perhaps she felt things more
keenly talking in British, she thought for a moment, a
language of childhood chatter with nurse, and not of grand
formalities. It would be safer to use Latin. And Latin
would surely be better for Arctus? She paused a moment
and, feeling a vague sense of guest-courtesy above a mass
of confused thoughts, she nevertheless found herself
speaking in British, impelled by obligation, saying rather
more than she felt comfortable with. "*I've been remembering
so many things in the last few minutes,*" she said. "*I and my*

brother were so affectionate once, I realise, and stayed close in many ways, even after we started to grow up. I remember us trying to be strong and virtuous together to comfort our mother after our father's death. We didn't always succeed, but in a way it was a kind of conspiracy together, relying on each other, hiding it from her, and it was something which brought us together even more. And I remember the excitement, a few years later, of setting out on our grand tour to Trier and Rome, and when it all ended in catastrophe he was so kind to me.

"I knew, in logic, as soon as I got that letter in Cormerick, that he must be dead, but I wouldn't believe it. And now I've no choice, and I feel confused as if I'd had no chance to prepare for the news at all. And I feel bursting somehow, so full of things I can't explain." She lapsed into a sullen silence, disturbed by her confusion of feelings.

After a while Arctus addressed Stephanus. "Is it true about the barbarian conspiracy?" he asked. "Should we be in danger here?"

"We may be, it is true," he replied, "In broad terms, anyway; I cannot make out the politics of it. In fact it may be even worse than Titus thought, and the Saxons may be involved as well as the Picts and Attacotti and Irish. But I think you would be in no danger here. Our little farm is not wealthy, and will not become so: I spend too little time hoeing the weeds and too much trying to plant the garden of men's souls. And our neighbours who fish at Kilderry and at Bysbie are peaceful folk, I don't think they are part of the High King's war-bands."

Flavia heard them only dimly, her mind dark and red. She stood up. "I am going out," she said rather thickly, "going for a walk."

"I'll come too," said Arctus.

But she replied "No! I need to be on my own," and strode out of the house. She walked directly away from it, and from his fading anxious voice. After a time she found herself heading southward up a hill and breaking into a run. She reached the top and saw down the slope ahead a little fishing village, where a small stream suddenly swelled into a generous harbour, and beyond it a great arm of the sea, and in the far distance the land again. To the west of the village was another hill, taller and long; she veered towards its western side and carried on down. To begin with she moved fast, running and jumping over clumps of obstructive heather; then, finding that this sometimes landed her leading leg thigh-deep in boggy mud, where getting out was difficult and left her covered in dirt, she tucked her skirt into her girdle and began to move more cautiously, trying to recognise the greener patches that betrayed soft ground. It was confusing; vegetation here was so different from that of the Cormerick fenlands. At last she was on a rocky low cliff overlooking the shore, and she cast herself down on the heather.

She was still panting, and could feel the blood flowing in her veins; her shins were scratched by the undergrowth, and her thighs aching from hills steeper than she was used to. But she felt alive, looking out over the water; the wind roared in her ears and the gulls shrieked. The sea was still, but tiny squalls beat on it: they made little patches go suddenly light or dark, or blew the surface in small circles like dust-eddies. Some large black-and-white birds, about the size of geese and seemingly flightless, were playing like fish in the water, chasing and ducking and diving. The sun came out and warmed her. She turned over with her face to it, yielding to it, uttering a fragmentary prayer. The heat absorbed her. Her mind gave itself up to her body's relaxation, and went blank.

She became aware that she was lying on another hillside, on the island of Elba, in a keener heat; scents of pine resin and wild thyme came to her, and the distant sound of gentle waves lapping a rocky shore. She felt the contentment of sexual satiety, and a regathering vigour through her limbs, but all her experience was slightly remote, as if perceived through a pane of glass. She was naked and lying on a heavy cloak, and she rolled over, burying her nose in it, enjoying the smell of sunshine-heated wool. She looked up, and saw that her movement had attracted the attention of Cæcina Priscus, who stood a few yards away, his hair still tousled, wearing a still-ungirded tunic. He smiled affectionately and admiringly at the sight of her. She felt residual delight, a lingering slight loneliness for his touch, a sense of contentment at being with him, a satisfaction with her own body. "I always pictured you Roman nobles caring about nothing but your own pleasure," she said drily. "I never thought that you would trouble about a mere woman's."

"It's all part of our family duty," he replied in a similar tone. "Pindar reminds us that it was limping Vulcan who was conceived when Juno was angry with Jupiter: unless both father and mother take delight in the moment of conception, the children will be flawed. So one needs some practice, of course, before one starts begetting them. But there are other reasons for it as well, you may be aware." He smiled complicitously.

She returned the smile, and stretched. "I'd better get dressed," she said, getting to her feet. "It won't do to get browned by the sun: it's too obvious in the baths." Cutting across her feelings, in a way that seemed strange, as though she did not really have access to it, or perhaps as if she were two separate people who felt differently, was a sense of foreboding.

"That's a shame," he said, stepping towards her and stealing a kiss on her breast while she stooped to pick up her dalmatic, so that she chuckled and pushed him gently away while she gathered it up. He helped her pull it over her head, and straighten the folds as they fell. "When I was small, and still allowed into the women's baths with my nanny, I remember one day when a German woman got herself sunburned. She was from beyond the frontiers, the wife of a chieftain who had joined the officer corps and achieved some distinction. As you know, even in the huge courtyard in the Baths of Caracalla where there's always lots of space, all the fine Roman ladies avoid lying in the sun for fear of getting tanned. But this German woman

loved the sunshine. One day she stayed out in it too
long, and was in pain. I remember being struck by
the way people gossiped about it: they obviously
felt she had done something shameful. To begin
with I wondered if the problem was that she had
made her skin darker: that people with darker skin
were less respectable. But I gradually realised that
it wasn't about what her skin colour was: it was
what she had done to it. She'd changed her
complexion in a way that linked her with slaves
and working women. It was that which was
disgraceful, and their talk put it together with the
fact that she was a barbarian."

They were sitting on the ground now, side by
side, looking out over the strait, for a while in
companionable silence. Then Priscus opened his
mouth to say something further, but Titus came
into view round the shoulder of the hill, and he
hailed him instead. Titus smiled candidly in
response, extending the greeting breezily to Flavia,
and they exchanged some conventional remarks on
the topography or the weather: she wondered at
Titus' easy acceptance, at his lack of curiosity.

She realised she was cold, and opened her eyes. She
was back, awake, on the barbarian coast of north Britain.
The sun had gone in again, and the long twilight was
beginning. It was late. She sat up, and saw Arctus
squatting a dozen feet away, watching her. "How long have
you been there?" she asked, half appreciating his loyalty,
half displeased at being spied on.

"An hour or so, maybe? I didn't run into you by
chance: I followed you. You're not within the Wall now,
you know. It's a dangerous thing for a woman to be
wandering the wild hills alone."

She stretched her long legs and arms, and kneaded at
her calves solemnly, looking out without interest over the
sea to the south, still clear, where an indecipherable ship

was visible against the distant blue coast. "That's nonsense. The people here may live in roundhouses and pay fewer taxes, but they're much the same as at home. I had no trouble making myself understood by them yesterday, did I?"

But it wasn't really true, she thought to herself, as they set off back to the White House. Everything was different here, really, if not different from the way things were at the Wall, then certainly different from the way they were back home. People spoke with a curious accent and used strange words; they probably wouldn't understand at all if you spoke in Latin. Ordinary people had fewer clothes of fewer different kinds and dyed fewer colours; they seemed to have fewer things generally. Perhaps it was no surprise if they wanted to take the Romans' possessions. They would have their own strange gods. Perhaps they even had human sacrifices, as Cæsar had said the Gauls had, before the Romans arrived.

Reaching the top of the hill, Flavia expected to see the White House sitting in its valley, but there was just a moorland dale, with to the west a burn running down to the sea and a wood beginning and, yes, a couple of deer just visible at its edge. Arctus struck out confidently and Flavia followed; she must have come further than she had thought. The journey lasted some time, and Flavia was tired again, as well as cold, when as dusk became night they stumbled into the little farm. A fire burned, making the room very smoky, and Stephanus and the old man sat by it with another man of about thirty-five and a boy of maybe twelve. Stephanus welcomed them to the hearth, and they approached gladly. They were given water to drink, and a vegetable soup enriched with eggs, and barley bannocks.

"*Has your journey healed you, Flavia?*" said Stephanus as he gave them cups of beer and returned to his place.

"*I'm not quite sure what you mean.*"

"*I think that you left the house full of anger, anger at those who killed your brother, yes, but also anger at him for going to the north and at yourself for letting him go. Is the anger still hot in you?*"

She bridled silently at her thoughts being invaded, and

was about to gainsay him, but then with a shock realised that what he said might well be true, and subsided. "*It is not, it is quieter. I prayed to the god Apollo and he sent me peace.*"

Stephanus put his hand on the old man's knee, as if to still him. "*Perhaps it is the Lord Jesus who sent the Holy Ghost to heal your soul,*" he said to her. "*But we shall not speak of such things now. You are hurt in your spirit and will take a long time to be restored. Your trust in yourself will be weak for some time, and it would be wrong to press the Gospel on you at such a moment. Later, perhaps, when you have had a chance to reflect, you may turn to God.*"

Flavia was irritated, and replied in Latin. "You should not claim too much for your Christ and deny the true gods. What of Arachne or Alcyone, who challenged the gods and were destroyed? Don't you know the story in Plutarch of the Governor of Cilicia who put the oracle of Mopsus to the test, whereupon the god anticipated his question and confounded him? Or of the little children playing in the court of the temple at Memphis, who in their innocence called out words which carried a divine meaning?"

Stephanus replied gently. "*We have many such stories among the Christians too. Leave them for now. We can discuss them another day, if you wish. Tell me what you saw when you went out.*"

Flavia reflected that she had a sense that this man's soul was close to the gods, and that she owed him much. She abandoned the argument, and instead told him of the fishing village and of the ship at sea, and asked him what they would be.

"*The village will have been Bysbie, which is our nearest harbour. That's where Theagenes here and I landed when we first came. The ship is more difficult. From that cape you can see four coasts: eastward the shore south of Goatend the way you came, westward the Rinns of Galloway, southward Manavia Island, south-eastward the coast of the Roman Province around the fort of Gabrosentum. Glannoventa at the mouth of the Esk, which is the next fort south and too far to see except on the best of days, has a good harbour, and a number of warships assigned to it. You may have seen one of them, or a supply ship from Carlisle — or just a merchant vessel on its way to Ireland, perhaps.*"

They spoke of geography for much of that evening, looking over itineraries and drawing rough maps on wax tablets, though Flavia soon felt sleepy. She also showed Arctus Titus' letter, and he read it, frowning. They slept, each in a blanket, on the floor of the house.

The next day was the unlucky day after the Ides of June. Flavia went outside early and combed out her hair, pondering her situation. She asked Arctus to come with her on another walk, and they set out westwards. The day was overcast but bright.

"My brother is going to get tarnished with this conspiracy," she announced fiercely, as soon as they were out of earshot of the White House, "even if that strange letter from Constantinople isn't a plot against him. I need to clear his name. I want it for himself, but also for myself and the family. Otherwise our estates will be confiscated, no doubt about it: there'll be no end of petitioners for them, ready to swear his treason. What do you make of this story of the Pictish prince?"

"I don't know what to make of it," answered Arctus. "The political analysis is plausible. But surely the situation's not quite as you say: after all, your brother's been acting on the orders of the head of the *arcani* in Augusta."

"Whether that is worth anything remains to be seen. Certainly I know nothing about this Dagwald; he could be playing games with us, too. And anyway he doesn't seem to have been able, or willing, to clear Titus' name straightaway: he told him to stay out of the way, north of the Wall."

"That might have been just to give him time to take action. But I suppose that if you could lay your hands on this Pictish prince Tiotagus it would prove your brother's good faith. You'd need to be careful, though. If Faber and the Easterners win, then you wouldn't want to disprove your brother's support for them."

"Titus is supposed to have sent this Tiotagus to Cormerick in September. But there was no sign of him by the time I left in early May. It doesn't take seven months to get from the Tweed to Cormerick, even with a lot of contrary winds."

"The winter's a bad time for sailing. Your brother's friend might have refused to leave till the spring."

"What, and feed and entertain him all the winter, a youth used to all the luxuries of Gaul? I hardly think so."

"Well, I suppose it's either that, or that he sank at sea on the way, or that there was some lesser trouble with the ship and they were marooned on the coast somewhere."

Flavia tightened the corners of her mouth, grimacing in vexation. "I suppose you're right. Well, if he's lost at sea, or if he's fallen into the conspirators' hands, there's nothing to be done. Nor can we search the whole east coast of Britain for him. And even if we do know the boatman's name, it must be days from here to the Tweed, and days more from its source to the coast: it just wouldn't be practical to look for the man." They had reached the edge of a pinewood, and a few trees away a squirrel, startled, made rapidly away at a great height in the trees, a scrap of red slipping from branch to branch with a single long sinuous motion. "Honestly, of all the boatmen that Titus could have asked for help from, he chooses one on the longest river in Britain! What do you think we should do now?" she asked.

"Hard to say," he replied. "If there is going to be a barbarian invasion we don't know if it will be this year or next. But if it's this year it'll be very soon now, or they'll be too late on in the season. Perhaps we should hurry back. At least we're on the west side now, where we can reach Augusta without going through Sanctus' province. Perhaps we could buy passage from a fisherman and cross direct to Glannoventa, or even Lancaster or Chester."

"Yes," she said, a little absently. "The problem is that we know so little about these political intrigues which cost my brother his life. I'm not at all sure that he will have tracked them to earth properly. And then again there's the letter that went astray. It may easily simply have got lost. But there's obviously a good chance that it got into the hands of this Serquina. It's very compromising. If they had any thought that we knew its contents it would be fatal to put ourselves in their power."

"Didn't he say that the army was independent of the *arcani*, and imply that there was no love lost between them?"

"Yes, but that doesn't necessarily mean it's true. It may be an impression they try to convey, and which Titus fell for. Or there might be individual army commanders who are in Serquina's pocket – more than likely, perhaps, if he's planning to betray the defences to the barbarians."

"What about the fact that we got here at all? Doesn't that suggest that we aren't known?"

"We might simply have moved too fast for them. Or they may have expected us to come to Carlisle, and we may have been lucky to have crossed the Wall at Banna, and avoided a trap further west. Or they may just not have suspected that I, as a woman, would have come north. We certainly made no great secret of who we were or what we were up to at Coria or Magnis. The more I think about it now, the more naïve I feel we've been. Nearly as naïve as Titus." No sooner were the words out of her mouth, than she regretted them.

But Arctus appeared to see nothing blameworthy. "What about Stephanus?" he asked. "They must surely know that Titus got here. And if the October letter has fallen into their hands they would know for sure that Stephanus had dangerous information. So why haven't they done anything here? Or indeed why didn't they get to you at Cormerick?"

"If they didn't pursue me to Cormerick before I left, it might have been merely timing again: the letter could have taken as much as some months to get into their hands, I suppose, and more time to get back to Serquina, so that even if he took quite prompt action his agents could well not have reached Cormerick till after I left on, what, the fifth day before the nones of May. But as for Stephanus, yes, I suppose he is much closer to Carlisle than Cormerick is, and Serquina would surely have been able to reach Stephanus by now if he'd wanted to. Can Stephanus be trusted? Look at him. Surely he *can't* be an agent for Serquina?"

"It seems hard to credit. But remember, he *is* in the middle of nowhere here. It's possible that they just thought it wasn't worth chasing him for the moment, that he wouldn't get word out. After all, he's not interested in politics, so far as one can tell. And it must be a very busy time for them, especially if the barbarian invasion is planned for this year: unless they had someone coming this way for other reasons, to go to Ireland or whatever, perhaps it wouldn't be worth sending someone specially. They must have to make judgements about uncertain things, like anyone else. We can't know, really. But perhaps the safest thing would be to stay here until things are clearer. If danger approaches, perhaps Stephanus would be able to get us away."

They walked on for a space. "I'm worried by what he said about a Saxon invasion," said Flavia. "Cormerick is not far from the coast, even if it is shielded by the marshes. A Saxon ship would only need to evade the fort at Branodunum. And if the army are distracted by a northern invasion there could well be trouble."

"Well, that's no reason for going back. You can't fight off a Saxon war-band by yourself."

"No, of course not. But I could help to plan and to get people and things to safe places: we could maybe move some of the stock to my cousin's place in First Britain, for example, which would certainly be safer. And this Tiotagus man might turn up. And I need contact with Cormerick; I draw my strength from it, like Antæus from the earth. And anyway I can't stay here for months on end: I've got work to do."

Arctus was silent for a moment. "Is this your writing you're talking about?" he asked, and she gave him a glance, defensive, defiant, self-satisfied. "You're an unusual woman, Flavia," he said. "Most would be worrying about their hair or their clothes in a place like this. What is it you're writing?"

"Nothing that would be of interest to you, I suspect," she said.

"Ach, come on, Flavia! Don't be so cold! I've not followed you to the ends of the earth to be treated with quite such disdain." And he made a half-angry half-playful lunge at her.

She let out an ambiguous cry and ran away, and he pursued. They were in a craggy dell. She dodged around outcrops and thorn-bushes for a while, laughter starting and growing, and then was caught: they fell to the soft ground and lay a while in a heap, partly winded and partly glad of the excuse not to talk. Little stroking motions began, it was hard to say where, and then he bent his head and she was kissing him urgently till their heads swam. After a while he started to raise her dress, but she suddenly began to feel withdrawn. He freed her girdle and slid his hands up her flanks, but she only felt more remote. She lowered her own hand to cover his. "Arctus, I'm sorry, no, not now."

"What do you mean, Flavia?" he murmured. "Do you want more time?"

"Yes, more time, but not now." She shifted her weight on the ground, then grasped both his hands with one of hers and pulled him to a rather chaste kiss with the other.

He dropped his hands and got up, expressionless, then went a few steps away and turned back to face her. "This may be a poor moment for this, Flavia," he said, "but I think you're behaving badly. Twice now you've acted as though you want me as a lover and then refused me at the last minute. And I have given up my own business and followed you now for a month now, even into barbarian country: you owe me some consideration."

Flavia's heart sank; she had been dreading this. Of course she warmed to Arctus in a number of ways, and just now she had been trying to ignore an awareness, in the light of what had happened at Pontefract, that she had been giving way to a moment's enthusiasm when he might expect more moral discipline. But she hated thinking about this. Well, there was no use in quoting at him the capriciousness of Catullus' Lesbia: this was not parlour games in Rome but reality, a reality in which, as he had said, he had already made a kind of commitment, even if a partial and provisional one. She sat more squarely, and folded her legs under her skirt, looking up at him solemnly. "Arctus," she said, "I'm sorry if I've been confusing, or confused. I think I should tell you that the last time I loved a man it went wrong."

Arctus was silent, waiting.

Flavia wished she could sound lighter, less ponderous. "It was during this journey I made to Rome," she went on uncertainly. "I... He..." She paused, wondering what to say, embarrassed that Arctus was probably thinking she was comparing him to some fancied idea of the time she had had with Priscus. She drew her knees up to her chest. "I think it has made me very...cautious. I'm not a young girl of thirteen: I'm a woman of twenty-seven and I must live with my experience of the world. I'm sorry if I've been inconsiderate. I can only... I shall try to be more straightforward." He was looking at her earnestly, searching, wanting to believe. Then he put out his hand silently; she took it, and squeezed it for a moment.

But despite her reticence about her work, the next day, after taking Hipponoë out for exercise, she found herself talking about it. "The *Timæus* is one of Plato's most important works," she explained. "It's his book that explains the whole world: it describes the great God's making of the universe, the four elements which make up all matter, the creation of man and the evolution of the animals, and human biology and psychology. And it's never been translated into Latin.

"Of course everyone may not agree that Plato's right about these things, but they do recognise that he's one of the greatest thinkers ever, about science as well as about other things. For example, he was the first, I think, to say that the world isn't flat but spherical, as everyone now accepts. And a lot of what he says is just common sense: for instance he explains that fire burns because it's made up of tiny particles that are very sharp, so that they easily make their way into things, including people, and of course that hurts. Or that the reason things fall downward is because the element of earth in them is attracted by the concentration of earth in the world underneath us. Even if you don't agree with every detail it's terribly important.

"And it's awful that there are so many people in the West who can't understand Greek and never have a chance to read it. It's quite difficult Greek too, anyway, so even people who have a little Greek aren't likely to get much out of it without help. And that's why I'm writing this translation. I've got a first draft done now and I'm polishing it. I shall send it to Rome for publication next year, and then I shall follow it up with a commentary explaining it and relating it to other writers like Aristotle, and the Stoics and Epicureans, and Plotinus and Porphyry."

"Will you become famous?" asked Arctus, listening attentively but with a twinkle in his eye.

"I hope so!" she laughed, responding. "And there've been very few women philosophers, you know, just three that I've heard of. That could work both ways. It might make me better known, because I'd be unusual. Or it might mean that they try to ignore me and say that I couldn't be as good as a man. But Plato himself thought that women were as good as men. In the *Republic* the Guardians, the rulers of his ideal state, are both men and women, and he returns to the idea in the *Timæus* too." She smiled at the ease with which she remembered both the Greek text of the passage and her own translation, though in fact it had been one of the first bits of the dialogue to fix itself in her mind.

Arctus had a smile on his lips too, but of a different kind, warm and sceptical at the same time. It seemed to say that the *Timæus* might or might not be important, and that he would judge that for himself in due time; but that what was important to him about it now was not the work but her enthusiasm for it, and that that deserved respect. It struck her that Arctus did not take her as seriously as she took herself, but that in a curious sense that was actually, in a way, to take her more seriously...as though he appreciated her soul and not just her intellect, perhaps. This lightness of his was good for her, she thought.

That night Flavia felt strangely fatigued again and retired early, and the next morning she thought she understood why, when she woke with a heavy cold – listless and hot with a sore throat and a congested head, as though before disordering her humours the sickness had been waiting politely for a pause in her travels. She kept to her bed for most of the next few days. Dried cherries, her usual remedy, were not available, but Stephanus agreed to seek out some feverfew and make a decoction, which she tied to her head as a poultice.

She was not so unhappy to be confined to bed for a while, since in the days that followed she needed time in quiet for her own reasons: sharp memories came to her of Titus, mostly from early childhood, some of which she kept to herself and some shared with Arctus. And despite the confirmation of Titus' death and the discovery of danger to themselves, it seemed somehow to be a relief to both of them to have reached the end of their quest. The weather was warm, and the food simple and good, and even when Flavia was quite recovered neither of them was inclined to make an early move: they agreed that it seemed unlikely that Philip and Rúari and Erdigorra would be in any danger, and there seemed no hurry to decide what to do. They exercised Hipponoë or wandered in the low hills round about, or Flavia studied while Arctus went hunting for hares or fishing for trout, for fun and to earn their keep; once, he came back excited to have killed a deer, and made Stephanus and his servant boy Toutius go and help gralloch it and carry it back to the White House.

After about ten days it was midsummer. Stephanus announced it to be the day that Christians marked as the anniversary of a man from Verulamium called Alban, once put to death for hiding a priest. He took Theagenes and the two servants to the other end of the building, to a room that the visitors were not allowed to enter, and voices began to emerge. They sounded to Flavia similar to those of the worship of any of the gods.

But she and Arctus wanted more than simply to be shut out of the Christians' celebration: they wanted to do justice to the holy day of the sun-god. They set off for a place some six miles to the north-west, a ring of standing stones set up by the Old People, which they had visited on their walks. In the Province such places were of no account, but the gods here, they had been told, thought them important. On their way they passed a group of giggling girls from a nearby farm who made saucy eyes at

Arctus, and they reminded each other, smiling, of the story that a woman gains a perfect skin by rolling naked down a grass slope in the midsummer morning's dew.

Arriving at the circle, they offered mead and made some simple prayers to the Sun and to Apollo; when they were finishing they saw the farm household arrive, and waited while these made their own offerings. Then they all ate together, bannocks and eggs and cheese, with oat-beer. The Novantans were cheerful and friendly, pleased perhaps to find some relatively normal people at the White House: they were clearly not impressed by the Christians. They had a slow way of speaking and some strange words, and narrow horizons, with none of them having been more than twenty miles away, save one old man who had travelled to Ireland in his youth.

In the late afternoon Flavia and Arctus returned to the White House; she missed the elaborate ceremonies at home, with the mumming and the druid's teaching.

CHAPTER 5

"*"And if in that shape he still does not abstain from evil, he shall be changed every time, following the nature of his evil, into some animal which is in accordance with his own nature, and in these changes he shall not be free of suffering."*' The words came unbidden into her mind. Herself, Flavia was unsure what she thought about transmigration, though she remembered the druid talking about it one festival when she must have been ten or eleven, being portentous and evasive, answering any question with an elaborate tale about the cauldron of Brân or the pig of Manawydan from which she was expected to distil an answer for herself. But now she looked with new attention for a moment at the hare sitting upright on the skyline, not very far off. Suddenly it started and leapt off to one side, like a splash of water running down a rock.

It was about ten days after midsummer. Toutius had gone down to Bysbie to buy fish, and she realised that it was he on his way back who had startled the hare. As he came in sight of the farm his little figure on the horizon broke into a sprint, and he kept it up all the way down the hill, his string bag filled with fresh mackerel bouncing incongruously about. By the time he arrived he was quite out of breath, and they had to wait nearly half a minute before he could speak. "*It's the invasion!*" he gasped. "*It's started! The Picts have attacked the Roman fort at Cramond!*" A trader from Ireland had got the news at Dumbarton, he said, and passed it to the village at Girvan when stopping for fresh water; it had come over the mountains from there. He talked excitedly of a massive army swarming across the wide Forth at night with each of its coracles lit by a flaming brand, and burning the fort to the ground before pressing on southwards, compelling into arms the high king of the Attacotti at his stronghold on Traprain Law.

Though this was an alarming picture, the countryside that Flavia and Arctus had themselves seen locally was as peaceful as anywhere, and debating what the story meant they decided it should still be possible for them to move freely. But they felt they should not now delay further, and pressed Toutius about when the attack had actually happened. He had had little interest in this, and could not answer, but the detail of what he had been told seemed persuasive: they would have to assume it was true. They reckoned it would now be dangerous to try to cross the Solway in a Novantan boat which might be inspected or even attacked by the Roman naval squadron; and that crossing the Wall anywhere other than at one of the main roads might be difficult, especially if they wanted to be inconspicuous. Thus the only route would be back to Blatobulgium and the main road through Uxellodunum and Carlisle itself. This seemed a big risk, if Serquina's men might be looking for them, yet if they stayed at the White House a number of dangers threatened, and their freedom of action might disappear, while with luck, even if they were being looked for at the Wall, there would be enough confusion there for them to get through unapprehended.

Flavia washed their clothes, hanging them like a peasant on the heather to dry in the sun, and they got their baggage together. Arctus, who had let his beard grow since Banna, now shaved his chin clean, and cursed as he nicked himself in a task he was used to leaving to a slave. The following day, the day before the nones of July, they left, quite late in the morning. They thanked Stephanus and gave him money. "I hope that you make some converts," said Arctus politely.

"We've been here eight years now and no-one has listened to us," laughed the priest. "My bishop in Carlisle says that the demons are powerful here. But perhaps we have sown a little seed, and those who come after us may get a better harvest."

The journey to Carlisle took longer than they expected. Although they were only a man and a woman travelling alone there was anxiety in the settlements they passed, which led to questions and delay; and it was clear that not just the Attacotti were at war. At Bladnoch they found grudging lodging for the first night, and were told that a boat from Ireland had come into the estuary a week earlier, having broken a halyard on the way to attack Anglesey and then been driven north by the weather before repairs could be made: once safe on land these Irish, angry at missing their chance of loot, had made trouble for the village, the better half of whose young men were away with the war-bands that had already gone south.

The next day, in the cities, it would be the annual holiday of maidservants, and Flavia vividly remembered it in Gaul ten years earlier: the spacious town of Vienne with its streets and cafés thronged with excited girls, free for the day to do what they wanted, the figures dowdy but dashing in their mistresses' still-nearly-fashionable cast-offs, the voices quarrelling over how to spend the precious time "Let's go to the baths!" "No, the games!". That must be, what, a thousand miles away now? But it seemed like a hundred thousand, as they plodded through whin and heather up the little hill north of the settlement, and a skylark poured out song overhead. About six miles north of Bladnoch they reached the river Cree again, near a well covered in flowers, offerings to the local goddess for men who had gone to the war. There they stopped for a while to eat some of the bilberries fruiting beside the path, and then, following the river, turned north-west. After another three miles they reached Minigaff. It was clouding over now, and, even though Arctus put Flavia onto Hipponoë for the crossing, they both emerged from the ford wet and uncomfortable, each secretly relieved not to have been swept away in the swift current.

The inhabitants were not interested in this pair of strangers, and Arctus and Flavia wandered through the dozen large roundhouses and down a track a mile or so to a tributary stream, and then south-eastward down the Cree again. Soon there was another stream, and some time later a small river. At last, perhaps ten miles but many hours from Minigaff, they arrived back at the village where they had been given a ferry-crossing, almost a month ago. The woman who had found them the boat on the way out was returning from a spring with water; waving to her, they turned eastward and started straight up the hill.

It was on the fourth day afterwards, the fifth before the ides of July, that they once more came in comforting sight of a road, its precise square stones set together, the drains neatly following the carriageway as it marched irresistibly over the hills. They set off down it eastwards, and after three days came again in sight of the fort at Blatobulgium. Nobody stirred outside the walls; but the wooden galleries round the stone towers each contained soldiers on watch, and after they had been in sight a few minutes there was movement. Three horsemen rode out of the nearer gate and approached them at a trot, armed with bows as well as swords.

The leading rider approached them, a well-knit man in his forties who on foot would be short of stature. The symbol of his regiment was a blue disc with a black rim and yellow hub: his shield was marked with it, and over a sleeveless coat of ringmail he wore a fawn cloak marked with two similar circles, along with fuscous leggings, brown boots and a dark rabbit-fur pillbox hat. "Who are you?" he called roughly, putting an arrow to the string.

"I am the Most Perfect Count Arctus, and this is the Most Perfect Flavia Vindex."

"My lord, I ask your pardon," said the soldier, without softening his manner. "Can you show your identity in some way?"

Flavia realised that Arctus was not wearing the symbols of his status. He opened the left-hand pack on his horse, while the trooper maintained a watchful distance, and got out his codicils of rank. But anyone, after all, might have picked such things up, especially if a Count had been so foolish as to wander beyond the Wall. "Here, soldier, this should be enough for you. I have no interest in concealing my identity to test you, like Ulysses with Eumæus."

"Thank you, my lord," replied the soldier, still watchful. "It is a pity that we have to ask honourable persons such as yourselves to identify yourselves in this way. We are poorly rewarded for such embarrassing tasks."

Arctus reached into a pocket and drew out a woollen purse, tossing it to the trooper. "I am concerned to hear it. Perhaps you and your colleagues would entertain yourselves on our account, to sweeten the memory of the occasion." The other inclined his head, motioning them onward, and Flavia and Arctus passed.

It was a tedious day and a half, across the bleak Solway mosses, until they again saw the strange white line of the Wall. At last, travelling down the last half-mile through barley-fields splashed with the violent red of poppies, they made for the fortress at Uxellodunum. It was set about with trim bastions, each with a war-engine, and crowned with the banners of a dozen regiments whose detachments were part of the garrison, as well as with the insignia of the Duke of the Britains, the commander-in-chief of the northern frontier. Once past, they found that it was only a furlong across a fortified bridge over the River Eden to Carlisle itself, where slaves sullen from overwork were loading half a dozen ships at the wharves, their overseers cracking whips and shouting with a shrill edge to their voices.

Willow trees grew at the gates, and the town was filling with people from round about, anxious to shelter behind the walls. Flavia first sought out a priest so as to discharge her vow to the god Cocidius, giving him money to sacrifice a lamb in thanks for their safety north of the Wall, but she did not wait to see it done: then both she and Arctus were asking urgently after their servants, doing their best to do it discreetly. They had no luck that day, and had to sleep communally behind one of the larger inns, in a store-room with an old stink of linen-retting. The next morning they had word of Rúari in a cottage under the southern walls, and went straight there.

It was a small wooden building with a thatched roof and a little window upstairs. Three other cottages clustered about it in a cobbled alley off a back lane, the buildings beset by tall elder and blackthorn bushes, and by long grass and mosses. Arctus went up to the door and knocked, ignoring the interested gaze, from the doorway of the next house, of a silent three-year-old with mud-stains on her hands and knees. Flavia heard the wind in the boughs of a hazel-tree, the song of a thrush, the noise of someone hammering metal in the next street. She thought of her earlier worries about Philip's welfare, her good intentions about keeping an eye on him, and that she had done nothing about it. There was a movement from the next doorway: the arms of a woman emerged from the darkness and dragged the little girl indoors. Then Rúari and Erdigorra opened the door together. "Aha!" said Erdigorra flamboyantly, doing a theatrical double-take, and beaming. "Welcome, my lord. Come in."

Arctus ignored this, and looked back for Flavia; both of them entered, finding themselves in a small room with a battered couch, two chairs and a low table; two bundles of possessions lay in a corner, and a dim light came in, making its way, through a back extension used for cooking and washing, from a doorway leading onto a small yard with a mossy apple tree and clumps of nettles.

"But where's Philip?" cried Flavia, seeing only two of them.

"*He is not here,*" said Rúari. "*He's gone back south.*"

"*What happened? Is he all right? Is he safe?*"

"*Well, we think he is,*" said Rúari. "*What it's like, you see, your honour, is that we wasn't here more than three weeks, just before the summer festival, and no word from your Lordships, when folk started to tell rumours in the streets about how the Picts were marching out and on the way to invade. And then wasn't it just two weeks ago that the news comes of the attack on a fort up in the north somewheres, and the Duke gives orders for transport to be requisitioned? And then Philip gets in a passion like a lawyer, and doesn't he go and berate the Duke face to face, swearing by all the gods and goddesses of Rome that he won't give up your waggon that you came all the way from Durobrivæ in, and that the Duke'll be answerable to the Emperor himself if he takes*" it, and then he harnesses up the horses and rides it out to save it in the very teeth of the Duke's soldiers. That man is the hero itself, your honour, and he has certainly saved your waggon, for if it had been taken by the soldiers then for sure they would have had it for firewood by now."

This was a bizarre story. "Is this true?" asked Arctus of Erdigorra, then studied him more closely. "And have you two been drinking?"

"Well, the days are long up here and there's not a lot to do, apart from trying to turn the odd denarius," said Erdigorra with a bright smile. "Yes, it's all more or less true, so far as I understand the language, though of course Philip didn't see the Duke himself, just bribed the soldiers to let him out. He was concerned for the lady's property as much as for the waggon itself, and he took pretty well all of her stuff with him."

"Was he going to wait for us or just head straight home?"

"He was a bit vague, really. I think he was scared, and wanted an excuse to get out of the frontier area. Not sure I blame him, really; the last time the Irish and the Picts attacked here, six or seven years back, they say there was a lot of damage, and casualties too. Look, he left a letter." And rummaging in a bundle Erdigorra handed back two writing-tablets bound with string. Flavia went over to the doorway for better light.

To the Most Perfect Lady Flavia Vindex from her loyal freedman Philip, greetings.

I regret that, as I hope your slave Rúari will inform you, your property here is under threat of military confiscation, so I am taking the liberty of interpreting your orders with latitude, and removing it to safety. I shall make every expedition to York, and attend there until such time as instructions may be sent to me care of your Ladyship's cousin Ïullinus. I am leaving with Rúari 30 solidi from the money you left in my care, in the hope that it will be sufficient to cover your expenses on arrival. I hope that this will meet with your approval.

Farewell.

"This letter is no good at all!" exclaimed Flavia.

But Erdigorra was still deep in the bundle, and now

reached out a scroll-tube, labelled to *the Most Perfect Lady Flavia Vindex* with several crossings-out: first *in the presence of Æmilius Pacensis at Trier*, then *at Cormerick near Durobrivæ*, then *at the posting-house at Carlisle.* She opened it, and after she had glanced at a sentence or two began to read it aloud, derisively. Arctus looked on as if he had never seen this Flavia before, which in a way he had not.

To the Most Perfect Lady Flavia Vindex from Calcidius, Archdeacon to the Bishop of Cordova, the tenth day before the kalends of February, in the consulships of Fl. Lupicinus and Fl. Iovinus, the ninth year of the indiction.

I heard you some years ago in the house of Themistius in Trier, speaking of the wisdom of Plato, and have been told that you have now taken it upon yourself to seek to translate the words of Plato's <u>Timæus</u> into Latin.

Know that with the help of God I have already accomplished this, and will bring the words of the Philosopher to the people of the West. You are a woman, and as such you have a weaker constitution and a weaker intellect than a man. You should be glad that on your part further labour on this task is now unnecessary.

You should also be told that the ideas you were expounding at Trier about the void are wrong. For you said then that Plato stated that there was no space between the atoms, when he said "the whole within which the elements are held, since it is spherical and therefore naturally aspires to fall in on itself, hems them in and allows of no empty space." But Aristotle says in his "Concerning the Universe" that the diverse shape and varying size of the atoms never allows them to fit completely into each other; and it follows from this that there must be a void between them. Hence your view of the void is incorrect. You should be glad not only that another of a more worthy sex has achieved the translation, but that you have been saved by him and by the grace of God from misleading men into error.

Farewell.

Flavia clenched her jaw. She had invested so much of her time and herself in her translation that she was vexed that another had been made, and would sap the use and impact of her own. But what was much more serious, she told herself, was that it should have been made by such a fool, and by a Christian with good connections (and of course a man) who would probably have no trouble in publicising it.

She did not remember meeting this Calcidius in Trier, admittedly ten years ago. However, she told herself, in any event his letter was ridiculous. Firstly, he claimed that Aristotle said there was a void, yet Aristotle had argued the opposite very clearly both in his *Concerning Generation and Corruption* and in his *Physics*; secondly, it was true that Aristotle had made the remarks referred to in his *Concerning the Universe*, but the inferences Calcidius drew simply did not follow; finally, although Flavia herself had expressed at Trier the opinion attributed to her, that had been an opinion about what Plato had meant, and not, as Calcidius seemed to think, a statement of her own view.

"Look at it!" she said to Arctus. "It's from a man who has written a flawed translation of the *Timæus* and presumes to condemn my own. He can't be allowed to get away with this nonsense. He's careless with reasoning and evidence; he'll get everything wrong. He won't be doing it for the sake of seeing that people learn, or of making sure that the truth is known: just for the fame and the money."

She drew a breath, and started to pace up and down in agitation. "I shall have to publish my own translation at once, and follow it with the commentary when I can. It's hard to make your work known, too, I know; I've spoken to others. Unless I can persuade or commission others to do it I shall have to give readings, and trail round western cities, probably Trier, Arles, Milan, Rome, Capua, perhaps Carthage and Sirmium... The sooner I can get to Gaul the better, once we've seen that Cormerick is all right. And it'll be an added struggle for a woman, for of course everyone believes that women are unsuited for philosophy, despite the myths of Athena and Tiresias, despite Empedocles' "Once I was both girl and boy", despite what Plato himself wrote."

"Flavia, how did this reach you?" asked Arctus.

"It was addressed via the post-house," Flavia said, her

speech slowing as she realised what he had said. "I see what you mean. By the Good Goddess, who knows we're here? Erdigorra! How did you get it?"

Erdigorra shrugged and looked at Rúari. Rúari looked confused, and Flavia repeated the question in British. The answer came at once, "*One of the slaves from Cormerick brought it, Lanucus, the skilled hand who works in the apple orchard.*"

"*What was he doing away from the farm? Where is he now?*"

Rúari smiled. "*His Honour Sallienus sent him with the post.*"

"*Is he still here? Were there other letters?*"

"*Surely no, he went back with Philip. He'd be wanted for the harvest, wouldn't he?*" He paused. "*And indeed there were other letters. Erdigorra, what have you done with them?*"

Erdigorra was delving in the bags again, and already had a little pile of letters in front of him, all of them tied bundles of alderwood wafers. "Here they are!" he said, and after a final grubbing reached them across.

Flavia looked at the superscriptions: To the Most Perfect Lady Flavia Vindex from the Honourable Abascatus; To Flavia from Vedia; To the Most Perfect Lady Flavia Vindex from the Most Perfect Tranquilia Severa; To Flavia Vindex from Pedius Blæsus; To the Most Perfect Lady Flavia Vindex from Sallienus. She opened them in order. The first four were simple, from Abascatus a note of thanks for her visit in May, from Tranquilia Severa an invitation to dinner, now months out of date; from Vedia in Cirencester and Blæsus in Trier recommendations of travellers who were likely to be passing through Durobrivæ. Sallienus' letter was also short:

To the Most Perfect Lady Flavia Vindex from Sallienus, the day before the Ides of May, in the consulships of Fl. Lupicinus and Fl. Iovinus.

There were a number of letters shortly after you departed, and I thought it best to send them on. I am sending Lanucus, who is reliable and will not be wanted till July. I have asked him to be discreet if he can on arrival, but he will leave the letters at the posting-house and return at once. All is well in Cormerick. You can *reassure Philip that his wife is healthy and happy.*

"This needs thinking about," said Arctus. "Flavia, it's not just the question of this Calcidius; whatever happens it'll be some time before you can do anything about that. If the posting-house was alerted to report these letters, as seems likely, then Serquina will know you are expected here. We should leave at once. The question is which way to go. Tell us, Erdigorra, what's the news of the invasion?"

"Confused, sir, to be honest. You will know about the attacks on the Wall, first in the East, then in the West. The Irish have attacked two places further south in the diocese, one called... Anglesey, yes, and now, ten days ago, Lancaster and Bremetennacum as well. Some of the crack reserve detachments of the Vicar and Count are said to be moving west from Augusta in response."

"We heard that Cramond had been attacked by the Picts."

"That is true, I understand. But in no case has a fort been taken: it looks as if it's still true that barbarians can't take a walled fort or town. Carlisle is full of people, as you know, and also of rumours of invasion, though few have actually seen any fighting, I think. It's said that the garrisons at Newcastle and Wallsend were summoned to Coria on a false alarm, and that the main force of the Picts and the Attacotti crossed the Wall and the river in their absence, and are now well to the south."

"But it's all quiet this side of the mountains?"

"Yes, so far as one can tell: the Irish were given a bloody nose by the regiment at Bremetennacum and went home. But Fullofaudes, the Duke of the Britains, marched east from here, a week or so back, with an army drawn from most of the western Wall forts. Perhaps he will catch the northern barbarians before they get too far, and throw them out as well."

Flavia remembered the fortress at Uxellodunum flying the Duke's flag as if he were still in residence, and felt anxiety, wondering why the current commander saw fit to make such a show, and if it might imply bravado covering a weak defence. "Have you heard anything of the Theodorus we followed north?" she asked.

The two servants looked at each other, Erdigorra's

superiority for a moment lost in an unaccustomed complicity. He was silent, but before two elaborate seconds had passed Rúari had stumbled in: "*Well, we didn't like to be making enquiries, mind, my Lady, being like that it was a delicate matter, but it did come to our attention that a man answering the very gentleman's description was said to have been in the city, and to be leaving two weeks ago on the road south, towards Chester.*"

"Did you hear anything else? Have there been official enquiries about us?" she asked, but, apart from extracting twenty-eight of Philip's thirty *solidi* from Rúari, she was unable to get anything further, other than an impression that whatever the servants had been up to in Carlisle they had comported themselves relatively discreetly. But Arctus took Erdigorra outside later on, and they did not return until after Flavia, exhausted but delighted to have a real bed in a room to herself, had gone to sleep upstairs.

Their stay in Carlisle was as short as possible. Most of the next day they spent bribing army quartermasters with gold coin so as to get food and gear at extraordinary prices. But in the mid-morning, as they were leaving a granary where they had been buying dried fruit, Arctus took Flavia aside from the busy streets, telling Rúari, who was acting as porter, to take his current load back to the cottage and return. They crossed a muddy area between some houses, and mounted into the quiet portico of a small temple, a timber floor in the shelter of four wooden columns before the panelled door of the cella, once painted red and now rotting at the lower edge. A mudwort grew tall next to them, brushing Flavia's shoulder with its tiny white flowers.

"I took Erdigorra to task last night," Arctus said. "He admitted to me that all three of them were interrogated by the *arcani*. I'm not sure I managed to get all the details out of him, but they were asking about you and your plans and also about Titus. We must leave today if we can: there is a lot of confusion at present, which is probably how we've escaped attention so far, and may be good enough to get us out again if we move fast."

"But I want to talk to Junius Alfenus before we leave, the commander at Uxellodunum," demanded Flavia vigorously. "I want to make sure he understands that Titus was no traitor. And I want to talk to him besides that: he may have been the last Roman to see Titus alive, apart from that Christian priest."

Arctus paused, searching her eyes. "I think that's just too dangerous," he said. "Quite apart from the delay, it would attract much too much attention to you. Anyway, Alfenus is commander of the largest cavalry unit on the Wall: the likelihood must be that he's gone east with the Duke of the Britains."

"That's no reason why we shouldn't look for him."

"Well, maybe we could ask," said Arctus doubtfully, before concluding: "No, it wouldn't do. You saw what Uxellodunum was like when we came through yesterday: there are lots of detachments of different units there, and we should need to ask about a good deal and draw attention to ourselves."

"Oh, come on, he's the commander of the resident garrison. Everyone would know him."

Arctus seemed to be searching for why he was opposed to this quest, or perhaps for a way of framing his reluctance which would find favour with her. "Flavia, I don't think it's feasible. Carlisle is Serquina's headquarters; he may well have had notice from that letter that you were on your way; the city will be full of his agents. We really can't go about attracting attention to ourselves by demanding interviews with the authorities."

"It wouldn't be a matter of demanding interviews. We'd just turn up at his morning reception, when he greets clients and hears complaints."

"What, and just come out with it in public in front of his apparitors and petitioners? Oh, I don't think so, Flavia. Anyway, Alfenus may well be in with Serquina."

Flavia stepped away to the end of the temple plinth, staring angrily at the decaying limestone wall of a garden, tufts of red stonecrop in its crevices and spikes of green-white pennywort standing sentry on the top, then turned. She could see the sense of what he said, but resented him for it. "Very well. But we'll make inquiries anyway about whether he's here, ask the servants at least."

They returned to their negotiation with the

quartermasters, but when at last they got back to the house, with Rúari clutching a bag of fresh minnows to fry up as whitebait, they found Erdigorra waiting for them in a state of high excitement.

"Haven't you heard the news?" he exclaimed. "The Duke's been surrounded by a large force of Picts at South Shields, with no more than his bodyguard and a handful of troops – invalids and veterans left behind in the fort. There've been two attempts to relieve him, both have failed, and the barbarians have dug an earthwork right round on the landward side. Most of our ships had already been sent south on expectation of Saxon attack, and our remaining boats on the Tyne have been burned by the enemy."

"So is the Duke completely cut off?" asked Arctus.

"Completely. Junius Alfenus here should be in charge in his absence, as commander of the principal regiment on the Wall, but Hartulf at Coria is claiming precedence as being on the spot and more familiar with the east side of the mountains, and has the support of Serquina. There's to be a conference of the frontier unit commanders at Banna to decide the issue, but meanwhile the barbarians are all over the eastern side of the province."

He paused, as Flavia and Arctus began to digest this news.

"I've been to the quays," Erdigorra continued. "There is a packet leaving at dawn tomorrow with despatches for Gaul, and I've spoken to the captain. We can get on it, if you are willing to pay twelve *solidi* for each place. I haggled him down from twenty. We should go, my Lord: we have been away too long."

"That's enough!" cried Flavia. "Did you say that Alfenus was here in Carlisle?"

"Flavia!" called Arctus, with a warning note in his voice. "It really won't do." She wondered for a moment if it was her shortness with Erdigorra that was annoying him, or her persistence about seeing the commander. "What if he *is* in league with Serquina?"

"What do you know about that, Erdigorra?" asked Flavia. "Is Alfenus loyal to the Emperor?"

Erdigorra, watching them carefully, spread his hands.

"Who can say? He stayed behind when the army marched out, and some people said it was so that he could stay free to join the winning side. But people often say that of generals, I think."

Flavia and Arctus waited, but Erdigorra said nothing more. "You see?" said Flavia.

"No doubt he would do as he was ordered," exclaimed Arctus irritably. "But is it worth taking a risk for? You won't get any news about Titus' prince Tiotagus here whatever happens. Come to Gaul on this ship, and we'll sort things out when events have quietened down."

This talk of Gaul, thought Flavia, was a betrayal of Sallienus and everyone else at home. "Certainly not! Why in the world should I go to Gaul? Cormerick is where I belong."

"It would be much safer, Flavia. If you want to vindicate Titus' reputation, and you have this book of yours to defend, then it's much better to go to Gaul: you'll have better access to the Court for the first, and better access to the literati for the second. The chance of anything happening there or on the way is minimal. But if you try to get to Cormerick, the whole country is full of marauders, and anything could happen."

"You don't believe that. You've just decided you want to go home, and don't want to lose touch with me, and that's why you're making all this fuss about going to Gaul."

"Flavia, you're not being fair. I admit that I'd like to be home, and I'm worried about my mother, but what I say about you is true."

"Well, you can go home to Gaul if you want, but I'm going to Cormerick."

Arctus raised his eyebrows and gave way. That afternoon, Erdigorra was sent to Gaul alone, with gifts and messages.

But packing up took time, and deliveries from the granaries were late. It was not until noon the next day, a Wednesday, despite Arctus' urgency and reports of new Irish landings at Lancaster, that the other three set off south, requisitioning two more horses for the journey at the posting-station, with the aid of Arctus' postal warrant and a heavy bribe. They joined a group of soldiers' families being evacuated south to First Britain, and an escort of nine soldiers from the garrison; at the last moment a young drill-sergeant of the rank of *campidoctor* joined the party.

It was an ill-omened day when they left Carlisle: the anniversary of the Battle of the Allia nearly eight hundred years before, the worst ever defeat of Roman arms, when the legions had been crushed by barbarian Gauls near the Tiber. As they quit the city the sound of ritual lamentation drifted from the temple of Mars, dampening the spirit. Louder cries came from a gang of five housebreakers hanging from crosses outside the walls, this defiance of the Emperor Constantine's prohibition on crucifixions showing the panic of the authorities. As they proceeded through poppy-studded meadows along the banks of the Ituna, they passed small farmers labouring hard and early to get in the hay. But it was not long before the road went through a large estate. There, on the other side of spiny blackthorn hedges, slaves, sullen and naked, toiled under the whips of armed overseers, while white bryony and snapdragon flowers smiled heedless in the field margins and the woodland edges.

The road marched up a ridge to the west of the river, and their party managed about nine miles that first day before stopping in some huts below a signal tower. Flavia was to be quartered with some shy young women anxious away from home, and spent the evening with Arctus, but when the two of them wandered out of the camp for a walk the young *campidoctor* attached himself and seemed interested in where they were going; they became curt and unfriendly until he took the hint and went back. Flavia turned to watch him go, and stared at the tall stone tower stark against the darkening horizon. "He must be a spy, don't you think?" she said. "Not just lonely?"

"He behaves like it," agreed Arctus. "But he doesn't seem very dangerous, and I wouldn't worry about him." His eyes were drawn away by a buzzard, and she thought that he was estimating the point to aim for if he was going to hit it with an arrow. "After all," he added, "if they'd wanted to arrest us or do away with us they could easily have done it in Carlisle." But Flavia did not feel happy about the *campidoctor*; she could imagine half a dozen reasons for Serquina not to have taken action against them in Carlisle, but still to want to do so at a distance.

On the Friday, the thirteenth day before the kalends of August, they arrived at Brocavum, where four roads met. One they had been following themselves, one wandered westward towards Ambleside and the coast, a third climbed south-east up the valley of the Ituna to cross the mountains towards Catterick, and the other pressed onward to Bremetennacum and the south.

The fort was garrisoned by a small detachment from Uxellodunum, and the commander, beset by rumour and hungry for reliable news, asked Flavia and Arctus to dinner along with the decurion who commanded their little party. Down the eastward road, he said, had come word that bands of Picts and Attacotti were already at Catterick; up the southward, that the Irish had landed on the western coast and spread much terror until they had been dispersed by the crack troops at Bremetennacum.

There was a despatch waiting for their party, or rather for the soldiers' families and their escort, announcing that the southward roads were now unsafe, and ordering them west to the coast to be picked up (perhaps) by a naval vessel. While they ate vegetable soup with olive oil and barley farls, Flavia and Arctus debated whether to join this westward march.

The reports of Picts east of the Pennines seemed reliable enough, but it sounded as though the attack to the south had been warded off, at least for the moment, though no-one could swear the Irish had actually withdrawn. They would be more vulnerable on a naval vessel, if it were in the hands of Serquina's friends. The other choice was to wait things out, either back in Carlisle or in one of the coastal forts. But Flavia still insisted on getting back to Cormerick, and once they got south of York, she argued, they would surely be safe from the northern barbarians. At last the best plan seemed to be to go on to Bremetennacum, turn east there across the mountains to Tadcaster, and then take the road south, the same road through Doncaster as they had taken going outward: it was surely unlikely that they would have trouble going through Lincoln now, when Sanctus' attention, like everyone else's, would be on the military situation.

The next day they left early on their own, the river Ituna still on their left, and climbed up towards a high pass, looking across the valley to the west where the little party they had travelled with now toiled up a hill themselves on their way to Ambleside and Hard Knott; Flavia tried to make out the *campidoctor*, but they were too far off. It was a land where shepherds feared eagles more than barbarians, and where the cry of wolves from the western fells broke the night. They camped at the summit, and the next day followed a new stream downhill as it grew into a river, swift-flowing and full of shingle banks. Arctus tickled three trout and gave them to Rúari to cook for their breakfast. They pressed on south.

The rain sheeted down again, and they breasted a hill, oakwoods on either side, the margins thick with tall purple foxglove. The ancient military surveyors had laid the road like an arrow towards a large fort, whose limestone walls, battlements and towers could be seen vaguely through the flapping curtains of water; behind it would be a bridge over a broad, full, peat-brown river, the Belisama. To their right was a cottage. Perhaps it was abandoned, for jays were eating their fill of the bean-rows in the garden. It suggested to Flavia Ovid's words, '*Now there are fields where Troy once stood,*' and she ran over the journey in her mind: they had seen several houses empty in the Lune and Hodder valleys, one of them burned, some of them obviously rifled – had the barbarians been there, or had it only been looters? Perhaps it would not matter to the people who lived there, when they came back.

Then they heard a jangling of harness, and a troop of a dozen fully-mailed cavalrymen, each with long braided brown hair, appeared out of a birchwood to the east. They were arriving at Bremetennacum. The troopers escorted them to the fort and took them straight through to the commander, who brought them into the headquarters and questioned them on what they had seen.

He was a colourless man in his forties, with flat dark hair and a neutral accent, who behaved as if he had been awake a long time. Wearily, as though he had recently done it often, he explained that they should not be worried by the strange manners of his troops or by how few of them there were. Thousands of Sarmatians had been settled in the area centuries ago, he said, by the emperor Marcus Aurelius, and most of his troops came from their descendants; they still spoke both Latin and British with an unusual accent and might look rather strange, but they were not barbarians and there was nothing to be feared from them; they were crack troops, proud of their equipment as mail-armoured horsemen, and of combining the skills of heavy cavalry and of archers. In any event, many of them had been detached to meet important requirements elsewhere before the invasion, and there were few in the fort at present.

He mentioned that he came from the upper Danube, and had been in post for over eight years. He asked the arrivals for their names, and paused when Flavia gave hers. "I think I met a cousin of yours two years ago at Bath: Numeria Vindex," he said, with the ghost of a smile. Flavia wondered that this grim man had a social life; as if he read her mind he picked up a stylus and turned his attention to some kind of inventory, and his visitors were shown out.

When they went out of the headquarters to be shown to refugee bunks, improvised in barracks and segregated by sex, they noticed not just that the buildings they were shown to were empty of regular troops, but that many of the men they saw holding torches on the walls were slaves and not themselves troopers. As they crossed the fort, Flavia suddenly heard a loud melodious rumble. Turning, she glimpsed in the shifting torchlight a soldier blowing a huge circular horn as tall as himself, with an elongated bell curving away behind his thigh and then back forward again two feet above his head: his face red, dripping with rainwater and full of concentration, he ignored her, stealing an occasional glance at a cornet at his side. Now she recognised his instrument: the commander's horn used only for major military deployments, which she had not heard since watching a gladiatorial display in Rome.

At last she found herself in a long room: it had seemingly been first filled up with truckle beds, and then crowded again with talkative women and fractious little children. People pressed up to her as she entered, demanding news: their voices were half drowned in the rain hammering on the wooden roof, and some spoke in languages she didn't know, or of places she had never heard of. Trying to keep a friendly smile, she manoeuvred her way through the throng, denying much knowledge, and found an apparently empty bed. She dumped her bag and sat, combing her wet hair out, but people were still crowding on her: "They say you came from the north – did you see the barbarians?" "*Did you pass our Trenos, a little boy with brown hair, about eight years old?*" "*Was there an old man with a cow on the road?*".

She felt curiously alone, she realised, as her coldness and her lack of response set a wall about her, and they drifted back into their own discussions and disputes. In a way she'd been alone all her life, except for Titus, and he – he'd always been different from her, and was gone for ever now, anyway. She was used to being alone, but usually in her own surroundings. This room, roughly washed with distemper, packed with people and bundles, was a desolate place to be alone in. Life around was breaking down, she thought. And she was not protected from it: her life was being destroyed as well.

Even if Cormerick was safe – and who knew about that, a hundred, two hundred miles away? – life in the Britains would never be the same again. The Britains had been settled, ordered, peaceful; for generations there had been no real trouble. In the future, even if everything was restored, people in Bremetennacum would be like people in Strasbourg or Vienna or Budapest. They had always feared disease, and bad harvests, and unjust officials, but now they would have this permanent extra worry: they would fear the barbarians as well, armed men arriving in sudden boats out of nowhere, burning and stealing and enslaving.

It all seemed so much to cope with. She wished she hadn't been separated from Arctus. She laid out bits of clothing as bedding, and lay down, closing her eyes as the voices went on. *"You know that long fell you can see to the east as you come into the fort?"*

"I do, it's called Pendle Hill, isn't it? It's the one where they say, 'If you can see Pendle it's going to rain, and if you can't see Pendle it's raining?'"

"One can tell you come from these parts! That's the one. Well, Bacura says she was up there two nights ago and found two witches casting a spell to bring the barbarians here. They'd just killed a cat and were taking the guts out and stringing them on twigs in the shape of a cross above the ground, and they were singing incantations, they were, magical ones."

"No, really? A cross, you say? Were they Christians then?"

"No, she didn't say that. But she did say they sounded just like the language of the Irish."

"How would she know that? She's never seen a Irishman in her life!"

"I tell you it's true! She swore it by the Goddess Brigantia."

"The Goddess Brigantia spends her time a long way away from here – Bacura chose well, if she's going to be forsworn. I daresay she got a fright last year when she thought she was so clever at the village meeting swearing by Diana that she hadn't been going with Arcavius – and then Tancorix was out getting firewood and caught them at it together in the Badger Wood just at the next full moon."

Reminiscent giggles broke out, and Flavia's drowsy thoughts slowly took over from them in her mind.

The next morning at early dawn Flavia emerges from some dull dream, hearing a child singing quietly to herself somewhere. Vaguely she takes in the refugees' barracks, and in her mind's eye she sees a shipload of twenty or thirty huge moustachioed Saxons marching through the woods at Cormerick: they hear a child's singing coming from an invisible window, and turn aside; finding the household asleep they get out bales of hay (where from?), pile them against the walls and set them aflame; as people run out of the doors they are killed, first Atra, then Banta, then the others, one by terrified one; they lie in a heap with blood disfiguring their bodies, their eyes full of accusation. The last to appear is the little girl, whom Flavia does not recognise. The Saxons take her and throw her up in the air, holding up their spears to see if she will fall on them. They throw her up again and again, laughing as the crowd in the arena laugh at a stupid gladiator, and each time the child falls closer to a spear-head.

Then Flavia understood that the little girl was herself, and waking further threw back the covers of her bed. She got up chilled by more than the morning cold, and stumbled out of the building unwashed, her skin feeling stretchy and old.

She met Arctus in the yard between the barracks, and looked for Rúari to send for water for breakfast. She eventually tracked him down deep in conversation with some other Irish slaves, and he went off to his duties with ill grace. With the water they munched some dry biscuit.

They were about to get on their way out of the fort when the commander came up, the lines about his eyes still heavy, even in the morning. "Most Perfect Lady Flavia!" he called as he approached, and they stopped. He came right up to her, confidentially. "I think you should know there's a *campidoctor* arrived from the Wall, who's been suggesting I should detain you."

His manner suggested that he was not going to do anything of the sort, but Flavia, unsettled by her half-waking dream, felt a tenseness come into her body. "What does he accuse me of?" she asked.

"Theft of military funds at Uxellodunum," he replied. "Frankly, unconvincing. And an offence more plausible in someone like him than in you, anyway. Even if I didn't know a bit about you I'd trust your word against his. But I don't know what his game is. Perhaps he did something like that and wants someone else to pin it on: but if so you're a silly target for him to choose. Could be following you for some reason, I suppose. Do you know why he might?"

Flavia felt an urge to confide, and a cautiousness forbidding her to. She chose prudence. "No, no I don't."

The drooping eyes held hers for a moment. "Don't feel obliged to press on."

Should they stay? This was one of the army's best units: they would surely be safe here. The invasions seemed to be worsening all the time. But suppose orders arrived for him to arrest them? "No, I have duties in the south: I must go."

The commander shrugged his shoulders and turned away; an orderly immediately ran up and engaged him with a problem about a catapult windlass.

Flavia and her companions left the fort, crossed the river, and turned left up the road that ran into the mountains on its way to York. Despite the commander's sympathy, the Bremetennacum garrison had commandeered their two post-horses, and again they had to walk and to rely on Hipponoë as a pack-animal. They had one leather tent which was much of the mare's burden, and high in the mountains they pitched it for the first time, not far from the ruins of an ancient fort. Arctus insisted on posting a watch, and that he and Rúari should share it, and Flavia fell asleep.

Then she was emerging from a heavy dream, to the noise of light rain on the tent and Arctus gently shaking her; the dim light of an occluded sky leaked through the tent flaps. "Wake up, Flavia!" he said. "Bad news. I can't find Rúari anywhere. I think he must have taken the chance to disappear in the night."

Flavia dragged herself into awareness, trying to work out what this meant. She realised she had been expecting it for days. "I suppose he's gone to look for the Irish, and get back home. They are his people, it's understandable," she said as she sat up and hunted for her wrap. Shrouded by it she pulled on a woollen top and over it her leather jacket, and also a pair of leggings. There was no chance of a fire in this rain, and when they looked for a drink of water they discovered that their water-bottles had disappeared in the night, along with Rúari's own stuff and a few other things that had been lying near the tent flap. Flavia scrabbled through her possessions anxiously, and then more anxiously. "Arctus!"

"Yes?"

"Have you seen my books, in the oiled packet?"

Arctus helped her search again until they were sure that the books were gone. Flavia sighed deeply and looked at him. "What can I do?" she asked. "Why will he have done this? He can't even read!"

Arctus looked at her. "I wonder," he said. "There's a lot of respect for learning in Ireland, as well as here and in Gaul. Though the druids and the bards boast of committing everything to memory, I think they use books quite a lot. I shouldn't be surprised if Rúari was looking for something valuable to take, and that, with money and jewellery on our persons, and Hipponoë likely to make a fuss if he tried her, the books were the only things he could get at. But, you know, he may have a wholly inflated idea of the price he could get for them. I saw him looking at you in Carlisle when you opened that papyrus letter: you know, while talking about the Spanish priest you said that he would make a lot of money from his translation, or something like that." Flavia's expression was one of utter defeat. "You stay here," he continued. "We'll take the stuff into the woods, out of sight of the road, and I'll go after him: he can't have got far." He began to saddle the horse, while Flavia began to feel a sentiment that was becoming familiar, of gratitude mixed somewhat with resentment at her dependency.

She sat on a damp rug folded on a rock just within the woodland, while the rain continued. From where she was she could see, to the north, a mound of their bags and packages piled up against an oak tree. To the south, through the twigs of a hazel, she could just make out the road. Dusk was falling. Nobody had passed. She had studied all the trees and the underbrush in the neighbourhood, and gathered a large pile of chanterelle mushrooms. She had pondered Titus' death and their own situation. She had written a letter to her mother. She had set herself to remember the *Iliad*, starting at the beginning. To her annoyance she lost the place somewhere in the Catalogue of Ships in Book II, and could not pick it up again properly until the breaking of the truce by Pandarus in Book IV. But soon she was again running through the words effortlessly, and at last reached the scene with Hector and Andromache in Book VI:

> "Yet, come it will, the day decreed by fates!
> (How my heart trembles while my tongue relates!)
> The day when thou, imperial Troy, must bend,
> And see thy warriors fall, thy glories end.
> And yet no dire presage so wounds my mind,
> My mother's death, the ruin of my kind,
> Not Priam's hoary hairs defiled with gore,
> Not all my brothers gasping on the shore;
> As thine, Andromache! Thy griefs I dread:
> I see thee trembling, weeping, captive led!
> In Argive looms our battles to design,
> And woes, of which so large a part was thine!
> To bear the victor's hard commands, or bring
> The weight of waters from Hyperia's spring.
> There while you groan beneath the load of life,
> They cry, 'Behold the mighty Hector's wife!'
> Some haughty Greek, who lives thy tears to see,
> Imbitters all thy woes, by naming me.
> The thoughts of glory past, and present shame,
> A thousand griefs shall waken at the name!"

She paused, halted by the image and its uncomfortable relevance. She appealed to the Good Goddess, muttering under her breath, "Grant that the people at Cormerick never come to such a pass!", and to anchor her mind in practicality she turned it to what would be happening on the home farm. If the weather were better than here, then they would have started the barley harvest by now, and nearly all their efforts would be at that. Otherwise, they would still be busy with a hundred tasks: sowing cabbage-seed, hoeing turnips, pruning trees, gathering peppermint and elderflowers for the still, harvesting the camomile, gathering cranberries and mushrooms, checking the kitchen-gardens, weeding, looking after the cattle, seeing to the dairy tasks; and the bird-boy still watching the corn crops.

She heard an unfamiliar noise, and looked up: Arctus and Hipponoë were already leaving the road and coming towards her. Her heart beat faster, and she chided it, and moved forward out of the shadow of the trees; but Arctus, now clearly in sight, smiled and patted a saddle-bag. He rode up, and carefully passed down her two books of the Plato, safe and sound, still wrapped in their oiled cloth against the damp. Then he picked up their water-bottles from the other side of the saddle-blanket, and tossed them onto the ground at her feet, together with a large hare. Flavia never discovered the details of how Arctus recovered her books, whether he had come across Rúari straight away or whether hours of skilled and patient tracking had been needed; whether it had been a matter of threat or force or bargaining. Arctus seemed to take a pleasure in making a mystery of it, as if he might be a magician who had just had to wave a wand and make the books appear. They pitched the tent again, and Flavia set to cleaning and skinning the hare.

In the morning the rain was even heavier, and despite her leather clothing Flavia was soaked to the skin by the time they set off, but the breeze was quite warm and she did not feel uncomfortable. A mist started to gather. They had not gone more than a mile when a cart appeared, driven towards them by a man who goaded his oxen unmercifully, apparently to no effect at all. He was tall and shabby; a sharp-faced woman, two small children and a dog sat in the cart, all looking exhausted.

As he came up to them he spoke, sneeringly: "*Back you go, fine folk; the barbarians are coming.*"

"*From the east? How far away?*"

"*Near enough. They've burned York and Isurium, and now they're burning Ilkley, just a few miles up the road. You'd see the smoke if the bloody weather were any better.*" He jabbed again at the flanks of the oxen; already he was passing them.

Arctus turned and called after him as the cart disappeared into the mist: "*Be careful. The Irish are down in the western valleys.*"

"What now, Arctus?" said Flavia. "Do you think it's true?"

"Why not? They could easily have got this far south by

now."

"I somehow doubt they've sacked York. I've never heard of barbarians capturing a major fortress or city."

"I daresay you're right. That doesn't mean they're not around, though. We must turn south, off the roads. They'll never hunt us up in the hills when there are easy pickings in the valleys. We'll walk south through the open mountains, like your forefathers before the Romans came." He smiled.

"All right," said Flavia, finding this patronising. "How far do we need to go?"

"It's hard to tell. There's at least one more route going across on its way up to York: we'd better not take that. After that, if we make our way to Buxton there's a road to Doncaster. That would do. It'd be maybe five days' hike, pretty mountainous. I'll check in the itinerary later."

"Mountainous, eh? Well, if I could manage the hills north of the Wall I daresay I'll manage these, even if I am a woman."

Hipponoë seemed unenthusiastic about leaving the road, perhaps wondering whether to go along with this apparent pretence that she was a donkey, but in a few minutes they had turned south along a rough path and lost sight of the road behind limestone outcrops and stubby thorn trees.

To begin with, the way led through the edge of a straggling woodland. Huge mature elms overshadowed them with thousands of tiny leaves, and though these gave shelter from the wind they offered none from the stilling, relentless rain. Arctus went ahead leading Hipponoë, and conversation failed.

Flavia's mind drifted back, as so often when unoccupied, to Plato. His remarks on the elements in the *Timæus*, she began to think, depended very much on how the actual elements in the world participated in the ultimate Ideas of the elements, and he was quite obscure about that – at least at that point; perhaps he had explained it better in the *Parmenides*, but she couldn't remember that now. Anyway he might have changed his mind between the two; though she hadn't settled her mind on which came first.

She thought once again of the great Reality which Plato and all his followers said was the ultimate truth of things, and union with which was the proper destiny of mankind. How could one achieve that?

Socrates himself, if he had been reported correctly, had thought it was something fairly straightforward, not much to be worried about for someone who tried to live well and to study truth. Though, admittedly, if one accepted the idea in the *Philebus* about there being "true pleasures" such as the search for truth and "false pleasures" such as food and sex, then she herself was not as free of the second as she should be.

But perhaps it wasn't a question of absolutes but a matter of proportion and limit, as the Stoics said. There were other views, too, of course. There were those who said that one had to use all kinds of theurgical practices to bind the gods to one's will, and learn the secret passwords to the seven heavens before one's death. Flavia couldn't summon up patience with any of that: she held to what she saw as the common-sense views of Plato himself, which after all had been followed by Plotinus. Plotinus had said on his deathbed, '*Give back the divine in yourself to the divine in the universe,*' and perhaps that ambition was intelligible and praiseworthy enough.

For the world, she thought, must be a matter of representation and reflection: after much questioning and much study she could not believe otherwise. The World Soul was surely a reflection of the Divine Mind, just as the latter was a reflection of the One, and that relationship was itself reflected throughout all the universe. Not only did it account for the similarity between the great and the little, but it was the only intelligible reason for the imperfection, the evil, which infected the world about us. Even in her own little case she could see it, where her own innocence had been lost in Præneste, and this was now reflected in the violence of the invasions which were overthrowing the Britains, and that in turn set within the wider insecurity of the whole Empire since, well, the days of the emperor Severus, perhaps.

Flavia let out a little involuntary sigh of sadness, and wondered to herself at the comprehensiveness of the barbarians' invasions. They came from the north, from the west, from the east, all at once. It seemed as if the whole island was being overrun: it was like the sea, washing in on all sides, irresistible, now lapping up here at the spine of Britain.

Arctus looked round. "Are you all right? Do you want a rest?"

They had left the woods behind them now, and were walking across open fells, the grass cropped short by goats and deer and hares; they could not see so very far through the rain, but the path was clear enough. Suddenly there was a noise to the left, and turning she saw a huge bird she had never seen before, but which must surely be a great bustard, heave itself startled from the ground and wear into the rain like a ship, with laborious flaps of its six-foot wingspan.

"I'm all right," she said, catching him up as he slowed his pace. "I was thinking about the invasions: they seem so thoroughgoing. I daresay there'll soon be news that the Saxons are attacking Chichester and the south coast, as they did in our grandparents' time before the Saxon Shore defences."

"Yes, it's bad," he agreed. "I doubt we've seen anything like this even in Gaul, at least since those same days. But you need to remember that rumour gives fear wings: we've not actually seen any barbarians yet, well, not since we got back inside the Province. It may not be as serious as it seems to us."

"Maybe not, but it's surely bad enough in all honesty."

"Do you think Faber is pushing at an open door, then?"

"What do you mean?"

"I've heard one or two remarks. Your grandfather lived in the time of the autonomous British emperor Carausius. There are still those here who look back to those days – I heard a couple of them in the men's quarters in Bremetennacum. They were saying that in Carausius' day taxes were lower, or even if they weren't lower at least you knew that they weren't being wasted far away but spent in Britain. And they said that tenants on a lot of senatorial estates had very high rents which they were able to stop paying at that time. There's probably truth in that, at least

– and it stands to reason that it couldn't do Britain much good to have so much gold leaving the diocese and not returning."

"Maybe. Though, from what I gathered from Titus when he was in the Sacred Largesses, Britain may not do so badly. There really are a lot of army units here, and their wages and allowances and donatives add up to an important sum. Remember how prosperous the Wall area was: not just the official granaries in Catterick and Carlisle, but all the tradesmen right along the line of forts, butchers and brewers and bakers and builders and bargirls... If you think of it all together it's like a great city, right at the edge of the Empire, and it can't all be funded by British taxes."

Arctus did not reply. He was peering into the rain preoccupied. Flavia could see nothing of interest, except that the day was growing dimmer and there seemed to be nowhere to shelter from the weather.

"What's the matter?"

"We seem to have been going downhill for too long. And if you look at this tree you'll see that most of the lichen is on the right: it usually grows strongest on the north side. I have a feeling we're coming back down into the western plains again. Let's go cautiously for a bit." Arctus led the way for a distance, and then two people loomed in the rain ahead. The taller put his hand to his lips, and as they came closer two large dogs bounded up out of the mist.

"*A good day and a long life to you!*" called Arctus.

The elder figure was in early middle-age: a mountainy man, tall and rangy and carrying a shepherd's crook. His companion was a boy of about nine or ten. "*And a good day to you, sir!*" came the reply. "*Are you going far this day?*"

"*We are going to Buxton,*" said Arctus a little slowly, perhaps realising only as he spoke that this was perhaps not a prudent admission to a stranger, "*though we know it will still be three days' journey.*"

The shepherd laughed. "*You will not travel it all the way to Buxton in three days,*" he said. "*especially on this road. But perhaps a stranger like yourself will not be knowing that.*"

Flavia became concerned. The dogs were large, and she

didn't like them; and there would be other shepherds nearby. She could see how, to a stranger, Arctus' Gallic accent sounded foreign and suspect; he might easily be taken for an Irishman by someone who had never travelled. Why had he not spoken in Latin?

"*It's true, I'm from Gaul,*" said Arctus. "*I'm certainly not familiar with this area.*"

"*So what are you doing so far from the roads?*"

"*We were driven from our path by the barbarians.*"

The shepherd's brow darkened, and he glanced at his boy, who dropped a bag of clam-pegs and stooped to pick them up. "*Barbarians? Where?*"

"*Have you not heard?*" asked Arctus, thinking that the mountain people must be very remote. "*They are all around. We were near them on the Wall and in Brocavum, and had to turn aside at Bremetennacum, but they are on the east side as well.*"

The shepherd gave a shallow grin. "*Aye, that's true enough. But they've not been seen in the mountains yet, and I never or heard that they had been any time,*" he said. He turned to his boy. "*Looks as though these folk've been straying from their path, eh? For if they go on the road they're heading they'll be back down in Bremetennacum ere long. Might get more than they set at down in the valleys these days.*" He gave a laugh.

"*Can you direct us, then?*" asked Arctus, adding after a moment. "*We would be glad to pay you for your trouble.*" Oh, thought Flavia to herself, that was a bad move. He really shouldn't have tried that in British; it's easy to get the wrong tone.

The shepherd turned slowly to face them and studied them carefully, hefting a bag on his shoulder. "*We don't get many of your sort in these parts,*" he mused. "*Get left to ourselves in the summer, we do. Can you do a turn? Could come along to the steading, maybe, and we'd see.*"

"*I'm not sure...*" said Arctus, and turning to Flavia he said, "A turn? What does he mean?"

"Some kind of performance, probably a recitation," she explained quickly.

Arctus addressed the shepherd. "*I could present to you a hunting-song from Aquitania,*" he said.

"*That where you be coming from in Gaul?*" asked the shepherd, and Arctus nodded. "*Might do, I 'spect. We'll put it to the company.*" Without another word he turned and plodded off into the mist.

After a mile or so Flavia and Arctus were led to a group of round wood-and-wicker huts. Flocks were grouped about, some separated by watchful dogs or in folds marked by walls or hurdles, and one or two women were milking ewes in each; to one side four men laboriously worked on a drystone wall so as to extend an area set aside for cows. Their host led them to a large hut. Outside, a group of women were cooking a communal pot of barley and garlic over an open fire. Flavia went over at once and, despite an alarming crowd of dogs coming to investigate the newcomers, did her best to help and to be agreeable. After a while a man came up from the valley leading three donkeys with big panniers, and unloaded oatcakes from them, filling them with cheeses before setting off back down.

Suddenly a shout went up, and looking round Flavia saw a figure climbing over the brow of a hill: it was the *campidoctor* who had left Carlisle with them, now dressed like the shepherds. He was not welcomed with embraces, but he was clearly known to the village. She and Arctus went forward with others, and caught him saying in return for some taunt, "*No, I don't mind if I do fight, then. Who's to be put up against me?*" Then he looked up and saw Flavia and Arctus, and began to smile broadly.

A call went up without prompting, taken up by several voices: "*It's the stranger that has to fight!*", and a group of shepherds gathered excitedly round Arctus. An old man addressed him: "*You'll have to give us a fight in the wrestling, stranger. It's the custom.*"

Men appeared from nowhere. "*Stranger, this is Molacos, who you'll be fighting, from Papcastle. What's your name? Where are you from?*"

They seemed disappointed to hear that Arctus came from Gaul rather than more locally, but men laid a row of stones along the ground to be a fighting ring. "*Indeed, let Sarimarcus be referee!*"

Sarimarcus, a bearded, dark-haired man of thirty or so,

came over: "*You can have a little while to prepare.*"

Arctus had had a long day, and Flavia wondered how she might help. She took him behind the huts and offered to massage him, but he refused, and stripping covered himself in olive-oil, and then began to exercise, limbering up as if for a bout on the palæstra. "What will they do if he wins?" he asked.

Flavia was anxious for him, but laughed. "We're not Læstrygonians in Britain, you know: we don't feast on human flesh! Nothing will happen. Not that you wouldn't do well to concentrate on winning." But she had seen wrestling matches at Cormerick which had ended in men being crippled, sometimes for life. Often enough it was friendly, but it could be a way of settling scores. Though her anxiety could not stop her admiring the fine, well-toned shape of Arctus' body.

"But will they bet? Will you be safe?"

She had not thought of this, and realised again that she was much more dependent on Arctus than she would like. How could she know exactly what would happen? But these were Britons in a village, even if the village was just summer-quarters; they were not barbarians or a savage group of gladiators; they might be of the Brigantian canton rather than the Corielsolilian, but that would hardly matter. This community of mountain shepherds, though, where nobody bathed or knew a word of Latin, or had heard of London or of cooking with wine-syrup – this place was very different from Cormerick. It was like going back in time hundreds of years, to before Cæsar had come to Britain, a strange time, a wild and dangerous time. But she made herself laugh. "Of course I'll be safe, idiot!" she said. "You're the person you need to concentrate on. They'd soon take action if he did anything out of order, but you do need to be on your guard all the same."

"Find out if I need to wear clothes," he said, presumably knowing that it was unusual for provincial village customs to approve of the Greek and Roman practice of naked wrestling. But Flavia knew that in Britain (and she had thought in Gaul; had she seen such wrestling in Soissons?) it was quite normal, and was explaining this when Sarimarcus appeared. He gave them hardly a glance. "*It is time,*" was all he said, and turned to go back.

Arctus followed. "There's one essential rule: you lose if you lie on your back, or if opposite knee and shoulder touch the ground together," added Flavia to him urgently; though why, she asked herself, should the rules here be the same as at Cormerick? As he came into view the low hum of conversation in the circle of shepherds livened. "*Short-cock Gaul!*" cried somebody, and there was a medley of voices and a chink of coins. The supposed *campidoctor* was at the other end of the ring, talking rapidly to a fat young man, but turned: clothed, Molacos had been short and unimpressive, but naked he was muscular, and his shoulders were covered in black hair. He began to advance into the ring. "*Short-cock Carvetian!*" shouted another voice: not very imaginatively, but at least it showed there were people betting on Arctus too. Sarimarcus stepped into the ring and beckoned to Arctus, then stood upright and spoke loudly and rapidly in dialect which Flavia could only follow with difficulty.

Arctus apparently did not follow it at all, since as the referee rapidly stepped back the soldier darted forward, seized Arctus' ankle and tipped him over. Immediately he jumped back, then as Arctus slowly raised his torso, a smear of blood coming from his head, Molacos leaped on him from behind. He tried to engage his arms round Arctus' neck, but Arctus grasped his wrists and ducked, dragging the other over his head so that he hit the ground headlong.

Then both of them were up and circling warily round each other, while the circle of shepherds bellowed encouragement. Flavia moved closer to see better, and an unwashed smell came to her in gusts from the onlookers. She glanced at their eager faces, spit flying from gap-toothed mouths as they urged on their fancy, and then heard an involuntary grunt from the ring. The two were locked together, hip to hip, striving for a throw. Arctus' face was taut and grim, the other's split by a fixed smile; all their concentration was in the struggle. Now one foot and then another edged in search of a better purchase, but the seconds went past and the two stood there swaying, hardly mobile, their eyes bulging, their muscles swollen, the sweat dripping and darkening their hair. Suddenly Sarimarcus raised his arm high, and a boy blew a ram's horn surprisingly loud, a short blast on two notes. The referee stepped forward and separated the combatants. The soldier turned back to the edge of the ring, where he picked up a drinking-horn and tossed the contents down his throat.

Arctus came over to Flavia. She looked round for a little girl she had spoken to earlier, who now came running with a wooden bowl of water and a rough goat-hair towel. Arctus leaned on Flavia, then drank deep from the bowl and sat down on the ground. She wetted the towel and dabbed his brow, cleaning the scratch and wiping away the sweat. "He's quick and he's strong," he murmured. "I hadn't been expecting him to be so formidable." He took another draught of the water. "Are there any tricks I can use within the rules here?"

Flavia had no idea what rules Arctus was used to, but though feeling anxious and angry did not criticise the question. She searched her memory: she had been to few enough of such events. "Don't try any obvious fouls," she advised pointlessly. Then a shepherd came up, a burly blond young man. "*I got money on you,*" he told Arctus. "*I been expecting some of that professional Greek stuff you get in the big baths, see? I want you to do better than you have so far. You need to be on your guard. That Papcastle man's waiting his chance. I can see his eyes. He'll try and get you in the groin when the referee's not looking. If there's an obvious distraction, watch out.*"

Arctus gave Flavia a glance which seemed to mean, "This man's serious; I'll listen to him," but the boy was already winding the horn, and the two combatants warily approached each other again. A desperate thought occurred to Flavia, however, and she whispered in the ear of the little girl who had brought the towel, and who now looked in the direction of a boy who had been giving water to Molacos, and giggled, looking at something she was holding in her own hand. The wrestlers came together in holds twice, then three times, and each time it seemed that Arctus was gaining an advantage when the other broke away. Then Molacos seized Arctus round the thighs and lifted him clear from the ground. A roar went up from the spectators, but the grip slipped in the oil on the skin, and Arctus fell back on his feet, thrusting the other away. As he did so a large pebble came flying from the back of the crowd and hit him a glancing blow on the temple; and then Molacos brought his leg up towards Arctus' groin, and Arctus let out a cry and doubled up.

Sarimarcus seized Molacos, stopping the fight, and called for another man to hold him, while Flavia ran over to Arctus. "*That was foul play!*" cried the referee, going over to Arctus himself. "*Where did that stone come from?*"

"Managed to take most of it on the thigh," muttered Arctus painfully to Flavia. "Be all right in a minute." Flavia saw that he could stand, and checked the new wound on his head, which was only a bruise.

"*It was that young lad was with the Papcastle man,*" came a voice. The circle had broken up and men were roaming about. Arctus was now hobbling to and fro, trying to distract himself from the pain. Suddenly Molacos broke free of the man holding him and ran off into the woodland, grabbing his clothes as he went. Sarimarcus watched him go, shook his head and went to the middle of the circle, hauling Arctus after him. "*Hey, shepherds, listen!*" he cried loudly. "*Arctus the Aquitanian is the winner! Give him beer!*" Cheers came from the surrounding crowd. Arctus' supporters pressed round, and a drinking-horn was thrust into his hand. He was embraced and his hands pressed, but after a few minutes the throng dispersed; the women were making ready for the meal.

"What was all that about?" asked Flavia. "Are you really all right?"

"Fortunately, yes," said Arctus with a wan smile, "thanks to that timely warning."

Flavia sighed. "But where's he gone, and will he be back? I'm going to carry a dagger in my boot from now on."

When, after the meal, they drank sour beer and called for songs, Arctus' promised offering was greeted with enthusiastic applause, and they then courteously received Flavia's folk-tale from the fenlands. The next morning they were told the way without trouble. The interminable rain had stopped, and the sun was rising above the eastern hills. A curlew cried its mournful note not far away. They boiled water and drank some hibiscus tea that Flavia had brought from Carlisle to guard against chills, then packed up and set off.

The high hills now seemed deserted, except by occasional groups of sheep and goats, and by the wildlife: red and sometimes roe deer, hares and squirrels; once a bear in an oak wood, once an otter by a river; the dark calls of owls and nightjars, and twice of wolves; skylarks in the morning and blackbirds and thrushes at sunset, swallows and finches darting about, and on one memorable occasion two capercailzies displaying their fanned tails at each other, great two-foot birds with rich green breasts and a shot of bright aggressive red in the dusk above each eye. Arctus proved skilled or lucky as a forager, and they seldom had to do without fresh food – grayling or trout from the stream, or a hare from the moor with salad herbs of marigold or dandelion; once he found a large puff-ball, and twice a patch of delicious wild strawberries.

As time went by Flavia became used to walking, even more than she had in the country of the Novantans. She started to revel in the distance travelled each day, and in the satisfaction in her body; the earlier sense of strain and exhaustion in the evenings was now finally replaced by one of honest work done.

Six days after they had turned off the road, however, the outside world intruded again. From these high peaks they could see for miles to the east, to the edge of the fertile plains, but an ugly dark smoke now rose up there, and they agreed that it might be Doncaster. Flavia thought of the woman with the two children who had helped her get into the baths there, and wondered what was happening now in Durobrivæ and at Cormerick. For a while the ethereal beauty of a lark's song hovered overhead, and it was difficult to focus on far-off, hypothetical problems.

But as she walked along, league after league, up and down hill, she found dark thoughts encroaching on her. Again they pitched their tent under a tree.

The next day they had been walking for a couple of hours through very broken country when on the side of a hill a fort came into view, banners flying from its towers. They pressed ahead, and within half an hour were standing on a metalled road beside it. People came out to see them from the houses standing near, and said the fort was called Navio. They told that the garrison, the First Cohort of Aquitanians, had been summoned urgently to York ten days ago; only a handful were left: the sick, or late returners from leave. Many of the crowd were wives of the soldiers who had suddenly been ordered away from home, and they asked anxiously for news.

But these people already knew more news than they got: invading Picts, they said, were at Isurium and York, and Nectaridus, the Count of the Saxon Shore, had been killed at sea by an unlucky arrow while attacking longboats off the Rhine estuary. Virgil's First Eclogue, thought Flavia gloomily: *'The Britons wholly isolated from the entire world.'* She and Arctus did not want to linger. The eastward road led to Doncaster with its uncertain smoke, so they took the south-westward way to Buxton.

CHAPTER 6

'"...that those whose task was to fight in defence of the City must behave only as such, and be vigilant against any foreign or domestic enemy; and that they should judge gently those under their guidance and be their friends, but act ruthlessly towards those they meet in battle."' Flavia's mind wandered from its perennial rehearsal of the *Timæus* towards other cities, and towards Buxton in particular. It would be a small town, she seemed to remember, certainly a lot smaller than Carlisle, but important beyond its formal status, for it had a sacred grove known throughout the north of the island, and had become an important spa over the centuries of the Roman province. It was not on the main road, and, tucked away in the hills, might feel quite remote.

It was less than ten miles through light rain before the road climbed to another summit, and they paused, seeing it plunge down into a deep hollow carved by the river Wye, and reach the grove and spring of Buxton within. Neither had been here before. They could see a tall round hill near the middle of the town, covered in soft grass and bare to the winds, and surrounded by a band of huge ancient trees, many of them dark yews. The north-western quadrant of this belt, towards the river, was disturbed by a building complex, mostly in limestone, which looked like the baths. Beyond the hill, a walled *enceinte* enclosed another part of the town which seemed entirely normal, though quiet: a market was under way in a small forum, and busy comings and goings from the basilica suggested that if only the weather had been better there might have been more happening in the open air.

They went on down, heading straight for the extensive posting-station. They found it full and over-full with refugees. Unlike those at Bremetennacum, these were refugees of quality: indeed, they included a senator named Nummius Secundus, an Imperial Messenger called Siricius, the widow of a Vicar of the Spains named Lucilla, and various officials from London who had been cut off by the invasion. There was also an energetic officer cadet from the Imperial Guard called Quintinus, who seemed to use the posting-station for little more than sleeping in, having taken it upon himself to recruit and drill volunteers and to organise defence.

Flavia was allocated a room in a different part of the building from Arctus. She found herself sharing a large bed with an elderly lady called Magunna from Manchester, whose conversation was dominated by the improbable dutifulness of two nephews whom she claimed to live in Buxton itself, though during all her stay Flavia would never see any sign of them. She tracked down Arctus again, and, having rested a little and dried off, they went out to take the measure of the town.

It was already late in the day, but there was not a great deal to examine. Rather than temples, it was the sacred grove, carefully tended, which was still the most important place of worship, and there were a number of druids and bards on the streets, some of whom did not even seem to speak Latin. This provincial spa, Flavia concluded, was no rival for the more metropolitan Bath, where she had been several times and which could securely boast a sophisticated society drawn from two or three dioceses. They ate together in the common-room at the posting-station, along with various hangers-on of the more important visitors.

In the early twilight she was woken from a troubled sleep by someone shaking her shoulder rather violently. "*Wake up, dear,*" said Magunna. "*You're too young to be wasting your time in bed on a day like this!*" Her knobby hand peeled the bedclothes back from Flavia's shrinking form, letting in the cold morning air.

"*Leave me alone,*" said Flavia angrily, but to no effect.

"Now, now," said Magunna, *"You're only fussing because you spoiled your beauty sleep staying up with that young man of yours. A young woman like you ought to be with her children, not gadding about the country with men. There was a young lady like you in Lancaster I knew not ten years back, who came to a bad end, exiled from the canton by the magistrates, and it was lucky for her that was all that happened. She'd lost her honour, dear, and that you can't ever recover, you know. She was lucky not to be sent to the amphitheatre as a circus turn."*

Flavia was obliged to get up, muttering excuses. It was scarcely dawn, and the servants were not yet out of bed to stir up the fires; at this time of year sunrise came very early.

She walked down to the river and tried to compose herself, bad-tempered among the blackbirds and willow warblers, eventually making her way back to the posting-station. A freedman was setting out breakfast in the common-room, and seemed to give her a roguish glance she didn't like. She felt tired and vulnerable, and went up to fetch a book from her room, only to find Magunna systematically going through her things. She packed a few precious ones into a satchel and brought it downstairs, hiding in a corner of a sitting-room behind a book.

It seemed like a long time before Arctus arrived. "Yes," he said when she explained, "There were a few remarks passed to me last night about you and me. You're obviously going to have to be careful here."

They had breakfast separately, and Flavia wondered what they should do now, with barbarians all about and this town such a miserable place. Arctus had gone to consult a more detailed itinerary, which was kept in the private quarters of the posting-station manager, when a girl of about seventeen came up to her.

"I've not seen you here before. Have you just arrived?" she said. She was slightly shorter and a little heavier perhaps than Flavia, with good clothes, thick dark hair and a gentle smile.

"Yes," said Flavia, "I got here last night. My name is Flavia Vindex."

"Hallo! I'm Balbina Clementina. My mother is called Lucilla, and we're staying here. Isn't it dreadful about the barbarians? Have you come far?"

"I'm from the Corielsolilian canton, from near Durobrivæ, but I've come rather a long way round."

"You're not all alone, are you?" asked Balbina, seeming rather impressed by the idea.

"No, I'm travelling with my cousin; he's gone off to look for something. Where are you from?"

"Oh, we live up in the Fylde, not far away, about two days," said Balbina. "But my mother got advice that it wasn't safe to stay there with the attacks going on, and decided we should come here. She's found this wonderful villa on the other side of the river, called the Unellian's House, and I think we're going to be living there until things are sorted out."

"That sounds nice. Where's your father?"

A shadow crossed Balbina's open expression. "He died a few years ago. We were back here for a few months from the Spains where he'd been the Vicar, and he'd been appointed Proconsul of Africa: a great honour, of course, and we were all very excited. My mother was corresponding about buying a house in Rome. He'd been very busy with making preparations, and went ahead of the rest of us to take up office, but his ship was sunk in a storm in the Channel."

"I'm sorry," said Flavia, unsure what to say, and adding, "As Horace says, '*We all go to the same end.*'"

For a moment Balbina looked older. "He was on the threshold of high office," she said. "It was a pity." She smiled, and her face was restored. "We have some relations in Durobrivæ, I think. Who is your father?"

"He's dead as well," said Flavia, "but some time ago now. He was Florian Vindex. And my mother is Helpidia Valeria."

Balbina's eyes softened to show sympathy that Flavia had lost a father too. "Helpidia... the name rings a bell. I'll ask Mummy. I don't know where she is at the moment. Until the lease comes through she's had to take rooms here in the posting-house: there's quite a few of us, including our household servants, so it's all a bit of a jumble. I hope we'll see a lot of you while you're here, anyway. Will you be staying long?"

"We don't know really. We need to see how things are." She felt a momentary warmth towards the girl and grinned. "But we've been travelling a lot. I could certainly do with a bit of a rest."

Balbina smiled back, thinking. "Is your cousin that tall dark man I saw you talking to in a corner of the common-room last night?"

"Yes."

"He looks nice. What's his name?"

Flavia thought rapidly: should she tell the truth? It wouldn't do for it to get about that she wasn't related to Arctus, if Balbina and Lucilla really did know her family. But if she pretended he had another name, that couldn't easily be concealed either. "Arctus," she said. "He's quite a distant cousin. He comes from Bordeaux."

She saw a glimmer of intelligence in Balbina's eye. "He looks nearly as handsome as my fiancé," came the response.

Flavia smiled. "Who are you to marry?"

Balbina smiled back. "He's called Marcus Minicius. He comes of an old family from Brixia in Æmilia, but his parents live on an estate near ours. We haven't got a date for the wedding fixed yet, and I can't wait. I hope this trouble here is over soon."

She looked as if she was going to say more, but Arctus appeared, and drew Flavia away, out of doors. She wondered if he had something confidential to say, but it occurred to her that he often seemed more comfortable in the open air.

"The manager says that things are bad all over the north," he reported. "The barbarians have definitely reached York – which hasn't fallen, of course, you were quite right – though they may be moving less fast than we heard on the road: he thinks they only got there last Sunday week. And there are bands of Attacotti far and wide on the west side of the mountains now too: they've got to Bremetennacum, and though it seems that there the main party were dealt with by the Sarmatian Regiment, they may be anywhere in the countryside in small numbers. Then there've been raids by the Saxons on the north coast of Gaul, and it's supposed they'll turn their attention to

Britain as well. And the Irish have been seen at Anglesey, Carmarthen, and Cardiff, and he's had word this morning of a raid by them up the Avon against Bath, though he's not got much reason to think the report reliable."

His British geography was good, she thought, for an Aquitanian; but it did seem to interest him, for he never lost a chance to look at maps or itineraries. "So what's the army doing?"

"The news isn't good there either. He says it's true that Fullofaudes, the Duke, has been cut off in South Shields; and the units on the Wall still seem to be in disarray as we heard before, disputing who has authority in his absence. It's also true that the Count of the Saxon Shore has been killed; and it seems that his deputy – who's based at Boulogne – is concentrating on defending the coast of Gaul. And of course there isn't a Vicar and Count in Augusta at the moment. Individual unit commanders seem to be holding their own but not doing much to concert action. The Emperor is in Paris, and – this is the worst bit – he's seriously ill: the story is that he's dying."

"Dying? That's awful." She thought rapidly. "If the Emperor dies it'll be ages before anyone pays any attention to us here. Even now they'll be manœuvring around him in the Court: there's no heir in the West, and Valens in the East is a long way away. What will happen?"

"Well, apparently Valentinian had already ordered the Count of the Household Guard to Britain, and he's supposed to be on his way now. Cintusmus' advice is to stay here. I think he's right. We're in the mountains away from where the barbarians are known to be, and Quintinus is gathering a militia. So we're probably safer here than anywhere else much at present, other than a major city perhaps, which it would be dangerous to try and reach. It won't be long until the new troops arrive from Gaul, I expect, and then we can go down to Cormerick as you wanted."

Flavia tried to digest all this news. She pulled a face, shaking her head. Perhaps she shouldn't have held out against going to Gaul after all. "Oh, Arctus, all this is very bad, isn't it? How far can we count on this relief force? And this town is a miserable place to be cut off. But I suppose you're right. We'll have to make the best of it. What are you going to do now?"

"I'm going to have a look at the itinerary I've borrowed from Cintusmus, and copy down as much as I can: it may help with our route. Do you want to look at it too?"

"No, I've had enough of all this. I'm going to go into town."

She set off, shooing away beggars, and lost herself in the covered market. She wandered through the first stalls, of bakers, with strange styles of scones and buns unfamiliar in the fenlands. Then she came across shoemakers, and here too a kind was popular which she had not seen before, a sandal with the backstrap not anchored to the sole, and she spoke to a cobbler, discussing its merits in climbing hills. She wandered on, pausing at a perfumer's and finding a stale bottle of jasmine oil, and then suddenly discovered herself at the baths, an extensive establishment with separate men's and women's suites, and common areas for promenading and entertainment.

To her left was the sacred grove, but straight ahead the entrance to the women's baths beckoned, two ten-foot wooden doors, bound with iron and ornamented with rather good inlaid bronze panels showing mythological scenes – she identified Europa borne away by the bull, Leto and Jupiter being transformed into quails, Maia giving birth to Mercury on Mount Cyllene in Arcadia. It was early to go in, but she did so, and realised that at some stage a lot of money had been spent here, though sometimes to rather mixed effect. Even in the ante-rooms there were too many florid effigies, and too many of them had clearly been put there just to curry favour, either with the governor of the day or with some other worthy.

She stopped to pay, and saw behind the slave taking entrance fees a notice: *During July and August on Wednesdays, at the sixth hour in the Small Assembly Room, Olorus the famous slave of the Most Renowned Quintus Nummius Secundus will give readings from the Odes of Horace.* There were other notices advertising the services of doctors and specialist therapists, but she did not study them; she went in, and lay in the steam room long enough to fall into a nap, emerging with her spirits somewhat healed.

As she came out into the main hall she found round the plunge-bath an extensive tessellated pavement heated from beneath. Statues of provincial governors and of local dignitaries were crowded thickly round the walls, many painted in colours slightly too vigorous to be natural or in the best taste, and several decorated with golden or gilded torcs, rings or belts. A woman, her pale skin glistening like lard, lay face-down on a couch being pummelled by a dark, plump eunuch, while another, her hair carefully arranged, stood nearby draped only in a huge multicoloured chiffon shawl, which half-hid a dazzling display of jewels round her neck. The standing woman was in her fifties and fair-haired, rather ravaged but not gone to seed. "And you know Frontinus was there," she said to the other, waving absently and rather regally to acknowledge Flavia's entrance. "That man can make a party go just by leaving it. The conversation was so desultory you could have recited a book in each of the silences. What he thinks he's doing here I simply have no idea. No idea at all."

"But I thought he had news," said the other. "Ah, yes, down a bit there, Hyginus, yes, yes!"

The fair-haired woman paused imperceptibly for this interruption, and then replied. "Yes, he did have news, and he imparted it in the most inconsiderate way. He announced in front of everyone that the Count of the Household Guard, Severus, who is supposed to be on his way to Britain, isn't coming after all. I take it very badly: I had only yesterday bet Aula Verecunda five *solidi* that York wouldn't fall to the barbarians before the year was out, and if I'd had prior news of this I could have laid the bet off at decent odds."

"I suppose everybody was round Frontinus after that," said the other.

"No, not at all, weren't you listening, Pacata? He may have blurted out his story in public, but no-one was the least bit interested in him. It turned out he had no details to offer in any event, just the plain news passed to the *curator* at his house this morning. The reason's not far to seek, though: anyone would be *mad* to leave the Court when the Emperor's dying, and Severus, they say, is far too fly to let that one go by. The last thing he wants is to be away from the action when a new Emperor's acclaimed and he could be in line for the post of Master of Soldiers, or I suppose almost any plum position if he played his cards right."

"I suppose so, Vellibia."

"No suppose about it, my dear Pacata, believe me. Now show me the enchanting little enamel brooch you bought from that awful refugee woman."

"It's with my clothes, dear."

"Of course it is, darling. But send Hyginus away for five minutes; he can finish you later. Show it to me now, because I can't stay, I'm expected at Olbia's before lunch."

The other woman signed to the eunuch, who took a cloth, wiped the surplus oil from her back and withdrew, returning with a tray piled with neatly folded clothes. Pacata sat up, burrowed into these and found a brooch which she gave to the other woman, who examined it closely.

"My dear, it's quite divine! *How* much did you say you paid for it?"

"Half a *solidus*, Vellibia."

"*Half*!" She laughed prettily. "You know how to drive a bargain. It must be worth two at least. Certainly it ought to fetch that in Chester. Well, these refugees may be cluttering up the town and eating us all out of house and home, but there are some things they're useful for, I suppose. I must keep an eye out for that: I'm sure there will be other opportunities for all of us.

"Well, I must be getting on. Sita!" she called. A young slave-girl standing immobile in a corner, whom Flavia had not noticed, came forward with clothes and helped Vellibia into them. "*Lovely* to see you, Pacata. Will you be at Nummius Secundus' soirée tomorrow? Let me know: I want to make sure that we're not both wearing similar things. It's such a problem using the same dressmaker as someone, don't you think? These little provincial towns do have their burdens."

She swept out, and Pacata called the masseur back,

ignoring Flavia. Flavia plunged into the pool and swam up
and down for what seemed a long time.

Eventually she made her way back to the posting-
station, and the doorkeeper told her that she was wanted by
Balbina's mother Lucilla. Feeling slightly nervous, and
annoyed with herself for feeling so, she was shown into a
private sitting-room. Here she found an impeccably coiffed
lady of about thirty-five, dressed in a deep blue dalmatic
edged with gold embroidery in the height of fashion, and
with a bright saffron silk scarf dropped around her
shoulders and half-obscuring a complex necklace. She
turned away from the tapestry she was working on, an
elaborate scene showing a plainly allegorical interpretation
of the abduction of Ganymede by Eôs. Flavia suddenly felt
acutely conscious of her own travelling clothes, and glad
that at least she had just been to the baths. The servant
declared who she was, and left.

Lucilla got up, showing she was about the same height
as Flavia, and looked at her carefully for a moment. "So
you're Flavia Vindex," she said levelly, "travelling with
your cousin Arctus."

"That's right," said Flavia. "I think I met your daughter
earlier on."

"You did indeed, my dear. And I think that you're the
daughter of Florianus Vindex and Helpidia Valeria, and
grand-daughter of Lucius Aradius Valerius Proculus, are
you not?"

So she knew the name of Flavia's famous grandfather.
"Yes, indeed."

Lucilla smiled. "Well, my dear, your mother's great-
grandfather by the maternal line, Valerius Maximus, was
my own grandfather, which makes us first cousins twice
removed." She embraced Flavia lightly. "But I know
nothing of this Arctus person. And there is talk about you
already in Buxton, talk which is not good for you. I think
you'd better sit down here and tell me all about it."

Flavia had heard of this branch of the family only

vaguely, and knew nothing of Lucilla. Feeling at a disadvantage, and uncertain of her reception, she gave a version of her adventures since she had heard of Titus' posting to the North, trying to make it circumspect, and guessing that Lucilla divined more than she intended.

"I see," said Lucilla, when the long tale had wound to a close, and she had evidently listened carefully to every word. "Well, you seem to have acted well enough in all the circumstances. I am sorry about Titus: I met him once in Augusta, and I liked him: he was a bit of a fool, perhaps, but he had a sense of honour such as few have these days. He got it from your father, of course; my side of the family has not been able to boast such a thing for many a long year.

"But you had better move rooms, you know, or you may do yourself harm: this is a small town, and the respectable people are very small-minded. I have taken this wing of the posting-station until such time as I find a house; the servants make sure of who goes in and out, and, besides, I have a reputation which can cast a helpful shadow. I think you had better share with Balbina. You're not exactly of an age but you're both young, mature and unmarried, and I daresay you will get on well enough. Will you do that?"

Flavia felt a treacherous weakness stealing over her, a feeling that after so much worry about Titus and herself and Cormerick and Arctus, after so much fighting alone, at last someone, this competent woman, was offering to relieve her of it for a moment, and to take responsibility for her. "Yes," she heard herself say.

"Good. Go and get any special things you need now; I'll send a slave to pack up the rest of your stuff and move it. Will this Arctus have anything of yours that you need?"

Flavia thought quickly. "Probably one or two things. We weren't able to keep our stuff separate on the move."

"Don't go and fetch it yourself: get a slave to do it. And be careful of time you have with Arctus: you don't need to avoid him, of course, but don't spend too much time with him, and never alone." She paused, studying Flavia closely.

"But apart from all that nonsense, you're in an unusual

situation now. Technically, Titus would have made your marriage arrangements, but now that's not possible, and with your mother so far away you're very much able to choose a husband for yourself. Well, you're not a flighty fourteen-year-old: I suppose you should know your own mind. But you've been through some strange experiences lately. I wouldn't be surprised if you felt attracted to this Arctus man after spending so much time with him. Are you?"

Flavia had been watching this question arriving with alarmed fascination, as if it were an African snake. She realised with dismay that she didn't really know quite what her own feelings about Arctus amounted to, quite apart from the problem of how prudent it would be to admit the truth to Lucilla, whatever it might be. She was confused, certainly; she found him irritating and patronising at times; but she had grown... "Yes, I am attracted to him," she admitted, bridling as she said it. "But, as you imply, I'm old enough to be aware that one needs to make decisions on marriage very carefully."

Lucilla's eyes narrowed. "Hmph! That's very diplomatic. Suspiciously so, some would say. Well, normally I'd say to an unmarried woman of your age that you ought to get a move on: you're nearly as old as the Vestal Virgins are when they get released from their vows. But I don't think I will say it in your case, not just now – apart from the fact that you will have heard it often enough, I've no doubt.

"I suggest that you be careful of this Arctus, though. Don't forget that though he may be a Count he's a man of mystery as far as his family goes, and that's much the same as a man of no family, I'm afraid. I shouldn't have to tell you of the uses of such things as opoponax oil, when you've reached the age you have, should I?" She read an angry understanding in Flavia's eyes, and rang a small hand-bell. "We shall talk more of this." A slave entered. "Mainaino, will you please show Lady Flavia here to Balbina's room – oh, and tell Quarta that the lady needs her hair done. When you've done that, I'll speak to Marcus Troianus, and you can bring us a small jug of the Loire wine, watered to one-sixth." She kissed Flavia on the cheek, putting a surprising warmth into the gesture. "I'll see you later, my dear."

Flavia found Arctus in a quiet corner of the courtyard as the evening was starting to draw in. "I wasn't able to see you earlier: I've been taken under Lucilla's wing," she said.

"So I hear. I'm sure it's a good thing for you; from all I gather it should stop the mouths of gossip effectively. But I shall miss being able to chat, the way we could before." Arctus looked concerned; was he also a little bit hurt, or was that her imagination?

"I heard news in the baths that the relief force has been countermanded."

"Severus has been reassigned. The report came in to the manager while I was in his office today. But the relief force is still being prepared: another commander is to be appointed."

"Well, that sounds a little better. Do you believe it?"

"Why not? It's a great opportunity for a good general, after all. The Britains are an important diocese: there's a huge amount of grain, no shortage of livestock, the mines – lead, silver, iron and tin – and a large garrison. The man who rescues the Britains will have his career made. And if he's confident of his own abilities he may think it's a safer bet than hanging round the Court jostling for preferment along with countless others, all with good connections of one sort or another."

Flavia hoped this was an impartial assessment rather than an attempt to reassure her or persuade himself, and, not much wanting to know the answer, led the conversation elsewhere. Not long afterwards Balbina came out and lightly suggested, Flavia guessed on her mother's behalf, that she might want to go up to bed. It was a sensible suggestion, and Flavia was grateful at the care it implied. A few minutes later she made her way upstairs. The room was small, with space for one large bed and two chests, and a little to spare: her bags were piled up, still not unpacked or stored away. She set to work on them. Balbina put down some needlework she had already gone back to, sat on the bed and threw herself back, staring at the ceiling.

"I cleared the chest with the mauve drape on it," she said. "I can get Xanthe to do that for you if you want."

"Thank you," said Flavia, opening the chest at once. "No, I'd rather do it myself so I know where things are." She started to stow at the bottom things she would not need for a while, like her travelling boots and leather cloak.

Balbina sat up on the bed. "We're not going to that house my mother was going to take, now. She's heard the owner is letting it to somebody else. It's a pity. It was very beautiful, with a lovely peristyle garden and fountain. It was a bit outside town, mind you, though it *was* on the right side for the baths. Perhaps it's more fun to be in town itself, after all."

"I don't know," said Flavia, feeling suddenly tired and irritable, and wondering if a pair of socks could do with darning. "I suppose it goes both ways. Depends if you know a lot of people or not, perhaps."

"You soon get to know them in the baths here," said Balbina, "especially if you have introductions, though a lot of the people here aren't really our sort, tradesmen supplying the army and things. You *are* a relation of ours, aren't you, though I've never met any of your people? I've heard talk about your brother Titus. They say he's very handsome."

Flavia paused over a pair of leggings, wondering for a moment whether Buxton would be too respectable to make them wearable, and decided that it would. "My brother's dead," she said briefly.

"Oh, how awful!" cried Balbina. "And he was only, what, thirty or thirty-one! He'd become an army officer, hadn't he? Was he killed by the barbarians?"

Flavia felt that, quite apart from the overlay of treachery and plotting, Titus' death was a private matter, not to be discussed with some remote cousin she had not seen before. "Yes, he died north of the Wall," she said evasively.

"I'm so sorry for you!" said Balbina, impulsively coming over and giving Flavia a hug.

Surprised, Flavia turned to her, an unguarded expression of hurt and sadness momentarily in her eyes, and smiled wanly. "You're very kind," she said, wondering whether she'd been unfair in some way. "How long have you been here in Buxton?"

"Oh, we've only been here since the day after the nones of July. What's that, about three weeks, isn't it?"

"And have you seen any barbarians?" asked Flavia, unbundling some tunics and folding them carefully. "These could do with ironing. Do you have a maid who could do it?"

"Xanthe's not very good at that. She's quite new: she was given to me at my birthday last Spring, I think because Mummy thought she'd be good to take with me when I go to Paris. But, though she's clever, there're some things she's not used to yet. Better have Comindos do it. Get them ready and I'll call her. Look at that dress: the pleats are in a terrible state. No, we didn't actually see any barbarians, though the Irish have made several raids, you know, and been driven back each time by those brave cataphracts at Bremetennacum. It's been quite scary. They say that when there's a west wind the coracles can sail right up rivers faster than a carriage can travel."

"Does your fiancé live in Paris, then? I thought you said his estate was next to yours in the Fylde."

"Yes, well, his father's is. But he's a military tribune, and at present he's deputy commander of a field army regiment in Paris. I'm very cross with Mummy about him just now, actually. It's been agreed that Marcus' family will contribute to the dowry, but I think they are having a bit of trouble raising it, and she's insisting on full delivery by the time of the wedding."

"Well, it does make sense. What would happen to you if something happened to your husband in the wars?"

"Flavia, it doesn't bear thinking about! But I suppose I'd inherit his estate."

"Supposing you quarrelled with him; he could leave it to someone else."

"Well, it's hard to imagine. But couldn't I challenge

that in the courts?"

"You could, but it would take time and trouble and money, and you might well still only end up with a *legitim* of a quarter of your inheritance."

"Anyway, all kinds of things could happen. His estates could be overrun by barbarians, and then it wouldn't matter whether they were part of my dowry or not."

"They could, but nowhere has ever been permanently overrun by barbarians, except Dacia beyond the Danube which wasn't even Roman until the Emperor Trajan's time."

"You're good at history!" laughed Balbina, and went off to find Comindos, while Flavia went back to unpacking.

The next morning was fine and warm, and the town filled rapidly with noise and bustle: the Celtic feast of Lughnasa would be the following day. Out for a stroll, Flavia overheard complaints about the country people seeking safety in Buxton, many of whom had made their harvest earlier than usual because of the troubles, and had come in with great waggons laden with as much as they would bear. Few of these carts would fit within the town, and the owner of one of the inns, it seemed, had rented a small field on the outskirts and arranged, for a fee, for a watch to be kept on goods there.

In the late morning a dishevelled messenger came in to the posting-station to change horses, blurting out that the Picts and Attacotti had reached Leicester, and cut the road to Augusta. He soon disappeared on his way to Chester, but the town *curator* appeared within an hour and was closeted until well after midday in the posting-station manager's office, along with Quintinus, Nummius Secundus and Siricius the Imperial Messenger.

Then apparitors made their way through the town, announcing that the Most Renowned senator Nummius Secundus would hold a public meeting in the afternoon, at the ninth hour from dawn. As the sundial in the courtyard reached towards the seventh hour a messenger from Chester arrived, and shortly afterwards another from York. News of these movements went through the streets like a weasel.

Flavia dimly remembered aged relations' stories of such emergency meetings in the bad days before the emperor Diocletian had restored the frontiers, way back a century ago. It made her think of records of the past in Tacitus' histories – a past which, though far more remote, seemed curiously more real, perhaps because of the brilliant descriptions she could remember word-for-word. Either way, the present news seemed depressingly familiar. Now she did not want to be involved in a sweaty press of people being told half-truths, and she buried herself in her books to ignore it all. But Balbina came and bullied her.

"I don't know how you can bear not to be there, Flavia," she said. "It's only in the Forum, underneath the Grove. I'm sure the whole town will be out; even your Arctus." And Flavia had allowed herself to be persuaded to go to the first floor of the basilica and look out through the windows. On the paving of grey Pennine limestone a daïs had been set up with tawny rush matting, blue cushioned chairs, and towards the back a rich brown awning.

Two soldiers went to the forward corners of the stage and sounded long trumpets, and the hubbub of the large, anxious crowd gradually diminished. A procession of men in rich clothes ascended to the podium and filed in front of the stools: she could recognise Nummius Secundus, Quintinus in a crimson military cloak, Siricius and Cæcilius September the *curator*; there were two others she could not identify.

Nummius Secundus was bent and decrepit, and had trouble with the steps, leaning heavily on his nomenclator. But once the others were ready he stepped forward alone and suddenly straightened to his full height. Without apparent effort his voice rang clearly across the forum.

"If there is any one of you, citizens," he said, "whose spirit is at peace and whose mind is free of worry; if there is any of you who stays quietly at home about his ordinary business; if there is any of you who follows his daily round without disturbance – if there is any such, let him speak!"

He paused, throwing wide his arms with a dramatic flash of his deep white sleeves, and the already-quiet assembly froze. "But there is none!" he cried, and paused again briefly. "Indeed, how could anyone here in Buxton be so foolish? Under the prudent and wise tutelage of the goddess Arnemetia, this is a city which is renowned throughout the Prefecture of the Gauls, from the dank marshlands of Yarmouth to the torrid sands of Tangier: known for the wisdom of its priests, known for the skill of its physicians, but above all known for the good sense of its people. And possessed of that good sense, you are well aware – how could you not know? – that this is a moment of peril for the state: peril alike for the integrity of the Setantian republic of which you are part, and for the dignity of the Eternal City which you equally represent.

"It is said that when the Roman King Tarquin wished to build a shrine to Jupiter, and fastened upon the Capitol as the most worthy and appropriate site, he found that it was already in use by Terminus, the god of boundaries; and that this explains why to this day, in the temple of the chief of the gods, the stone of Terminus remains. This story, my friends, is not simply a piece of antiquarian lore. It has a deeper, a symbolic meaning: a glimpse of the truth which lies at the heart of things.

"What is that meaning? It is that we Romans will never give up a place that is in our possession: no-one will ever move our Roman frontiers. The gods themselves tell us, then, that the Roman republic is firm and steadfast. We can be assured that though the barbarians may slip into our country by deceit or by deception, though they may raid and ravage, though they may bluster and burn, they will never alienate our land, nor bring despair into the true and steadfast hearts of the Roman people.

"Who can be so impious as to doubt the word of the gods in such a matter? And yet we have a firm security in this sublunary world as well. For we know that in this very prefecture there sits, in the ancient city of Paris, an emperor august and venerable, powerful and wise. We know that his care is constantly exercised, both for his people's welfare, and for his citizens' good. Behold him now, as he sits in his great hall of state! The magistrate's toga is on his muscled shoulders, and the military *cingulum* about his narrow waist, while the purple robe of empire shields the feeble eyes of his subjects from the dazzling radiance of his divine form! His brows are crowned with the laurels of victory, emblem of his success over the wild Alamanni; he frowns as he meditates their final destruction.

"But see! The curtains of the sacred chamber tremble, and an Imperial messenger nears; entering, he prostrates himself before the Omnipotent Ruler with new fear added to his natural awe, and in broken words he gasps out his dreadful tidings: that the Britains have been slighted by the Picts and Attacotti. The messenger stammers to an end, and for a moment there is a hush. Then the great Valentinian – Valentinian the all-powerful, Valentinian the all-merciful, Valentinian the saviour of his people – rises to his sacred feet. A chant for a moment rises up from those about, a wailing cry. 'The Britains!' they chorus with one voice. 'The Britains! Alas! Alas! For the Britains were always the best-loved of the Emperor's provinces! How many times did he not say that the great lord Constantine himself was crowned in the Britains, that his successors must ever cherish those islands, and hold them in the highest esteem?'.

"But now the mighty Emperor raises his finger. On an instant, silence descends. His piercing eye darts like an arrow at the Consul and Master of Soldiers, Flavius Jovinus. The latter needs no words. At once he draws his sword from the scabbard, casts one meaningful regard at the altar of Mars, and addresses his weapon thus: 'Sword, you have slain Alamanni, and Germans, and Franks. All the enemies of our lord Valentinian have you slain! Now I swear death to those savage swarms that disturb the Diocese of the Britains. Until they have been expelled for ever from the lands of the Romans, you shall not be sheathed again!' He speaks, and he is gone. Listen! Without, there is already a noise of marching, a noise undiminished for many hours. It is the tread of multitudes of men, men determined for battle.

"Citizens in the town of Buxton, these are the events which even at this moment unfold but a short distance away in the Diocese of the Gauls! Our enemies know this well: their hearts fail, their right arms hesitate, their thoughts turn anxious to their own country. So our father, the Emperor, keeps his faith with us. Now it is up to us, for our part, to keep faith as well with him. Stand ready, you who are of military age, to take up the sword, and to defend this town from the enfeebled inroads of the barbarians! You who are older, be prepared to secure our women and children, and to marshal and support the defence! See how the gods stand by us as we defend our hearths and our homes, and how radiantly the Goddess Arnemetia glories at their head! Citizens in the town of Buxton, the days of this time are indeed urgent days. But while for our enemies they are days of bitter regret, for us they are days of glory!"

The figure of Nummius Secundus stepped back and seemed to diminish in stature, but a roar went up from the crowd, a clamour of approval and enthusiasm. For a moment Flavia heard a group of voices rise above the noise in unison, repeating "May the Emperor, pious and felicitous, pacify the world and rule for many years!", and then subside. Then another chant could be distinguished, "Long life and health to the Most Renowned Nummius Secundus!" and again "He honours his clients with generous donatives!", after which all was lost in the hubbub.

Flavia had had enough. Now Quintinus was moving forward to the front of the podium. But she slipped away, and in ten minutes had reached a spot she had already grown fond of, next to the river, upstream, and just outside the town: a small temple to Faunus. The shrine was of good sandstone, with pillars at the front in the form of atlantes supporting a simple frieze and a pediment adorned with figures. But the paint had disappeared from all the statues, and they had been weathered almost out of recognition. Reddish-purple cranesbill and tiny white rock cinquefoil flowers pushed their way through cracks between the stones. The spot was peaceful, and Flavia sat for a while watching a moorhen and a pair of tufted ducks. After a while the distant sounds from the forum ended. Damselflies gathered as the evening approached.

The sun was halfway below the crest of a western hill. But as it vanished a trumpet sounded an ancient call, a summons from the days before the Romans came to the Britains. Then, reflected from somewhere out of sight, sprang the glow of a great bonfire: it must be the celebrations for the festival of the god Lugh, one of the great feasts of the Britons, an event that everyone marked every year without fail, an event that took precedence over invasion or emergency. There were indeterminate cries; after a while a sound of singing; then a shouting of many voices. Flavia wandered back to the posting-house, not far, and on the same side of the town, and found Balbina on the verandah. As the darkness of night became full they heard snatches of the voice of a bard rising on the air, singing the tale of Lugh's defeat of the wicked Black Chrom, a tale that must be told every year.

Outside, the celebrations went on all night. In the posting-station there was at first an atmosphere of some tension, some people's sympathies being with the revellers and others being for some kind of disciplined vigilance against the barbarians. The major-domo, at a loss whether to put on the customary feast, had allowed himself to be confused by the fact that there were too many guests for the main banqueting-room, and yielded to pressure from his staff for leave to go and join the festivities outside. Ultimately he found himself constrained to offer a simple meal focused on lentils, but made up for this by broaching a large amphora of impressive Tuscan wine, and the result seemed broadly satisfactory to both camps. Flavia found herself at dinner reclining on the next couch to Lucilla, who asked her what she had made of Nummius Secundus' speech.

She felt it best to be quite open and recalled her impression. "Quite competent, I suppose. But too short to carry much literary weight. He didn't give himself space to develop his arguments properly. And though it wasn't badly constructed, there was clumsiness in the phrasing.

To be honest, though, my main objection was its excessive sycophancy."

Lucilla laughed. "I know what you mean by the last. Pliny somewhere describes his uncle's substantial literary output. One of the works was called *Problems in Grammar*, and he says that he '*wrote this during the last years of Nero, when the slavery of the times made it dangerous to write anything at all independent or inspired.*' But you should be careful what you say, you know: real slaves have ears. And Nummius Secundus is a man who has seen action in his day: he was a regimental commander in his youth, in Constantine's victory at the Milvian Bridge. But in a situation like ours it's not really literary merit which is the true test. What I really meant was, how was it received by the crowd, where you were?"

Flavia realised that Lucilla was even better read and informed than she had thought. She reflected, not having attended much at the time to how the speech was received. "I think it went down quite well. It was well-delivered, of course, too, and that in itself met people's expectations of a senator."

"I have a feeling that we'll be safe enough here in Buxton, but it would be useful for Quintinus to get willing recruits, and for there to be a feeling of hope and loyalty about in the town.

"I'm glad you've come to stay with us, Flavia, and I hope you'll be able to have fun with Balbina. I notice you've made a good start in keeping the right distance in public from your Gallic friend. You'll find it worth while, and not just here in Buxton: it's a small world and word gets about. We ought to find you a maid to look after you here; I'll see if anything can be done, but in the meantime you must share Balbina's Xanthe."

The day after the festival there was a feeling of waiting. A small group of Christians defiantly commemorated the execution of one of their fellow-believers in Exeter fifty years earlier, until a band of young men, still drunk on beer and excitement, forced their way into the house and drove them out with threats of arson. In the afternoon a company of soldiers arrived from Chester, from a detachment of the First Legion stationed there, and it was announced there would be conscriptions into Quintinus' improvised defence force. At evening a messenger came with news of Picts at Manchester, much to Magunna's disquiet. Flavia lacked the discipline to work on her book, and took the advice that it would be dangerous to wander outside the town. She roamed the streets looking for diversion, but found little.

No barbarians appeared at Buxton the next day, nor the following day, nor the day after that. People grew used to seeing Quintinus drilling his militia in the forum, leading them out on route-marches, training with javelins in the fields outside the town.

Then a messenger arrived from the commander at Chester: he had defeated the barbarian bands at Middlewich and reopened the road. The messenger had other news, too: of Saxon attacks on Caister and Colchester on the east coast; of Attacotti again besetting Leicester, and arriving at Durobrivæ (at this Flavia, hitherto lulled by the unreality of the news, suffered bitter pangs of anxiety); that the Master of Soldiers and Consul, Jovinus, was now in person to take command of the force to relieve the Britains. The messenger returned to Chester.

Time passed. News of the invaders came daily, and was endlessly dissected. Now there were reports of Picts and Attacotti as close as Derby and Towcester, but no sign that they were coming nearer. News came from further afield again, of Saxons on the south coast at Chichester. On the great feast of Diana, on the Ides of August, when slaves had a day's holiday, the guests at the posting-house were shifting for themselves again at a cold buffet when news came that twelve boats of Saxons had arrived at York, only to find it already besieged by the Picts. The supposed allies had come to blows, and after a while the Roman forces had made a sally. They had killed and wounded many of the enemy and burned six of the Saxon boats, but then the barbarians had rallied together and driven the Romans back within the walls.

The next evening Flavia made another visit to the little temple of Faunus. She had taken to making short prayers when she went there, and sometimes took a small offering, a cake or a fruit; from time to time she would return to find the god's animals, field-mice perhaps, devouring these on his behalf. This time she came away to run into Arctus on the terrace.

It was some days since they had met, and she realised she had missed him. He was seated on a stool at a small table, with a pewter jug of wine and a dish of almond-stuffed olives, looking over the posting-house game book. She joined him, depositing a small tapestry clutch-bag beside her. From her seat she looked eastward up the Wye, and could just see her little temple half-hidden behind an oak spinney. He snapped his fingers at the slave to bring her a goblet. He smiled, and surprised her with a quotation from Virgil: '*Night rushed upon them, folding earth in its dusky wings.*'

"Though in quite a slow rush at this time of year!" she commented. "I've been thinking, Arctus, how long are we going to stay here? It doesn't look as if things are getting any better, and there seems to be no sign of the famous relief force."

He brightened a little, pleased, she hoped, to see her, though at the thought she felt guiltily that she had neglected him. "Yes," he said. "Jovinus was a curious choice as commander. As Consul and as Master of Soldiers he has many responsibilities. The Rhine frontier still seems unstable, despite the defeat of the Alamanni, and the Emperor's sickness must make it difficult for the Master of Soldiers to leave the Court. And the commanders here in Britain don't seem to be making much progress. But at least we seem safe here for the moment. I don't know. What do you think?"

She sighed. "I'm not sure, either, Arctus. It's true that the barbarians don't seem to show much sign of coming here to Buxton, but they seem to be prowling all around. And though there are walls here you wouldn't get all these people inside them, at least not with enough food to last long."

"It's true. But there's no sign that the barbarians have

tried a major siege here in Britain, except at South Shields and York, which are special cases really, with the one being about containing the Duke, and the other the second city of the Britains."

"Yes. And the troops at Bremetennacum and Chester seem fairly active, thanks be to Jupiter."

There was a pause. "Flavia," said Arctus. "What *do* you believe in? It's clear you're not a Christian. But do you really think the gods are there?"

Flavia considered her reply carefully. "I suppose I've never had a religious experience, not in the sense of visions and so on such as you read about in Apuleius or whatever, or such as the Christians talk of – or like what they say happened at Lydney last year. Though I have had dreams that I think must mean something, and I do feel a sense of awe towards the gods quite often. I don't believe in the stuff you find in Homer, with Mount Olympus as the home of the gods, or Hades and the Elysian Fields in the after-life – it's only simple people who do that.

"I've always been attracted by the Platonists, by the idea of there being an ultimate good God, and the world making sense, and the seven heavens with Powers in each which intervene in the world here and which we call gods and pray to, and us purifying ourselves through each heaven after death, gradually losing our mortal contaminants until we become pure soul with God and are readied for rebirth. I certainly believed in that at one stage. I'm not so sure I do now, not in detail anyway: the idea of there being a good God seems more difficult, and sometimes I think we may not be meant to know how the cosmos fits together. Though I still think there's something so beautiful in Plato's idea that God allotted each of us a star, which our soul comes from and where we shall eventually return.

"Perhaps God is neutral between good and evil; or rather perhaps he is above good and evil as we know them. But I think there *are* Powers that can intervene in our lives, and I do feel sometimes, when I pray or make an offering to the gods, that I'm communicating with them. I'm sure it doesn't make any difference whether I call a god Mars or Rigonemetos, or whatever name the Syrians or the Goths have for him: I still feel there is some Power there who is sometimes listening." She smiled rather wanly. "But I often feel very alone, as if, even if there are gods there, they mightn't be very interested in me, or even in human beings in general, like in Lucretius." She paused, as he took her hand and squeezed it. "What do you believe, Arctus?"

He sat quietly for a moment, holding her hand. She turned to look at him while he concentrated on what to say, and despite a slight anxiety that someone would see them holding hands her smile became fonder. "I don't think I know what to think, really," he said. "I've obviously studied nowhere near as much philosophy as you (I remember, when we first met, asking if you could speak a few words of Greek: you must have found that rather quaint, with all your learning).

"My mother brought me up to worship the gods like anyone else, but it didn't seem to have a lot of substance to it, and I became very sceptical. I've never much believed the stories of healing cures at the shrines, or gods actually appearing to people in their dreams, though I can see that strange things do happen, and I do have one cousin who really was cured of a nasty skin disease by praying at a temple in the Pyrenees.

"I was always worried by the Christians: they say there are no gods except their own, and they claim to have healing powers just like those in the gods' shrines. And I always felt that, if the gods are as powerful as people say, then they wouldn't have let the Christians become as many as they are, with all the emperors Christian since Constantine (even Julian, before he came to the purple), and more and more people becoming Christian every day.

"But there again, the poet said 'Those who the gods wish to destroy they first make mad', and there have been many impious people and impious emperors. So I have some sympathy with those who say that some madness has seized Rome, and that the gods have let the people turn Christian so that they themselves can destroy the Romans without impiety." He paused.

"When I was in Beirut," he went on slowly, "I went through the initiation as a follower of Isis, the whole thing, fasting and shaven head and all. While I was in the Isiac community there, it was the most important thing in the world to me. When I finished my studies, I was going to live with Isiacs in Antioch, and make my life there."

"What happened?"

"I don't know quite. About that time, my mother became ill, and I came back to Gaul to look after her, and on the long journey I met a number of Christians and realised that there's not that much difference between them and the Isiacs. And that worried me. I mentioned once before that I don't like the Christians' hypocrisy. And I started to think about my Isiac friends and think that theirs was perhaps rather similar: they had the same way of taking money off wealthy members by talking about the spiritual value of giving and of poverty, and so on. Then there weren't any Isiacs near us in Second Aquitaine, and after I'd been back for a couple of months I began to feel that it had just been a young man's enthusiasm, and didn't really relate to real life at all. And of course I started to wonder too whether my mother's illness had been chance, or whether it had been destiny, in some way, to set me free from the Isiacs."

They sat in silence for a moment. It was now almost quite dark, and Flavia said, "I feel rather cold. Could we go indoors?"

They went in to a small upstairs sitting-room alone, violating Lucilla's rules. There was a little fireplace, with peat sods burning in the grate, giving a pleasant scent. A cat by the hearth stretched as they came in, and then settled again. For a while neither of them spoke.

"What was wrong with your mother?" asked Flavia gently.

"She had an illness of the mind," said Arctus. "She had always been so strong, but one day she started to behave very strangely, to shout at people when they hadn't done anything wrong, and to have ideas that strangers were going to get into the house and assault her and steal her belongings. I think if it had been physical illness I might not have come home, but I got such strange, terrible letters from her that I felt I had to."

"What happened to her?"

"Well, the family were very worried, of course; beside themselves, really. Most of them thought she was possessed by an evil *dæmon* and should go to one of the healing shrines, perhaps the one where my cousin was cured. Some said that magic was the answer. I had one cousin who'd gone Christian and wanted to get one of their exorcists, but the exorcist refused to come because my mother wasn't a Christian herself." A slave came in to check the fire, saw them sitting there, and silently withdrew. "Then her elder brother, Marinus, who lived in Tolosa, arrived one day and just took charge. He brought a doctor with him, a follower of Galen, who declared that there was no supernatural problem: the balance of her body had been upset, he said, and put it down to a court case she had lost which had made her worry and not take proper care of herself."

Yes, good, thought Flavia, probably an excess of saline phlegm and bilious humours, but did not interrupt.

"He administered a strict diet with baths and exercise, and over a period of six or eight months she became herself again. I got home when she was already a lot better, and I found it at first hard to believe what everyone said had happened; until I looked back at the letters, anyway."

"It was very good of your uncle. It must have cost him a lot of time and money."

"Yes, I'll always be grateful. We became quite close: he still lives in Tolosa, and I go to visit whenever I get the chance. I have a property in Spain, which I live off, so I need to pass that way now and then."

"What about your father? Was he able to help at all?"

Arctus returned from the past and looked at her. "Yes, I suppose I could tell you about him." He was silent a moment, looking about at the simple room with the firelight flickering on the red and yellow painted walls, mustering his thoughts, or perhaps his courage. "My mother's illness actually happened at the time of my father's greatest power and influence. His name was Ursulus, and he was a Cabinet Minister, a member of the Emperor's Consistory: he was Count of the Sacred Largesses under Constantius. I don't know a great deal about him: I was illegitimate, and my mother would never talk of him, so I've had to piece together what I could.

"I think he was very scrupulous, very correct. He must have been the perfect man to be in charge of the Empire's finances. But he must also have been very ashamed at knowing that he had taken my mother's virginity, with all that would mean for her if it were ever known: and in fact it *was* known, of course, since, once there was a baby, that couldn't be hidden. He met her when she was only fourteen – in Gaul we keep closer than I think you do to Roman ideas of when girls are ready for marriage – so she would have been very innocent, and very easy for a great man to seduce."

"Perhaps you judge him harshly," said Flavia. "Young girls often know what they are about, especially if they expect to be married within a year or two. If there was a fault it was surely her family's."

"I'm sure I judge him no more harshly than he judged himself. He refused to recognise me, and when he died all his property went to his daughter. Well, most of it: the Imperial Treasury got some. You see, he helped Julian when he was Cæsar in Gaul, but Julian when he became Emperor set up the Commission of Chalcedon to investigate actions by senior officials under Constantius, and they had my father executed. But the Emperor saved most of his property for his daughter."

"I'm sorry."

"He hadn't done anything wrong, I'm sure of that. But I've been told that he accused the military of extravagance more than once, or perhaps even of corruption, both in Gaul and during the Persian campaign. And that enough people wanted to get rid of him for the setting up of the Commission to give them their chance." He paused. "Sanctus' son, Lucanus Talisius, was one of the most en- ergetic secretaries of the Commission. They say that is how Sanctus got himself nominated for the governorship in Flavia Cæsariensis. When I saw the way he looked at you in Lincoln I was furious. I was delighted to be able to get you out of his hands."

Flavia waited for a moment before speaking, respecting Arctus' feelings, in case he was going to add anything, and smiled her gratitude for her escape. "Did you ever meet your father?"

"No, never. I wrote to him once, secretly, when I was sixteen, and I got a reply from a secretary telling me never to write again."

"Did you not even hear from him?"

"No, never directly. But he paid for me to be educated, and settled on me the estate in Spain, to give me an income. And when he became Count of the Largesses he arranged for me to be given honorary codicils of rank of a Count, and the postal service warrants we've been using. So I'm sure he thought he had done the right thing by me."

"I'm sorry, Arctus. You've had a hard time."

"No harder than many, and a lot less hard than many, too. A lot of men would have thought no more about an illegitimate son, and done nothing for me at all."

And many people lose fathers they know well, not ones who are no more than ideas to them, said Flavia to herself, and then regretted the thought as ungenerous.

He sighed. "Even now it's a relief to tell the story to someone, though. There are very few that I've dared trust with it."

"And your mother's family stood by her?"

"Yes. What else were they to do? The disgrace would have been even worse otherwise. My uncle Marinus told me that there were terrible scenes when the pregnancy became known, and that he was sent to take her to my aunt in York till I was born. The idea was that I should stay here in the Britains, and they would pay to have me adopted, but after I was born my mother refused to give me up, and also the news came of my father's gift of the land in Spain, so in the end I went back with them.

"They arranged a marriage for my mother, to a small farmer about twenty miles away, and I was given out to be his, though my mother insisted on calling me Arctus in memory of my real father. Her husband was quite an old man, and died within a couple of years; I don't remember him at all. But that's where we still live." He fell silent, and looked at Flavia.

He looked sadder and more vulnerable than she had ever seen him. She took his head in her hands on an impulse, and kissed him on the lips. He responded, hugging her body to his. She felt herself wanting to lose herself in him, but at the back of her mind there lurked a fear of something. She was aware that part of it was a fear that she would humiliate herself and hurt him by rejecting him again, and it dawned on her that in this mood he needed looking after, and she must be careful of him. He was urging her back against the couch they were sitting on, but she pushed him away gently. "No, Arctus," she murmured, "not now. It's...I don't know...I'm sorry...I think I'm still not ready. Can we just sit for a little?" They sat side by side on the couch, their bodies pressed together, their hands and forearms intertwined.

The Attacotti at Derby moved away south, and soon it was said they were near Verulamium. Then one Wednesday, ten days before the kalends of September, there was news that the Saxons had tried to sail up the Thames, and had been stopped by a chain across the river at London, and nine of their boats sunk by catapults on the bridge there; Flavia had never heard of catapults mounted on a bridge, and doubted the story. People spoke impatiently of the relief force: when would there be news of it?

Flavia went into the women's baths in the afternoon, as she often did these days, and spent a strenuous half-hour throwing a heavy exercise ball with Balbina. Afterwards she took off the band she had worn to stop her breasts swinging and went for an olive-oil massage. Later she was lying relaxed in the cool room, the slave-girl scraping her off with a strigil, when she heard a quickening murmur from some couches in a corner.

Balbina, who had been on the edge of the group, came across, full of some news. "Flavia, do you know what? They say that Valentinus Faber is arriving here in Buxton!"

Flavia's awareness suddenly focused. This was the name in Titus' letter, the exile who was conspiring with

Serquina. "And who is Valentinus Faber?" she asked. Surely there could not be two of them? The slave was just starting to clean her legs; Flavia sat up, dismissing her, and took the strigil herself.

"Don't you know about him? He's very dashing, but he's under a cloud. We meet him from time to time. He's in his forties, I'd say, tall with dark hair greying just a little at the temples: very handsome. He has a huge villa, a day or two west of Chester on the north-facing coast, on the edge of the mountains. We went there once, early last year I think. It's completely fortified – the governor turns a blind eye, he said – and it has fantastic views. He's very rich, but he lives very soberly."

"Where's he from?"

"They say his great-uncle was Prefect of the City under the Emperor Constantine, and his sister is the wife of the Maximinus who is very well in at Court. He comes from Valeria in Pannonia, on the west bank of the Danube just beyond the Iron Gates, and had vast estates there, but he was convicted of seducing the Emperor's niece Grata. Of course his secretaries say there wasn't a word of truth in it and it was just trumped up by his political enemies, but who's to say? And his properties in Pannonia were confiscated and he was banished here. But he has very extensive lands in the Britains, and must be very wealthy, though he isn't a senator; I don't know if he used to be, before his disgrace. They say he's arrived here in Buxton now with an escort of fully-armed cavalry and infantry from his own lands, and a hundred servants and followers, plus a lot of troops assigned for his protection by the First Legion at Chester."

"What's he doing coming here?"

"Nobody knows. It must be a lot less secure than his own estate. Aurelia's brother says that it shows how safe we are here, because Faber would never come if it was dangerous."

"Extra troops here can do no harm, I suppose, whatever else all that is about. Where's he staying?"

"That's the other thing. He's staying at the Unellian's House. They say the person who was going to rent it isn't now, and that Faber's going to take it instead, though

Claudia said that this other person was just a front and that
it was always Faber who was going to get the lease. I
expect it means we shall spend lots of time there after all,
because Faber entertains a lot. In fact we'll get the best of
both worlds: we'll be able to use the peristyle there to rest
in, and yet still be in town when anything's happening."

Flavia wiped the strigil with her left forefinger, flicked
the muck onto the marble floor, and turned her left knee
inward so she could get at the top of the calf. It was always
easier there if you could hold the thing with your left hand,
but a problem if you were right-handed. She saw it as a
little private discipline not to get a slave to do it instead.
"Did you say he was here already?"

"He's supposed to be arriving this afternoon. There are
secretaries and slaves at the Unellian's House already,
getting the place straight. You must meet him, Flavia: he's
really nice. We should make plans to go and pay a call
tomorrow morning."

"All right, let's think about it. I'm finished now. I'm
going to go for a bit of a walk. Do you want to come?"

They went through to the changing-room, called for
their clothes and dressed, tidied their hair and put on a
little make-up. Then they climbed up the knoll in front of
the entrance. Sometimes a worshipper was at the edge of
the sacred grove, but now there was nobody about. It was
quiet, shielded by the thick belt of yews from the rest of
the town, and they heard no more than the steady chipping
of a mason doing repair work at the baths, and occasional
noises of street-cries or of harness from further away. They
discussed where they might go next. Then they set off
through the streets, planning to walk out along the south
road to a farm where there were some attractive horses
which reminded Flavia of Cormerick, and which Balbina
enjoyed feeding.

On the way they went up to a stall in the upper gallery
of the basilica to buy a little malted barley for the horses.
Balbina was making her purchase and Flavia staring idly
down over the forum, when she noticed a short, burly dark
man walking very briskly away. It was the speed of his
movement that attracted her attention: she wondered if he
might be a thief, and she did not recognise him as one of

the locals. "Balbina!" she said. "Do you recognise that man just making for that alley now? There, by the pastrycook's stall!" Balbina turned and craned her neck, and as she did so Flavia saw another man following the first; he stopped for a moment, saluting the pastrycook with a curiously Italianate gesture that seemed familiar, and as he disappeared she realised where she had seen the sharp nose, freckled face and floating red hair before: they were those of Theodorus, the features she had seen long ago in the fens.

She ran to the steps and down them, two at a time, raced out into the street as fast as her too-narrow gown would allow, and made off down the alley where she had seen him vanish. But it was hopeless: the press of people made it impossible to move fast, and anyway there were off-vennels all along, and she learned nothing by asking passers-by. She made her way back to the basilica and found Balbina at the entrance looking about for her.

"Flavia, what happened to you?"

"I saw someone I know."

"You look angry. Come and have a cup of cider and tell me about it."

"No, it'll wait. I have to talk to Arctus about it, though. Do you know where he is? Would you mind postponing our walk?"

"No of course not. But I haven't seen him all day. He's usually still exercising in the men's baths at this time, isn't he?"

"Yes, I'll try there. See you later."

"All right. I'll go and call on Maternilla, if she's at home. Tell Mummy I'll be back for supper."

Flavia headed back to the baths, and at the entrance told a slave to look for Arctus. She waited. The bath-house was of limestone, and full-size statues of Hector and Achilles stood on either side of the door, each bearing a spear with its gilding stripped by pilferers for the bottom foot or so; Hector had blue eyes with his dark hair, which made him look implausibly British. The ungainly concrete domes of the hot rooms loomed round the corner. The sun was shining, and there was a smell of ordure from somewhere. A few yards away patrons' dogs were tied to a post under the supervision of a slave, who was having trouble stopping them from fighting. Flavia felt anxious and uncomfortable, and was relieved when her messenger returned and told her that Arctus had been found and was coming out. She tipped him four *nummi*, and was buttoning her bag again when Arctus appeared, still combing his hair. "You were quick."

"I'd finished: just had to throw my clothes on."

She led him for privacy to the densest part of the grove. Here the yew trees were thickly hung with votive wooden figures and an occasional animal skull. As they stood under one, its huge girth implying an age of hundreds of years, and its needled fronds dropping like a shroud around them, she became keenly aware of the numinousness of the place, and her spine was suddenly wrenched by a single shudder. "Help us," she muttered quietly to any local god who might hear. Then she spoke up aloud to Arctus. "I've seen Theodorus," she announced, and when he was silent added impatiently, "You know, Theodorus who visited me with the letter from Constantinople and led us such a dance north. He was in the forum not an hour ago."

"Yes, I know who you mean," he said cautiously. "Are you quite sure?"

"Of course I'm sure. I met him face to face in Cormerick: I should recognise him when I see him."

"All right. Anyone with him? Where did he go?"

"I don't know and I didn't see; he disappeared down an alley. He might have been with a short dark type, a bit like – oh, gods, I wonder if it was the man you had to fight in the mountains who called himself Molacos, the one who'd followed us! And do you know about Faber?" He had not heard, and she explained what Balbina had told her. "We ought to be pretty familiar with the people marooned in Buxton by now," she added. "If we see Theodorus now, then either he's been hiding for nearly a month or he's just arrived. Which is more likely?"

"And if he's just arrived there's probably some connection with Faber," remarked Arctus.

"Yes, but which way round? Is he here as an agent of Faber's, or to check up on him for someone else? Even if it was Molacos I saw, that doesn't really bear out either possibility."

"Does it matter to us?"

"Yes, it does. Theodorus delivered that letter to me; he can recognise me if he sees me, and may have done already, though I don't think so: in the forum I wasn't hiding, but I was on the upper floor of the basilica, and people don't look upwards as a matter of course. Faber probably knows that Titus was spying on him, and he may well have had him killed; if he finds out that I'm here I'm in trouble – I have a motive for revenge and could be dangerous, or at least a nuisance. So, if Theodorus is with Faber, then I need to disappear; if not, then it's not so urgent, and we might have a chance to find out what that letter was about, and in particular whether my brother has been implicated with anything else."

"Yes, that all makes good sense. I agree. You'd better stay quiet for the present. I'll make what inquiries I can manage."

He made discreet inquiries over the next few days, but nothing was seen of Theodorus or Molacos. Flavia did her best to stay indoors. And Balbina did not press her to go out: Faber proved far less sociable than had been expected, with his secretary Miltiades giving callers the unconvincing news that the master of the Unellian's House was not at home, offering them a drink and a snack in a small reception room near the front door, and sending them away.

The following Sunday Arctus, who had heard of a wild boar seen in the hills around, decided to go out hunting, alone, though he was universally urged to take companions. At about the fifth hour of that day another messenger arrived in town, this time from York. He was a tribune, grim-faced and courteous, with armour that bore the marks of battle, and the servants reported that he would drink no wine: muttered anxieties ran through the streets. He rode straight to the posting-station and demanded the immediate presence of Cintusmus the manager, Nummius

Secundus, Quintinus, Siricius and Cæcilius September. A servant went directly to the Unellian's House, and the conference did not begin until Faber and one of his secretaries had arrived at a canter.

The meeting took place in the main hall of the building, and, as it began, many of the residents anxiously clustered round the oak-panelled doors to the room. Occasionally an apparitor entered or left, pushing his way tight-lipped through the crowd. Flavia was unsure what to do, and reluctant to trust Balbina or anyone else with her affairs. She joined the waiting group, trying to stay out of view of the doorway of the conference room, and various speculations took flight about the nature of the message: Augusta had fallen to the Saxons; the Duke had been killed; the Emperor had landed with a relief force.

Within an hour the meeting was over, and the door opened. The first to leave was a tall man with dark hair greying at the temples, with a bearing that commanded acknowledgement and a full-length cloak of wolfskins. He was talking rapidly with a deferential Theodorus, but the latter nevertheless caught sight of Flavia at once. He in turn was closely followed by Molacos, armed and in military dress.

Theodorus spoke to him briefly; seeing him pointing to her, she quickly dropped to the back of the crowd, then slipped round a corner. Picking her skirts right up, she raced along the corridors, hearing equipment chinking on someone in hot pursuit. But she thought she was gaining as she dodged through doorways, hoping her follower was unfamiliar with the building.

As usual, a Nubian slave was on guard at the entrance to Lucilla's wing, and Flavia darted over the threshold, telling him not to say she had come past. In a moment she heard the Nubian arguing with someone, then the voice of a young woman: "I'm sure it was Flavia, but she may have gone past; there are lavatories out this way..."

Flavia felt sick with fear. Where were they, how could she get out? Panic kept blotting at her mind, and she groped her way up to her bedroom and locked the door, in the hope that in the familiar surroundings she would be able to think. She kept trying to force herself to work out what to do. She asked herself questions – how can I get away? how can I reach Arctus? – but she could not hold to them for more than a few seconds. She set herself to be calm, began to breathe deeply, and directed her mind in prayer to the Good Goddess. By the time a voice sounded at her door she was in a better state.

"Flavia, it's Lucilla, with Balbina. May we come in?"

Flavia composed herself. "Yes, come on." Her voice was normal. "Thank you," she breathed to the Goddess as she let them in.

"Flavia, there was an officer looking for you after the meeting; I think you know that. He could not find you and has gone, but he will certainly be back. He was with a civilian, who I think is the one who recognised you. What sort of trouble are you in?"

"I'm very frightened, Lucilla," said Flavia, realising that this was a time to speak up. "It's like this. Titus was working in the *arcani*, and discovered that Faber was involved in a treasonable conspiracy. In response, there was an attempt to impugn Titus himself. I suspect that the man who recognised me, Theodorus, is seeking me because he thinks I would testify to this."

Lucilla made a *moue*, and paused a moment. "That needs thinking about, indeed; I had no idea that you were involved in such high politics. We shall have to consider what is best, but there is very little time. The news that the tribune brought from York is out now, by the way, and it is good, in part anyway. Valentinian is still sick, but is now expected to recover. He has moved from Paris to Trier, and has declared his boy son Gratian as co-emperor, so as to regularise the succession. The bad news, for us, is that the Master of Soldiers Jovinus is now needed, it is said, at Court, and will not come to Britain, so the relief expedition is being delayed yet again while still another commander is found."

This went largely over Flavia's head. She was wondering if there was anywhere, outside the town but in the neighbourhood, which could be a rendezvous, where she might meet Arctus. With luck Theodorus didn't know of Arctus, despite Molacos' presence. "Suppose I slip out to the farm with the horses, you know, Balbina, the one on the Derby road. Could you get word to Arctus of where I've gone and ask him to meet me there with our gear?"

Lucilla considered. "It's very close to the town, and Faber has a lot of men. If he's looking for you I can't see you getting away. I could protect us here if you escaped, so I can't object on our own account. But I wouldn't advise it."

"Can you think of anything better?"

"I'm wondering. The town's like a bowl: I doubt you'd get up the mountains without being spotted. There's little traffic leaving at present because of the emergency, so you couldn't try to elude them concealed in a waggon. And it would be hard to hide against a determined search. No, I can't think of anything better at present. I'll arrange a horse; at the worst you may be able to try running for it."

Flavia set to packing up her stuff, helped by Balbina, while Lucilla gave orders for the wing to be guarded and for a fast horse to be readied without fuss; she also sent a servant to pack Arctus' things and saddle his own horse. In less than half an hour Flavia was ready, dressed as a man in trousers and leather jerkin, her hair piled into a light round fur hat. Balbina pushed little packets of raisins and hazelnuts into the heavy saddlebags. Flavia embraced both her relations, stepped onto the mounting stool and swung her leg across the saddle. There was still no sign of Arctus. "Tell him that if I'm not still at the farm I'll have set out for Doncaster," she said. "Thank you again!" And she was off.

She cut at a walk down a lane to the west of the walls, well out of sight of the Unellian's House, and without passing near the forum. She made her way onto the Derby road beside a large timber building, the Christian church, its doors still scorched from the Lughnasa fracas. Soon the buildings dwindled and it was open country, and she kicked the horse into a trot. In a few minutes the town had disappeared for a while, and after a time her destination, the farmhouse, came into view. As she approached it, she slowed to a walk again. There came a tall brick wall, overtopped by branches heavy with ripe plums and growing apples. Then suddenly another horse moved out from behind the corner and a hand laid hold of her bridle.

She gasped.

"Well, Lady Flavia, we meet again," said a familiar soft voice. "I noticed the last time how excellent a seat you have on a horse. On this occasion, however, I regret that I am obliged to ask you to descend. I feel that our business this time will be more securely conducted with both of us on foot."

"Theodorus, I have no inclination to interrupt my journey. Please let go of my horse at once."

"I regret that I cannot allow that." Theodorus loosened a sword in its scabbard. "If you are not willing to co-operate I am afraid that I shall be obliged to hurt your animal. Please be more reasonable."

Watching him carefully, Flavia swung her left leg over the saddle.

"Sorry, the *other* way, if you would be so kind."

Flavia moved the leg back, and followed it with her right, then jumped down on the same side as Theodorus. "That's kind of you, Lady Flavia," he said. "Now just give me a moment..." Less agilely, Theodorus slid to the ground himself, and clipped both the horses' bridles together. He folded his hands on his chest and considered her.

"How did you know I would come this way?"

"A guess, my Lady, though I did have other routes under observation as well."

"And why did you not just send a troop of soldiers for me?"

Theodorus smiled. "Well... The truth is that I am a bit of an independent operator. I wanted you to myself. You have something I would like. Well, I *think* you have it, anyway; and it is worth a little risk. And you, after all, are a woman; you are no threat at all, really." His smile was plainly now bland, superior, insulting.

"What could I possibly have that you could want?"

"Well, curiously enough, it's that letter. That very letter that I gave you at the end of April, what, four months ago now. Doesn't it seem a long time? There's been a lot flowing down the river since then, and though one may never step into the same water twice one doesn't necessarily always find it so different, perhaps."

"Is that why you want the letter back now? To destroy

the evidence of the Eastern conspiracy?"

"Well, circumstances have changed, if you like; the letter might be of... some value now, to a certain person. But as to the Eastern conspiracy...well." Theodorus laughed. "I think I can be quite open with you at this stage, under the circumstances.

"There's no Eastern conspiracy," he said. "Faber grew up in Pannonia with someone called Maximinus, who married his sister. It's Maximinus who's my own employer. He's never got on all that well with his brother-in-law, and was thinking to denounce him in the expectation of being rewarded with his estates: Faber had blotted his copy-book once before, so a denunciation would not need very much evidence. Unfortunately Faber's barbarian invasion has come rather sooner than we thought, and if his insurrection should prove successful it would be Maximinus rather than Faber who was in trouble: I may need some fast footwork to restore the balance.

"But I think we needn't worry too much. His communications here may not prove as effective as he hopes. And the latest news from Trier plays into our hands, too, and will mean that a number of army units will be more loyal to the Emperor than Faber was counting on. They may now start to move quite effectively against the barbarians, now that there's less temptation for them to sit on the fence."

Flavia felt more afraid. He had no need to tell her all this: that he was doing so showed not just vanity and self-indulgence, but too much confidence, too threatening a confidence. "Why are you telling me this now?" she asked.

"Oh, for my own satisfaction. It's nice to have someone to confide in from time to time. There is very little opportunity for that in my chosen profession." There was a viciousness behind Theodorus' smile, and Flavia recalled Tacitus' comment '*It is a characteristic of the human mind to hate the man one has injured.*'

"But what you wanted to know about was the 'Eastern conspiracy'. You need to understand that the Eastern interest is quite separate, really. The way it goes is this. Maximinus has an associate called Festus, who's the governor of Syria, and Festus has his own reasons to want to get rid of Lupicinus, the Master of Soldiers in the East. So what could be more convenient than to implicate him in the Faber insurrection? Well, it hasn't been that easy, actually: we haven't really known the right people with contacts both in the East and in the West. But fortunately your Titus came on the scene, and I think that we've now been able to use him quite nicely to make the link."

There was a short pause. This was why he was telling her all this, realised Flavia: cruelty. He was doing it to reveal how thoroughly he was going to destroy her family. Then Theodorus widened his right eye. "Now, Lady Flavia, would you by any chance have in your baggage that letter we were discussing?"

Surely he would kill her once she produced it. Would the people at the farm help, if she ran for it? He might have missile weapons concealed, a throwing dart perhaps. Would it be worth the risk? But it would do no good just to claim that she did not have the letter.

"I packed in haste," she said. "I hope I still have it." She went to open her saddlebag, thinking to delay in case some expedient occurred to her. Theodorus stepped back a few paces, as if wary she might have a weapon concealed in her bags, and she wished she had thought to do just that.

"I've had an unexpected time over the last few months," Theodorus mused, "with a lot of travel, some of it in quite difficult circumstances. We've had to denounce you and your brother fairly widely, of course; one tries to be as economical with these things as possible, but it was inevitable, I fear. Still, evidence has been a bit of a problem, sometimes. It was indeed very fortunate that your brother agreed to conduct that Pictish prince back home from his meeting up north of the Wall: that will be the thing that convincingly establishes him as traitor, and hence as a key link in the conspiracy. If it hadn't been for that, I daresay that the trial judges might be tempted to reach the wrong conclusions. Ah, I think you may have found it now."

Flavia, feeling unable to delay any longer, lifted the letter out of her bag.

"Just put it down on the ground there, if you would. And do you have any recent letters from your brother?

Perhaps you would be so good as to let me see those as well."

Flavia was powerless: he would surely search her anyway. "I do have one letter from him."

"I'm truly sorry to deprive you, but it may not be for very long. Please."

Flavia spent as much time as she dared searching in the saddle-bags again, and eventually came up with Titus' third letter, the one given to her by Stephanus.

"Pass it to me now, if you would."

Flavia reached the bundle out to the man, and he took and untied it. He read it carefully. "Ah, this is good. This is excellent. Yes, I am afraid I shall be keeping this for a time."

"Now Lady Flavia, I'd like you to mount again, if you would, and we're going to take a little ride further along the road. But first I'm afraid I'm going to have to hobble your horse to make sure that she doesn't move faster than is convenient. Will you please stand well back under this elm tree, just over there..."

Flavia went over to the trunk of the elm, and watched as Theodorus knotted a leather strap firmly between the front knees of Flavia's horse. The mare tried to scratch it off a couple of times, then gave up.

"Now mount, if you would be so kind." Flavia got back on her horse, and Theodorus carefully packed the two documents into his own saddle-bags and picked up a spear which she had not noticed, propped against the wall.

"I should explain that some friends of mine from Ireland will be arriving up this road shortly. I understand that there is currently what one might describe as a glut of slaves on the market there, but I nevertheless consider they would be prepared to pay rather well for a slave who is as healthy, as educated and as beautiful as you, Lady Flavia." Theodorus studied her face, raising an eyebrow as he speculated. "Your commercial value is of course obvious, but if I were you I wouldn't worry too much about the danger of being hired out in the service of a number of men from day to day, as it were. I'm sure that with your persuasive gifts you would be able to ensure that you avoided that, for the sake perhaps of more confidential duties."

This had not occurred to her. Suddenly the scene ten years ago at Præneste was filling her mind, and abject terror was on her. She found herself clenching her stomach muscles to avoid crying out; she could feel a deep shudder beginning, and struggled to compose herself. She focused on Theodorus' face, clinging to the need not to show him weakness, not to allow herself to crack. Determinedly she drove her mind elsewhere, and heard herself speak in a voice that was almost normal. "What about Cormerick?" What about Sallienus and Atra, what would come of all they had done there?

"Ah, yes, your little estate. I left a message for the governor in May suggesting your brother's treason, but I gather that he has been reluctant to act upon it because of your family connections. Still, with the aid of this letter I should be able to secure action by the Privy Domain, which is of course entitled to the property of condemned persons...

"Unless of course anyone successfully petitions the Emperor for such an estate. I'm sure I cannot imagine who might. Though it would probably be rash for anyone to do such a thing in the current situation, at any rate until we are quite sure who is to be Emperor next year." Theodorus gave a little, contented laugh. "Ah, well, enough of these conjectures. It is nearly time for our meeting with my friends. It shouldn't take too long to reach the rendezvous. Shall we set off?"

A blackness sat all about her, like a bad dream. Theodorus hoisted himself up on his horse, swinging clear away from her for a moment, and picked up the reins. As he did so, there was a sudden whizzing sound, and giving out a cry he pitched straight forward over the horse's shoulder. Startled, the animal trotted a few paces and then stopped, looking idly round. Theodorus twisted on the ground, trying to sit up. "Brigea, help me!" he prayed to some god through clenched teeth. Each time he breathed in he moaned.

Flavia could see a feathered quarrel protruding from his shoulder, and bright red already beginning to stain into his chestnut cloak. She looked round, feeling the long sobs of releasing pain already starting to clutch at her throat. About forty yards away, closing the distance fast, Arctus was running towards them, carrying in his left hand his crossbow, and in the other a short hunting spear.

CHAPTER 7

'"*So this nation, gathering all its powers, made a bid at one time to enslave not only your country and ours, but all the lands within the Straits. It was then, Solon, that the manhood of your country showed itself conspicuous for valour and courage in the sight of all the world.*"' So ran Plato's story of Atlantis; but would the Romans, would the Britains, be as fortunate this time and avoid being overrun? So Flavia asked herself, as they made their way down from the hills through valleys full of frantic activity: lines of people were scything down wheat and barley and sometimes coming to blows over whose was to be reaped first, while the air was full of wood and peat smoke from kilns set to dry prematurely-harvested grain.

They were able to turn off at Rotherham before reaching Doncaster, and joined the route of their northward journey at Bawtry. Again they crossed the river Trisantona at Segelocum, and past Scampton joined the road from Petuaria and turned due south. The road now ran down the narrow spine of the Lincoln Edge, just to the east of its summit, giving a view over the miles of flat-lands and salt-marshes to a spacious bay, with the fortified port of Bannovalum lying under chalk hills in the distance, its harbour crowded with shipping. On one occasion they saw what might have been Saxon boats in the Wash; three times an ugly black smoke rose far away, once on the north coast, and twice behind the Edge to the west.

At last they could see the city of Lincoln again. From this elevated approach it was not as spectacular as from the south, but it was still by far the largest city on their journey, and its extensive walls were impressive. Perhaps they had impressed the barbarians: at least, there was no sign of major damage to the suburbs, though four individual houses they passed on the road showed signs of fire or looting, and the towers and walls seemed thick with soldiers, while workmen were felling trees to the west, perhaps to deprive attackers of cover or firewood.

"We must be circumspect here, Flavia," Arctus reminded her. This kind of protectiveness still irritated her, and she thought that he had become more so towards her since Buxton, as if his rescuing her, or perhaps his confidences to her there about his illegitimacy, had given him a right to it. It seemed paradoxical, but perhaps they had. Certainly the two of them, in discussing their route, had already gone over the question of how to act when approaching Lincoln: the danger of Sanctus' troops being on the watch for them (minimal), or of actually meeting him (remote), and his likely reaction if they did meet (unpredictable).

Carried with a throng of people, they made their way unchallenged around the walls, and getting down to the Witham found a group of soldiers from the crack Second Legion stopping all traffic. These carried spears each tipped with a foot-long iron shaft and a barbed head, like the ancient *pilum*, and wore corselets of scale armour and bronze helmets with white crests, matching the white symbol set against green on their oval shields.

"Halt!" cried a swarthy young soldier, striding towards them. "All private horses are being requisitioned for the use of the army. I must ask you to give up these animals."

"I am the Most Perfect Count Arctus, and I have important business. I will not give up these horses."

The soldier looked at them. Flavia wondered if he was weighing the significance of her presence against the undeniable motifs of rank that Arctus was wearing on his cloak. She felt a pang. She had grown fond enough of the strong and docile mare that Lucilla had given her in

Buxton, but Hipponoë was a different matter: she had been with them all their journey together, and Flavia knew that Arctus had had her for years. She had grown used to her foibles, and she felt a sense of curiously keen outrage at this proposal, almost as if something more than the loss of a horse was in prospect. Seeing the soldier pause, his officer came over, resplendent with gold inlay on his helmet. "What's up, Delphinus?" he asked.

"Gentleman won't give up his horses as per orders, sir."

"Very well." He turned to Arctus, unhurried, assured. "I'm sorry, my Lord, but you're aware of the present situation. Unless you can show a specific Imperial warrant for duty in the current emergency I must ask you to surrender your horses. You'll be in no danger if you wish to go into the city: it's only twenty minutes away at most, and you and your wife will be quite safe behind the walls."

Flavia repressed her anger. She looked at the panniers holding all their luggage, including the leather tent, and wondered how on earth they would manage without Hipponoë and her own beast. Arctus showed his postal warrant, but the officer was not impressed. Arctus tried again: "Many people would give a good deal of money to hang on to a horse like this one..."

But the officer laughed this off. "I must ask you to start unloading the animals now, sir, or we shall have to take them and your baggage as well."

Arctus began to unstrap the panniers, and with help from Flavia managed to get them off quickly. The soldiers led Hipponoë and her stall-mate away. "I couldn't try and insist, Flavia," said Arctus. "It might easily have led to us being taken into the city and brought before Sanctus."

"Don't worry," she said, and smiled at him, unable to resist adding in Cicero's words "*'Law is dumb in time of war'*". Inwardly she was so angry that she was finding it hard not to weep. It was very bad luck to lose the horses now, having come so far but with quite a distance still to go; and it tore at her heart to lose Hipponoë.

They set off along the riverside towpath for nearly half a mile to the start of the fenland canal, laboriously going to and fro with the baggage so as to keep it in sight all the time. Already here it was less busy, and they then set to hump the loads up to a more secluded point past the first lock, intending to sort through it in the morning, and set off with the little they could comfortably carry. It was now late in the day, and they came across a number of abandoned barges. The waterway was deserted, and shielded from the sight of the city by a spinney. They searched about carefully before choosing a boat that seemed fairly dry and relatively comfortable, then gratefully set down the heavy bags in it and camped for the night.

The next day Flavia woke at early dawn, rocking unfamiliarly, to see Arctus regaining his balance, having just stepped back down after a visit to the bank. He stopped, and seeing her awake said, "Flavia! There are poles in the boat! I wonder what else there is."

Flavia sat up, little interested, reached down into the water and rubbed her eyes with it. Meanwhile Arctus found a large locker under the rear thwart and half-disappeared in it, emerging with coils of rope and the end of a large piece of cloth. He pulled the fabric right out, and rummaged further, finding wooden pins and pegs, a paddle about five feet long, a net and a leather water-bottle. He examined them carefully. "I think this boat may be very useful," he said. "We have a punting pole, a mast, a yard and a sail, in addition to a fishing net. This could be a much easier way of going wherever we want than walking." They made a meagre breakfast and discussed what to do. Then, making new plans, they cast off the little yawl and set out down the canal.

The next few days were quiet and idyllic. The waterway was nowhere far away from the Wash, and in this section no more than thirty-five feet wide. It had usually been busy, Flavia recalled, since weather was such a hazard on the open sea. But now hardly a boat was to be seen. The canal did not only carry traffic, but was a drain for the area to the west, which its high banks also protected against tidal floods. These dykes shielded Flavia and Arctus from sight on both sides, and they passed cocooned through a troubled land.

At some places the banks were damaged by tree-growth, or silt had made it scrapingly shallow; at one, beavers or otters had undermined the edges. But everywhere the route was too important to have been left in decay, and corvées had evidently grubbed out infill and rebuilt mounds. The few people they passed were in terror of the Attacotti and the Saxons, but near Sleaford they found a work-gang still busy maintaining sluices and repairing winter frost damage. They bought the services of two men to punt them for a ten-mile stretch, relieving Arctus' aching and still-unaccustomed muscles.

The fifth day on the canal was a Saturday, and from early morning Flavia began to see familiarity in the pottery-buildings coming into sight, though the banks were ominously empty of people and livestock. After a while the boat began to push sluggishly against weeds, but continued to make progress. Eventually they won their way to the wharves. The sheds were burned to stumps, and there were two great barges charred down to the waterline. Flavia jumped out and secured the painter. Arctus hopped to the bank, and the two of them hauled the yawl to the side and made it fast to the staithes. Here they were about three miles from Durobrivæ, but the town was hidden by a thick belt of trees.

They concealed their packs and set off cautiously through the woods, which to begin with were mainly elm, ash and elder. After they crossed a stream there came a loud roaring about them. They stopped, and it ceased. Then they realised that as they moved they disturbed clouds of little flies feeding on the flower-strings trailing from the nettles on each side of the path, flies like small translucent green bees, which buzzed angrily until the intruders went on and they could settle again.

However, perhaps a hundred yards further on they

found a different kind of fly clustering. Investigating while the bluebottles crowded round their heads, they discovered the corpse of a man lying face up, half-hidden under a bramble bush. The red shift he was dressed in was torn at the neck, showing a ragged tear in the shoulder lying wide open; and the grass and moss below were black with blood.

Arctus took Flavia's hand for a moment, putting his finger to his lips, and they went on. Gradually the forest changed; willow and oak became more common, and the nettles and their denizens died away.

Soon they found themselves coming towards the edge of the woodland, and suddenly heard loud voices speaking a strange, guttural language. They moved quietly and carefully away from these sounds, and then edged forward until the city came in sight through the trees: they could see armed men moving around the suburbs, and one house and then another kindling in smoke and flames as they watched.

They froze: but nobody seemed to be nearby, and the city itself seemed safe: men stood guard on the battlements, and as they watched a catapult bolt flew from one of the towers and landed somewhere behind a suburban building, while distant men and horses came into view scattering from its path. They took each other's hands again, and Flavia murmured in Arctus' ear, "Let's get away."

They moored again in the river Farcet, where it joined the canal, drawing the boat in under overhanging elder-bushes. As she pressed ahead up the rise below Cormerick, images crowded Flavia's mind: the late summer garden with its luxuriant growth of purple asters and scabious; the slave-boy with a scythe, and the smell of mown grass; her study, pregnant with the rich life of its books, a volume lying open at a picture of a woman waiting for her lover, the dust dancing in the warm sunbeams above; evening on the lawn with Titus or Tranquilia Severa, the murmur of insects and the cups of good Gallic wine. And fear was there too: of accidental fire, of riots by frightened tenants, of barbarians destroying, destroying, as they had seen in Second Britain. Was there a scent of smoke in the air, that acrid smoke that meant destruction? Or was it a false memory of the Pennines?

She reached the crest, but could not see the house: it was still concealed by a copse of hazel and willow, and by banks of thorn and honeysuckle grown full and bushy through the summer. She made herself wait until Arctus caught up, with long regular strides, and they approached the thickets together. Her mind now was on her books, on the long afternoons spent poring over them: the work on Plato, the comparisons of the *Timæus* with the *Critias* and the *Republic* and the *Laws*, the meditations on Plotinus and Longinus and Porphyry; but also the time spent hunting down other paths, absorbed in Galen's or Soranus' descriptions of medicine, lost in Virgil or the Greek poets, or diverting herself rather guiltily with Heliodorus' romance or Lucian's satirical stories.

As they finally came round the edge of the bushes they saw the first wisps. The house must have finished burning only some hours before, for a little smoke was still rising. The walls had already mostly collapsed. Flavia walked up slowly to the ruins. Odds and ends lay about where they had fallen in the disintegration of the building, or in the act of removing them.

This was the stables, she thought, coming to the nearest remains. They had mainly been of timber, with hay in the lofts, and there was little left. Somewhere here must have been Ario's stall, and here Xerxes'. Argulus had looked after the old horse kindly; she wondered if he had been able to get away. She began to feel a sort of numbness coming over her.

Her feet seemed to take her onward of their own accord, and soon she was standing by the sewing-room looking straight into the courtyard through what ought to be walls. She stepped over the stub of stones with difficulty; the ground was uneven, with charred bits of flooring, and she could soon feel the ashes working their way in between her foot and her sandal. She remembered her mother long ago: "You must get your back-stitch tighter than this, Flavia, if you're going to get a neat result. You may not always have slaves to do it for you, you know," while all the while she herself, ungratefully contemptuous of needlework, only longed to get back to Ovid's *Metamorphoses*. She thought of the afternoons which Atra had spent here more recently, pretending to sew and mend, when her eyesight was no longer good enough and it really had to be left to Prudentia.

The only substantial piece of wall still standing was on the right side of the courtyard, and she picked her way across. She stood on the stained and broken remnants of the verandah flooring. In the main kitchen behind a fallen beam she could still make out remains of the brick cooking range, and there and in the scullery twisted iron utensils; she recognised a cake-mould which had always been used on her birthday. In the next room, the pantry, the fire had been hot, and there was little to see; the next again had been the still-room, and the fused fragments of glass on the ground suddenly brought back hours of studying herbs, hunting and picking them, and then heating them and floating off the essential oil for perfume or for medicine. She felt increasingly as though she were someone else. Then with dismay she realised that she had been avoiding remembering the library.

Her study had been at the opposite side of the peristyle, on the southern corner, and she knew already that there was nothing left standing there. But she found herself walking across to it, over the courtyard gravel which was almost the same as it had always been. She stepped up onto the verandah and looked into the remains of the room. It was a jumble of broken brick and charred timber. She could identify a corner of her desk, always carefully varnished with Mauretanian gum sandarach, the desk where she had spent so much of her life since her return from Præneste; but that was all. No trace of books was to be seen.

She stepped blankly to the right, into the garden. Heavy objects had been dragged through the lawn and the flower-beds, tearing them up, but she scarcely took it in. A scene played itself back again and again in her mind, of a time when she must have been about five. She had sat just here by the stream under the cherry-tree, surrounded by its white blossoms, while Titus, ten years old and so proud of his reading skills, had carefully shown her a little illustrated book and slowly read out stories from it. The language had been elevated and mysterious, but very beautiful, and she had been mesmerised by the rhythm of the poetry against the noise of the running water, and by the solemn attention of her brother.

Arctus had kept a respectful distance, but now came up. "Flavia..." he said, but she did not reply. He reached out and grasped her shoulders, and she looked up as if she did not recognise him, then tightened her mouth and started to try to respond.

"Arctus," she began desolately, and then stopped, not knowing how to go on.

"There are other buildings a furlong or so to the east, which are also destroyed," he said.

"That's the home farm," she said. She hunched her shoulders, covering her mouth with her hands, breathed in deeply, and raised her head, blowing out the breath, then tossed her hair back. "There's little point in going over to the stud-farm, I think. Let's make for the house of a neighbour and see how things are there: it'll take about an hour."

"We must be very careful," he remarked. "This was done recently: they can't be far away."

Flavia pointed the direction. "Æneas said to his followers, '*You have endured worse, and God will grant an end even to this.*' " The sentiment seemed quite unreal to her, she knew as she spoke it, but at least it was some kind of claim on proper behaviour, and a link with normality. They picked their way from the ruins and set out. The last time she had trodden this path, on the way to the festival of the Good Goddess, she had been in another world. Now the familiar route to Aculeius' house ran through a strange, deserted country, its fields of spelt and barley half-harvested, and full of undisturbed partridges and buntings feasting on the corn. They stopped at a cottage, and then another, but pushing through the doors found them empty: one looked as if it had been disturbed, perhaps only by foxes.

Nevertheless, Aculeius' house was occupied, for as they approached they could see everything in order: haystacks built tall and carefully thatched for the winter, stable-boys cleaning harness in the yard, chimneys smoking domestically.

Coming up to the door they found a massive soldier in full armour standing in the porch, but as he smirked and started to put out his hand for a tip Pappitedo, the steward, pushed past and waddled out to meet them, dressed unseasonably in a heavy dark grey robe with a light fur collar. "My dear Lady Flavia, what a relief to see you again!" he exclaimed, leading them indoors. "There has been no news of you at all since Philip returned, and with the terrible stories from all over the Britains we all feared the worst, the very worst. I am so pleased, so pleased, and the Lord Aculeius and Lady Severa will be enthralled at the news. *Ressona! Take the guests' bags and cloaks, wash their feet and bring them some refreshment: redcurrant water I think, and some of the spiced buns with raisins which were baked this morning for the soldiers.* Lady Flavia, who is your companion? I don't think we..."

"What has happened at Cormerick, Pappitedo? Where is everyone?" Flavia broke in urgently.

Pappitedo raised his hands. "Oh, my Lady, don't say you have been there? It's terrible, terrible, isn't it? But, my Lady, don't worry too much. It's bad enough, in all conscience, quite terrible destruction, such a beautiful building and the gardens, but all the rest of your property is safe. Yes, indeed, quite everything on the estate, and all the people as well."

Flavia forced herself to composure. "My dear Pappitedo, you're as kind as ever. When we saw what had happened to Cormerick we couldn't hope that Aculeius' estate had survived, and I am so glad that all is well here," she said, sitting down as the servant came in with a jug of warm water and an earthenware bowl, removed her heavy sandals and began to wash her feet with deft fingers and lavender-scented soap. Courtesy demanded introductions; they should not be further delayed. "This is the Most Perfect Count Arctus, of Bordeaux; Most Perfect Count, this is Pappitedo, the steward of Aculeius, who is bailiff of this estate on behalf of Our Lord Emperor."

"I could not say that all is well, my lady," continued Pappitedo, seemingly with hardly a pause, "but we are fortunate so far to have escaped the marauders' attention. It is such a tragedy that they reached Cormerick yesterday, when the house had survived so many months of these uncertain times. Your home, my lady! You must be quite distraught! I am so sorry that you should have seen it already. No doubt you stumbled upon it with no warning or preparation. Are you safe?" Distracted by her impatience to hear what had happened at Cormerick, and also by the blissful bathing of her feet, Flavia had trouble attending to these ramblings and making appropriate signals in response. "There were I trust none of the hooligans lurking there still? I hope not indeed. I sent two of the soldiers across there first thing this morning to check the place, for we saw the smoke late yesterday afternoon. It was one of the soldiers himself who saw it first. They are indeed most scrupulous men, and keep watch like eagles."

"Where do the soldiers come from? And where are they now?"

"Oh, they were sent from Augusta several weeks back now. It was an inspiration from the gods, from Jupiter himself I have no doubt. It was the Lord Aculeius and the Lady Tranquilia Severa. They went to Augusta before the end of July, and spoke with the Comptroller of the Privy Domain for the Britains, and such was their influence that they persuaded him to send a squad of soldiers to defend us against these pirates. The soldiers have met the Saxons more than once, Lady Flavia, and acquitted themselves most valiantly, they assure me. But they are *such* a burden. Nothing is too good for them, you know. I am *so* glad we are not in a frontier region and have to put up with this all the time; it makes managing the household quite impossible. You know they have done their best to safeguard other properties as well, Lady Flavia, and I am deeply sorry that they found it was not possible to protect Cormerick yesterday, but your stud-farm buildings have been spared, at least, and there is a limit to what can be done, you know. They cannot be everywhere at once, and they have been very industrious, very industrious."

"I am sure they have, Pappitedo," said Flavia, urgent within herself for news, but letting her body sit back on the couch now and nibble at a bun while the servant turned her attention to Arctus. "But what has happened to everyone at Cormerick?"

"Why, it was Sallienus, Lady Flavia, it was all his doing. Let me see, it was around the nones of July that we heard of the attacks in the north and the west, and I remember Sallienus across here one evening saying that he would surprised if this would be the last of it and that this time would be a bad one. He said, you know, that he had spoken to a wise-woman who had seen a sea-eagle mobbed and killed by gulls, out on Riduna Island in the Wash, and that she had said that it presaged a defeat of the Romans by the Saxons. So he had made plans before ever we had news that the Saxons had landed at Caister and Colchester, and started to put them into effect, too. We told him he was foolish, and that you would not be pleased when you returned, but it turns out that we were wrong, I don't mind admitting it.

"So when it finally happened, around the Nones of August, before the news came of them even at Chichester, pretty well everything was packed up. Luonercus, now, who was in charge of the home farm, he turned out a bad lot, and just ran off, I'm afraid. But Sallienus left a letter for you. I'll go and look for it now. Oh, but no, now, there's your guest that arrived all those months ago!" He clutched at his forehead. "How could I have been forgetting him? Oh, Lady Flavia, you'll want to be seeing him at once. He's in a room, a nice room, in the west wing, come along."

Flavia looked up. "I think I'd rather look at Sallienus' letter first," she said. Pappitedo's brow creased, and he went off, muttering. She looked at Arctus. "I don't know who this guest could be. But I wonder whether it could be the mysterious Tiotagus, that poor Titus sent here," she said, with a glint in her eye.

Pappitedo returned with a letter. "Here it is, Lady Flavia," he said, handing it to her. "You'll excuse me, if you don't mind; I must go and speak to the soldiers."

Flavia untied the string.

To the Most Perfect Lady Flavia Vindex from Sallienus, the third day before the ides of August, in the consulships of Fl. Lupicinus and Fl. Iovinus, the tenth year of the indiction, greetings.

Following rumours, firm information came some weeks ago of a great barbarian conspiracy for the destruction of the British provinces, and the day before yesterday there was news that Saxons had landed at Yarmouth and at Colchester. We have done our best to secure the estate. The stock and most of the staff went off almost four weeks ago to your cousin's in First Britain, which I judge to be much safer than here; with luck and the blessing of the gods they will be there by now, though there will necessarily be some losses on the journey.

I had planned to send most of the other servants and movables there too, but news is of Picts and Attacotti moving very fast, and it may not be safe, so they have gone to London instead, and I am now setting out to join them there myself. I took enough gold for our needs – a fair amount, for there are many mouths to be fed – but will not take more. There is a lot, since as you will remember I called in debts in case we needed to ransom the Lord Titus, so for safety I have buried the rest in an amphora on the south side of the tree which your brother planted on the day he came of age (you will know the place, but no-one else).

Aculeius assures me that he will keep his estate occupied, and plans in London to arrange with the Comptroller of the Privy Domain to have guards sent. We had a visitor not long after you left, and Aculeius has kindly agreed to let him stay with them to await your return. And by his leave we have left in his buildings as much as we could not move: most of the barley and spelt harvests that we managed to get in, and some bulky items such as cupboards, tables and curtains. I hope that I have done right, including in sending the letter on to Carlisle.

Farewell.

Flavia felt a great relief: the people she was close to seemed safe. It was important that they had saved so much of the property too, and it seemed to her that she felt this not out of selfishness or avarice but because it was the basis of their way of life, both her own and the entire household's. And what a hero was Sallienus! Though the house had been destroyed, her home was still intact. It seemed to be an omen, a symbol of herself, and the news made her feel whole and protected. But would she and hers remain so safe? She passed the letter to Arctus for him to look at, and called Pappitedo. "I should like to see the guest now, please," she said.

He took her out to a courtyard, apologising, and in at another door. "He's not been at all well, of course, you'll know that he was in a poor state of health, and he had to be brought here from Cormerick on a litter. I thought he would be better off in the wing here where there is more peace and quiet." It was a roughly plastered corridor, and he opened a door and stood aside.

"Thank you," she said in a dismissive voice, and went in. On a bed lay a young man, propped up on two pillows. A girl was sitting on his bed, a slave in a loose dress, her pendulous breasts half out of it; he had his hand on her wrist, as if to stop her from getting up. He evidently saw Flavia's entrance out of the corner of his eye and suddenly turned to face her, letting go of the slave and batting dismissively at her arm.

This was certainly unexpected. Flavia studied him. He looked rather pale and wasted, about eighteen years old, in a light shift square-cut and embroidered at the neck, with lank dark hair and rather too bright pale blue eyes; and only slightly embarrassed. "They tell me you're a scholar," she said in a dubious voice.

"You'll be the Most Perfect Lady Flavia Vindex," he guessed aloud, perhaps in case she might correct him. His voice was slightly shrill, and he spoke Latin with a respectable accent. He raised himself slightly on his pillows. "You have me at a disadvantage, madam. My name is Tiotagus. I'm not sure how much you know of me. But you should know that I'm a prince of a not insignificant house, where I come from, and we are grateful to you for your hospitality."

"So you are Tiotagus," she said. "I should have

expected you to arrive earlier. You're the son of the High King of the Northern Picts, I understand." What was all this about illness? Still, he was in bed, and looked sickly: it was consistent. But the picture of him in Titus' letter had been of a studious young philosopher, not a pompous, lecherous asthenic. For a moment her sense of tiredness and disappointment quickened to nausea, and then through a fog of emotion and unwelcome novelty, through a sense of all she had been through to find this at the end, his patronising and self-important words began to register.

She found herself filling with pent-up indignation. "Your rank is petty," she replied. "Do you know who my grandfather was? He was Lucius Aradius Valerius Proculus *signo* Populonius, Augur, Senior Pontiff, one of the Fifteen for the Performance of the Rites, Flavial Pontiff, Tutelary Prætor, Regulator of the Census in Gallæcia, Governor of Numidia and also of Byzacena, Consular of Europa with Thrace and also of Sicily, Count of the First Class, Proconsul of Africa, Vicar of Africa, Prefect of the City of Rome, and Consul." Not since she had been a child had she boasted of her family like this, but she could not feel that it was unwarranted: as she recited the dignities and offices her own spirit, so trampled by its defeats and degradations, filled against the young man, lifted and took on vigour again; and she saw with satisfaction the dismay coming into his eyes.

He raised himself up further on his pillows, and inclined his head. "I beg your pardon, Lady. I did not intend to presume."

Now behind Flavia stood King Numa, Quintus Scævola, the Twelve Tables. "I gather from my brother, who is dead, that he did you a service, and that you can yet be of service to the Emperor."

Tiotagus peered anxiously at her stony face. "I did not believe he was dead," he said quietly, looking away. "I am very sorry. He was a good companion, and a good man."

Flavia gave a dry, conditional smile, and sat down on the bed. "You had better tell me about it," she said.

Tiotagus dropped his hands in his lap. "It's a long story. But you seem to know that Titus saved me from being sent home. You spoke about my being a scholar... I suppose I led him on a bit about that; I'm keen on rhetoric, certainly, but I'm no philosopher. But I've no intention of going back to Caledonia if I can help it, when I could stay in Trier or Argentoratum with all that a great city has to offer. To be quite frank, I am betrothed to a lady, as well." He suddenly burst into a coughing fit, and started to make a whooping noise for a few breaths, then controlled it and took a drink from a cup on a bedside table.

"So I'm immensely grateful to your brother. I was effectively kidnapped by an agent called Venocarus, and it was Titus' doing that I escaped. He took me to a place where the Gala Water joins the Tweed and put me in the hands of a Votadin trader and fisherman." He paused for a moment. "He expected me to be in Cormerick within a week or two; but we had bad weather, and then I grew very ill. I think that the Votadin expected me to die; I did myself at one stage. But the result was that we had to wait for several months. At last I recovered enough to resume the journey, and eventually made it to this part of the world." He paused again, but Flavia was silent. "At Cormerick I had a relapse, and wasn't well enough to go to Augusta with Sallienus, though he urged me to make the effort. Happily, Pappitedo agreed to take me in and await your hoped-for return. And I've been improving here ever since."

This, thought Flavia, was a disappointingly prosaic tale. But it was still important to get the man back to Trier, as living evidence of Titus's loyalty. At least he seemed properly grateful for what had been done for him; perhaps he did take advantage of slave-girls, but that was only a minor discourtesy to his host, something that men would usually do when they could. "Are you well enough to travel now?" Though he wouldn't think he was, otherwise he'd scarcely still be in bed.

"Not really, I'm afraid."

"I know a little of medicine. I'll have a look at you tomorrow. But you're obviously aware of your obligations to my family, and you can imagine the kind of dangers we might be in at present. I expect to leave shortly to go to Augusta. But after the current disorders are sorted out I shall require you to report to the authorities, either in

Augusta or, better, in Trier, and make clear the part Titus had in preserving you from returning to your family, and hence in discouraging the rebellion of your people."

"Very well, Most Perfect Lady."

"Swear it."

He placed his hand on his breast. "I swear it by the gods of my own people, and by Mercury."

"Very good." Flavia's stern features softened into a tired smile, and Tiotagus gave a relieved grin. "You had better write it to me as a letter, too; I may need it in Augusta. I'll have pen, ink and tablets sent in. Get some rest. I'll see you tomorrow."

Flavia left the room and went out of doors, pausing in thought for a little. Then she went down to the little temple of the Good Goddess, and offered a prayer of thanks. Behind a clump of box-bushes grown there for the purpose she took her clothes off, and then slipped into the river-pool.

The pool was quite large, and she swam vigorously, and began to feel her first composure slip, and underlying anxieties surface. For so long now, she had lived at Cormerick. She had been born in that house, and grown up there. After her mother had left, no, perhaps ever since her father's death, she had ruled the household, a place where everyone looked to her. She had kept the stud-farm going, and built it up. She had laboured there for years over her books. Her home, her household and her books had seemed all she had and all she was: now they were all gone, and what would become of her? Images from the past entered her mind again: her father telling her to marry and her sullen refusal; her mother announcing with triumph her aunt's invitation to go and live in Constantinople; Titus packing his things to go to London.

Then the Goddess whispered in her ear, and her world began to be lit from another quarter. She saw that her book was written, and finished, and safe in her bags. She saw that the stud-farm was thriving, even though its horses and people were elsewhere for now. She saw that the work she had done for the household had indeed borne fruit, and that her achievement had been kept intact in its time of danger. True, Titus had gone north and Titus was dead; true, her grandfather's house was burned. But, though the gods had sent these things to her, nevertheless, through her and her people, in the midst of destruction, they had saved what she had done. There was a link, perhaps, with what had happened earlier: she herself had been hurt to the core at Præneste, yet she had defied that and built things: she had done her duty and done it well. It was time now to acknowledge this, and to make it her own.

A sense of new strength flowed into her, and she understood that in this dangerous and vulnerable world she was herself active and robust, and had her own power, a power that lived in her and was not dependent. Unbidden, the image of Arctus came to her, his warm eyes and the patient, mischievous smile that seemed to give her permission to laugh at herself. She recognised that another thing that she had built over the last months was her friendship with him. That might or might not endure, but it was now quite clear that it still wanted fulfilment. Choosing to endorse it fully, she thought, would mark her acceptance of the whole, and she newly found within herself – familiar, to her surprise, as if it had been there for ever – a sense of freedom and of strength to give and receive that endorsement. She smiled to herself.

She paused at the turf altar, and kissed it, having nothing else to offer to the river god. Then she crossed the stream and emerged, dried herself on her gown, cut a few strands from the ends of her hair, and laid them before the shrine of the Good Goddess, pausing a moment in prayer.

She went back indoors, and told Arctus of her interview with Tiotagus. They dined well on samphire omelette, a spit-roast hen and fresh loaves and honey-cakes, with, for the first time since Buxton, good Gallic wine. It had been a hot day, Sunday, the fifth day before the Ides of September, and as the long dusk began to fall they went out to wander in the garden. Cool breezes blew in the warm dark, and soon they found themselves out of sight of the house on the edge of an apple-orchard, the trees now heavy with fruit.

They looked up at the sky as the stars became visible, and Flavia traced the constellations. Pisces was just rising. It was a dark night, with no moon, and no obvious planets, and though her sidereal calendar was lost she thought she remembered that Saturn would be near the south-western horizon if the visibility was good, probably in Scorpio or Ophiuchus. She wondered if it was true that she had her own star, and whether it was somewhere there in that night sky.

"Do you believe in astrology?" she asked.

"No," Arctus replied with a smile.

"I used to be so fascinated by it," said Flavia. "I had copies of the books of Nechepso-Petosiris and Hermes Trismegistos, and I studied intensively for three years, after I came back from Rome. I cast horoscopes, especially my own and Titus', until I was perfect at it. But do you know that the seven planetary spheres, in their order from us, carry the Moon, Mercury, Venus, the Sun, Mars, Jupiter and Saturn, and that the astrologers follow that order; while the Babylonians, who originally invented astrology, thought they had a quite different sequence: Moon, Sun, Jupiter, Venus, Mercury, Saturn, Mars? It was when I discovered that that I started to doubt the truth of astrology."

"What do you mean? Why?"

"Because, when the astrologers discovered that the real sequence of the planets was different from their assumptions, they didn't vary their methods or the mechanics of the calculations. They only altered the results to fit. The whole basis of the science assumes that the astrology of the Babylonians was a perfect insight into the workings of the world. It doesn't make sense that, after the planets were known to have a quite different order, you could cast a horoscope for the same person in the same way and end up with the same results."

"So you don't believe in it any more?"

"No. I think I was comforted for a while by the idea that the stars controlled our every action – if everything was fated, it meant I didn't have to feel responsible for what I had done, or what had happened to me. But in the end I grew disgusted with myself, and decided that one can't just shrug off responsibility for things. One has to confront one's own actions. As Phlegyas says to the damned in the *Æneid*, *Learn to be just and not to slight the gods!*" She twisted her mouth a little and laughed rather ruefully. "But I still sometimes feel that the dinner-party astrologers are right when they say, for example, that someone born under Virgo is meticulous or someone born under Leo is mercurial: that does often seem to be true."

She felt his hand on her arm and turned towards him. She put her hands on his belt, pulling him closer, and giving her an unfathomable glance he wrapped his arms about her and hugged her. "Let's go to bed together tonight," she murmured. "I think I feel different, now." They turned, and hand in hand went back to the house. Pappitedo was waiting up for them, and gave them a night-drink of wine mixed with honey, cinnamon and poppy-seeds.

While he went to bar the doors they started upstairs, and both went into Arctus' room. Flavia's attention was on him, but she was at first also dimly aware of the yellow paint on the walls, a chest and some hooks for clothes, an upholstered stool, a wash-stand, a low bed. Arctus turned and took her by the elbows, looking into her eyes, his gaze assuring her of himself, asking if she was ready. In herself she felt affection, desire, a slight habitual sense of challenge: a need to overcome the fear she had felt before, and a feeling of trust in herself that she would; a need not to be taken for granted. Arctus opened his mouth as if to say something, and then, surprising her with his suddenness, crushed her to him and kissed her hard. Equally suddenly he released her, bent, picked up the finely-embroidered bedspread, all reds and greens, and threw it into a corner.

She felt herself responding instantly to his kiss, with a suddenly-awoken desperation to be closer to him, yet at the same time a hard bubble of excited fear seemed to rise from nowhere and lodge in the pit of her chest. She reached to her brooch and let her cloak fall to the ground. He came back to her and held her again, more gently this time, and she loosened his own cloak before losing herself in kissing him. Then he was taking out the pins at her shoulders, and her dress was brushing roughly past her nipples; she felt a brief involuntary shudder as its fall left her naked, unable to identify what she felt, trying to focus on the strength of her desire. He ran his hand up and down her back, pushing her stomach in against the brasses and hard leather of his four-inch deep military belt. She pressed him away for a second and hauled at the belt to undo it, not quite possessed of the person who was suddenly laughing at him: "Little gods, how do you manage to wear a thing like this all day and every day!" He disengaged the *cingulum*, and awkwardly hauled the shoulder cross-strap over his head; she pushed up his red woollen tunic at the same time, and he pulled that off as well.

"Come on!" he smiled, pulling her down on to the bed. They lay for a moment in each other's arms, adjusting to the shock of each others' bodies after so long a forbidden awareness, then threw themselves hungrily at each other. Her senses swam with the feel of his skin, and with the desire running through her; and she drew the intensity of his smell into her, familiar and secure from so many months on the road together, lulled by the reassuring growl of his voice, until she realised that the hard little bubble of fear in her chest had disappeared. She felt herself rolling onto her back; he held himself away for a moment, but quick and wordless she pulled him on top of her: a thrill rushed all through her. As she returned to awareness of the world she realised that she had been crying out, and that Arctus too was already finished, the burden of him heavy but comforting.

They lay for a long time wordlessly. After a time he shifted his weight a little so that in part it was taken by the bed, and his breathing became regular. Her mind began contentedly to drift free. It stopped at a phrase of Plutarch's, 'the act of sex is the beginning of friendship, a sharing, as it were, in great mysteries'. It waited for a moment, idling relaxed and free, and moved on to Sappho. 'I prayed that for us the night could be twice as long' she thought, and then leaned over and kissed his eye where it joined the nose, and murmured the words aloud. He smiled, and moved up, kissing her on the mouth, then settling again. She lay with a dreamy sense of completion as well as satiety, though hazily aware perhaps, as she fell asleep, that in a remote part of her mind a new secret arena was beginning to open, one where a new Flavia, rearmed after many years, was preparing to arise and crush old ghosts.

Once in the night, their appetite once more slaked, Flavia found herself hovering again on the edge of sleep when Arctus spoke quietly: "We shall need to decide what to do tomorrow."

Lost in her satisfaction, and in a sense of other things redeemed, she replied with no more than a grunt, just enough to signal her wakefulness. But after a pause he continued, slowly, perhaps thinking aloud; his attention, she gratefully remarked as she emerged from her reverie, was focused on her own concerns. "There's surely nothing to stay for at Cormerick for the moment," he murmured, "and little other point in stopping here." She felt his chest vibrating with the gentle rumble of his speech. "I think your main problem is the safety of your estate. If Faber's rebellion were to succeed, then it would clearly be vulnerable: Theodorus may be out of the way, but he presumably wasn't the only person to know about Titus and Cormerick, and others could make the same accusations and claims."

She stretched out her legs, and rubbed her cheek against his shoulder. "You mention him in the past tense, but he may have survived," she muttered. "That kind of wound isn't invariably fatal, and there were some good doctors in Buxton."

He pursued his thought. "But, either way, if someone took such action, there would be nothing you could do about it other than get yourself away before you were arrested."

But who was to say the insurrection would succeed? "Most rebellions seem to fail, as Magnentius' did a few years ago. It may not be a bad risk to take."

"No, but even if Faber were successful only for a while, and only in the Britains, you would still be in danger yourself. People might be after the estate, and the estate might survive to a restoration of order after a usurpation, but if you were in the way you would be at risk." She felt him turn to face her, and opened her eyes, seeing his expression, grown serious, in the flickering shadows thrown by a single candle across the room. She felt herself smile, simply with gratitude for his concern. "And even if the current authorities have so far taken no action against you, you do need to lodge some kind of effective official claim of Titus' loyalty."

She focused on the problem, pressing aside self-indulgence. Maybe Dagwald, the head of the *arcani*, could be relied upon to sort that out, but that could scarcely be taken for granted. Who knew what agendas he might have? She laid her left hand on Arctus' cheek. "You're right," she said. "I need to lodge an authoritative affidavit from Tiotagus. I doubt that he should be moved at present, so he can't go in person. I've thought of that, so I've already asked him for a letter, and that will have to do for now. I can present it to the office of the Vicar of the Britains at Augusta. It'd need to be followed up later. But though the soldiers just here now are few, they seem reliable enough. Surely they'd be unlucky not to hold off casual Saxon raiders: Tiotagus ought to be safe where he is until he's needed."

"Flavia, my love, I don't think that's good enough. You can't trust people's loyalty at Augusta, I think, not even right now, let alone at some time in the future, when Faber may have succeeded in carrying sentiment there. Or he may have done that already, for all we know. Much better than going to Augusta would be to go straight to the Prætorian Prefect of the Gauls at Trier. Besides, an affidavit by itself won't be enough, in the end: the authorities will want Tiotagus himself as soon as they can get him, for he'll surely be a negotiating counter for them to use with the Pictish king. In fact they'll ask why he wasn't sent back to them at once. You'll need to be able to show that if you kept him here it was for good reason, if you want to be seen as truly loyal."

Flavia remembered the ashes of Cormerick, and all the people from there who still depended on her. She could not abandon them and leave the Britains, not even for Arctus. "There's the translation as well," she objected. "Sallienus is in London with it."

"You have your own copy. And the best possible place to publish would be Trier, the seat of the Imperial court, where your work would become most easily known, since communications with the rest of the Empire will be the best there are."

These arguments were very plausible, Flavia thought. But she knew Arctus was eager to get back to Gaul; perhaps still he would seize at any straw to persuade her. She felt somewhere that she should not give way, and began to feel impatient. "I don't know," she said. "Let's decide in the morning."

"Delay brings delay," he said, "and if we leave it till the morning we may not reach a decision. It would be sensible to cross to Gaul straightaway. I know that the yawl we found isn't the most seaworthy of craft, but I understand sailing. I'm sure we can make it safely."

Flavia put her hand over his mouth, then suddenly shifted down the bed and begun to lick the insides of his thighs. He laughed. "I'll tell you what, though," he managed to utter, though increasingly impeded by his own moans, "it's not a good idea to go anywhere overland now. We could go to Augusta in the boat and decide..." He could not finish the sentence. Flavia raised herself and moved up the bed again, and prevented him speaking more by stopping his mouth with her own.

The next day they lingered in bed, and the morning was advanced when they went downstairs to a large living-room panelled in dark elm, with a fire of apple-wood burning brightly in a hearth. Pappitedo opened the door, a tall and chubby figure full of smiles, with a large tray of beer, eggs, fruit and bread. "*The eggs are this morning's,*" he announced, pleased with himself, lapsing into British in his excitement.

Eventually they announced that they would leave, resisted Pappitedo's blandishments to stay; accepted a slave to help with portage as far as the boat. Flavia gave Tiotagus the medical examination she had promised, taking his pulse and feeling his temperature, and judging his breath for depth and sweetness. She found him indeed on the mend, but not yet ready to travel. Then she took the letter giving evidence of his oath, and gave Pappitedo instructions for his care: "I should myself have chosen a somewhat different regimen. But if the treatment should be changed abruptly, there is a risk of some newer danger from the change. Continue as you have been, and allow him to rest. And see to it that he is served only by the older slaves, whose humours are more stable than those of the young." The last part of it was not strictly true, she thought, but would do the young man no harm.

By this time the morning was gone, and she and Arctus took a brief meal. At last they left, heading for the river, and trekked across the empty fields until they reached it; stowed their remaining baggage, and climbed into the boat.

Arctus glanced around to check that all the luggage was on board, and saw that the slave who had helped with it was already trudging home, looking anxiously about. He unmoored and pushed away from the bank, and began to punt slowly downstream.

They moved through the reeds in silence for a time, the peace broken only by the occasional kingfisher darting in little stages along the line of the waterway, or a flight of teal or scoters startled into the air. The day extended; they paused to take a drink and eat a little, snatching a long kiss or two, and continued. Gradually the dusk came down, and it grew chilly. Arctus guided the craft into the reeds, plunged the pole into the mud, and tied the painter to it. They snuggled together in the middle of the boat, and beneath the warm shelter of a rug found themselves raising each other's tunics and renewing their closeness of the night before.

Flavia was racing Titus on horseback on a great
estate in the hills somewhere west of Durobrivæ,
helter-skelter down a broad drove-road between
bramble hedges. Without warning, Xerxes threw
her; she lay in a roadside ditch staring through
delicate lilac-flowered stalks of vervain, while
German auxiliary troops started to camp nearby,
their language full of throaty gutturals, and of
sentences suspended looking for a sudden verb.
She tried to call for help, but nothing would come.

Flavia realised that she was awake, and that she really could hear strange voices, coupled with straining ropes. A ghostly hand closed over her heart: Saxons, she thought.

There was still no moon, but the sky was fairly clear of cloud and the stars gave light. Arctus was asleep. She saw his lips move silently, as if he were on the edge of murmuring. She put her hand over his mouth, and he started awake confused, to find her whispering urgently in his ear, forming the words with hardly a breath: "...Saxons, Saxons, Saxons, Arctus: wake up. Be quiet! Are you awake yet?"

CHAPTER 8

She peered through the reeds; she could make little out. Now the Saxons were gliding past upstream, only a few fathoms away. Again the *Timæus*, she thought: '*There have been and will be many different destructions of mankind. The greatest are by fire and by water, but there are other lesser ones by many other means.*' Torches, faintly and flickeringly, showed maybe a score of tall, burly figures shrouded in rough cloaks, and gleaming spear-heads. One of them seemed to have a huge scar all down the side of his face. She held her breath, suppressing her panic. Silently she prayed in Catullus' words, '*Grant me this, gods, for my piety's sake.*'

When they were quite out of sight, she and Arctus embraced, and rested in relief for a while. Then he stood up, freed the pole, and punted the boat forward a space. The tension ebbed, and Flavia felt her tiredness invading her again. The shock of so keen a danger had easily made her defenceless, she thought, and a memory occurred to her from many months ago at Cormerick, of thinking of life as a Saxon slave; she thought of Theodorus' plans for her, and her lip twitched. In the end, perhaps, what she had achieved at Cormerick was not enough: she needed the gods' healing for herself as well: robust she might be, and wholer of heart than before, but there was still something within her knotted up, that could suddenly unravel when she needed her strength most. She repeated the prayer she had made, and closed her eyes.

She realised she was arriving at the villa at
Præneste with Titus and Cæcina Priscus. They had
come out from Rome by carriage the previous day,
and stayed in the little city overnight while a
servant went ahead to ready the house. They had
marvelled at the town's towering citadel, at the
enormous temple of Fortuna Primagenia and at the
Imperial palace built by Hadrian; and they had
noted the presumptuous new Christian church near
the main gate. Priscus had reminded them that the
town had been founded by Cæculus son of Vulcan.
He had pointed out where King Pyrrhus of Epirus
had turned back from his advance on Rome over
six hundred years ago. He had shown them the
place where the younger Marius, defeated by Sulla
in the civil wars of the Republic, had taken his own
life. At dinner they had tried the wine
recommended by Athenæus and the walnuts
extolled by Cato, and they had lamented that it was
too early for the roses praised by Pliny. It was not
yet mid-April; there was still snow on the high
Apennines as their open carriage negotiated the
hill-road. The sun was hot and the breeze crisp.
Spring flowers bloomed in the meadows: white
saxifrage and narcissus, and yellow tormentil and
wolfsbane. The rhythm of an early cicada struck
the air.

Cæcina Priscus had left his majestic formal
toga behind in the City. Now he looked more
dashing, in a white silk dalmatic tunic tailored to
his broad chest and slim waist. Both its deep border
and a matching girdle were heavily embroidered
with threads of green and purple and gold, and with
it he wore fine supple purple boots, a heavy gold
wrist-band over half his forearm, and two antique
gold rings, one set with a ruby and one with three
amethysts. She looked at him fondly, vaguely
recalling hours of pleasure at his family's palace on
the Quirinal Hill. Titus, still wearing a brown
woollen *birrus* bought last year in Lugdunum, and
more suitable for travelling than for show, let her

down by comparison, she thought. She hoped that she herself showed to better advantage in an outfit acquired in Rome: a pale blue linen *othone* set off by an indigo *maforte* which floated round her shoulders and protected the high hairstyle that it took half an hour for a maid to arrange each morning. She had jewellery too, a graceful silver and jet necklace inherited from her great-aunt with matching ear-rings, and a gold armlet in the form of a twisted torc.

They were laughing and joking as they turned out of sight of Præneste and entered an ancient oak wood. Suddenly they came out of the trees and saw the villa. "A mere rustic cottage," Priscus had called it, but it was not that at all: it seemed huge. Flavia whooped in delight: "Priscus, is this it? It's wonderful!"

"Yes, this is our little country retreat," smiled Priscus. "At the front you see it's an old Latian farmhouse, with the traditional little atrium courtyard where rainwater falls off the roof into a central pool. A hundred years ago, my ancestor built an addition in the Greek style with a pillared courtyard, and to the other side you can see a suite of baths, added ages before, under the emperor Trajan. Look! The furnace chimney's already puffing blue smoke: they're ready for our arrival!" Roofs beyond hinted at other buildings, perhaps stables and slaves' quarters. The coachman urged the horses forward. "Water comes by a covered aqueduct from high in the mountain, to avoid pollution by animals," Priscus went on, "so there'll be no repetition of the illness you had at that inn on Elba, I think! And if you look to the left you'll see a grove of the lemon trees that so impressed you in the City."

There was a barking of unseen dogs as the carriage came towards the door, and they saw a line of domestics drawn up to greet them, a dozen or so in all. "Very well, Rautio," said Priscus crisply to a burly major-domo, "Get them about their business.

Our guests have travelled from the City. They need wine and a bath." Chests and bags were unloaded as the arrivals were ushered through the old farmhouse and the peristyle into spacious rooms. A large goblet of well-watered wine was brought, and each took a deep draught.

"Come on," called Priscus, "race you to the baths!" Titus and Flavia caught his mood, and rushed after him like children through the corridors, past the noise of servants, through an open space and into a small quiet room with stools to sit on and hooks and shelves for clothes, a warm moist air leaking into it from next door. "Sit down, Flavia," said Priscus, in charge again. "Sanna here will help with your hair." A slight Syrian-looking girl came forward, and began to take the pins from Flavia's *maforte*; a young boy was already unbuttoning Priscus' dalmatic; a half-black youth approached Titus. The men were soon undressed, and went through to the next room.

Flavia had not before been naked in the presence of men apart from slaves and family, though she knew that mixed bathing was fashionable in some circles in Italy, and now her vulnerability made her all the more aware of the exotic, luxurious villa. She felt shy as she prepared to go through, carrying a linen towel, her hair in a rope. The others were sitting together on a couch, chatting. "Ah, here you are," said Priscus, smiling; his eyes dwelt with gratifying pleasure on her, but there was something there for the first time, some hint of self-serving power, which she felt somehow she did not quite like. "It's chilly in the *frigidarium* at this time of year. Come straight on through." They went out into an open courtyard with a plunge bath, into which Priscus jumped straight away, drenching the others with cold. They shrieked and laughed and threw water for a while; then the men chased each other into another doorway, still shouting. Flavia followed them cautiously through a warm chamber into a hot dry room, covered in duckboards to keep the superheated floor-bricks from the touch. In the dimness she could see the others stretched out on benches, excitement spent, one of them humming a tune in the silence. Flavia lay prone on a third couch, spreading the towel below her breasts in case the cedar-wood was too hot, and folded her arms under her head.

She must have slept, because then the young Syrian girl was waking her and saying lunch would be soon and she should get ready. She led her into the warm room they had come through, polished her skin all over with a towel, made her lie down again and massaged her briefly, at the shoulders, the small of the back, and the feet; then turned her over and delicately worked over her cheeks, her forehead and her scalp: her touch was firm and sure, trained and practised. Then she gave her a heated wrap and led her back through the house to her bedroom.

Flavia felt released and relaxed. Another maid was waiting to dress her. She made no protest as one strange perfume was applied to her temples, another to her breasts, armpits and waist, and a third to her wrists and ankles. Then she was dressed, simply but elegantly, and her hair arranged. In the baths Flavia had been reflecting how brief and intense her liaison with Priscus in Rome had been, and how little they knew of his character beyond it; now she remembered her unquiet feeling about his look when she had come into the *frigidarium*. "What is your name?" she asked the maid, who looked about seventeen, and was pretty, with short black curly hair; she tended to hold her head a bit to the left, and there was something about her appearance that Flavia couldn't quite place. "Judith, Noble Lady," replied the maid.

"So you are a Jew?" asked Flavia, for the name was distinctive, and when the other nodded, said, "And how do you come to be a slave? Were you raised in the household, or were you involved in the revolt in Judæa under the Cæsar Gallus?"

"No, my lady, that was only a few years ago. I was enslaved as a little girl."

"Tell me about it, Judith," said Flavia, and the maid explained how her father had been a silversmith in a city across the Persian frontier, on the river Tigris in Adiabene, and how while going to visit her uncle during the emperor Constantius' wars they had been taken by a Roman patrol on the open road; her father had died on the spot as a result of some confusion, her mother of a broken heart on the long march to Antioch; she had been brought to Rome and sold to the Sabini family; at first she had letters from her brother in Adiabene, but now she received none.

She had obviously told the story many times, and was in a hurry, anxious not to make it tedious for this sympathetic listener, so the details were hard to follow. But her loneliness was clear, and faced with this grim comparison Flavia began to think her own fear about Priscus just now was rather foolish. "Tell me about the Lord Priscus, Judith. Does he treat the servants well?"

Judith looked wary. "The Cæcinæ Sabini are a great family, as my Lady will know well," she said. "The household has both slave and free, but we slaves are well treated: we each keep our own property undisturbed, and we all buy our freedom sooner or later. I hope some day to go back to Persia, or at least to find a Jewish man in Rome to marry."

It was so difficult getting the truth out of slaves, Flavia thought: the hope of freedom was always with them. "But Priscus himself, does he treat you properly as master, even the women?"

Judith made a sudden involuntary movement of her head and arm, and caught Flavia's glance for a second. There was an increased cautiousness in her eyes, but at the same time a kind of sympathy – perhaps the kind that Flavia had sometimes seen in other women conscious of a shared experience of men across all classes and conditions, perhaps a sort of pity. "It is not for me to make comments on my masters, Lady," Judith said primly. "I am sorry to have taken up your time with my troubles. You should be going in to lunch."

Flavia realised that she could not insist. Judith led her through to the dining room. At its door, as the maid turned to leave, she could no longer conceal the left side of her head, where most of the ear was missing.

There was a round of courteous applause as Flavia entered, and she found that Titus and Priscus were not alone. Two other young men were there, both short and chestnut-haired, the younger distinctly plump. They were brothers, said Priscus, Apollonius and Opramoas, from Sardis in Asia Minor, who had looked in as they were passing and would be staying for a few days; they had both been to Constantinople a number of times; perhaps they knew Titus' and Flavia's relations there. The guests exchanged news of half-acquaintances; Flavia, like Priscus, sought to be social and draw the party out, and Titus' reserve began to thaw, helped by a heavy southern wine. The newcomers spoke Latin with a strong Greek accent, and sometimes became stuck for a word, passing it off with engaging laughter.

Then the talk was of hunting, and Priscus mentioned a mountain a day's journey or so away, beyond a village called Sublaqueum.

"Yes, it's an excellent place," said Apollonius. "You remember, Priscus, we hunted there when I was last down, in November. What a bag we got! Do you remember that mouflon which led me half a mile along a cliff crevice until only he could get further, and I took three hours to creep back? Titus, you in Britain are famous for your hunting! What say you we set out for Mount Auctor and put in a couple of days?"

"Good!" said Titus, brightening, as he always did when sport was in prospect. "I feel I've been in the city too long. I should love to get out into the field. I have a favourite bow in my bags, if our host could find us mounts and javelins."

"Gladly," said Priscus, "though I won't come myself, if you don't mind. I want some peace and quiet, and there are estate matters to attend to here. You two go off with a couple of beaters, and I shall stay and look after your sister. But I'm delighted you're taking a real interest in this part of the country; I shall look forward to comparing notes when you get back, and hearing how things differ here from in the arctic wastes." He chuckled to show he meant no disrespect to Titus' home province, but Flavia realised with dismay that this would leave her alone in the villa with him and his friend Opramoas, and she remembered her sudden mistrust for Priscus in the bath-house. She looked for a way of keeping this proposal open for the moment, until she had a chance to talk to Titus alone.

"That sounds a marvellous idea, Titus," she said, "but do you think this is the time to go off into the country? You've only just arrived; you need to settle down and enjoy Priscus' lovely villa for a bit. Besides, it's hardly courteous to our host to go off so soon, and taking his horses and equipment. Give it a few days." This was a mistake, as she realised as soon as she had said it.

"Nonsense," said Priscus. "If Titus and Apollonius want a few days' hunting I'm delighted; I wouldn't begrudge them for a moment, and it would be an excellent introduction to the area – give Titus a chance to find his bearings."

"Really, Titus, are you sure?" she persisted embarrassed, staring at Titus with narrowed eyes, trying to will him to say no.

"Listen to what Priscus says, Flavia," said Titus with a slight irritation in his voice. "He's clearly quite happy. Apollonius and I will be fine."

It might be Flavia's imagination, but there was something strange about Priscus again when he glanced in her direction, something new and detached, observing or controlling. She had a sense of uneasiness again. "Well, if you're really sure it's all right I think I'll come along too, if you don't mind. It's a long time since I've been out as well, and I could certainly do with the exercise."

"Oh, we can't be having that," said Priscus with an easy and authoritative smile. "I don't know what you do in Britain, but you're in Latium now, and it just wouldn't do for ladies to go on hunting expeditions here. The days of Diana and Hippolyta are past, you know. There are lovely walks in the woods here, Flavia, if you need exercise."

Titus smiled apologetically at Flavia, as though to convey that he sympathised with her desire to come but that they had to accept their host's decision and no real harm was done. The arrangements were settled. The meal came to a close, and Priscus went off with Titus and Apollonius to give instructions to the beaters, the grooms and the chambermaids.

Flavia made for Titus' room, and worked herself into increasing anxiety until he arrived to superintend his packing. "Titus," she hissed, beating him on the shoulder with frustration. "You *can't* leave me here alone with Priscus. We're miles from anywhere. Anything could happen. You're *responsible* for me."

The maid came to the door. Titus closed it telling her to wait, and then turned, and took Flavia's wrists gently. "Little sister," he said, in tones which had infuriated her for fifteen years, "take it from me, nothing bad is going to happen.

"Priscus is an honourable man from a noble family, and that wasn't your story back in his parents' house in Rome," he chuckled. "Look. Both you and he are very fond of each other. There are servants in the house, and that brother of Apollonius'. You'll be fine. I'm going to go away for a few days' hunting in the mountains, and when I come back we'll have a marvellous time together.

Now go and leave me to pack." And he opened the door and pushed her out into the passage, admitting his maid.

Flavia retired to her own room, giving it out that she had a headache, and lay down, trying to recover the peace of mind she had felt on awakening in the bath-house. Priscus called through the door to ask attentively after her health. And it did not seem long before Titus came in, his bags packed and the horses saddled. He was high-spirited and cheery; there was clearly no point in reopening things. Flavia was withdrawn; they kissed and made their goodbyes.

She did not want to go out, but felt a prisoner in her room. Dusk came early in Italy in the spring, she thought; she asked for something to read, and was brought sweet beeswax candles and a copy of Gellius' *Attic Nights*. She slept poorly, and had dreams which left no memory, save a vague impression of huntedness and violence.

Judith came in the morning with some almond biscuits and a hot drink of lemon flavoured with honey and cinnamon, and Flavia wondered how to deal with the day. Eventually she dressed and ventured out. The sun was hot and the villa was beautiful. Priscus was attentive, courteous, gentle as ever. Then he excused himself, pleading estate business, and she sat in the shade in the peristyle picking at embroidery for a while, an occupation famously respectable, but in her eyes as boring as watching whitewash dry.

Lunchtime came, and with it Opramoas emerged; they all three sat down to an over-elaborate meal featuring dishes such as larks' tongues, and pastries delicately moulded in the shape of mythical animals. Priscus and he were playing some kind of game over the meal, showing off to each other in some way she couldn't quite fathom. It wasn't really exclusive, it was done in a way that was undoubtedly entertaining for the observer; it reminded her a little of student competitiveness. Once or twice they joked to each other in a rapid demotic Greek she could not follow. The men drank a lot of wine, though not to the point of drunkenness; she had intended to avoid it, but as the meal wore on found herself unable to resist sipping some and then more to quell an uneasiness somewhere.

As they rose from their couches at the end of lunch Priscus came up to her and murmured the suggestion that she should come to his room. He was gentle and loving, and she felt reassured. She smiled, and washed and changed, and went. He was his old self, as he had been in Rome, and her vague fears were soon gone; they cuddled and kissed and explored each other again and went to bed; they shared a pomegranate, giving each other the seeds with their lips; at last they made love. They lay spent, recovering their forces, and began to talk of the house, and its surroundings of Latium and the mountains and the old myths.

"And here you are in my house, my little British warrior-queen," he said, raising himself on his elbow and admiring her body, "and you have eaten my pomegranate seeds. It reminds me of Proserpine, who ate Pluto's pomegranate seeds and was bound to stay with him. I think you should stay with me."

She looked at him seriously. Was he thinking of marriage? She had hoped he might, though his exalted family might be hard to handle. It would be more proper for him to speak to Titus. But, after all, she was a woman of seventeen, not some little fourteen-year-old who wouldn't know her own mind; he might well want to make sure how the land lay with her first. "What do you mean?"

"I am very fond of you, you know," he smiled, "and I think you are of me as well."

"Go on."

"As you know, my family is noble. My father Antonius Cæcina Sabinus was consul; one of my two brothers is a senator. I have held no office as yet, but I shall be a quæstor next year and admitted to the Senate, and I expect, the year after, to be governor of Lusitania, thanks to the recommendation of Eusebius, the Preposite of the Sacred Bedchamber. I may have to travel a lot over the following years, and don't want the responsibilities of marriage yet. But I do need a concubine." He smiled again. "You are beautiful and learned and witty. I could do a lot of good for you and for your brother's career. Will you be my mistress? It could be for a fixed term, and you would still be young enough to find a husband at the end of it. I would settle land on you to ensure you were not short of money. What do you say?"

She stared at him for a moment uncomprehending, working out what he had said, and then was invaded by a pain and anger that she had never felt before. Tears came into her eyes. She squatted up on the bed and clenched her fists. "I say that is a wicked suggestion, especially after I trusted you so far," and then more shrilly, as she saw him unmoved, the anger bloomed uncontrollably in her mind and she blurted out words without thinking. "You are shameless and without dignity! I have never heard such nonsense! A secret affair far from home is one thing, but who would want me after five or ten years as another man's open mistress? What if I got pregnant? And how dare you make such a proposal to me, treating someone of equestrian rank as if she were a slave or freedwoman! You demean yourself and you demean your family." She began to see what she said going home, and a fierce joy of her words took hold of her. "Nobility lies in words and actions, not simply in blood. Someone who could say such things is no better than a slave himself, and a son of slaves!"

His mouth had been narrowing and his face darkening during this speech. "Shut your mouth, scum!" he cried, his voice heavy with rage, and threw himself at her. "Your father was a nothing and you are a nothing. You shan't speak of the Cæcinæ Sabini like that, and I'll show you what happens to people who do." He wrestled with her, forcing her down with difficulty.

"Your family must be ashamed that they could produce a man so dishonourable." She was losing the struggle, but perhaps not the contest: her voice rang clear, and triumphant she could see clearly in his eyes the damage her words were inflicting. "Your father says to your mother, 'We have two sons to be proud of, but one who is a disgrace to us all. Like Lucius Cantilius he is a seducer of virgins.'"

"You British bitches are stronger than decent women, but you shall see how you get treated." He pulled her hair sharply with one hand and hit her head hard with the other fist.

With the blow, her world became confused for a moment; he had disengaged himself and she started groggily to raise herself again, but now he was behind her seizing one arm, pulling it violently and slipping a loop of cloth over her wrist. Distracted by her own indignation, she had realised too late how excited he had become. Fear was rapidly swallowing her anger, and she struggled to turn and lash out at him, but her head still rang and she couldn't get her legs to move fast enough. Now one of her arms was pinioned, and he had got hold of the other, pulling her over on her front, and was tying that down too. Her head was suddenly hit again; then he was moving round and catching an ankle to fasten that as well. Then, breathing heavily, he leapt on the bed, aroused by the violence, pushed open her buttocks and forced his way in. Humiliation ran to her core, and her anger instantly vanished; she was suddenly a small thing within her body, shrinking from its sensations, pallid and hunted. "You pathetic bitch!" he said as he thrusted twice and finished, then got up.

She heard him go to the door and call for Opramoas. Both of them came in, and turned her over on to her back, limb by limb. Her mind became full of sudden white blossomings, blotting out everything else; her vulnerability was all that she could find to be aware of. A corner of her raced with imaginings of what they might do next. "I suppose you thought you could wheedle your way into a noble family by marriage. You silly provincials disgust me. But you will take what you deserve." She was full of sobs and terror, trying not to show it.

Then three of her limbs were securely bound to the bed, and Opramoas smiling and holding down her other leg, and Priscus was astride her. He twisted a breast violently and hit her about the body: at each blow she tensed, and it seemed that whenever she began to relax another would fall, the chunky rings on his fingers sharpening the pain: she tried to cut herself off from her sensations, but whenever the pain fell it dragged her back. Soon, aroused again, he entered her, and afterwards rolled off and got up. "Well, that will do for now. We shall go and think of some other entertainment. Shall we do the other side again next? Or do you think something more inventive would be appropriate? There are branding irons for the slaves, of course. Or we have some very savage hunting dogs, Opramoas, have we not? Yes, have you thought, my British bitch, what it's like to be eaten by the beasts, yum yum, with their hot meaty breath?"

The pain of his violence competed with her fear and humiliation. "Priscus, please," she moaned.

"My little philosopheress is finding it hard to keep her academic detachment, her stoic tranquillity, isn't she? Perhaps we ought to go and find a book for her to read. Paxamus' *The Twelvefold Art* is very inventive about sexual positions, as I recall. With the right partner she should find it very educational." She could not bear to have her eyes open, nor closed. Squinting, she saw him grin at Opramoas, look down at the swelling bruises with satisfaction and put on a cloak. Both men left the room.

She had no idea of time. A pause had come. It might have lasted for five minutes, or five hours.

Then the door opened. Someone behind her struck her head with his fist again, and her arms were loosed, and then her feet. Priscus, not addressing her, simply gave orders to two muscular slaves whom she had not seen before, both with noses cut off and livid brands on their foreheads. They tied her wrists and ankles together with a long leather thong, and bore her through the door and out of the back of the buildings; their bodies stank. She heard the noise of barking dogs become louder and more excited, and was taken past a row of what must be kennels. A door was opened and she was thrown casually in, falling shoulder-first on a heap of fresh animal ordure, disturbing its acrid, revolting smell, and the flies, all the flies which were crawling on it, and which rose up to settle on every part of her body. Her gorge rose, and she vomited again and again.

Yet there seemed to be no dogs in the hut. She lay there for hours, and as her faculties began to return it began to come to her that he had probably, so far at least, done nothing which would do her body permanent damage, nor that would even be much visible once she was cleaned and dressed. Surely it was not pity or compassion. Perhaps even a poor relation of Quintus Aradius Rufinus Valerius Proculus, owner of the palace of the Valerii on the Cælian Hill – even if she did come from a remote province, even if she was connected only through her mother's side – perhaps even she was worth a vestige of respect from the grand Cæcinæ Sabini. Perhaps at least, if she survived, the story of what happened would not get out and destroy her reputation, her chances of marriage. It began to grow cold, and she lay there in a stupor where memories of gentle Priscus and cruel Priscus mingled bewilderingly, along with muddled memories of some poor man she had recently seen cuffed apart by a bear in the arena, and a glimpse in some aristocratic hall of alabaster figures showing Callisto hunted down by Diana's hounds.

Some time in the night Judith came, seemingly very frightened, and untied her. She put a rug round her, gave her water to drink, then helped her, dumb and shuddering, over the frosty ground to the house and to her room, and bathed her in hot water in a wooden tub.

Flavia started awake, and convulsively grabbed at Arctus' cloak. The skiff pitched and rocked as if it would capsize, and he sat down with a thump, losing hold of the pole. She crawled forward, oblivious, cried his name twice, wound her arms round his knees, put her head in his lap, sobbing. Then, brokenly to begin with, she spilled out all the story of what had happened at Præneste, all those years ago. Out and out it came, in all its cruel detail, and as it came she began to sense that it might be being taken away from her at last, even if its exhaustion drained her quite empty.

He cuddled her to him, stroked her hair and murmured endearments as the story went on, while the green streaks of light in the eastern sky grew, slowly, slowly, through yellow and pink and red towards full dawn. At last she fell silent, and there was only the sound of their breathing, of the river-water lapping at the boat, of the breeze soughing in the rushes. Shadows of reed-beds, and of low banks scrubby with samphire and spurrey, moved slowly past them on the stream or the tide. The semi-darkness was pregnant with the limitless vista of the marshes all around. A flight of shelduck passed high above, brilliant in the new sun which had not yet reached the river. A rustle came from the reeds, a waterbird or an otter. She raised her head and looked into his eyes.

"I couldn't bring myself to talk to Titus about it, though obviously he knew something awful had happened. But I see now somehow," she muttered with a deep breath that went out as a great shuddering groan, "I see now that I've been angry with Titus ever since: I wouldn't admit it to myself, but I felt that it was all his fault, that he should never have gone and left me when he did. My whole life has been consumed by the anger, it seems to me now, and it poisoned the rest of my time with him. And now he's dead and it's too late to forgive him, too late for him to forgive me, too late to make it up." Her body shook with sobbing, again and again; she gasped in lungfuls of air and let them out in long deep convulsing moans. "It's too late...it's too late..." He raised her tear-filled face to his wordlessly and kissed it again and again, stroking her gently until she lay quiet. Then they were still.

They stay there together, oblivious of time, knowing only pain and comfort. At last, not releasing her head between his hands, he raises his gaze. They are out in the broad main stream of the river, maybe two furlongs from the nearer bank of reeds, drifting uncontrolled towards the sea. In the flat lands the skies are huge above them, pure as the limitless spaces of the heavens which only the gods see. Far above, the autumn's first geese are crossing the coast southwards, and faint fragments of their remote trumpeting reach even down to the water.

Then, in ungainly, startled haste, a swan paddles into his view from behind. He looks round, and there, holding course toward them from up-river, not three hundred yards off, is a tall war-galley, oars raised and sails furled, ready to heave to. Men are gathered in the prow.

"Ahoy! You in the boat!" cries a voice over the water. "Romans or barbarians?"

Arctus gets up on his knees and shouts an answer.

"Stand by to come aboard!" comes the call again. He can just see them adjusting the steering. Commands are called, the oars sink. The ship comes to a halt beside the little boat.

A rope descends. "The Most Perfect Lady is in no condition..."

"Stand by!" A sailor works a second rope with bewildering speed, then slides down the first into the boat. Kindly but briskly, he passes a loop over Flavia and under her armpits. "Is that comfortable, Lady?" he asks, but not waiting for an answer looks up and calls, "That's it, sir!"

"Haul away," cries a voice, "gently, mind!" Arctus tries to support Flavia's weight as she is hoisted upwards. As she disappears onto the deck the sailor helps him to scramble up the rope into the warship, then throws their bags up after them onto the deck. The officer is checking that Flavia can walk; he leads them down the ship to a bench near the stern. He calls to someone unseen. "We'll get you a drink," he says. "We've nothing warm until the breakfast fire is lit, so it will have to be wine for now." Orders are shouted, a bugle call sounds, and a drum begins to beat: the oarsmen set to their labour.

"Where have you come from?" asks Arctus.

"From Durobrivæ. The city's still cut off, but that won't last long: Count Theodosius landed at Richborough last week with a big army. Augusta and Colchester are already relieved." The officer's drawn, bearded face lightens into a grin. "We're off direct now, all the way to Imperial Headquarters at Trier on the Rhine. If this wind holds you may see the Emperors Valentinian and Gratian in person by Wednesday night." He turns away. "Wine and some biscuit for the refugees, Messala! And bring a couple of heavy cloaks!"

Arctus feels Flavia shivering, whether from cold or grief he cannot tell. He takes his cloak off and wraps it round her shoulders, hugging her to him. She looks up at him gratefully, and lets herself topple into his lap, her head on his shoulder, giving a little smile, feeling safe and consoled, like a small animal in a nest, and knowing that for now that is enough. Presently a sailor reaches down two wooden cups of red wine and some rusks. Flavia takes her food and drink, and nibbles and sips.

Gradually, strength begins to glow in her again. Præneste is a long time ago, she tells herself, and she is all right now, and whole: the gods have been with her. She has suffered and made mistakes, but here she is secure, and also Arctus is by. As for Cormerick, Sallienus has dealt well with the problems of the invasion: he will not need her guidance to get daily life under way there again, so soon as the island is once more secure. And it is true, in fact, that Trier, the capital of the Gallic prefecture and headquarters of the western Empire, is the place for her now: there they will be able to stay with her acquaintance Blæsus, and there, better than anywhere, she will be able to act early and effectively. If she wronged Titus in the past, she will redeem it now by clearing his name. And she will also publish her book promptly. Perhaps before beginning a tour of the western cities she will accompany Arctus to Bordeaux, and explore where he comes from and what it is like. She smiles to herself, and snuggles up to him.

They lie too far below the bulwarks to see the marshes and rushes and winding channels that are the scene of their journey out through to the river-mouth, the new journey that is leaving the Britains behind, perhaps for ever. But directly ahead of the ship, through the ragged remains of storm-clouds, an irresistible sun gradually, imperceptibly, buoys itself into view. Pure, serene, and comforting as a god, it begins to warm them both.

SUPPLEMENT

I

ADVERTISEMENT

This story is of course based on real history, and (despite the destructiveness of the events described) on history at a time at least a generation before serious barbarian pressure on Roman Britain seems to have begun. Any reader new to the period will find that the various academic schools – the classical historians, the church historians and the archæologists – can be each jealous of their own patch, and that there is often a desperate lack of evidence. So there is debate about the most straightforward things: the size of the British population, the normal age of marriage, who spoke British and who Latin and how much, how easy it was to have affairs without being executed for it, where the coastline was, whether citrus fruit was available... There is almost no evidence about native British religious ritual. So I have had to make some arbitrary judgements in fierce academic debates, or just invent details to make the story work.

However, the basic political facts <u>are</u> historical: there <u>was</u> a "barbarian conspiracy", the *arcani* and Valentinus were somehow involved, and the successive proposals for relief expeditions did happen; Fl. Sanctus, Phronimius and various others were real people (and Ausonius' lubricious poems, and Calcidius' translation of part of the *Timæus*, still exist). Flavia and Arctus are invented, but I have related them to historical people: Flavia's grandfather Lucius Aradius Valerius Proculus, Arctus' father Ursulus, Lucilla's father Proculus and husband Clementinus. Ælius Cæcina Priscus is a name I have given to a historical figure in the great family of the Cæcinæ known to the learned authors of the *Prosopography of the Later Roman Empire* only as "Anonymous 140", but the people I have made his father

(Antonius Cæcina Sabinus) and his influential contact (Eusebius, the Preposite of the Sacred Bedchamber) are also figures known by name. There is no evidence of the White House in Galloway so early as 367; but later on it was to be the base of the mysterious bishop St Ninian, according to legend the first to Christianise a part of Scotland.

Of course, little is known even about the historical figures, and I have almost entirely made up their personalities (there is room for debate in the case of Ausonius, about whom more is known than others, and whom I have presented in a worse light than most historians would offer – though he did have a poor opinion of Britain, so it might have been gained at first hand: see *Epigrams* 108-112). Most of the personal names, including the British ones, are recorded somewhere as ones actually used in Britain, though often at an earlier period; but for Valentinus I invented the sobriquet of "Faber", which you could render as "crafty", since early drafts of the book confused friends with too many mysterious dignitaries whose names began "Val..." – all of them unfortunately historical, so that they couldn't satisfactorily be changed at the stroke of a pen.

In social description I've tried to keep to the known and the academically-preferred as far as possible, and otherwise at least to be plausible. I will certainly have missed things; and even where I haven't there will no doubt be objects dug up next year which will turn accepted wisdom upside down (it was only in 1964 that S J Hallam discovered that there had been villages in Celtic Britain, not just isolated farms). But I've tried. For example, I've modelled the ritual of the Good Goddess in Chapter 1 on records of the real thing published in the Leyden series on ancient religion, and the information on contraception follows Soranus. My only deliberate error has been that I discovered too late Salway's 1981 remark that it "now seemed increasingly unlikely" that the Car Dyke canal was used for transport; I didn't want to lose this aspect of the story, and left it in. In addition, I have assumed that in practice the offices of the civil Vicar and military Count of the Britains were combined: there is no authority for this, but such an arrangement is known elsewhere, and given that few holders of either office are known, and that by comparison with other dioceses the British troops were mostly in the ducal frontier commands, making the Count's job a rather small one, I feel this is a justified simplification and might even have been true.

Place-names are a problem with historical writing, and there is no real solution to it. Calling Rome "Roma" is pretentious and distancing, while you have to be a local to find "Chesterholm" any clearer than "Vindolanda". My basic rule has been to use the Latin name for a place if it is known, and the English if the Latin is not. But I have used English anyway for well-known places, sometimes preferring a better-known place a mile or two away at the price of precision (and even then I have made an exception for the special case of London, whose late official name of "Augusta" is used in contexts where characters might have insisted on that instead of the longer-standing "Londinium"; I have also used "Britain" for the island and "the Britains" for the four Roman provinces). To make matters even worse, modern names are a special difficulty in Britain in that they usually carry quiet ethno-historical messages in themselves (any native can guess that Llantrisant is in Wales, Ipswich in southern or eastern England, and Inverkip in Scotland); hence for Flavia's estate I invented a name, Cormerick, which, though plausible – since brutalised from the Cornish for "snow-valley" – does not seem wholly outlandish in East Anglia.

All translations are my own, apart from the Homer, where Pope's version was irresistible. I could not have written this book without my long-ago studies in Classics under the excellent and long-suffering Denis Henry†, Freddie Turner S.J.†, and Michael Bossy S.J. at Stonyhurst; and Ted Kenny at Cambridge.

NOTES

Page 5 For it is impossible to disbelieve the children of gods, &c: Plato, Timæus, 40.

Page 6 Placenames are explained in section I of this Supplement.

Page 9 This is the Emperor Julian, known as "the Apostate" (since, though raised as a Christian, he returned to paganism), who died on campaign on the eastern frontier of the empire in 365.

Page 10 The *arcani* (or perhaps, less intriguingly, *areani*) are only known from one brief mention but are generally thought to have been somewhere between a military and a security unit; they seem only to have been found in Britain.

Page 18 There is no virtue without work,: Seneca, *De Vita Beata*, 25 5.

Page 29 Eighteen was early enough for bearing children, as Rufus of Ephesus recommended: Rufus of Ephesus, Book II, quoted by Michel Foucault, *The History of Sexuality vol 3* (Penguin 1990, trans Hurley) p 130.

Page 46 And we spoke about women too: we said that they were to be brought up and educated in the same way as the men, &c: Plato, *Timæus*, 18.

Page 48 A huge new temple to Jupiter or his Celtic equivalent was built in Lydney on the Severn in the fourth century, for reasons which can only be speculated on. Flavia refers on page 195 to some kind of theophany there, a possible inspiration of the new building. This is, it may be inferred, the cause of Flavia's friends' pilgrimage.

Page 54 If you respect the jovial and content, And keep the festal days with merriment, Ausonius, *Commemoratio Professorum Burdigalensium* 7.

Page 55 'A pretty new book, now who's to receive it?' Long ago said a poet of Verona: Ausonius, *Eclogæ* 1.

Page 55 Let's live, my Lesbia, and let's make love: Catullus 5.

Page 56 Syrian Eunus, you're a gastronome of groins, And under Phyllis' teaching you're a Master now of Loins!: Ausonius, *Epigrams* 87.

Page 64 This pass'd on earth, while in the realms above Minerva thus to cloud-compelling Jove: Odyssey XXIV.

Page 67 Emperor Constantine Augustus to the People: If any man who has not made an agreement with the parents of a girl should take her against her will, &c: *Codex Theodosianus*, 9 24 1.

Page 76 The Goddess founded this whole order and system when she framed your society &c: Plato, *Timæus*, 24.

Page 85 Words that have once been uttered have already flown past recalling: Horace, *Epistles*, 1 18.

Page 105 "If he's away," said Socrates, "It's for you and the others" &c: Plato, *Timæus*, 17.

Page 120 The circumstances of Vulcan's conception are referred to by Michel Foucault, *The History of Sexuality vol 3* (Penguin 1990 trans Hurley) p 206, where he summarises Plutarch's *Dialogue on Love* but does not give the Pindar reference to which he alludes.

Page 130 "very few women philosophers, you know, just three that I know of": Flavia probably means Plotinus' pupil Amphiclea, Iamblichus' pupil Arete and perhaps Sosipatra of Ephesus or Pergamum.

Page 133 And if in that shape he still does not abstain from evil, he shall be changed &c: Plato, *Timæus*, 42.

Page 157 Yet, come it will, the day decreed by fates! κτλ: Iliad VI.

Page 150 Now there are fields where Troy once stood: Ovid, *Heroides*, 1.

Page 160 Give back the divine in yourself to the divine in the universe: Porphyry, *Vita Plotini* 7.

Page 170 The Britons wholly isolated from the entire world: Virgil, *Eclogues*, 1 66.

Page 171 ...that those whose task was to fight in defence of the City must behave only as such: Plato, *Timæus*, 17.

Page 174 We all go to the same end: Horace, *Odes*, 2 3.

Page 192 He *'wrote this during the last years of Nero'* &c: Pliny, *Letters*, 3 5.

Page 195 See note to page 48 about a temple to Jupiter in Lydney.

Page 194 Night rushed upon them, folding earth in its dusky wings: Virgil, *Æneid*, 8.

Page 211 It is a characteristic of the human mind to hate the man one has injured: Tacitus, *Agricola* 42.

Page 216 So this nation, gathering all its powers &c: Plato, *Timæus*, 25.

Page 218 Law is dumb in time of war: Cicero, *Pro Milone*, 4.

*Page 224 Æ*neas said to his followers, '*You have endured worse* &c: Virgil, *Æneid*, 1, 199.

Page 234 As Phlegyas says to the damned in the *Æneid* &c: Virgil, *Æneid*, 6, 620.

Page 236 the act of sex is the beginning κτλ: Plutarch, *Dialogue on Love* 769.

Page 236 I prayed that for us κτλ: Sappho, fragment 197.

Page 141 Once I was both girl and boy: Philostratus, *Vita*

Apollonii 1, 1.

Page 240 Risks in changing medical treatment: Galen, *On Hippocrates on the Nature of Man* 120.

Page 242 There have been and will be many different destructions of mankind &c: Plato, *Timæus*, 22.

Page 242 Give me this, gods, for my piety's sake: Catullus, 76.

Page 255 Paxamus' *The Twelvefold Art* was extant in late antiquity but is now lost.

III

PEOPLE

Abascatus	city councillor at Durobrivæ
Aculeius	bailiff of an imperial estate near Cormerick
Alexander	former tutor of Flavia
Alfenus, Junius	military commander at Uxellodunum (Stanwix near Carlisle) on Hadrian's Wall
Antonia	girl-friend (?) of Titus
Antonius Cæcina Sabinus	father of Cæcina Priscus
Apollonius	guest of Cæcina Priscus
Arcavius	subject of local gossip at Bremetennacum
Arctus	visitor to the Britains
Argulus	a groom at Cormerick
Ariobarzanes	a horse
Arruntius Niger	commander at Chester
Ateanctos	wife of Marcius
Atra	aged slave at Cormerick, once Flavia's nurse
Aula Verecunda	a betting woman at Buxton
Bacura	subject of local gossip at Bremetennacum
Balbina	daughter of Lucilla
Banta	housekeeper-slave at Cormerick
Blescius	*duumvir* or council leader at Durobrivæ
Cæcilius September	curator at Buxton
Cæcina Priscus	young man of exalted family at Rome
Cæcina Sabinus	see Antonius Cæcina Sabinus
Calcidius	author and Archdeacon to the Bishop of Cordova
Calenus	worker on Cormerick stud-farm
Caracalla	third-century Emperor famed for buildings
Carausius	commander in Britain at end of third century who was locally declared Emperor and ruled independently for a time
Chrysippe	wife of Felix
Cintusmus	manager of posting-house at Buxton

Cipius	ship-owning friend of Titus among the Votadins
Cocidius	god worshipped in north Britain
Comenio	dragoman of Flavia and Titus on journey to Rome in about 357
Comindos	slave of Lucilla at Buxton
Constantine	Constantius II's predecessor as emperor (converted to Christianity and repealed penal laws against Christians)
Constantius II	Julian's predecessor as emperor
Cresconii	family friends of the Vindices living near Durovigutum (near Huntingdon)
Curatia	slave at Cormerick
Curiata	aunt of Arctus
Dagalaifus	*magister peditum*, translated as Master of Soldiers (commander-in-chief) of Western Empire up to previous year
Dagwald	head (*tribunus*) of the *arcani*, an official intelligence agency in the Britains and northern Gaul; the whole organisation of the *arcani* is conjectured (even the name may really have been *areani*)
Decimius Magnus Ausonius	lecturer, poet (his works survive), and tutor to the Emperor's son Gratian
Diocletian	emperor at turn of third-fourth centuries, founder of the characteristic institutions of the late empire
Erdigorra	Arctus' servant
Eusebius	Preposite of the Sacred Bedchamber, the most influential Court official in the Western Empire
Faber, Valentinus	Illyrican magnate exiled to Britain
Felix	Imperial town manager or *curator* of Durobrivæ
Flavia Vindex	*passim*
Flavius Gratian	the emperor Valentinian's son [historical]
Flavius Lupicinus	Master of Soldiers (i.e. commander-in-chief) of Eastern Empire [historical]
Flavius Sanctus	incoming governor of province of Flavia Caesariensis, married to sister-in-law of Decimius Magnus Ausonius [historical]

Florentius	Master of Soldiers (commander-in-chief) of Procopius
Florianus Vindex	Flavia's late father
Frontinus	man at Buxton
Fullofaudes	Duke of the Britains, the commander on the northern frontier [historical]
Gervidianus	councillor at Durobrivæ
Gervidianus	soldier in detachment at Temple of Cocidius with news of Titus
Gratian, Flavius	the emperor Valentinian's son [historical]
Hartulf	army commander
Helpidia Valeria	Flavia's mother
Hipponoë	Arctus' horse
Hyginus	eunuch in baths at Buxton
Jovinus	Master of Soldiers (commander-in-chief) of Western Empire and Consul for the present year [historical]
Judith	slave of Cæcina Priscus
Julia	acquaintance of Titus in Augusta
Julian	last emperor but one previous to the action (Julian the Apostate); threw off Christianity and tried unsuccessfully to restore pagan cults as the official religion [historical]
Julius Limisius Noricus	visitor to Flavia Caesariensis
Junilla	grand-daughter of Tranquilia Severa
Junius Alfenus	military commander at Uxellodunum (Stanwix near Carlisle) on Hadrian's Wall
Limisius, Lucius	fiancé of Paulina
Lucilla	cousin of Flavia; her late husband, Clementinus [historical], had held office as Vicar in Spain in 357
Lucius Aradius Valerius Proculus *signo* Populonius	Flavia's maternal grandfather
Lucius Limisius	fiancé of Paulina
Lucius Palatinus	commander of detachment at Temple of Cocidius
Luonercus	manager of home farm at Cormerick

Lupicinus, Flavius	Master of Soldiers (commander-in-chief) of Eastern Empire [historical]
Lycontius	former governor (Vicar), and field-commander (Count), of the Diocese of the Britains [a historical figure of this name was a vicar in the West at this time]
Magnentius	former usurper in Gaul [historical]
Magunna	elderly lady at Buxton
Mainacrius	hunting acquaintance of Blescius
Mainaino	slave at Buxton
Manillius	acquaintance of Marcius
Marcian	governor of province of Maxima Caesariensis [a historical figure of the same name held a higher office later]
Marcius	owner of leather-works and councillor at Durobrivæ
Marcus Troianus	fiancé of Paulina and visitor to Lucilla at Buxton
Melania	slave of Titus
Nectaridus	Count of the Saxon Shore, that is, commander in English Channel and nearby seas [historical]
Nepotianus	former governor of province of Flavia Caesariensis [a historical figure of this name was a governor in the West at this time]
Niger, Arruntius	commander at Chester
Nonico	servant of Marcius
Nummius Secundus	senator in residence at Buxton
Opramoas	friend of Cæcina Priscus
Orestes	dignitary in Eastern Empire
Pacata	a lady at Buxton
Palatinus, Lucius	commander of detachment at Temple of Cocidius
Pappitedo	steward on estate of Aculeius
Paulina	neighbour of Flavia's
Philip	freedman, worker on Cormerick stud-farm
Phrantzes	deputy head (*primicerius*) of the *arcani* for the Count of the Saxon Shore
Phronimius	exalted dignitary in Eastern Empire (Prefect of the City of Constantinople)[historical]

Priscus	see Cæcina
Probus	see Sextus
Procopius	rebel [historical]
Proculina	cousin of Flavia
Proculus	see Lucius, Valerius &c
Prudentia	slave at Cormerick (f)
Quintinus	officer cadet from the Imperial Guard (protector) at Buxton
Rautio (i)	soldier in Lincoln
Rautio (ii)	major-domo of Priscus at Praeneste
Ressona	slave on estate of Aculeius
Rúari	slave of Aculeius, rented to Flavia for her journey
Rutuleius	family friend of the Vindices living at Shepreth
Sabinus	see Antonius Cæcina Sabinus
Sallienus	bailiff managing the Cormerick estate
Sanctus, Flavius	incoming governor of province of Flavia Caesariensis, married to sister-in-law of Decimius Magnus Ausonius [historical]
Secundianus	official of provincial governor Marcian
Secundus, Nummius	senator in residence at Buxton
Senopianus	deputy head (*primicerius*) of the *arcani* for the Count of the Britains
September, Cæcilius	curator at Buxton
Serquina	deputy head (*primicerius*) of the *arcani* for the Duke of the Britains at Carlisle
Severa, Tranquilia	wife of Aculeius
Severus	Count of the Household Guard (*comes domesticorum*)
Sextus Claudius Petronius Probus	tipped as next Praetorian Prefect of the Gauls [historical]
Siricius	Imperial messenger at Buxton
Sophia	oldest inhabitant in Cormerick area
Stephanus	Christian priest in Galloway
Tancorix	subject of local gossip at Bremetennacum
Tasulus	bard from Cambridge

Theodorus	bearer of a message to Cormerick &c
Tiotagus	prince of the northern Picts
Titus Vindex	Flavia's brother
Toutius	boy attached to Stephanus
Tranquilia Severa	wife of Aculeius
Trenos	a lost boy
Troianus, Marcus	fiancé of Paulina and visitor to Lucilla at Buxton
Trophonius	mythic hero given "his heart's desire" by the gods, which turned out to be death; worshipped with divine honours
Urbica	wife of Valerius Proculus; Flavia's aunt by marriage
Valens	Valentinian's brother, and emperor in the East [historical]
Valentinian	current emperor in the West [historical]
Valentinus Faber	Illyrican magnate exiled to Britain
Valeria, Helpidia	Flavia's mother
Valerius Proculus	Flavia's maternal uncle
Vellibia	lady at Buxton
Venocarus	officer of the *arcani*
Verecunda, Aula	a betting woman at Buxton
Vindaticius	finance officer of Durobrivæ council
Vindex, Flavia	*passim*
Vindex, Florianus	Flavia's late father
Xerxes	a horse

IV

PLACES

Argentoratum	Strasbourg
Attacotti	probably the generic name for tribes between Hadrian's Wall and the Forth-Clyde gap
Augusta	the fourth-century name for London (it means "Imperial": the city must have been given this name in honour of some service to an Emperor, but no record survives)
Banna	Birdoswald, fort on Hadrian's Wall, about 15 miles east of Carlisle
Belisama	river Ribble
Blatobulgium	Birrens, outpost fort about 20 miles north of Hadrian's Wall on road to Clyde valley
Branodunum	fort at Brancaster on what is now the north-west Norfolk coast
Bremetennacum	Ribchester, near Preston
Brocavum	fort at Brougham near Penrith
Brocolitia	fort at Carrawburgh, more or less in the middle of Hadrian's Wall
Castra Exploratorum	Netherby, outpost fort about 10 miles north of Hadrian's Wall
Cilurnum	Chesters, fort on Hadrian's Wall
Coria	Corbridge, eastern base-town of Hadrian's Wall, some 20 miles west of Newcastle
Cormerick	home of Flavia in modern Cambridgeshire
Dalmatia	province on east coast of Adriatic
Durobrivæ	town in fens at modern Water Newton, near Peterborough; believed to have been capital of city-canton of the Corielsolilians
Durovigutum	town on London-Lincoln road, near present Godmanchester, close to modern Huntingdon
Epiacum	Whitley Castle, near Alston: fort in the remote Pennines south of Hadrian's Wall, where there were lead mines

First Britain	Roman Britain in the mid 4th century was governed as a diocese divided into four provinces. The province names are known but their locations are conjectural; I follow the usual modern guess. On this basis Britannia Prima was the British province containing the rich Cotswold estates, and ruled from Cirencester, with an eastward boundary running maybe through Winchester, Oxford, and Worcester, and then to Leintwardine and up the Welsh border to Chester.
Flavia Cæsariensis	the British province assumed to be ruled from Lincoln, and to stretch roughly from Norfolk and Lincolnshire west to the Welsh border.
Gabrosentum	fort at Moresby near Whitehaven on Cumberland coast
Galatia	province in central Asia Minor (modern Turkey), settled by marauding Celts in early historical times
Gaul	More or less, France plus Belgium and the bit of Germany west of the Rhine. Also (in singular or plural), a diocese (group of provinces) created by splitting the original Gaul into two: the diocese of the Gauls was the northern and eastern part, and the south-west became the Seven Provinces
Glannoventa	fort at Ravenglass on Cumberland coast
Isurium	Aldborough near Boroughbridge about ten miles north-west of York; a small town but capital of the huge city-canton of the Brigantians
Lebadeia	city in Greece
Longovicium	Lanchester, about 6 miles north-west of Durham
Luguvalium	Carlisle
Lusitania	≈ Portugal
Magnis	Carvoran, fort on Hadrian's Wall
Mauretania	≈ Morocco
Maxima Caesariensis	the British province assumed to be ruled from London, and to stretch west to Chichester, Silchester and Oxford, and north to Northampton, Cambridge and Suffolk.
Manavia Island	Isle of Man

Navio	fort at Brough in Pennines, about 10 miles west of Sheffield
Noricum	province approximating to what is now Austria
Novantæ	tribe in what are now Dumfries and Galloway
Pannonia	province on Danube, ≈ modern Hungary
Panticapæum	Greek colony in the Crimea
Phoenicia	province in the East, ≈ modern Lebanon
Præneste	small city south-east of Rome, now Palestrina
Rerigan	(Latin, Rerigonium): place on north-west coast of Britain, probably at or near Stranraer, and the tribal capital and royal seat of the Novantae
Sarmatians	Asiatic barbarians defeated by the emperor Marcus Aurelius in the second century in central Europe
Saturnalia	≈ Christmas
Second Britain	the British province assumed to be the northernmost, ruled from York, and stretching from Northwich and Middlewich through Buxton and Doncaster to the south Humber; and northward to the Wall.
Seven Provinces	diocese (group of provinces) in what is now southern France
Styx	mythical river at entrance to underworld
Temple of Cocidius	Bewcastle, outpost fort north of Hadrian's Wall
Traprain Law	stronghold of Votadins on the summit of a volcanic extrusion in present East Lothian
Uxellodunum	fort on Hadrian's Wall just north of Carlisle: Stanwix
Venta Belgarum	Winchester
Vercovicium	Housesteads, fort on Hadrian's Wall
Verulamium	≈ St Albans
Vindolanda	Chesterholm, fort on Hadrian's Wall
Vindomora	Ebchester, about ten miles south-east of Corbridge
Votadins	tribe in what are now Lothian and the Borders; in Roman writers as Votadini, in Welsh as Gododdin